Erotica Omnibus Two

Erotica Omnibus Two

Musical Affairs
Stephanie Ash

Eternal Kiss
Anastasia Dubois

Shopping Around
Mariah Greene

X
LIBRIS

An *X Libris* Book

This omnibus edition first published by X Libris in 1997
This edition published in 2001
Copyright © Stephanie Ash, Anastasia Dubois,
Mariah Greene 1997

Musical Affairs copyright © Stephanie Ash 1996
Eternal Kiss copyright © Anastasia Dubois 1996
Shopping Around copyright © Mariah Greene 1995

The moral right of the authors has been asserted.

A CIP catalogue record for this book
is available from the British Library.

ISBN 0 7515 2226 0

Photoset in North Wales by
Derek Doyle & Associates, Mold, Clwyd
Printed and bound in Great Britain by
Clays Ltd, St Ives plc

X Libris
A Division of
Little, Brown and Company (UK)
Brettenham House
Lancaster Place
London WC2E 7EN

www.xratedbooks.co.uk

Musical Affairs

Stephanie Ash

Chapter One

JERRY ANSON LIKED to get surprises on his birthday. Well, thought Amelia, he certainly would be surprised when he woke up on this particular birthday. Very surprised indeed.

In fact, Jerry wasn't asleep at all. He was lying in bed, eyes half closed, listening to the sounds floating up from the kitchen. Crash, bang, shatter. Amelia boiling an egg. Jerry smiled slowly. She was useless in the kitchen. Fabulously beautiful, with the body of a goddess, but useless all the same. Which was why, he justified to himself, he hesitated over making an honest woman of her. And why he didn't feel too guilty about always keeping one eye open for someone new.

And that, unbeknownst to Jerry, was why Amelia was in the kitchen. Not, as Jerry thought, preparing him a sumptuous birthday breakfast but packing up her share of the kitchen crocks. There had been one blonde hair too many on her side of the bed.

Crash! She'd always hated that bloody novelty teapot.

Jerry pulled the duvet up to his chin and rolled over, unperturbed. He hoped Amelia had remembered that he'd recently given up taking sugar in his coffee.

Click. That was an incongruous sound in the breakfast repertoire. Slam. So was that.

An hour of silence passed before Jerry sat up in bed and allowed it to cross his mind that something might be wrong.

By which time Amelia was en route to a new flat and a new start in Kentish Town in Jerry Anson's own new car.

'Damn, damn, damn.'

Amelia stalled the jeep at the traffic lights for the second time in as many minutes. 'Why are there so many bloody sets of traffic lights in this damn town?' she asked no one in particular very loudly.

A middle-aged man in a white Porsche Carrera with the top down smiled up at the outburst. He gave the pretty red-haired driver of the Shogun what he assumed was a sexy wink. She gobbed her chewing gum out of her window and onto his passenger seat in reply.

'Oh no, not again!' Amelia cried. She could feel the tears welling up like an ocean behind her eyes. That was the exact same model of Porsche that Jerry had been driving when he took her on their first date ... The memory pricked her. Things were so different back then. He had opened the door of the car for her, taken her coat in the restaurant, pulled out her chair. So gentlemanly. So full of chivalry. Until he got what he wanted.

Amelia wiped her nose on the back of her hand.

'I'm not going to think about it,' she told herself.

She had held out for so long because she wanted to make sure that she was special to him. Not like all the other bimbos he met through his work.

Jerry Anson was a celebrated record producer. They had met at a music industry party. Amelia was there with an old friend, a gay pop singer, who was using her as a foil for the press. The headlines which appeared in the tabloids after that evening had been faintly amusing, Amelia remembered. Johnny had ended up punching Jerry and the tabloid press had reported that it was because Jerry had stolen Amelia, Johnny's beautiful mystery date, straight out from under his celebrated nose. Little did they know that the whole fracas had blown up because Jerry had insulted an inebriated Johnny's favourite orange Moschino tie.

In the circles in which Amelia had been moving at that time, relationships were based on strict theories of equity and exchange. At first glance, Jerry had seemed to Amelia to be about as attractive as an overweight bulldog chewing a wasp, but he wanted her and she wanted a record contract. He talked music, he talked production, he talked sessions. Even though they didn't turn out to be quite the sessions she had in mind.

But Amelia's initial pragmatism had been replaced by a very real lust. Like Titania in *A Midsummer Night's Dream*, she had emerged one evening from the ladies' room in Quaglino's or Le Café D'Amour (as they had romantically dubbed it), to see him chatting earnestly by candlelight into his mobile phone and fallen hopelessly in love. She couldn't explain it. Was it something to do with the soft wave of his hair, the square set of his jaw, the way his ears stuck out at 90 degrees . . .? Or the fact that he was talking to someone very big at Sony on her behalf . . .?

'For goodness sake, Amelia, he's so ugly!' she told herself vehemently, slamming her hands on the steering wheel. An elderly woman passing by on the pavement with her dog shrank back in surprise.

It was no use. It was hopeless. She was so deeply in love with that horrible little man, they would have to send Jacques Cousteau in after her.

As she wiped away her tears again she caught the lingering scent of Jerry's skin on her hand. His aftershave, his sweat, even his semen. It had been so hard to tear herself away from his side that morning. Even after her worst fears about his new PA had been confirmed by the blonde hair on her pillow and the naff silver earring under the sink. His hands could still mould her anxious mind as

4

they caressed her agile body. His lips could still take any unhappy words straight out of her mouth with one tender, careful kiss . . .

But last night they had made love for the last time. The realisation stuck in Amelia's throat as she waited for the go-ahead at another set of lights and she gave out a strangled sob. She had let him nuzzle her soft pink breasts and draw a last path slowly up the inside of her thigh with his velvety tongue. He had pulled her close to him and entered her so slowly, so carefully, so reverently, that it was as if he too had grasped the finality of it all. With her shuddering orgasm, she had shed hot and salty tears. But he had settled into a deep sleep straight after without seeing those bitter teardrops at all.

She would never, never, never let herself become so enslaved by a faithless man again. He may have given her flowers, and he may have given her earth-shattering orgasms, but, Amelia reminded herself, Jerry Anson had never once given her a piece of his heart.

In his neat Victorian terraced house in Kentish Town, Richard Roberts paced the little sitting-room, setting straight the African knick-knacks and tossing unspeakable debris into the raffia wastepaper basket that stood by the door. The ad about his spare room had only gone into *Loot* the day before. The paper couldn't have been out for five minutes when he got the first call. A girl. Desperate, she sounded. She said she didn't care

5

how big the room was, or how much he wanted for rent, as long as she had a bed and a piano. Ah yes, the piano. He'd put that in as a selling point and it had obviously worked, as a selling point that was . . . he wasn't sure about it's usefulness as a musical instrument.

Anyway, this girl had practically left him no choice. She was being made homeless, she said. She would have nowhere to go but the gutter if he didn't let her stay with him. What could he do when faced with such a dilemma? He told her she could move in the very next day. Richard glanced at his watch. She would arrive any minute now.

Amelia had said that she would pick up the keys from next door if he wasn't going to be in or up when she arrived, but Richard had called in sick so that he would be there to meet her. He was dying to see just what he had let himself in for. The feel-good factor of saving someone from a night on the streets had been replaced by a nagging question. Why did she have to leave her old flat so suddenly? He had a vision of a brutally murdered landlord on a brown carpeted floor. No, she didn't sound like an axe murderer. That was the worst case scenario. The best case was that she would turn out to be a complete stunner. Richard smoothed his thick dark hair down hopefully as he polished the mirror which stood on the mantelpiece.

Rat-tat-tat.

Richard swung the door open and in flew the

6

first of four suitcases.

'Give me a hand, will you?' shouted a vaguely familiar voice.

Richard trotted out to the Shogun, which was parked half on the pavement outside his house, and duly obliged the flame-haired siren who was slinging coats, vases and saucepans out of the passenger door and onto the pavement.

'That's it,' she announced, when Richard had been all but buried in a pile of cotton dhurry rugs.

Amelia slammed the car door and kicked it, hard. As Richard winced with that peculiar male automobile-empathy at the foot-shaped dent, she relieved him of a natural-coloured rough linen lampshade and marched into the house. There she collapsed, sobbing, onto the sofa.

Full of trepidation, Richard stretched out a welcoming hand.

'I'm Richard,' he said.

'Amelia,' she wailed in reply. Her shoulders continued to twitch up and down and she limply took his hand in hers. Her fingers were wet from wiping her face.

'I'm sorry,' she snorted into a handkerchief. 'I'm not normally like this, Richard. I promise.'

'Tea?' asked Richard suddenly. What else could one ask in such a situation, he thought.

Amelia nodded and Richard gratefully escaped his new housemate's company for the sanctuary of the kitchen.

From the kitchen door he had quite a good

view of the new girl. While the kettle boiled he sized her up. She was dabbing at her face with a scrunched up and fast disintegrating piece of pink tissue. Her eyes were red and piggy from crying. But on the whole, she looked OK. Richard definitely liked her coppery hair, which was unwinding itself from her kirby grips and falling in waves onto her black-clad shoulders. She was wearing black jeans and what looked like a black all-in-one that clung tightly to her slim arms. As she blew her running nose, Richard glimpsed her cleavage. Though she was slim, she wasn't at all flat-chested. A large pendant of amber hung like a golden tear between her breasts.

Richard found himself wishing he had made more of an effort with his appearance that morning.

'Milk?' he asked.

'Yes,' came the strangled reply, followed by the sound of a nose being blown.

'Sugar?' he asked.

'Yes. Two.'

He ladled them in with a cleanish-looking teaspoon. She had stopped crying now and was unfastening the latch on a square-shaped wicker basket. Richard stood with a cup in each hand, unwittingly awaiting the appearance of the second redhead to enter his life that day. Eliza the cat came hissing out of her box. Fat and grumpy and missing all her top teeth. She hadn't said anything about having a cat.

'She'd like a saucer of milk,' Amelia

announced. 'Not skimmed.'

Richard put down the steaming mugs and hurried back to the kitchen. A girl, a cat and a large quantity of those stripy Indian rugs he had always despised. Richard sneezed. Things around here, he thought, are about to change for good.

'Tell me about yourself,' Amelia had said before she promptly launched herself into her own life story. She was twenty-five, born in London to an English father and an American mother, now divorced. She had been educated in England, at a Gloucestershire convent school, but spent the summers with her mother in California. She'd been to college in the States too, before finally moving to England for good four years ago. That accounted for the strange accent she knew she had, she said. It was very slight and rather nice, Richard assured. She had two half-sisters from her father's first marriage, both older, both married, something which she would never be. Not after this last fiasco. She wrote songs which were a bit like Carpenters classics on the piano and wanted to play music for a living. She didn't have a day job but her wealthy parents still sent her 'guilt money' which would cover the rent.

The words became one long melodious stream of sounds in Richard's ears. Her face was less wet and blotchy now. The eyes, a watery blue, were fixed on the traffic-fume dirty window as she recounted a tale about her early life. Richard tried not to, but found he just couldn't stop his gaze from wandering down from her face on a journey to her hips. From her hips, down her legs to her . . . it was then that he spotted it. On the floor next to one of her dainty lace-up boots. The unmistakable red and black wrapper of a Durex Arouser, ribbed.

'Ohmigod,' Richard breathed, barely audibly. His horrified eyes were transfixed. Had she noticed it too?

'And you, Richard,' she continued, oblivious to his sudden discomfort, 'do you have any brothers or sisters?'

'What?' He couldn't tear his gaze away from the embarrassing piece of foil on the floor.

'Do you have any brothers . . .?'

It was too late. Amelia's eyes had followed down his line of sight. She shifted her right foot slightly to see what it was hiding.

'Oh,' she blushed. She picked the wrapper up and tossed it into the raffia bin. 'My favourite sort.'

Richard gathered up the mugs and retired to the kitchen until he could breathe properly again. Ah well. At least she wouldn't think that he was some sad guy who never scored.

Her first night in her new home. Amelia felt cramped and cold in the narrow single bed, with Eliza the cat sleeping on her chest. She surveyed the unfamiliar surroundings. The Liechtenstein print her best friend had given her on that flowery wallpaper. It just didn't go. But Richard had said that he would get round to doing this room up soon.

The piano mentioned in the advert stood against the far wall. It was a Victorian upright. With the original curly wooden legs still in place. Its lid was covered in piles of dusty old sheet music that she had yet to look through. She couldn't sleep. Amelia flicked on the bedside lamp and wandered across to her new piano. It was just a little different from Jerry's white baby grand . . . Tentatively, Amelia hit middle C and played a shaky chromatic scale. Not too far out of tune. She would have liked to have played more but Richard was probably sleeping. She had taken a peep into his room earlier and seen the double pine-framed bed. She remembered the condom wrapper. He must have a girlfriend, though he hadn't mentioned any names. He was a nice-looking guy, rugged even. Friendly. Tall. It would be a pity . . .

'No,' Amelia told herself, 'I have to live with the guy. You don't screw the crew.'

But as she settled down beneath the thin duvet, she couldn't stop herself from wondering what it might be like to unbutton his too-big jeans.

A picture came into her mind of Richard in the kitchen. Standing at the sink, washing their coffee mugs. His shirt half-tucked in, half-pulled out. Sleeves rolled up around strong and sinewy forearms. She would walk in behind him and silently slide her arms around his waist. He would be shocked, but say nothing, until her lips lightly brushed the back of his neck, still golden brown from two weeks in the sun. He would quickly relax into the embrace. He's been thinking about this moment too. Can't resist her, doesn't want to.

Chapter Two

AMELIA WOKE, AS usual, just too soon, and no matter how hard she tried, shutting her eyes just would not bring back her happy dream. The sun was streaming in through the thin yellow curtains which hung at the long window. Amelia made a mental note to get those changed. It was seven a.m. and it was Saturday. What a bloody disaster!

Eliza had also awoken early and was pacing the unfamiliar room which had no cat flap. She was mewling fiercely. Amelia opened her bedroom door and booted the fat tabby out onto the landing.

Meanwhile Richard lay in bed on the other side of the wall, listening out for sounds of lodger life. He was strangely nervous about getting up, about wandering down into his own kitchen in his off-white dressing gown and dinosaur-feet slippers. He didn't look good in the morning. Bianca had told him. Bianca from Barbados. Owner of the Arouser found beneath the settee. Another one-week wonder of a relationship, that was. She was only too delighted to be with him until she found out that his record company job was in the accounts department. Oh sod her, Richard told himself. She may have had the legs of a baby giraffe but she had the voice of a chain-smoking wart-hog.

'Yeowwl!'

Someone from the room next door was up. Richard poked his tousled head around the door to investigate the unearthly howl and came face to face with Amelia. Overcome with guilt, she was poking her head out of her door to see what had become of the cat.

'Hello.' Her blush gave way to a wide smile. Though her eyes were still faintly pink, Richard could see that Amelia was generally the kind of person who looked great in the mornings. Their disembodied heads swapped pleasantries around the door frames for a while, then they agreed to emerge, more fully clothed, in five minutes' time and grab some breakfast in a nearby greasy spoon.

Richard ransacked his room in the search for a pair of clean underpants. It was like going on a date. There were no clean pants to be found. Oh, well. He remembered Murphy's Law. If he was wearing a pair of tatty Y-fronts, she would be bound to want to take his trousers off.

Amelia knocked at his door to let him know that she was done in the bathroom. She was

14

dressed in a loose white cotton top with no sleeves and blue jeans. Most of her hair was scraped back from her face into an intricate plait. The amber pendant still hung around her neck. Richard found his eyes drawn to it as they talked. Amelia laughed nervously and folded her arms across her chest, feeling more than a frisson of pleasure at his obvious interest. On the way to the café, she linked her arm through his. It was warm outside already but the sweat which began to gather in the crook of Richard's elbow had little to do with the heat.

It was only a matter of time before Jerry missed his brand new Shogun. Probably longer than it would have taken the average guy, however, since he had a vague recollection of parking it outside Tramp on Thursday night and wasn't sure whether it had been stolen or he had just forgotten to drive it home. Amelia wouldn't have taken it, surely? He didn't think she even knew how to drive. When a sortie to Jermyn Street failed to come up with the wheels, he telephoned the police. They rang back quite quickly. They'd found his car. In Kentish Town.

'Kentish Town?' he said incredulously when the policeman let him know the address. He didn't know anyone there but he didn't like to request police back-up when he went to fetch it just in case the address turned out to be the vital clue to those missing hours on Thursday night.

He found the car easily, but didn't recognise

the house. He had just opened the Shogun's driver door and was climbing inside when a familiar voice screamed to him from a little way down the road.

'Stop, thief!' the redhead squealed. Jerry climbed back out of the car and waited on the pavement for Amelia to come hurtling up the road. She had just finished breakfasting and talking about her songwriting ambitions with Richard. He was following behind her. He had stopped at the shop on the corner to pick up some milk and twenty Silk Cut.

'Darling, what are you doing here?' Jerry asked warmly, arms outstretched.

'Don't you "darling" me,' said Amelia, wrestling the keys from his hand.

'What's going on? Where have you been? Who do we know in Kentish Town of all places?'

' "We" know nobody,' Amelia told him, spitting out the 'we' as if the word tasted bitter. 'I live here now.'

'What do you mean, you live here now?'

'I've left you, Jerry.'

'Left me? Don't be ridiculous. You haven't taken your curling tongs.'

'You can send them on. I've had enough of all your messing around. I know you're sleeping with that miserable little PA of yours. Well, I just hope she's good at shorthand . . .' Amelia accompanied her words with the most withering look she could muster when faced by the only man she had ever loved. Jerry's eyes narrowed.

She'd hit him straight on his Achilles' head, as it were.

'It was nothing, Amy.'

'And so are you, Jerry. Nothing but a part of my past. So, you can just take your stupid car – which keeps stalling anyway – and go.'

'Bunny, stop being a silly little girl and come back home with me. We can talk about this . . .'

He tangled loving fingers in her beautiful hair and fixed her watery eyes with his most penetrating gaze. Using her plaited hair as a line to reel her in he pulled her face towards his and parted his lips in readiness for a winning kiss.

'No,' she pulled herself away from his embrace unexpectedly. 'I can't. It's not just you who's found someone else, Jerry, I have too.' She looked desperately back down the street for her new housemate. 'His name is Richard.'

Richard was approaching them. Dawdling along, lighting up a cigarette as he walked. He had heard Amelia talking to someone as soon as he walked out the door of the shop and had heard the voices raised but decided to stay well out of it.

'Richard!' This time his name was being used as a command. Maybe she was really in trouble. Dropping his cigarette, Richard sprinted up the street like a knight in shining armour. Through the arch that Amelia's arm made with the car door, he could see a man, slightly shorter than she was. He was thick-set, clad in an expensive blue suit over a soft sage polo-neck jumper. He looked like an East End mafioso.

'Ah, Richard . . . meet Jerry, Jerry Anson, my ex. Jerry, this is Richard . . . my lover.'

Richard's face barely had time to register confusion before Amelia had fastened her lips to his and was forcing them apart with her tongue. His hands were raised in a gesture of bemusement and submission as her arms wrapped tightly around him and she kissed him frantically until they heard a vague 'Harrumph' and the sound of Jerry's smart leather-soled shoes beating a retreat. The door of the Shogun slammed shut, whereupon Amelia dropped Richard like a limpet letting go of its rock and fled back into the house. She collapsed on the sofa, sobbing, again.

Richard raised his fingers to his violently tingling lips and felt them for damage. Had that really just happened? Yes, he could taste lipstick. It had definitely happened. He watched the Shogun tear off into the traffic. So that was her 'ex'. Very flash.

Tentatively, Richard walked up to the front door and pushed it open. He crept over to where Amelia crouched and cried, sat down beside her and put an arm around her shoulders.

'So that was him?'

She nodded.

'He's a bit of a spud, isn't he?'

That line didn't succeed in stopping her tears, but it did drive Amelia further into Richard's arms. He felt the hot salt-water soaking through his clean cotton shirt and on to his chest. He squeezed her a little tighter to him and tenderly patted her slim back.

'Tea?' he asked, after he had been holding her for about ten minutes and felt that he was about to dissolve in her tears.

She nodded.

He pushed a piece of unused tissue between her fingers and left her to it.

Richard put the kettle on and then stood at the sink, looking out onto the weed-punctuated concrete that called itself the garden. He felt damp under the arms as well as all down the front of his shirt. He was still hot from the kiss on the doorstep. She was a strange girl. Incredible. Amazing. He didn't know whether to be angry or pleased. She had used him, hadn't she? But he supposed he had enjoyed it. He hadn't been kissed like that for months.

As he scanned the garden, he noticed that Eliza the cat was curled up in the tiny corner of the yard which was still in the morning sun. Amelia had brought that fleabag along without asking, he thought. Smeone who did that couldn't really have much regard for anybody else, or their feelings.

Amelia had got up from the sofa and stood at the kitchen door, unnoticed, watching Richard watching her cat. She liked the way his forearms looked in their rolled-up sleeves. His big, clean hands gripping the edge of the sink. His shoulders were broader than she had at first thought. Quietly she reached for her hair and began to unplait it, for effect.

'Don't turn around,' she begged Richard silently, as she crept up behind him and got almost close enough to stir the hair on his neck with her breath. She stretched out one hand and placed it on his hip, near his belt. He spun around in surprise and nearly knocked her over.

'Amelia, you nearly gave me a heart attack!'

'Don't worry, I'll make it better,' she told him, drawing herself level with his curious eyes. They widened involuntarily.

Now she was kissing him again, but this time, not because she wanted anybody to see.

Richard was frozen with shock at first but, as Amelia's soft lips wandered a little more gently over his face, he let his hands rest lightly on her shoulders. She brought her fingers up to cup his square, stubbly chin.

'Amelia, are you sure . . .?' Richard began to ask a question when she broke away from him briefly to get some air.

'Ssssh,' she replied, silencing him with a finger on his burning lips.

Richard leant back heavily against the aluminium sink and let himself be swept up in the moment.

His tongue pushed its way between her lips and began to explore her straight, white teeth. She stopped moving her mouth for a moment, just opened it a little wider and let him inside. He ran his tongue along the inside of her upper lip.

Tickling her. A satisfied sigh escaped her when he moved his attention to another part of her face.

Richard placed a kiss on each of her closed eyelids, which fluttered as he pulled away from them. Her mouth was curved into a contented smile.

'Amelia.'

He pushed her hair away from her face and kissed her exposed white forehead. Then he let his lips touch her alabaster cheeks, which were growing a little pinker now. She tilted her head back so that her lips were in the line of fire again. Her hands curled purposefully around his neck, then she slid them down, exploring his upper body, squeezing the muscles that she had imagined lay beneath the cool cotton chambray when they first met a day before. Her fingers found the front of his shirt. And the buttons.

'Amelia, do you think we . . .?'

She cut him dead with a kiss. He acquiesced to the hands which had now breached his shirt and roamed predatorily over his pleasantly hairy pecs. Still surprised by the whole chain of events, Richard hesitated to follow her lead, his hands still motionless on her shoulders while she delicately rolled one of his small, hard, nipples between her forefinger and thumb. He wanted to close his eyes and relax but before he could do that he had to believe that she wasn't going to wake up and stop kissing him any second now.

'You can join in if you like,' she told him pointedly.

Richard squeezed her shoulder blades and allowed himself to feel his way down her spine to where her soft jersey top was tucked into her jeans. There were no fastenings to be undone, so he merely untucked it and let his hands slip underneath. She shivered and stiffened at the coolness of his fingers against her back, but the chill was gone in a moment and she relaxed her body against him once more, her pink cheek against his bare chest, pressing herself into him like a cat.

She was wearing no bra, Richard discovered as he reached her shoulder blades without any obstruction. Her hands were now on his buttocks, pulling him away from the sink and closer to her. He lifted the jersey top up and out of the way so that they finally stood bare chest to chest.

Uncomfortable with the material bunched up like that above her breasts, Amelia let Richard go briefly and hurriedly stripped the vest right off. Richard couldn't stop himself from giving a little exclamation of pleasure upon seeing her white breasts with their pinky nipples, framing the amber teardrop that felt cold when it touched his skin. After allowing him just a few seconds of contemplation, Amelia reached up behind him to the bright yellow Venetian blind that hung at the kitchen window and pulled it quickly shut.

'This is it,' Richard thought. The future, or what was going to happen in the next hour at the very least, suddenly became blindingly clear.

In the semi-darkness, Amelia took hold of his

hand and led him out of the kitchen, through the sitting-room and up the creaky stairs. Richard followed willingly, wanting to say something, ask her if this was really happening, but afraid that if he did so the spell would be broken. They passed her room and went straight into his. Amelia had already ascertained that the bed in there was bigger than her own. Richard's untidy room smelt musty and warm, unaired, like a cocoon. Dust stirred in the narrow shaft of sunlight that pushed in through a chink in his heavy mustard velvet curtains.

Amelia backed herself up to the edge of the bed, let her knees fold and flopped backwards onto it. Richard stood in front of her, quickly stripping off his unbuttoned shirt. Amelia almost swam backwards up the bed, pushing aside the brightly coloured duvet and the pillow so that soon there was nothing on the mattress but her and the fitted sheet. She was fiddling with the flies of her jeans. She raised one foot at a time so that Richard could grab each denim leg and help her tug it off. Soon she was clad only in a pair of black jersey and Lycra panties that fitted perfectly the gentle curve of her hips. She parted her legs suggestively and writhed a little with her hands above her head. Richard was going to have to take off his own trousers. Amelia couldn't help smiling as she watched him hop from foot to foot in his hurry to get to her side, and then at the Mickey Mouse boxer shorts which he had put on that morning without expecting anyone else to see

23

them. The curse of the dreadful underpants had struck once again.

Richard knelt on the bed between Amelia's casually parted legs. She hooked her thumbs into the elastic of his funny shorts and tugged them down unceremoniously. Then she took hold of her own pants and began to do the same, bringing her legs up around Richard's body and together to get the black Lycra off.

Richard fell onto the naked body before him, peppering her breasts and torso with kisses like a traveller falling upon water in the desert. She squirmed delightedly as his hands explored every inch of her, massaging her long, slender thighs, caressing her delicately rounded stomach. She trembled as he bent to kiss the spot where her left leg flowed smoothly into her body, her most sensitive point, sending arrows of delight up to her head. She prayed that he would find it again soon as his mouth travelled upwards to her waist and followed the curve of her body as far as her arm.

Suddenly she took hold of him, more forcibly than he had ever imagined, and pulled him down so that he lay flat on top of her, his straight, firm penis nestling between her thighs. Amelia sought out his mouth again and kissed him hard, her hands clenching his buttocks rhythmically at the same time. One of his hands had insinuated its way between them and was beginning to caress her aching mons, searching for a way into her.

'Penetrate me with your fingers,' she whispered urgently.

Richard gulped but did as he was asked. As his middle finger slipped between her labia and found her already wet and slippery, she sighed audibly as though he had taken a pin to an inflatable dinghy.

'That feels good,' she said when Richard began to move the finger slowly around, in and out. He smiled with the thought that he was giving her pleasure. A pleasure which was as much his as hers. As he rolled back so that he was on his side with his fingers still in her, his cock rested for a moment on her hip. He felt harder than he had ever done. Ready to come in great gushing spurts without her even laying her little finger on him. She bucked her hips in excitement so that her flesh brushed against his balls. He let out a sudden gasp that made her open her eyes and look at him questioningly.

'I feel like I'm going to burst,' he said apologetically.

'So do I,' she said. 'Let's not waste it.'

Within seconds she had manoeuvred herself so that she was now astride Richard, who lay flat on his back. He looked up at her in shock and amazement. No one had ever taken control like this before. She was holding his penis in her hand, getting him into position beneath her. Tiny moans and squeaks of excitement escaped her pretty mouth as she began to move down and his purple glans touched her wet and ready pussy. She teased them both for a moment by rubbing the smooth head back and forth across her labia like a lipstick until the anticipation became too much for either him or her to bear. Then she used the fingers of one hand to open herself a little more and . . . suddenly she pushed herself down.

Amelia groaned in ecstasy at the sensation of being filled by his glorious dick. It went in to the hilt straight away, so that his balls touched her buttocks. The feeling of being entered so deeply and so perfectly with that first thrust made her giddy with delight.

Having savoured that first moment she put her hands on Richard's shoulders and readied herself to bring some movement into the act. Slowly she drew her backside up so that he began to slip away from her. All the way up so that only the very top of his penis still remained within. Richard burned with joy. He felt as if a host of tiny tongues were licking him all the way up the length of his shuddering shaft to the tip. His hands groped blindly for her thighs so that he could pull her back down onto him again.

But Amelia drove back down of her own accord soon enough, welcoming the invasion of his penis into her body like the waves of the tide rushing back into the shore. She felt so wonderfully wanton, with the shaft of sun cutting across her breasts and his willing body beneath her thighs. She closed her eyes and threw her head back in rapture as she worked her thighs slowly then gradually increased the pace.

Richard had given in to the sensation. He was no longer trying to hold back. Each time her body swept down to meet his, he raised his own hips and gripped her tightly to him. His stomach tensed. He could feel his balls stirring, his shaft stiffening to the point where it hardly seemed like part of his flesh at all. He strained upwards to meet her glistening mouth for another kiss.

'Come, come, come,' Amelia was chanting in a half human, half animal voice. She was moving up and down like a crazed machine, her face changing as the crisis approached. Her climax was gathering within her like a storm cloud of lust. 'Oh, please, come now,' she whispered. 'Come now, Richard. Please come now.'

'Yes, yes, yes!' Richard's grip on her thighs tightened, his fingers turning her skin white with their pressure. His face twisted. His eyes screwed shut. He was gritting his teeth as though to get to his climax he would have to break through a brick wall.

But get there he did.

The force of Richard's orgasm could have shot Amelia straight off the bed. He let forth an incredible roar as his loins pumped furiously beneath her. She was calling out too, her fingers digging hard into his sweat-covered shoulders. The muscular walls of her vagina were matching his rhythm, pumping him dry. As the waves reached their maximum intensity, they pushed their bodies together as though they were trying to make them one for all time. Amelia threw back her head and clutched at handfuls of her hair. Richard exploded into her. Finally, completely, losing all semblance of control.

As her vagina was flooded and overflowing with the mingled secretions of their passion, Amelia collapsed onto Richard and clung to him while the crisis of their climax passed, laughing and crying all at the same time.

Afterwards, as Amelia dozed in the heavy atmosphere of Richard's room, he ran a slow hand through her long hair and replayed the scene which had just taken place through his buzzing mind. For now he was a very happy man indeed but already he had the nagging thought that he was going to be able to repent this particularly amazing event at his leisure.

Chapter Three

'I'VE GOT A GIG!'

Amelia bounced into the kitchen where Richard was making toast. She had been living in Kentish Town for a week now and seemed much happier than when she had first arrived. She had made a effort to make herself known to the local landlords and promoters as a singer/songwriter and already it had paid off.

'That was Lawrence Willow on the phone. One of the acts for Thursday night has pulled out and he wants me to take their place. Me! It's at the Bull and Gate.'

'Great, that's just round the corner,' said Richard. 'I'll be there.'

'Er, well.' Amelia shifted from foot to foot. 'I'd rather you weren't, actually, Richard. It's just that having someone I know sitting in the audience always makes me feel a little bit on edge . . . And apparently there are going to be a couple of A & R men, talent-spotters, in the audience to see the headlining act, so I'd like to play as well as I possibly can. Could be my big break,' she added with a sorry smile.

'Okay.' Richard tried to hide his disappointment. 'I'll stay away. I'm sure you'll knock 'em dead anyway.'

'Do you think so?'

'Of course I do.'

'Really, really?'

'Yes, really. I've heard you practising. Your new songs sound great. Like Tori Amos.'

Amelia's eyes narrowed.

'Okay, not like Tori Amos,' said Richard, back-pedalling. 'Better. You will blow their socks off. I only wish I could see you do it.'

Amelia was smiling broadly. 'When I play Wembley Arena, I promise you'll be in the very front row.' She flung her arms around Richard's neck and let him twirl her around with her feet off the floor. 'Thursday night. I'm so excited,' she told him. Then she squealed. 'That's tomorrow. What on earth am I going to wear?'

Richard watched her retreating figure and felt a faint twang, like Cupid's bow snapping, in his chest. Since their surprising encounter on Saturday, they had not slept together again. In fact nothing had even been said about the incident. But she had been very affectionate, he supposed. Hugging him and kissing him, though just a little too fraternally for his liking. Richard had decided not to push it. They had known each other for just a week or so. Amelia was probably still smarting over that snake of an ex-boyfriend. Richard had all the time in the world, and he was sure his time would come again.

Jamie Nettles liked to think he was as 'dangerous' as his namesake. Dressed in the softest black leather jeans, with no underpants beneath to spoil the line, and a Byronesque white shirt, he waltzed into the dingy pub chatting animatedly on his mobile phone. He was fashionably late, as usual. The gig he was due to watch had started an hour earlier. The manager of the first of the three acts glared across at the errant A & R man, who was widely known to be the most asinine and arrogant but also, unfortunately, one of the most important and influential in the business.

'Awright, Dave?' Jamie nodded to the balding man. The group the bald guy managed had a modicum of talent but were too ugly to be of any interest to this particular impresario. No, Jamie was there to see the act that was on next. Girl singer. Half American, or something. Lawrence thought she had some style and was a bit of a babe, to boot. Jamie wondered whether, coming from Lawrence, that was really a recommendation.

'Drink, Jamie?'

A shadowy figure had appeared at his side. A girl with a complexion the colour of the powder she used up her nose, a centre parting and a smoker's cough. It was Marilyn, his constant companion and sometime lover. She was hanging around with Jamie because she wanted a record deal, and his babies, in that order. Jamie was with her because, while she was an appalling guitarist, she could always manage to get some good gear.

'D'you park the car okay?' he asked her.

'Yeah,' she drawled.

'Good.' Jamie hated parking cars. That was his only problem. The more successful he was, the bigger his company car, and the harder it became for him to park.

The death metal act on stage finished their encore to a round of polite applause from the assembled girlfriends in the audience. Jamie winced at the final ear-splitting chord and mused that it might be worth signing them up just to be able to ensure that they spent the next two years in a soundproof room. While his companion rolled another cigarette and the next act's gear was shifted onstage, Jamie scanned the dingy bar. He recognised a couple of faces. The new exec from EMI. Interested in Death Metal? That was a surprise. Lawrence, the no-hoper guy who promoted the gigs in this godawful place. No girls worth speaking of. This singer had better be good. There was nothing Jamie liked less than to spend an hour in a place where no one was worthy of his decorative presence. He leant on the bar and gazed at his reflection in the glass behind the optics as he rearranged a bright-blond wave over one eye. Not the trendiest of haircuts, as his prodigy bands often teased him, but the girls all loved it. His wraithlike friend nudged his arm and motioned the suggestion of another pint. He mimed a half over the sound of the next act setting up. He had to drive home.

Amelia trod nervously onto the stage. The previous acts had been ten times heavier than her and she was sure that at the first sight of her, with her elegant high-waisted black dress and pre-Raphaelite hair, the place would clear.

She sat down at the keyboards and cleared her throat.

'It's another bloody Tori Amos.' Jamie's companion affected boredom and checked his eyes worriedly for the favourable reaction she knew this pretty redhead would get. He hadn't heard her comment. He tucked his mobile phone tightly into his back pocket and moved closer to the stage.

Her voice trembling with nerves, Amelia announced her first song. Richard's words played through her mind. He had faith in her. He had sat up half the night with her telling her so. She was going to do just fine. She almost wished she hadn't told him not to come. Wished that she could look out into the dark hall and see a friendly face amongst the strangers.

'Heartbreaks and promises,' she announced quaveringly and began to play, hitting the first few notes of her newest song perfectly. She smiled and heaved a sigh of relief as she entered the first chorus. Her stage fright was gone, banished. It was all plain sailing from now on.

Jamie Nettles folded his arms and leaned back against a nicotine-stained pillar. He wasn't sure if the girl was good, but she was damn well gorgeous. So, he figured, he might as well reserve judgement until she'd finished her set and he had her safely en route to his bed.

'You were great,' said Jamie, flashing the girl what he hoped was a warm smile.

'Oh, thanks.' Amelia was still shaking slightly with nerves. Her chosen career was going to be a lot harder than she had ever imagined. 'I'm glad you liked it.'

'I'm Jamie Nettles.' He held out his hand. 'Gallagher Records. A & R.' He fetched out a business card from his back pocket and twirled it between his fingers before giving it to her. He had practised that move. Amelia's eyes flashed excitedly. 'Did you write those songs yourself?'

She nodded eagerly, reading his card. 'I did, yes. All of them. Gallagher Records,' she murmured. That label sounded familiar.

The final act struck up their first song and the room was filled with discord. Jamie asked Amelia another question, which went unheard above the noise, then used the opportunity to take her aside by the arm and whisper straight into her pretty little ear.

'Want to go someplace quiet to talk about your act?' he asked.

'OK,' Amelia agreed, giving him a quick up-and-down glance while he flicked back his hair. 'Lead the way.' Jamie sashayed on ahead of her. He had a beautiful ass.

Jamie whooshed Amelia straight past Marilyn, who dropped her half-finished roll-up in disbelief. He hoped she hadn't left any of her rubbish in his car. Outside, Jamie motioned the beautiful redhead towards his sleek black roadster. She raised an eyebrow approvingly but seconds before she got in, he noticed that it was clamped.

'That can wait until tomorrow,' he said casually, stepping out into the road to hail them both a taxi. He was secretly relieved that he wouldn't have to unpark. 'What do you want to eat?' he asked. 'Chinese, Japanese, Italian?'

Over chimichanga and tacos at a Mexican place on Upper Street, Jamie set to work.

'And then I signed "Stegosaurus" . . .' Amelia nodded politely between mouthfuls of her spicy rice as Jamie ran through his long and successful repertoire of bands. They were mostly heavy rock, which made her wonder why he was interested in her. But hey, this meal was on his company expenses. Jamie reached for the wine-bottle that stood between them and somehow contrived to touch her hand when asking her if she wanted a top-up. The butterfly of first lust beat its wings briefly against the walls of her chest.

'What was that last band you mentioned?' she asked, regaining her composure.

'Stegosaurus,' he replied.

'Oh, yeah,' said Amelia, 'I think I've heard of them.' She hadn't.

'They went top twenty with their third single on Sunday. It's called "I wanna be your underwear." Inspired, eh?' Jamie ran a hand through his hair. He'd be upgrading his car again if they had just one more hit. What a headache.

Amelia felt good. It suddenly struck her that she hadn't really thought about Jerry at all that day and even remembering that she hadn't thought about him didn't dampen the happy mood which was building inside her. She was in a restaurant, eating good food, drinking great wine with a guy who appreciated her music, and had the looks of an apprentice Greek god to boot. And this Greek god definitely seemed to fancy her back. Why else did his every move result in brushing her hand, or her knee beneath the table?

'More wine?' he asked again. She hadn't touched her glass since the last time he asked. He was nervous. She had him on the run. Amelia placed her hand lightly over the top of her glass in refusal.

'Let's get a coffee, yeah? And then I really ought to be going to bed,' she told him. Jamie smiled, acknowledging the undercurrent which made her say 'to bed' rather than 'home'.

'I guess that at this point there's only one thing

left to say,' Jamie said as the taxi hovered outside Amelia's door. 'Your place or mine?'

His place, she decided, and the taxi set off again. Amelia wasn't quite sure why, but she had been distinctly uneasy about taking Jamie back to her own house. At least if she was at his place she could be the one to take the initiative and leave when she wanted to.

Jamie's first-floor flat in Camden was sparsely decorated. It was painted cream throughout. The floors were of pale polished wood, studded here and there with brilliant woollen rugs. An intriguing blue-green painting of nothing in particular hung above the fireplace. Amelia wasn't sure whether it was the flat of someone with immensely good taste or just someone who hadn't bothered to do anything much to it since he moved in. Her host flicked a switch and the room was suddenly filled with a subtle pink light which emanated from a peculiar-looking lamp on a three-legged table beside the sofa.

Jamie emerged from the kitchen with two glasses of brandy. No, not brandy, he told her, Calvados. Ah yes, she nodded, savouring the vague scent of apples before she took a sip and seriously burned her throat. Jamie slumped back on to the king-size sofa beside her. His Cuban-heeled cowboy boots had gone and his feet were bare. Amelia, who for some reason was always acutely aware of people's feet, decided that his were nice. Long, narrow and brown. Nails nicely trimmed and no hairy toes. Jamie drew one leg up so that his foot rested on the edge of the sofa and studied her shy-looking figure from his position of carefully assumed indolence.

'Comfortable?' he asked.

Amelia suppressed a nervous giggle. She kicked off her own shoes and drew both her feet up onto the sofa between them.

'I am now,' she told him.

Jamie rested his wrist on the upraised knee so that his glass dangled just in front of his shin. Amelia fixed her eyes on the swirling contents to avoid the scrutiny of his gaze. She took another sip from her own glass, barely letting any of the vile-tasting liquid into her mouth. Her lips tingled hotly, and she was sure that he would be able to see them growing a deeper red as bad thoughts began to creep into her mind. Prickles of anticipation ran along the back of her neck and down her spine. She could sense him shifting. The inevitable approaching. Suddenly he changed position, put his glass on the floor, took her glass from her hot little hand and pushed her backwards onto the sofa, his entire body touching hers at the same time as his lips as they both sank heavily into the soft cushions.

'I'm sorry,' he said insincerely as he came up for air. 'I just had to do that.'

Amelia feigned surprise. It was always best to let the guy think that it was his idea, that things were proceeding at his chosen pace. Jamie looked beautifully dishevelled now. The second and third buttons of his shirt had mysteriously come undone and revealed a light covering of hair on his chest. A discreet gold chain from which dangled a simple crucifix nestled between his pecs. It moved with him, sliding over his collar bones as he repositioned himself at her side. His hand cupped the side of her face, her chin resting on its heel.

'You can do it again if you like,' she told him softly.

Jamie needed no more encouragement. He brought her face close to his and plunged his tongue between her happily parted lips. The air was forced out of her body by his ardent embrace. She breathed in through her nose, relishing the smell of his aftershave, which warmed each intake of oxygen with amber and other exotic spices. She let her hands settle on his broad, thinly covered back and moved them over the fine cotton, feeling the powerful lineation of his muscles. Here was a man who definitely worked out.

He was making soft mewling sounds and his touch, after that first clumsy attempt, was surprisingly soft and tender. He pulled away from her occasionally, his face cut across by a broad smile, almost as if he was checking that he still had her full and rapt attention. His hands flattened out on her shoulder blades, then he slid them up and down, bringing blood rushing to her cheeks in anticipation as he found the tiny button that fastened her dress at the nape.

He fumbled the button open but the slit which such an action revealed was barely big enough for his hand. He contented himself for a moment with a small foray across her chilly shoulders with his well-kept fingers. Then he found her bra strap, followed it a little way down but soon realised that he just couldn't get to anything this way.

Amelia meanwhile was dealing with the remaining fastenings on his shirt. They popped apart easily and soon the shirt was open to the waist. She pulled away from his kiss and looked down at his exposed torso. He was lean. The muscles on his abdomen showed clearly, highlighted by a covering of dark hair that ran in a line from his belly button and disappeared beyond the belt of his leather jeans. Amelia's hands grasped the tops of his thighs as she returned to the kiss. The leather of his expensive jeans was so soft that she felt as though she was already touching his skin. She shifted position until her long skirt was no longer trapped beneath her and Jamie could lift the whole black dress over her head and out of the way.

She heard him draw breath in approval when he saw what the unveiling had revealed. Amelia let her head fall back so that her long red hair tumbled around her bare shoulders. Her perfectly rounded breasts bounced proudly up like twin suns from an intricately lacy bra. She was wearing exquisitely delicate knickers and beneath them, a suspender belt to match. Even her fine black stockings had lacy tops to them. She always like to dress for all possible eventualities and was very pleased now, knowing that an eventuality had popped up and Jamie was about to become as malleable as a soft dick in her warm hand.

When she felt that he had had sufficient opportunity to take the vision in, she returned to the business of setting him free from his own clothes. The voluminous white shirt slipped easily back from his shoulders. Amelia quickly tugged it free from his leather pants and tossed it aside. It billowed in the air like a sail as it fell to the floor.

Now for his belt.

Her fingers found their way to the heavy silver buckle. Jamie only looked down at the hands which were undressing him and gave a tiny, strangled noise of approval. Amelia had gathered from a brief exploration of his buttocks while they were kissing that he was not wearing any underpants and, since the fine black leather was the last barrier between her hands and his total nudity, she wanted this particular moment to last.

The free end of the belt was loosened. Amelia slid the long leather strip out from the loops. The feeling of his belt slipping away from around his waist provoked another of Jamie's peculiar little mews. Once she had pulled it completely free, Amelia took the redundant belt in both hands and looped it carefully around his strong neck, using it like a lasso to pull him to her. His eyes were closed. Amelia noticed with pleasure that his dark brown eyelashes were long enough to brush against his cheeks. She couldn't resist rubbing her nose softly against his. His hands blindly sought her warm breasts in their lacy confines.

Amelia slowly undid one of the tight silver buttons on his trousers while Jamie deftly unclipped her bra with one hand as though he had been born for the special purpose of doing so. She exhaled in pleasure at the sensation of her heavy breasts suddenly swinging free, their nipples already hard and ready to gratefully receive his urgent kiss.

Pop went another of Jamie's buttons. The line of hair which originated at his belly button became altogether more prolific here beneath his waistband. Amelia ran a teasing finger through the tawny curls. His smooth penis, still held down by the tightness of his flies, seemed to be straining upwards. Jamie's fingers played along the hem of her close-fitting panties, slipping under the elastic until his hands were cupping the twin cheeks. At the same time his mouth fluttered down her throat to her shoulder. He was breathing heavily as she let the final fly buttons go. Amelia was sure that her entire body would be flushed and pink by now. The Spartan sitting-room, which had been slightly cold when they first came in was suddenly starting to feel very warm indeed.

Jamie got up from the sofa and stood before her so that finally she could more easily pull his body-hugging trousers down. His dick sprang free and stood straight out in front of him, level with her eyes.

'It's rude to point,' Amelia laughed.

Coquettishly, she lifted her hair up away from her neck with both hands and held it on top of her head while she took in the picture of Jamie in his naked glory. Jamie looked at her, then at his dick. At her red mouth, then at his dick. The invitation was only too clear.

Amelia let her hair drop back onto her shoulders and shuffled forwards to the edge of the sofa. Jamie got into position between her stockinged legs. Amelia wrapped a hand around each of his thighs and pulled him closer still, her mouth widening into a tantalising smile as she let the pinky-purple glans bob up and down, up and down, just millimetres away from her slick glossy lips. Jamie placed his palms on her shoulders. He could hardly believe his luck. Not only was she gorgeous, but she actually looked as if she wanted to do this. Gently, he pulled her towards him so that she had to open her mouth to let him inside. Teasingly, she pulled away again once more.

'Tell me if I get it wrong,' she told him with the earnestness of someone taking their first driving lesson.

'I'm sure you won't,' he replied calmly, while his body screamed at her to hurry up.

Amelia ran a provocative fingertip along the gully where his abdomen joined his leg. A soft chuckle escaped her lips. There was nothing submissive about this position for her. He was putty in her hands, about to become marble between her teeth. Her lips formed a perfect 'O' as she zeroed in.

'Mmmmm.' A sigh like escaping steam flowed from Jamie's mouth. The moment her lips had closed oh so gently on his purple head, he had taken her red head in his hands. As her tongue worked diligently around the tip, he scrunched up great handfuls of her hair, even rubbing some of it against his downy stomach. Amelia wasn't a deep throater. She liked to use her hands and tongue, gently massaging the foreskin up and down the shaft with her fingers while her tongue flickered across the smooth glans and sensitive raphe. She closed her eyes and savoured the taste of his clean penis, growing saltier with semen as she licked him, and listened eagerly for the sighs which let her know that she was doing it right. She worked all over the shaft with her tongue, and right down to his balls. Jamie's hands were going mad in her hair, twisting and pulling harder than he knew, but Amelia bore his clumsiness for now, guessing that it was a sign of deep, deep appreciation.

Letting his glans drag slowly out over her bottom lip, Amelia moved her attention to his balls. She blew on the hairy sacs which hung swollen and pulsing between his hard thighs. The skin on Jamie's balls moved in reaction like a covering of molten lava. Eventually Amelia cupped one in each hand and fondled them like two precious golden spheres while she licked sporadically at the bobbing glans. He was getting really hot now. She would have to use one hand to hold the shaft still while she licked at it.

'Amelia . . .' He breathed her name as though it were a word in a foreign language. His fingers tightened in her hair. 'Slow down, slow down, please. I feel like I'm going to burst. You are driving me mad . . .'

Reluctantly unfastening her tingling hands from his shaft, he pulled her up from the sofa so that they were face to face again. He had to stop her or he would be useless for the rest of the night. He kissed her again, her mouth salty with his own semen.

Amelia was still wearing her knickers. Jamie gave them a yank and they quickly joined the rest of her clothes on the floor. He didn't want her to take off her stockings and suspenders, not yet.

'You've got such a warm pussy,' he told her as he placed his right hand purposefully between the tops of her legs. Normally, she would have shuddered at such a description but somehow, that night, coming from him, it seemed right. His fingers brushed across her fast-awakening labia towards her tingling clitoris. It was her turn to tremble now.

'Is it as warm right inside?' he asked.

Unconsciously, Amelia spread her legs a little further apart and raised herself on tiptoe to make it easier for him to find out.

She sighed with a delirious mixture of pleasure and relief as the first finger slipped easily inside.

She was feeling so wet. So very hot. She ground her silky mons against his welcome hand, begging him without words to find her clitoris and fast. Jamie quickly picked up on her subconscious signal and was soon there. Amelia let out a shaking breath as she felt her newly-discovered clitoris begin to stiffen and grow large.

'Faster,' she murmured. Jamie obliged. Amelia's legs shook and became unsteady as the pleasure became more intense and she had to get him to let her collapse back down onto the bed-sized sofa again. He tumbled on top of her, still working his hand furiously in her body as though he was revving up the engine of a sleek red car. He thought that her face, in the throes of her lust, was even more beautiful than it had looked at the club and in the restaurant. Her darkening eyes had taken on a feline quality, seeming almost to draw out his soul, as she looked at him from beneath lowered lids.

'And harder,' she whispered.

Jamie's excitement grew in line with hers. He reared away from her and his dick waved between them like an excited spectator watching the big match. His feet slid backwards on the shiny wooden floor as he tried to put even more power behind his arm.

'More! More!' Amelia's breathing was getting so heavy now that Jamie could hardly hear her words. Her hands fumbled for his penis. No matter how many fingers he put inside her, it

46

seemed that they would never be enough to satisfy her desperation. Her eyes greedily took in his dick. Hard and straight. Big enough to make a difference. Amelia twisted around so that her legs fell off the sofa, her bottom at the edge. She opened her knees. Jamie dropped to his knees between them, still working her clitoris like a demon with his love-slick fingers.

'Fuck me, Jamie,' she hissed with a voice that was barely her own. She pushed his hands out of the way and placed her own fingers on her labia, pulling them apart so that the entrance to her vagina was explicitly clear. Jamie pulled himself into position, steadying himself with his hands on her creamy thighs. Her vagina was at the perfect height. Holding his dick in his hand like a weapon, he penetrated her. Her hands clutched at the loose soft cushions behind her head. Her arousal-pink face first registered a fleeting look of shock at the strength of his thrust, then pleasure, her eyebrows raised.

Open-mouthed with ecstasy, Jamie slowly drew back his hips and pulled his shaft a little way clear of its deep warm haven. Amelia groaned as her swollen lips vibrated softly with his passing and she grabbed for his waist to stop him from withdrawing too far. Jamie looked momentarily as if he were about to speak but was unable to find the words. Amelia used the sides of his slim waist to lever him back inside until his pelvis grazed her clitoris and his balls slapped against the cheeks of her bottom. Jamie's hands rested, one on each of her breasts, while he savoured the feeling of the muscles in her hot narrow pussy with which Amelia was holding on tightly to his shaft.

Amelia was sliding off the sofa. Gradually both she and Jamie slipped to the floor, still fastened together. Amelia groped for a cushion which she knew had fallen off the sofa earlier and wiggled it in beneath the small of her back. Her hips were raised to the perfect angle now. Jamie was as deep within her as it was possible for a man to go. He felt her hands take possession of his buttocks, kneading them, encouraging him to begin pumping again now that she was comfortable beneath him. Jamie raised himself on his arms so that their bodies were joined only at the pelvis. Amelia gazed in tacit approval at the taut tensed arms which held Jamie above her, then she looked down along her body to where his semen-shiny shaft was slowly gliding in and out.

The combination of the friction of Jamie's movements and the sight of them taking place were almost instantly too much. Amelia felt a spasm in her vagina, pushing a sigh from her mouth. She raised her knees and placed her feet flat on the floor for leverage. Her thighs were trembling with a sensation of melting as she brought them in tightly against Jamie's waist.

She longed to force him to speed up, to thrust into her as though he was trying to thrust through her, but Jamie was taking things at his own measured pace, using his shaft as an instrument of slow torturous pleasure, determined that he would not be the first to let go. Amelia's head rolled slowly from one side to another. Her eyes were closed now, her eyebrows knitted together. She was biting her lower lip. Around his waist, her thighs gripped harder and harder. Her hands on his buttocks were trying to flatten him into her.

'Aaaaah!' A cry she just couldn't hold inside told him that she was nearly there. For Jamie too, the restraint was at last becoming too much to bear. Like a stallion spurred on by the crack of the whip, he finally agreed to let her hands set the pace. Her pelvis rose frantically up to meet his. Their bodies crashed together as they raced towards the finish. He had collapsed down onto her now, his mouth at her ear. The sound of his panting, his passionately uncontrolled exhalations was arousing her still more.

Suddenly, Amelia felt as though she was a mighty river, rushing through a narrowing tunnel, the pressure building up until there was no option but to burst open the walls which were channelling her inwards. She lost her rhythm, could no longer keep up. Jamie carried on, his face changed above her, barely recognisable in his ecstasy. Amelia's hips no longer moved in time with his but pushed ever upwards as she was ripped apart by the first wave of her climax, to be joined, fractions of a second later, by his.

Like a single frozen frame of an all-action film, their bodies were still momentarily, pressed together and held there by the forces which still raged inside them. Amelia counted the tiny grunts which accompanied each spasm of her lover's thunderous orgasm, while hers rolled continuously, relentlessly, like the angry sea breaking through a dam.

When the crisis was over, they stayed locked together on the floor, neither wanting to be the first to pull away from the other's body. Jamie's softening penis still felt caressed from time to time by Amelia's pulsating vaginal walls. But soon she found she was growing cold, so Jamie pulled a throw off the sofa and laid it over the top of them both. They stayed there on the floor until the throw and the pink light could keep them warm no more.

Chapter Four

'NICE NIGHT?' RICHARD asked in a tone which told her that he really didn't want to know. 'You could have called. I waited up for ages. I was worried.'

'You needn't have worried,' Amelia breezed. 'I stayed with a friend.'

'I had to feed your cat,' Richard said accusingly.

'Thanks.'

As if on cue, Eliza appeared and wound herself around Amelia's silk-stockinged legs. Richard noticed the ladder which ran upwards from her left heel.

'What friend?' he asked. As soon as the words escaped his lips he wished he could have bitten them back.

'Someone in the industry. No one you know.'

'I am in the industry, remember?'

'Oh, yeah.' Amelia laughed. 'The singing accountant. I forgot.' Richard clenched his teeth.

'Who did you stay with? I'm interested.'

'Jamie Nettles, if you must know.'

Jamie Nettles. Richard paled at the name of that posturing idiot.

'Known him long?'

'Ages,' Amelia lied. 'I'm going to have a bath. Is there any hot water?'

As Amelia jogged up the stairs, Richard finally remembered to ask, 'How was the gig?' She gave him the thumbs up sign and disappeared behind the bathroom door.

Jamie bloody Nettles. Richard knew exactly what he'd like to do to that guy with a dock leaf. They had met at the record company's Christmas party, the only time of the year when creatives, like Jamie, mixed with the proles, like Richard, who actually kept the company going when A & R's 'next-big-things' went belly-up. He wore leather trousers and high-lighted his hair. There was nothing else Richard really needed to know. Their acquaintance would have been restricted to a hair-flick and a sneer had Richard not been standing next to the prettiest girl in Finance when Jamie walked into the room.

Jamie had sashayed by, pinched the girl's bum and Richard had landed the reciprocal slap round the face. Jamie saw Richard take the flak, bought him a drink for being such a good sport and, two weeks of being best buddies later, walked off with Richard's girlfriend of the time. That dalliance hadn't lasted long of course, but Richard could never feel quite the same about his one-time dream girl again. He wondered how well Amelia had known Jamie Nettles 'for ages'.

'I forgot,' said Richard when Amelia emerged towel-wrapped from the bathroom like Botticelli's Venus from the waves. 'Jerry's secretary came round to the house this morning – in the Shogun.' Amelia's eyes narrowed. 'She dropped off some post for you.'

'Where is it?'

'Over there.' He motioned towards the mantelpiece.

Amelia sorted through the not inconsiderable pile of envelopes until she came to one with an American stamp and very familiar handwriting. Amelia turned the blue envelope over in her hands a couple of times before she took a deep breath and opened it.

'It's from my mother,' she told Richard. 'She never writes unless something has gone desperately wrong or she's about to get married.' Amelia skip-read the letter. 'And this time she's about to get married.'

Her lips pressed together in a tight smile. 'The wedding takes place next Saturday. In Las Vegas of all places. To a guy called Doug Hertzberg. He's a dentist. And his clients include Tom Cruise.' She was reading out the letter in a strong West Coast accent. 'And Mom wants me to be there – as her matron of honour. Matron. I ask you . . . She says she has already booked the tickets in my name, so I guess I'm gonna be there.'

Amelia threw the letter down onto the coffee table.

'Damn it. That means I'll have to cancel my next gig.'

'But it is your mother's wedding . . .' Richard reminded her.

'You don't understand, Richard,' Amelia said with a world-weary sigh. 'It's my mother's fifth wedding. She does this every other year.'

Chapter Five

AMELIA WAS VERY glad of her dual nationality when the Virgin flight from London touched down in Los Angeles and she was able to walk straight past the queue of true Brits waiting at immigration. She hauled her cases onto a trolley, wondering briefly how a couple of pairs of shorts and a swimsuit could possibly weigh so much, and made her way to the arrivals lounge. Her mother had told her that she had just had her hair coloured mahogany, so she looked out for a head of that shade but could see none. She was just about to get to a phone and find out why no one was there to meet her when she caught sight of a very familiar head indeed. Not mahogany, but blond. Not her mother, but Amelia's ex-lover – mark one.

'Mimi!' he jumped up and down excitedly, waving a piece of card with her name scrawled across the front of it, as if she wouldn't have recognised him. 'Mimi, it's me, Marty, over here!'

Amelia hated being called Mimi. Well, she had hated that particular abbreviation of her name ever since she and Marty had split up. He pushed forward through the crowd of people waiting to pick up loved ones and planted a hot kiss on her irritated cheek.

'Let me take that.' He wrested the luggage trolley from her grip and began to push it towards the car-park. Amelia was suddenly hit by the heat as they briefly walked through the sun. 'Why didn't you let me know you were coming? Your mother just called me. She couldn't make it to the airport because she has a tennis match at two with Mrs Hobbs that she just clean forgot. And then a residents' meeting in Bel Air. She says she will see you at the house later this evening. I said I'd pick you up . . .'

'Oh, mother,' thought Amelia. She was still trying to patch up the long-dead relationship between her daughter and one of the most eligible bachelors on this side of the Atlantic.

Marty was like a dog with two tails. He slung Amelia's luggage into the back of his red BMW six series as though it was made of polystyrene and feathers, then picked her up just as easily and twirled her around.

'I am so glad to see you, Mimi.'

'Amelia.'

'Don't be so English.'

'I am, Marty, I am . . .' She sighed. 'Hey, Dumbo, just who is my mother marrying this time anyway?'

'Oh, Doug. He's a cool guy. He did these.' Marty bared his teeth for her to check out the dentistry. 'I dinged them on a rock when I was surfing off Huntingdon last month. Lost half of this one here . . . and this one was completely smashed.' He indicated a perfect denture.

'Oh, well,' Amelia sighed, 'at least I know my mother's molars are in good hands.'

Amelia went to get into the car and found herself unconsciously going for the driver's seat.

'Wrong side,' laughed Marty, using the opportunity to squeeze close by her to get to the wheel. He reached across the seats and flicked the passenger door open. She slipped in beside him, careful not to flash too much leg. Marty put the key in the ignition but didn't start the car.

'You're looking great, Mimi,' he told her as he looked deep into her eyes.

'Thanks.' She didn't like to return the compliment, though it was exactly what she was thinking. His blond hair was a little shorter than she remembered, with his heavy fringe swept back from his face. It was bleached bright blond by the sun and salt water. He smiled broadly, flashing his new white teeth, like jewels against his biscuity tan. He was wearing a light blue vest and brightly coloured board shorts that showed her that his body had lost none of its tone. As he lifted his arm to adjust the rear-view mirror, she caught a whiff of a familiar deodorant, mixed with familiar sweat, and was unable to prevent the rush of nostalgia which accompanied it. She closed her tired eyes and breathed in deeply and slowly.

'You look a touch on the pale side though, Englisher,' he was teasing her.

Amelia threw out an arm to hit him in the side. Just like old times.

'So, what exactly are you doing now?' Marty asked between mouthfuls of Caesar salad. Amelia looked around at the decor of the waterfront café as she considered her answer. What had she been doing? The sun bouncing on the water outside, the sound of ropes against sail-poles in the wind, the bronzed and beautiful people who passed them by . . . And to think that she had been living in dirty old Kentish Town when she could have stayed in her pretty summer villa on Balboa Island?

'I've been trying to get my act together.' The cliché had meaning for her in more ways than one. She had left LA for London because of the man sitting in front of her that very minute. When she had last eaten in that very café, where they were now having their lunch, she was twenty-one years old. He was six months older. Both fresh out of college. She had wanted marriage. He didn't, of course, and four years of reflection in British weather had made her see that it wouldn't really have been such a good idea after all. Compared to Jerry, Marty was still just a kid. 'Still writing songs?' he asked in a way which implied that he didn't really take her ambitions seriously.

'Yes,' she told him.

He looked surprised.

'I'm negotiating a deal, as a matter of fact.' It was a bit of an exaggeration but she was damned if Marty was going to make her feel small within an hour of stepping off the plane. And with a bit of luck, she would be making a deal in the not too distant future. Jamie Nettles had promised to look into it for her. 'And what about you? What are you doing with yourself these days?' She wanted to get Marty off the subject of her life before the holes started to become evident.

'Oh, this and that.'

As usual, Amelia reflected. Marty was fortunate to have a family rich enough to support him lovingly while he did just 'this and that', year in, year out. His father was a sought-after film producer, his mother, a fading Norwegian film star who had settled in Hollywood after a brief blaze of glory as a Bond girl in the sixties. With all that celluloid in his blood, Marty had harboured ambitions to direct, but unfortunately found it difficult to get up for anything in the morning other than the surf.

'This and that,' Amelia echoed.

'Brett and I are writing a screenplay based on the story of two surfers who find this really incredible break just off the coast of . . .'

Amelia wasn't tuned in to Marty's words. As he shovelled lettuce into his mouth and talked through it about his plans for the next year or so, she was taking in the familiar face. She took in his blue eyes, inherited from his beautiful Scandinavian mother, which sparkled excitedly as he talked about projected profits for his yet to be born production company. She took in the full lips she used to spend so much time kissing.

'You finished?' she asked him when the last mouthful of salad was gone. 'Let's go for a drive.'

Marty settled the bill with a flash of American Express and soon they were outside in the sun again. It had been warm in London but not nearly as warm as this. It was still well into the eighties though it was nearly dusk. Amelia surveyed the boats which lined the harbour as though the sight were completely new to her.

A lone roller-skater weaved in and out of the pedestrians towards them. He was oblivious to the rest of the world, lost in the music on his personal stereo to which he was no doubt matching his moves. The muscles in his legs, which flexed as he passed, touched something deep inside Amelia. She had a weakness for a pair of thick, firm thighs and the erotic possibilities which his brief appearance on the street awakened in her made her reach out and link her arm through Marty's as they walked by. He smiled at her sudden decision to touch him and resumed the contact by placing his hand on her knee when they got into the car.

It was cool enough to have the top down now. When he had picked her up at LAX it was better to have the top up and the air-conditioning on.

Marty flicked on the CD player and cranked it up as loud as it would go so that they would be able to hear the music above the roar of the powerful engine. As she settled into the deep and warm leather-covered seat, Amelia could already feel her inner thighs growing moist with the combination of the heat and the power of the automobile beneath her.

There was no doubt about it. A fast car was a great substitute for a small dick, but when the fast car was driven by someone who was not only well-off, but also well-endowed, the combination was fatal.

Once he got behind the wheel, Marty was a different guy. The aggression in his driving made him seem older somehow, more of a man. Amelia laughed to herself for thinking that the addition of a sixteen-valve engine could make him seem so much more attractive but she didn't move his hand off her knee and was disappointed when he had to pull away from her to change gears. Why the hell didn't he still drive an automatic?

They struck out onto the freeway, heading north to Malibu beach and the Bel Air beach club that Amelia had missed so much during the grey British winters. The road, busy with commuters, required a great deal of concentration and suddenly Amelia found that Marty just wasn't paying her enough attention. The engine growled beneath her, the rock music on the stereo was full of bass, making her heart beat faster, her breath come more quickly.

Now the sun was sinking and the sky turning from grey-blue to pink – a fantastic sunset being the one good side effect of the terrible smog. Amelia loved the pastel Pacific colours of Los Angeles. So different from the moody green and grey of the Atlantic beaches in Cornwall and Devon that she had visited a summer ago with Jerry. She reclined her seat a little more and looked up at the sky as they drove. From time to time a palm tree would lean over the road and cut across her view. Even the traffic lights which dangled from wires seemed exciting to her that day, especially when they were stuck on red and gave Marty the chance to turn his attention briefly back into the car.

Suddenly they hit a stretch of fairly clear road and Marty made straight for the car pool lane, making the most of having a passenger as an excuse to speed past the Porsche owners who languished one to a car in the selfish driver's queue. Amelia was lying right back, her seat fully reclined, her hair waving in the wind like a scarf, her feet braced against the floor of the car, her hand creeping down to the edge of her flirty flowery skirt.

Amelia pulled her skirt up and her pants down.

'Fuck, Amelia,' Marty gasped, as he caught sight of the action from the corner of his eye. 'I gotta concentrate on my driving.'

'I'm not asking you to join in, Marty. Just drive. Fast.'

Marty's foot went down and the sound of the

engine took on a different tone. They had to be doing a hundred now. The trees and traffic signs passing overhead became one long blue of green. Amelia opened her mouth to scream 'Yes!' but her exaltation was lost in the roar of the wind.

Her fingers, which had been twisting and tangling in her soft pubic hair, moved lower to find her fast-moistening sex. She found no resistance there, two fingers sliding straight in and out with alarming quickness. While her right hand penetrated her velvety entrance, her left hand toyed tantalisingly with her hardening clit, heightening the sensation and sending darts of excitement down her inner thighs. Using juices from her vagina, she gently lubricated the tiny clitoral nub so that she could vibrate it faster still. Her lower body was all a-tremble. Though she felt that she hardly needed to use her hands at all, lying back as she was in Marty's huge vibrator of a car.

Her mouth quivered, her face smiling and then looking as if about to cry by turns. Her breath was short, arrested, each sigh whipped away to the car travelling behind. Languidly, she turned her head to her left to look at the man beside her. Marty's hands gripped the wheel tightly, his forearms tensed. Amelia's eyes travelled down his body to his loose board shorts. An unmistakable bulge had lifted them away from his body at the crotch.

'Wanna park, Marty?' Amelia asked wickedly as she lazily continued to bring herself off.

Marty grunted a reply and turned off the freeway at the first possible opportunity, swinging the screeching car around as if it had hit a patch of black ice. Down a quiet road leading up into a junk-filled canyon, he pulled the car over onto a grassy verge that was edged by trees. Grabbing her by the hand he lifted Amelia out of the car and dragged her stumbling behind one of the parched pines, ignoring her protests that her legs were being scratched by the long, dry grass. With one hand he lifted up her skirt and, with the other, he pulled his dick out through the front of his shorts. The circumcised tip of his shaft was already glistening wetly with pre-come. Amelia divested herself of her flimsy knickers altogether and got into position.

There was no time for any more preliminaries.

'Ready?' he asked.

Marty hoisted Amelia up so that her legs were wrapped around his waist. He supported her with his strong arms while she shifted until his hard shaft hovered at the door to her desire.

'Yes. Now.'

Amelia used her thighs to pull herself in towards Marty's body and impale herself on his penis. They sighed simultaneously with the pleasure of the connection and for a moment everything seemed to be in slow motion while they enjoyed the melting sensation of coming together. Then, as though neither of them had seen a body of the opposite sex in the four years they had been apart, they began to move again.

Frantically. Sometimes in time, sometimes out of it. The powerful crashing of an ill-timed move only adding to the experience.

Amelia clung on tightly to Marty's neck, after a while letting him control the pace, pushing her and pulling her backwards and forwards. Marty had the biggest dick she had ever encountered. It stretched and filled her more deliciously than anything she had found before or since . . . And it was harder than marble now.

Marty grunted into her red hair with the exertion of holding her in position and the thunderous excitement which was building in his loins. Amelia leaned back all of a sudden and nearly pulled them both over by upsetting the balance. Marty shuffled about, with her legs still clamped around him, until he had backed her up against a tree. The dry bark scraped against her back as they moved, but she could hardly feel the pain . . . and right now she didn't really care.

Her pussy was aching for more and more and more. She knew that she was just about to come and by the frantic grunting in her hair, she could tell that Marty would not be far behind. She clutched at his shoulders, both to stop herself from falling to the ground and to have him as deep inside her as she possibly could. His fingers clenched her buttocks as he brought them into the home straight, crashing her body against his.

Marty's movements were going to pieces now as he reached explosion point. He flung his head back. His eyes were tightly closed as if his whole body was trying to squeeze the orgasm out. Amelia felt his buttocks clenching beneath her calves which were still crossed tightly around the back of his body. Suddenly, he stopped his thrusting and drew her to him one final time, holding her in place as she began to feel his dick stiffening to shoot. His semen seared its way inside her.

Amelia screamed with joy as her orgasm followed quickly after. Her pussy was drenched both with his come and her own, which was forcing its way out to soak her thighs and the front of his shorts.

They collapsed onto the grass, panting with exertion. Amelia gazed up at the reddening California sky and let out a joyful laugh as Marty leant up on his elbow, kissed her nose and told her 'Welcome home'.

An hour later, Marty turned his BMW into the driveway of Amelia's mother's house in Bel Air. He turned the engine off and waited expectantly to be invited inside. Instead, Amelia opened the car door for herself, fetched her own luggage from the trunk and carried it to the porch. The key she had carried in her purse for four years still fitted the hefty lock. She opened the door and walked inside.

Marty still sat in his car. Amelia poked her head out and waved him goodbye.

'Thanks for the lift, Marty,' she called to him. 'See you in another four years or so!'

The attraction was still there, she figured, but she'd had an itch and she'd scratched it. There was no need to rub herself all over with sandpaper. As Marty gave a shrug of his handsome brown shoulders and reversed his BMW out of the drive, Amelia knew that the best thing she could do now was stay out of his way. After Jerry, she had no intention of letting herself fall in love again, particularly on the rebound with the devil she already knew too well.

Marty waved. He'd be on the beach and she'd be out of his mind by the time the sun came up the next day. As she watched the back-lights of the BMW disappear around the corner, Amelia felt just the faintest cry of disappointment from between her sticky thighs.

Chapter Six

'DARLING, DARLING, DARLING!!!'

Amelia's mother Theresa wafted into the antiqued oak kitchen in a cloud of *Giorgio*. She looked slimmer and happier than she had when Amelia last saw her on a fleeting visit to the British Isles, as Theresa was wont to call them. Behind her hovered a tall thin man with very little hair on top of his walnut-tanned head but a set of teeth that the Cheshire Cat would have killed for. Amelia guessed that this must be Doug. He introduced himself as such and kissed her on both cheeks. She couldn't help but notice that he shared her mother's taste in overpowering perfume.

'I knew you'd come, Honey Bun. Hope you didn't have to cancel anything important for your poor old mom . . . I have the dress, it's in my dressing room – out of Dougie's way.' She giggled like a young virgin on her first marriage rather than a sexagenarian on her fifth. 'I was gonna get green for you because that goes best with your hair but the girl at the store said green's unlucky for weddings so I got you an Edwardian style robe with a burnt clementine velvet bodice and sleeves and ivory satin skirt instead . . .'

Doug had already wandered out into the carefully kept garden with its orange and lemon trees and was lighting up a pipe. Amelia deserted her bags on the spotless kitchen floor and followed her excited mother up the stairs to the room which had once been her own.

They flew to Vegas on the Saturday morning. Amelia's mother had tried to persuade her to have Marty there as her escort but Amelia was having none of it. True, he was a lovely guy, from a respected family, with a mansion in Stone Canyon that had an Olympic-sized pool, not to mention two ski chalets in Europe and a condo down town, but he was also the lovely guy who had once broken her heart. When the wedding was over, Amelia told Theresa, she would check out the MGM casino with the other witness, Doug's daughter Leah.

Leah was in her mid-thirties, tall like her father. She was married to an evangelist from Idaho who could not bring himself to smile on the remarriage of his father-in-law in such a city of sin. Hopefully, Amelia thought, Leah would retire at ten to say her prayers and she would be left in peace to enjoy Vegas as she really wanted to. At a blackjack table, on her own.

The drive-in wedding ceremony was suitably speedy. It was followed by a sumptuous meal in the pyramid-shaped Luxor casino-hotel. (Theresa's spiritual regressionist had told her that she was an Egyptian in a past life but Doug was unable to get the time off work to enable them to honeymoon in Cairo.) Throughout the meal, Doug and Theresa swapped glances and caresses that told Amelia they would be only too glad to see their witnesses buzz off. Amelia half-heartedly caught the bouquet her mother tossed to her as she disappeared with her new hubby into the elevator. Leah smiled approvingly and asked who was going to be the lucky man. Amelia wiped the smile off her face by saying that she was considering Mormonism since there were just too many to choose from at the present time.

The burnt clementine and ivory bridesmaid's dress soon found its way onto the bathroom floor in Amelia's slanting, windowed suite and was replaced by something a little more 'Vegas'. Leah, predictably, had wimped out of an evening at the tables. She was going to fly back to Idaho at the first possible opportunity and Amelia was free. She clipped on a pair of emerald earrings that Jerry had given her for her twenty-fourth birthday and pulled a soft green sweater embroidered with a butterfly in sparkly thread and sequins over her head. Her mother, who had bought the sweater, was right, the colour suited her daughter's hair and it didn't matter much about luck any more.

Amelia walked from the Luxor to the MGM which was just opposite, across the busy highway into a town that always moved at a snail's pace because people kept leaning out of windows to take photos and say 'oooh and aaah'. Stepping out into the gaudily lit street gave Amelia a head-rush like no other. Her pulse was raised immediately by the sights, the smells and the unnatural noise. She nodded happily at the huge billboards that flashed out alternately '$100,000 JACKPOT' and 'ALL YOU CAN EAT FOR 50 CENTS'. She looked down the road that led out of the town to the silent mountains surrounding this monument to Mammon. Then up at the indescribably gigantic lion that was the MGM hotel. She felt dwarfed, she felt exhilarated. She felt like she needed to have an orgasm.

Nearly crashing into a couple of real live cowboys with hats and rhinestones as she did so, she crossed the road and dashed inside the lion's den. A bundle of dollars which her new father-in-law had thrust into her hand after the wedding reception was burning a hole in her pocket. As the casino opened out before her, she didn't know where to start. Elegant croupiers with perfectly manicured hands dealt cards with the bored look of Oxford Street shop assistants. Theme-dressed waitresses weaved between them carrying free drinks for the punters. Young men and old ladies poured dollars into the slots of one-armed bandits as insistent as open-mouthed baby birds. To her right, a machine spilled silver dollar tokens out onto the floor. The player grovelled to scoop them up in his plastic cup while a loud electronic fanfare drew the rest of the casino's attention to the latest favourite of Lady Luck.

Amelia crossed the floor purposefully and slid silently onto an empty velvet stool at the edge of a blackjack game. She exchanged fifty dollars into tokens. The croupier dealt her in quickly and the game continued, so fast that there seemed to be nothing game-like about the whole business at all. The croupier went bust. Amelia gathered her winnings and prepared for the next game, doubling her stake. If you're going to gamble, Jerry used to say, you might as well gamble big. Well, ten dollars wasn't quite big, but by the end of the evening she would get there.

A waitress came and took her order, returning minutes later with a double dark rum and Coke over ice. And another. And another. Amelia sat at the same table until she had increased her pile of tokens to seventy-five and doubted that she would actually be able to stand straight if she did get up.

'Quit while you're ahead, eh?'

Amelia swivelled around on her stool, her hands full of bright plastic tokens, to come face to face with the last person she had expected, or wanted, to see in Vegas that night. His bow tie hanging undone around his neck, his waistcoat open – a sign that he had just had a pretty good meal – Jerry Anson stood behind her with a cigar burning in the corner of his mouth.

'Jerry? What are you doing here?'

'I could ask the same of you.'

'It's a small world.' Amelia's automatic reaction to the sight of Jerry's face, a smile, had been swiftly replaced by a less friendly façade.

'No,' said Jerry, about to use one of his favourite corrections, 'it's a big world and there are a lot of coincidences.'

Amelia stood up to go but Jerry settled himself on her stool, pulling her down onto his knee before she could protest. 'You can be my mascot, Amy,' he told her. He put his hand in his pocket and pulled out a crumpled fistful of hundred-dollar bills. The croupier changed a thousand dollars into gambling chips. Jerry put the whole thousand on the table and won first time.

'You are my lucky star,' he sang to the squirming girl on his knee.

'Let go of me, Jerry,' Amelia snarled. 'Your "Personal Assistant" might get jealous.'

'She isn't here.' Jerry's speech was slurred – the result of too many hospitality whiskies. 'She's looking after the office. And anyway, I wasn't sleeping with her. I was sleeping with Mac's girl . . .'

Before he could tell her that it was all over now, Amelia landed a stinging slap right on Jerry's jaw. He tumbled backwards, tipping her onto the floor as he fell. He hit his head on the edge of another table and lay, out cold, on the plush red carpet. The croupier had stopped the game. The punters gathered round him in a collective gasp.

'You all right?' asked a Texan gentleman who helped Amelia to her feet. 'Was he bothering you?'

'He's been bothering me for four years!!' Amelia shouted indignantly as she stood over Jerry's prone body, her hands on her hips. 'You low-down sonofabitch, why don't you just stay out of my life!'

Jerry clutched his head and groaned.

'Get up, you creep,' Amelia snarled, 'so I can knock you down again!'

The crowd was growing. This was better than a free trip to Universal Studios.

Jerry pulled himself giddily to his feet with the aid of a little blue-haired lady who didn't like the look of the harridan with the funny accent haranguing the poor English gent. He tried to look at Amelia, but his eyes wouldn't focus. Blood was beginning to seep from a cut on the top of his head.

'Oh mi gad!' the blue-haired lady shrieked. 'The man is bleeding. Will somebody purleese call a paramedic.' Mobile phones were pressed into action all around and within seconds a first-aider was at Jerry's side. Amelia was quickly forgotten as the crowd surged around her to be nearer to Jerry and hear the verdict. Someone got out a video camera and started to film the whole debacle but was quickly shooed away by the staff.

'Concussion,' someone said gravely. 'What's his name? Who's he with?'

Amelia was pushed to the front, protesting as she went. 'I am most certainly not with him—' but the first-aider only took in her vaguely similar accent and the brief look of recognition in Jerry's swimming eyes.

'She's his girlfriend,' said someone, who hadn't seen the punch, helpfully.

'Is he gonna sue the casino for having sharp tables?' said someone else, worriedly.

'I saw everything. I'll be a witness,' said the granny with the blue hair.

'I'm okay, I'm okay.' Jerry was shooing the spectators away with floppy hands. 'It's just a little cut. I just need to have a little lie-down.'

'Do you have a hotel room?'

'He's staying in mine,' said the blue-haired lady.

'Is that right?' the first-aider asked the inert body on the floor.

'No, it is not right,' Amelia outglared the blue-haired lady. 'He doesn't even know her. He's staying with me. I'm in the Luxor. Can somebody help me get him across the road?'

Two Texans obliged and soon a dazed Jerry was bandaged up and undercover in bed. Amelia's bed. She had to keep him awake, they said. To make sure that he didn't go into a coma. Jerry thanked them gratefully and waved regally as they left. Amelia sat on the edge of her lovely double bed, which was now full of her nightmare bedmate, and scowled.

'Do these beds vibrate?' Jerry asked. 'I stayed in

a motel here once where the beds vibrated.' He looked around for a slot to stick a dollar in.

'Don't make such ridiculous small-talk with me, Jerry. I'm already regretting rescuing you from that blue-haired witch. All I want to know is, what are you doing here?'

'You offered to let me stay in your room.'

'No, smart-arse, I mean what are you doing here in Vegas?'

Jerry took a theatrically painful drink out of the glass of icy water that stood beside the bed. 'I'm only in Vegas for the weekend. I got called in to sort out some fiasco of a second album The Dolphins were recording in LA. Their producer stropped off when he got rebuffed by the drummer, or something like that. Love, eh?' he added with a laugh. 'I've got a couple of days spare while they sleep off a big record company binge. Vegas is just recreation. I came out here to meet Michael.' The mention of Jerry's least desirable friend made Amelia snort with derision. 'But that's enough about me. What about you?'

'My mother got married today.'

'What? Again?'

'Yes. Again.'

'Anyone nice?'

'His name is Doug Hertzberg and he's a dentist to the stars, no less.'

Jerry spat a mouthful of water out with a laugh.

'It's not that funny.' Amelia flopped backwards onto the bed so that she and Jerry were now lying side by side. Him under the sheets. Her on top.

His hand tentatively sought hers. She brushed it away.

'I've missed you,' she thought she heard him say, as she started to drift into a woozy, alcohol-induced doze.

'Oh yeah.'

The combination of jet-lag and the excitement of her mother's fifth wedding were too much for Amelia and she soon forgot to check that Jerry wasn't slipping into a coma and fell asleep herself. When she awoke the next morning, he wasn't beside her. She wondered for a moment whether it had all been a dream. Then the sound of a running shower told her that it had not. She rolled over and buried her face in a pillow which reeked of Jerry's aftershave. Oh no, oh no, she thought. What had she done? She felt a little better when she noticed that at least she was still fully clothed.

Jerry emerged from the steamy bathroom, rubbing what was left of his hair dry with a fluffy towel. He tenderly touched the little bump which had formed at the back of his head and winced. He was still standing though and if he was perfectly honest with himself, a hangover probably counted for ninety per cent of the headache he was feeling right now.

He started to dress, chastely, beneath his towel. Amelia watched him, eyes narrowed, suspicious.

'I'll just get dressed and then I'll be out of your way.' His face had the look of a puppy that had just made a mess and was anticipating a kick. 'I'll check into a motel down the road and spend the rest of the day getting some more sleep. God knows I need it. Thanks for looking after me, Amelia . . . for making sure that I didn't slip into a coma . . .'

It was working. Amelia lay on her back with her hand over her eyes and sighed.

'Okay, okay. I've got this room for another night. You can sleep off your accident here.'

'Oh, thank you, darling.' He bounded over to the bed and planted a kiss on her forehead.

'But just don't touch me, OK?'

'What?' he asked. 'Not even a little bit?'

He grabbed her around the waist and dug his fingers between her ribs. The effect of his tickling was like an electric shock. Her body tensed and flipped about like a fish out of water. Jerry kept it up until she was writhing, helpless and breathless, all over the bed, knocking the pillows to the floor and grabbing at the sheets in a vain attempt to protect herself.

'Stop it, stop it,' she giggled ineffectually.

'Only if you'll kiss me,' Jerry said slyly.

'I'll . . . do . . . anything!' Amelia gasped in desperation.

Suddenly, Jerry ceased his torture and pulled her close. His face was serious, as was hers. Closing his eyes, he moved in for the promised kiss. Amelia kept her eyes open until he had come too close.

'Amelia,' he murmured, gathering her tickle-loosened body up in his arms. Momentarily forgetting they had ever been apart, she let her arms wrap languidly around his neck as their lips met and moved together, bringing back all the magic and erasing the pain which had forced her from his touch. Soon her hands were caressing him, twisting the slightly too long hair at the back of his head. Smoothing across his naked shoulders until she found her favourite little mole. His hands echoed hers through the barrier of her soft green sweater, until he felt he had probably regained licence to pull it out of the way.

'Amelia,' he whispered again.

They broke away from each other for just a second while Amelia lifted her arms to help him pull the sweater off. She was wearing a silky camisole beneath to stop the wool from making her itch. Jerry let his hands slide backwards and forwards on the silk for a while before that too found its way to the floor. He studied her face and smiled when he noticed that she was wearing the earrings he had given her and that the amber pendant which had been his last present to her still hung around her neck.

'I really have missed you,' he murmured.

'Yeah,' she said again, but this time there was a happy laugh in her voice.

Jerry dipped his head to the familiar breasts and carefully kissed them on each nipple as though he was greeting long lost friends. Then he returned to the first one, sucking the nipple into his mouth until it stood erect like a tiny ruby crown on a splendid dome. He did the same to the other, working it upright with his agile tongue. Amelia gazed at the top of his head for a while as he licked and kissed her, then closed her eyes, blocking out all sensation except touch. Jerry reached up and took her hands by the wrists and held them above her head while he let his lips wander across the sensitive join of breast and armpit. Amelia shivered at the faintly tickly feeling it gave her. Jerry's firm grip on her wrists prevented her from moving herself out of his way.

When he had kissed her from the base of her long throat to her waist, Jerry let go of Amelia's hands. She reached for him straight away, running her fingers lazily down his chest, through the greying hair on the tanned skin. Propped up on one elbow beside her, Jerry smiled contentedly as Amelia found the place where he had tucked the end of the towel in to secure it around his waist. She pulled it free.

'I've missed you too, Jerry.' It was her turn to say that now as her fingers lovingly caressed the familiar penis that had been hiding beneath the towel. The stiffening shaft pulsed ever so slightly as if in accord. Jerry traced the line of Amelia's body down to her navel and kissed her lightly on the nose. Then he gently removed her hand from his balls and rolled her over so that she lay on her back.

Jerry began to fumble with the belt at Amelia's waist. Impatiently she reached down to give him a hand, wriggling her hips free of the denim. Jerry clambered between her parted legs and pushed them upwards by the ankles so that her knees were bent towards the ceiling. Then he slid back down the silky sheets so that his chin rested for a moment on her belly. Amelia hoped she knew what was coming and shivered in anticipation.

She closed her eyes as she first felt Jerry's fingers find the delicate folds of her labia. Carefully, so carefully, he was parting them to reveal the succulent pink surface inside, which was already slick and shiny like the inside of a shell. For a short while, Jerry just gazed at the promise which lay before him, while Amelia breathed heavily but measuredly. Then it was time for Jerry to dip his head, to seek out her deepest secrets with his tongue.

As his tongue touched her clitoris, Amelia's legs bucked and twisted to one side. Waves of sensation rushed through her body to converge at that most sensitive spot. Jerry took her hips firmly in his hands and held her still, his tongue tantalising her like a live wire applied directly to her clitoris. Expertly, he flicked his agile tongue around and around, doing to her clitoris what he had latterly done to her nipples. Spurred on by the soft sounds of pleasure which floated down towards him from the pillows, Jerry increased his pace. Amelia's hands suddenly clutched at his head. She didn't know whether to hold him still, try to stop him from driving her over the edge, or to push his tongue down and further inside her.

Jerry pushed his tongue inside her. Gently probing at first, like a hummingbird in search of nectar. Flickering around the entrance to her vagina. Then going more deeply, until he was using his tongue like a penis to thrust into her, driving her so crazy with desire for him that she could barely lie still. When Jerry climbed back up the bed to kiss her, his chin was wet. He was smiling ecstatically.

'Can't think of anything I'd like better for breakfast . . .' he murmured.

She swatted him with a pillow.

'Come here,' she said, using his erect penis as a stick to pull him closer to her. Jerry moved towards her quickly, mindful of the potential for pain in the situation. Amelia wrapped one arm around his neck as she kissed him. Her other hand was busy down below, slicking the foreskin on his stiff shaft backwards and forwards until she was satisfied with the hardness in her hand.

'Will you make love to me, Jerry?' she asked him breathlessly. He didn't need to be asked again. He tipped Amelia carefully back onto the bed as though she were made of alabaster and positioned himself between her thighs. Her hand was still between them, helping Jerry to find her pulsing vagina the first time. As he penetrated her, he kept his eyes fixed on hers. They were swimming with tears which were strangely at odds with the smile on her lips. He moved slowly, as he had done the last time they made love, just hours before she left him alone in his flat. It was as if he was trying to make better the damage he had done to their relationship by using his body as a tool of worship. Amelia pulled his face down to hers and kissed him deeply as they moved together.

This was what they meant by 'making love'. This was sex that could heal, she thought. Sex that bonds.

Though they were taking things slowly, she could sense that Jerry was almost there. His face had taken on that peculiar look of mingled pain and pleasure. He was holding his breath, then letting it out in great, noisy gasps. Amelia clasped him tightly between her thighs and closed him inside her arms. Inside her, his penis twitched and danced, sending jets of semen deep into her. Her own body pulsed faster and faster at its depths, echoing each of Jerry's climactic thrusts. When they had both finished coming, she wrapped her legs around him so that he couldn't pull out. She wanted him there forever – again.

Jerry pushed the aerial of his mobile phone back down.

'I have to go, sweetheart. The bassist has finally woken up and we're going back into the studio this afternoon. Finishing off, I hope. I'll see you when I get back to London, yes? In about a week, maybe two.'

'You will call me, won't you?'

'Of course, sweetheart, of course.' Jerry kissed Amelia on the forehead, slipped the phone into his pocket and was gone.

Amelia had a brief rendezvous with her mother and stepfather in a restaurant at Caesar's Palace before they drove off to honeymoon for a couple of days in Palm Springs. When she had bid them goodbye, promising to be back in the States before her mother next changed her hair colour, she called the airport and changed her ticket so that she could fly straight to London from Vegas instead of bothering to go back via Los Angeles. She didn't really have anyone she needed to see there now. Jerry would be working in the studio and she knew of old that he wouldn't want to be distracted. Since she had been educated in England, she had no old school pals there and as for Marty, well, as she'd said when he dropped her off, she'd see him again in four years. No, she would go straight back to London and get on with her life. If she was going to get things together with Jerry again she would have to make sure that things were different this time. She would have her own career so that she didn't spend all her days moping about the house while he was working, and smothering him while he was at home.

She would make Jerry proud of her.

Chapter Seven

AMELIA WASN'T ABLE to get a plane home that night after all. The travel agent had managed to doublebook her seat and so she found herself stuck in Vegas until the next afternoon. She rang Jerry at the studio. He couldn't come to the phone. She managed to stop herself from dialling the final digit of Marty's number, just, even though she knew that he would drive out to meet her in a flash. She was just flicking through the channels on her three-million-channel cable television when the phone by the bedside actually rang for her.

Amelia snatched the receiver up.

'Hello?'

'Miss ... We have somebody for you in reception.'

'Really? Who is it?'

'It's a Ms Lusardi.'

'Lusardi?' Amelia heard the receptionist cover

the mouthpiece and ask her guest for her first name.

'Ms Karis Lusardi.'

'Karis?' Amelia shrieked. A broad smile of recognition spread across her lips. 'Karis Lusardi! I don't believe it. Send her on up.'

It seemed just seconds later that Karis Lusardi stood at the door of Amelia's hotel room with her Louis Vuitton overnight bag in one hand and a bottle of Bollinger in the other. Still reeling from the surprise of her old friend's sudden arrival, Amelia stood aside to let her in. Karis dumped the bag on the bed and handed Amelia the bottle. Then she hugged her so tightly, Amelia thought her ribs were caving in.

'Dump that in the chiller, thriller,' said Karis in her familiar rhyme. Amelia moved towards the mini-bar but was going too slowly for her impatient friend, who whisked past her, grabbed the bottle back and did the job herself, fishing out a miniature gin and tonic as she did so.

'Aaaah, that's better. Shame they make them so small,' she sighed as she knocked it back straight. Amelia winced. 'So, Miss English,' Karis began, 'just what do you think you're doing? Coming back to the City of Angels and not letting your very best friend and social adviser know that you're in town? I only found out you were over here because I bumped into that dork Marty at Salty Dog's. Marty Dorkface! I just can't believe you saw Marty Dorkface and you didn't come and see me. I don't know why I bothered to seek you out at all, you fair-weather friend. But for now I guess you are forgiven. Come here.'

Karis flopped onto the bed, her jet-black hair spreading out around her like a fan. She was wearing red, as usual. A tight button-through top that was only fastened as high as her black Wonderbra. Her legs were covered, in places, by a pair of ripped black jeans. She kicked off her shiny red high heels and made herself more comfortable. Amelia sat down beside her to offer an explanation.

'When I asked Mom if you were about, she said you had gone away to Alaska with some horny fisherman you met in Palm Springs . . .'

'What?' Karis looked momentarily confused. 'Fisherman? What fisherman?' She furrowed her brow while she mentally flicked through a card index of the last four years' hot dates. 'Oh, hang on, yes. I remember. His name was Andy. He had a cute body, great butt. To die for, in fact. But he wasn't a fisherman, Amelia. He owned a fishing fleet, for heaven's sake. Do you think I would go to Alaska to spend my life with some guy who comes home with his hands all covered in squid ink?' She rolled her eyes in mock despair.

'So what happened to him?' Amelia asked, more out of politeness than interest.

'I moved back down here with a writer I met in Anchorage.'

'Karis!' Like Marty, Amelia's best friend hadn't changed a bit.

'But that's all over now. He was into all sorts of

weird shit. Animals and stuff.'

'Don't tell me about it,' Amelia winced. 'But I imagine there must be someone new by now.'

'Well . . .' Karis's face took on the expression which signalled a new conquest and a big story. 'As a matter of amazing fact, I think I just may have met the love of my life.'

'The love of your life?'

'Yeah.' Her face took on a look of intense excitement. She sat up on the bed while she was speaking. 'It's early days.'

'How early?'

'Three days. Maybe four. What day is it today?' Karis counted the days back on her fingers. Amelia just rolled her eyes. 'But you know how it is when you just, you know, just know?'

Amelia guessed that a nod was probably the appropriate response at this juncture.

'I met him at The Batcave in Santa Monica. You won't have been there. It's new. Opened last October. Batman theme.'

'Funnily enough.'

'Anyway, I saw him across the top of my date's shoulder and it was like, wow. Drums crashed. Lightning flashed. There he is . . . There is the man for me. For ever.' She crossed her heart to illustrate the fact. 'So, while Butch was in the men's room I made maximum eye contact with this wonderful guy, which was reciprocated, of course, and I scribbled a little note on a page from my organiser which I slipped to Mr Gorgeous as I went to powder my nose.'

'Who's Butch?'

'Oh, some football player I met on the beach. Nice enough. You know the type. Big but thick . . .'

'And did Butch see you making a play for this other guy?'

'No, no, no! I was *très* discreet. Anyway, the note said, "meet you in the hallway in ten seconds". He followed me out there and we kissed.' Karis put her hand to her heart. 'Amelia, it was the most incredible kiss I have ever shared with a man.'

'You just kissed?' Amelia asked. That wasn't Karis's usual style.

'Well, we had a bit of a grope, but we couldn't do much because Butch was still there. So, anyway, we swapped vitals and agreed to meet in a sweet bar by the marina on Tuesday night.'

'What were his vitals?' Amelia asked.

'A good seven by the feel of it.'

'I meant vitals like his name, Karis.'

'Oh Amelia, you know me. I was off my head. I think it began with a J. Jeffrey. Yeah, that was it. Jeffrey. He's in music. Funny accent. I'll recognise his face . . . I hope. I can't wait to see if the engine matches the exterior, if you know what I mean!'

Amelia couldn't help laughing. It was always the same with Karis. Always in love with love. The more outrageous and mysterious and downright dangerous her meetings, the better. Picking up a new date while she was already out with one guy was nothing new or unusual for this particular good-time girl. Amelia remembered fondly the time when Karis had deliberately speeded backwards and forwards past a traffic cop she fancied until he booked her and she got his number on the back of her ticket.

'Is that champagne cold yet?' Karis asked.

'It's only been in the chiller for three seconds, Karis,' Amelia reprimanded. 'Can't you wait?'

'Oh well, I like it warm.'

Amelia retrieved the bottle. Karis sat on the edge of the bed and held out two plastic cups while Amelia popped open the cork. The warm champagne bubbled furiously and a great deal of the pale golden liquid missed the cups completely and dribbled down Amelia's arm until it dripped off her elbow. Karis grabbed her former playmate by the wrist and twisted her about until Amelia's elbow was dripping straight into Karis's open, scarlet-lipped mouth. She flicked out her pink tongue to catch the shining amber teardrops.

'Cut that out,' Amelia laughed. Even her elbows could be unbearably ticklish at times. Karis let go of Amelia's elbow and returned her attention to the plastic cups which were fizzing nicely. She downed her share of the booze in one gulp. 'I don't know how you can do that,' Amelia said. 'The bubbles in this stuff get right up my nose.'

'Practice, dear Amelia, practice. I like to line my stomach with champagne. It doesn't give you a hangover.'

'Karis, I think you may be a lush.'

'No, that's not true because if I was a lush I would drink all the time. I only drink with a meal.'

'We're not eating now.'

'No, but we will be. Come on, let's go and get something inside us.' Amelia winced at the innuendo with which Karis always invested her words. Karis jumped to her feet and crammed them back inside her dangerous red shoes. Grabbing the half-empty champagne bottle from Amelia's hand, she made for the door and stood there, waiting for the bemused redhead to catch up. 'What do you fancy? Champagne and corndogs?'

'Sounds great,' said Amelia. 'You're on.'

The array of choice for eating out in Las Vegas proved just too bewildering and so they eventually found themselves plumping for an 'All you can eat for $3' buffet in Circus Circus, the legendary casino where circus acts still performed nightly in the big ring which nestled between the slot machines and the gaming tables. Nobody really seemed to pay much attention to the girls on their flying trapezes any more. For the gamblers, the slot machines held a more personal reward. And now that Circus Circus had one of the biggest water-chute rides in the world dangling between casino and car-park it would take Elvis unicyling naked to bring the appeal of the Big Top back. Amelia sat opposite Karis on a plastic chair and picked at her potato salad, while

Karis filled her in on the comings and going of those simple Los Angeles folk since Amelia had left for England.

'Virginia Schneider,' Karis said, waving her fork to catch Amelia's full attention. 'Mousy hair, big nose? Now there's one hell of an unlucky girl. You know she got engaged to Mark Warbler straight out of college. Buck teeth, BMW six series? You know the guy, you do. Well, last October he left Virginia for some Swiss girl that his married sister was employing as an au-pair, and then, to top it all, Virginia got one of those exploding breast jobs. It was nasty, by all accounts. Silicone and heli-skiing just don't mix. Boy, am I glad these are real.' Karis cupped her own breasts and bumped them up and down. Amelia cringed and hid her eyes with her hand.

'Hey!' Karis's bouncing had earned her the avid attention of an admirer on the other side of the cafeteria. Karis tossed back her raven hair. 'Amelia, would you get a load of that cowboy?'

Amelia swivelled around on her chair to see just who Karis was raving about now. The cowboy tipped his studded white hat at her and smiled a slow, broad smile. Karis coyly feigned a flush and waved her hand in front of her face to cool her cheeks down. The cowboy was already purposefully getting to his Cuban-heeled feet.

'Amelia,' sighed Karis like a Southern belle, 'I think I just met the love of my life – mark four.'

'Well, good evening to you two lovely ladies.'

Now that he was standing right in front of them, the cowboy tipped his hat again.

'Good evening to you too,' replied Karis, mimicking his Texan accent as her eyes flickered between his cute little face and his tight denim crotch.

'Mind if I pull up a chair?' he asked, already drawing one up. He turned it around and sat astride the seat, his arms lying along the top of the back rest. He pushed back the brim of his hat with two fingers, like a child's representation of a gun, and his knowing eyes drifted lazily from one girl to the other, making it obvious that it wasn't only Karis who had drawn him across from his corner chair. Amelia focused on the little silver pistol motif which formed the fastening of his bootlace tie. Oh boy, she thought. Only that morning she had decided to make a go of her relationship with Jerry again and here was grey-eyed temptation, already putting itself very much in her way.

'So where y'all from?' he asked to break the uncomfortable silence.

'Santa Monica,' replied Karis.

'And you, little blue eyes?' he said, turning his unsettling attention to Amelia again.

'London,' she stuttered.

'London, England?' he asked, looking a little amazed.

'London, England,' she confirmed.

'Well, I ain't never seen such a pretty-looking English girl before. Do you want to come and have a cup of tea with me?' he said in his best Cockney accent. He laughed at his own bad joke. Amelia knew that she shouldn't be intrigued by this chap-wearing wide boy but there was something unnerving about his smile. Something sexual. And he knew it. Karis was laughing with him, throwing her head back to expose her beautiful lithe throat to him as she did so. Twiddling her hair flirtatiously. The presence of this handsome stranger had all but obliterated the friendship between the two women.

'And what're your names?'

'I'm Karis,' the dark-haired girl answered languidly, 'and this is my very good friend Amelia.' Amelia nodded.

'Well, I'm mighty pleased to make your acquaintance, Miss Karis and Miss Amelia. My name is Ricky and this here,' he gestured to another cowboy who appeared like magic behind him, 'is Bud. Say hello to the ladies, Bud.'

'Hello to the ladies, Bud,' parroted the standing guy. They were a regular double act. Amelia took the newcomer in. He looked a little older than Ricky, who must have been in his late twenties. A little taller, too. Thicker-set. A wide black moustache travelled across his upper lip. Ricky was clean-shaven. As fair as Ricky was, Bud was dark – even in the clothes that they were wearing. Ricky wore pale blue jeans and a white shirt with silver details. Bud wore an identical shirt in black and gold. Amelia wondered if these guys got dressed together for effect as she and Karis had done when they were younger.

'You girls want to come and shoot some craps with us?' Bud asked.

Karis was already on her feet. 'Yeah. Why not?'

As they followed the tight denim-covered butts out onto the gaming floor, Karis and Amelia hung back a little to get the evening's tactics clear.

'Ricky's mine, I think, little sister,' Karis purred, already sure that her catch for the evening was in the bag.

'Oh what?' Amelia protested. 'That's unfair.'

'OK,' Karis conceded. 'We'll shoot it out. Whoever takes most money away from the table in a half hour gets first choice.'

Chapter Eight

KARIS AND AMELIA sat side by side at the table. Bud was to Amelia's left, Ricky to the right of Karis. The boys were placing pretty big stakes, bigger than Amelia had expected. Ricky put down fifty dollars, Bud doubled his friend's stake and put down a hundred. He eyed the girls for a reaction. Karis raised her eyebrows to Amelia. To one of her regular dates, a hundred bucks was just the tip you left the coat-check boy. The croupier rolled her dice. Bud lost. Ricky collected his winnings and was unable to suppress a smile.

Bud pulled his chair a little closer to the table and to Amelia. His leg now rested against the length of her taut thigh. He shifted position and put a hand just above her knee to steady himself. Amelia felt a warm prickle run along the back of her neck. Yeah, Ricky was definitely the pretty one of the pair, but Bud had something altogether more exciting about him. It was almost as if he emanated danger. As the croupier began another game, Amelia felt Bud's arm slide slowly around the back of her chair. He was almost touching her . . . but not quite.

This time around, Bud's luck was in. Ricky nodded in defeat and pushed his hat back again so that its brim framed his boyish face like a halo. Karis had her shiny scarlet varnished fingertips on Ricky's thigh, right up near his crotch. Amelia felt a smile creep across her lips at the sight of Ricky's tightening trousers beneath that professional hand. His face was reddening involuntarily. Karis, however, looked straight ahead at the game with the inscrutable expression of the Sphinx.

Suddenly, while the table was busy with people collecting their winnings, Bud grabbed Amelia's hand and pulled it down roughly to his own button fly. 'Feel this,' he hissed, pressing her fingers down into the denim. 'This is for you.' Amelia was crimson. The assembled punters were too busy concentrating on the game to notice, or to care.

Bud held her hand so tightly to his hard prick that she felt the bones might crack in his crushing grip. His unexpectedly rough gesture had shocked her at first but now she could feel the blush which had started in her cheeks spreading elsewhere. She moved slightly in her seat until she could feel the seam of her jeans rubbing against her labia. Bud leant closer to her and whispered hotly in her ear. The croupier smiled as though she knew exactly what he was saying.

'What do you say we leave these two here and go back to my room right this minute, Amelia?'

Amelia swallowed nervously. A small voice inside her momentarily questioned the sense in going back to this virtual stranger's room. And the morality of it in view of that morning's renewed vows. But Bud's breath in her ear was fanning the heat building inside her and she nodded.

'I'll just tell Karis where we're going,' she gulped. 'So that she can find us later on.' He wouldn't try anything too funny if he thought that someone else might come looking for her. Bud smiled like a spider that was well-prepared to bide a little more time for his chosen fly. He turned back to the table for one last game.

Karis listened to Amelia's excuses and winked. She was pleased enough that she was being left to her own devices with the blond guy for at least a short while.

'So Ricky is mine for the night, then?' Karis whispered excitedly.

'I didn't say that . . . He is for now.'

'OK. We'll join you in an hour, yeah?'

'Just an hour?'

'I don't want you to wear Bud out before I've had the chance to take a ride on that moustache!'

Amelia cringed.

'Anyway,' Karis continued, 'I thought you agreed with me that the more, the merrier.'

'You know I do. But do you think these guys will be into that? Cowboys are normally pretty straight when it comes down to it.' At that moment, Ricky looked across to see what they were talking about and held Amelia's gaze for a second with his light grey eyes.

'All guys are into it, Amelia,' said Karis, as though she was talking about peanut butter and jelly sandwiches. 'And besides, I haven't seen *you* in so long.' Karis placed heavy emphasis on the "you" and laid her spare hand on Amelia's unattended leg. Amelia blushed still deeper. Her hand tightened involuntarily at a particularly vivid memory of a long ago beach party scene. Amelia's hand was still in Bud's crotch. He relayed his pleasure by gently squeezing her fingers.

'I'll see you in an hour, then,' Amelia said breathlessly. 'Chalet C 15. It's on the other side of the car-park. Oh, and you will make sure you knock before you come in?'

Karis gave a little chuckle and turned back to the game.

Seeing that Karis and Amelia had made their plans, Bud pushed his pile of chips over to Ricky. 'Don't lose it all at once,' he quipped. Then he got to his feet and dragged Amelia away from the table in the direction of the exit.

They had to pass through a dismal multi-storeyed car-park on their way to Bud's room. They walked a little way apart – he didn't even try to hold her hand – but, as soon as they were out of the general flow of human traffic, Bud suddenly pushed Amelia up against a cold, grey wall and began to kiss her. To devour her. His tongue forced her teeth apart and flickered inside her mouth like a serpent's fork. His lips crushed hers until she was sure that they must be bruised. His moustache was rough against her soft face.

There was no time for the formalities of polite courtship with Bud. As his mouth seemed to draw the breath from her body with its force, his hands were almost immediately beneath her sweater, pushing her bra out of the way to grab at her tender breasts, squeezing them tightly with almost total disregard for the fact that she was made of flesh and blood.

After ten seconds or so, he grabbed one of her hands and pulled it down to his crotch again. As he set about kissing her neck, biting a path down to her collar-bone, Amelia felt his hard shaft twitch beneath her palm and let out a gasp of anticipation. Through his jeans it felt so long, so rigid. She hoped that she wouldn't be disappointed. Quickly she set to work on his button fly. Bud helped her by loosening his belt. He worked his dick out through the narrow gap. Soon his shaft was bobbing in front of her in the still air of the car-park, then pressing into her stomach as he once more pulled her tighter against him for a kiss.

Amelia worked one of her hands between their frantic bodies and wrapped her fingers around the penis's wide girth. She began to slick the warm foreskin slowly back and forth. Bud was undoing her jeans now. Forcing his own hand down between the tight covering of denim and her skin until he reached her mound. Excited as she was by the build-up to this moment, which they had shared at the gaming table, and by the impressive size of the organ she now held in her hand, Amelia knew that she was already wet. Bud probed roughly at the lips of her vagina with the tip of his middle finger until he found a gap between them and was able to slip suddenly inside.

Amelia gasped with pleasure. 'Let's do it now,' she breathed low in his ear. The combination of Bud's hot breath on her neck and his fingers at her clit was almost paralysing her with desire.

'We can't do it here,' he replied gruffly, his voice muffled by the flesh of her throat. 'If you had a skirt on maybe, but not with jeans. You'd have to take them down and the whole world would see your ass.'

'I don't care,' Amelia laughed, but Bud was already extricating his hand from her pants so that they could abandon their bleak location and head for his motel room.

He had taken a cheap suite in one of the low blocks to the side of the car-park. He carefully guided her inside the anonymous chalet with an incongruously chivalrous gesture. The television was running, tuned into MTV. A hard rock band were thudding out a song about the blood of virgins, with a commentary by Beavis and Butthead. Amelia barely had time to take in the room, which was so different from her luxurious pad at the Luxor, before Bud was edging her backwards, slipping her sweater over her head and off as he did so, and pushing her down onto the scratchy, musty-smelling blanket that covered the bed. Her dusty shoes dropped from her feet to the floor.

Amelia's jeans were still undone from their tangle in the car-park. Bud tore them from her roughly so that she was dressed only in her bra and panties. His eyes were looking through her, seeing nothing about her but her body. They were hungry, desperate eyes that sent a shiver of delicious fear through Amelia's vulnerable bones. Bud pulled his own tight jeans down only as far as his knees. He wore nothing beneath and Amelia's eyes were drawn instantly to his dick, standing proudly out in front of him. She longed to take it inside her mouth and draw him, oh so slowly, to the brink of pleasure. She wanted to make a real meal of him. But she knew already that that wasn't going to happen.

Bud carelessly flipped Amelia over onto her front and tore her delicate white panties off. His hands slipped quickly beneath her waist, pulling her down towards him until she was half off the bed, her feet on the floor, her bottom high in the air. She could feel his dick already nudging insistently at her upturned labia. With just two determined thrusts Bud found the licence he was looking for and was suddenly deep inside.

The strength of his thrusting nearly threw Amelia flat on her face. She braced her arms, locking her elbows to keep herself steady as he pounded into her. His balls slapped against her each time he went in to the hilt, keeping time with the bass of the song which blared from the television.

After the initial surprise of his brutal entry, Amelia found herself pushing back to meet him, excited not just by the friction between their bodies but by the anonymity of the position she now found herself in. This man with his rough hands around her smooth waist could be anyone. Anyone at all. She hardly knew his face. Amelia screwed her eyes tightly shut and tried to focus on a face in her mind. She was nowhere near achieving a picture of her fantasy man when she felt Bud's fingers tighten harder and harder on her waist. His thrustings began to fall apart, become deeper, slower. His breathing staggered. He was almost wheezing. All the time he used his hands to pull her body more and more firmly against his.

He grunted suddenly. Amelia threw her head back in a sympathetic sigh as the hot spurts of his sticky semen began to fill her. He continued to thrust until it was all gone from him and beginning to run down her inner thigh. Then, without so much as a word or whisper of endearment, he withdrew from her abruptly, used her pretty little panties to wipe his dick dry, and collapsed on the bed beside her. His chest was heaving with the exertion of his climax. Amelia surveyed him from her position of all fours. He made as if to speak but the words came out only as gasps. Finally Amelia rested on her elbows beside him.

'Is that it?' she asked humorously. 'We haven't even started yet.'

Chapter Nine

EXACTLY AN HOUR after they had left the casino, Amelia heard the tinkle of familiar champagne-fuelled laughter floating in through the window of Bud's dismal room. Bud was fast asleep. That really did seem to be that . . . for the moment at least. Amelia lay on her back beside him and looked at the fan which was spinning lazily in the corner. Bud's efforts had only just warmed her up. Thank heavens the cavalry was about to arrive.

Karis was outside the door now, whispering loudly about not wanting to disturb any funny business. Ricky was protesting that they shouldn't look in on the others. Karis was insisting that they did. She hiccupped, and then knocked briskly at the door. Amelia swung it open and Karis, who had been leaning against it and not expecting such prompt attention, nearly fell in. Ricky tumbled in with her. He had been leaning against Karis.

Karis regained her balance and surveyed the room. She pulled a disappointed face. She surveyed the bed, and Cowboy Bud, flat out upon it. She pulled another disappointed face.

'That good, huh? How was the moustache?'

'I am going to have extremely bad beard burn,' was all Amelia could be bothered to say.

'Oh well.'

'How's it going with the Milky Bar Kid?' Amelia whispered.

'Not great,' replied Karis. 'After all that bravado in the casino, I think in reality he's just a little shy.'

Karis and Amelia turned to look at Ricky. He was still standing in the doorway, cowboy hat in hand. He looked as though he was visiting his grandparents on a Sunday afternoon.

'Karis,' he said nervously after a little while, 'I think we oughta go. My room's right next door.'

Karis strolled across and took hold of him by the bootlace tie. 'Is it now? Well, the bed in here is a bit busy, I guess.' She glanced back at Amelia and winked. 'Come on, Amelia, Ricky has invited us to go next door.'

He looked puzzled. 'Amelia's coming too?'

'Of course, dear Ricky, of course.'

In Ricky's room the narrow bed was flanked by two hard-backed chairs. Karis and Amelia pulled them out into the centre of the floor and sat upon them facing their companion. Ricky perched daintily on the end of the bed. Karis filled tumblers with whisky and ice from the mini-bar and handed them round. Ricky sipped his drink like a man condemned.

'Are you OK?' Karis asked him, full of faux concern, aware that even the way she and Amelia had positioned their chairs was designed to intimidate him. 'You look kinda scared.'

'Scared?' said Ricky in a little voice. 'Why should I be scared?'

'I don't know. I mean, it's not as though Amelia and I are going to touch you . . . or anything. You know, Ricky, we would just be happy to sit here all night and look at you. Being such a pretty boy, as you are.'

Amelia looked at her knees to suppress a loud outburst of laughter. Suddenly she knew only too well what was coming next, remembering the night at college when they had talked the butch football captain, Jim Fuller, into a bag of frazzled nerves.

'I bet you look even better underneath that lovely shirt,' Karis began.

Ricky flicked at his fringe.

'Don't you think so, Amelia?'

'I do, Karis, I do.'

'How about if we ask him nicely to take it off?'

'Take your shirt off, Ricky,' Amelia commanded with an executioner's tone.

Ricky was surprised by the uncompromising sound of the sweet one's voice. 'Aw, c'mon,' he said with a trembling laugh. 'You girls call that asking nicely?'

107

'Take your shirt off, Ricky,' Amelia repeated. There was still no hint of humour in her voice.

A look of panic flashed in Ricky's eyes. He licked his dry lips. What were they playing at? Did they both want him? Both of them? At once? Oh no. What if he couldn't get it up twice in a row? This was his dream and nightmare all at the same time.

'Is this going to be a threesome?' he asked hopefully, fearfully.

'Don't you know how to undo buttons or something?' Karis deftly avoided his question.

Yeah, thought Ricky, these girls want a kinky threesome. And I'm going to be at the centre of this all-girl sandwich.

'We're waiting,' said Karis.

Ricky's hand flew enthusiastically to the bootlace tie around his neck and he began to frantically tug it loose. Karis rolled her Egyptian-painted eyes. 'Oh, Ricky, Ricky, don't you know that half the joy of the present is in the unwrapping? Slowly, please. Take it a little more slowly.'

He slowed his pace immediately, undoing the pearlised buttons of his white shirt like a pro. Karis leant back in her uncomfortable chair, her fingers steepled in front of her mouth in the gesture that so many men had used during the humiliating casting sessions of her short-lived modelling career. She tapped her fingers thoughtfully against her lips. Ricky slid his arms out of their sleeves and let the shirt fall onto the bed beside him.

'You had better fold that up,' said Amelia, passionlessly.

Playing the game, Ricky did as he was told and sat up straight on the end of the bed, obviously wanting to make a good impression. His arms were tensed, his muscles crossed by veins which bulged in the heat. He had a tattoo of a cowboy's coiled rope on his left bicep and another of a swallow on the right side of his chest, simply outlined in blue ink. Karis and Amelia took the measure of his well-formed pecs, smiled at each other, but said nothing to him.

'Trousers,' Karis announced next. 'No, hang on, hang on,' she said as Ricky's hands flew to his leather belt. 'On second thoughts I think you had better start with your boots.'

Ricky bent down and rolled up the bottoms of his jeans until his snakeskin-detailed, Cuban-heeled cowboy boots were fully exposed. First he grasped the left one by the heel and began to tug it off. He strained and grunted. It was obviously a snug fit. No wonder Bud hadn't bothered with taking his off, Amelia observed. Beneath the boots Ricky was wearing white towelling socks. Karis grimaced. 'And those . . . quickly,' she added, indicating the offending items of clothing with a little wave of her fingers. Amelia bit the knuckles of her hand in an attempt to keep a straight face.

Ricky was breathing quite heavily already. His dark brown chest was covered with a slick sheen of sweat – from the heat of the room, the anticipation of his next order, or the exertion of pulling his boots off? The girls didn't really care.

Amelia rocked her chair back onto two legs. Karis lit up a Marlboro cigarette and let the smoke spiral lazily up to the ceiling fan.

Ricky shifted from one bare foot to the other, awaiting his next instructions.

'Now your trousers,' Amelia said.

Ricky stood up and took hold of his buckle.

'Do it nicely, though, eh?'

Ricky's eyes narrowed. Who did these two broads think they were? He hesitated, then dared to ask, 'Hey, ladies, let's just wait a minute. Am I the only one round here who is going to take his clothes off?'

'If you get it wrong, then yes, Ricky, you will be,' Karis said without a hint of a smile. Ricky looked to Amelia for an explanation or reassurance. She was trying to remain implacable but her lips were curved upwards in spite of herself. Of course they would get their clothes off too, Ricky assured himself. They just wanted to play a little game, that's all. Make like it was they who were in control of this situation. He had better let them have their fun if he wanted his. Boy, Ricky thought, if only Bud knew what he was missing.

'Trousers,' Karis repeated. Ricky undid his buckle, pulled off his thick brown leather belt and slowly rolled it up into a tight little coil.

'That's better,' Amelia murmured.

Ricky paused before carrying on, as if he had finally grasped the concept of dramatic effect. He hooked his thumbs in the waistband of his jeans. Karis was looking at a couple of smoke rings she had just puffed into the air. He waited for her to return her attention to him.

'Carry on,' said Karis suddenly.

Amelia crossed her legs as Ricky began to loosen his fly. She tensed her thighs so that they pressed hard, one against the other, gently squeezing her pussy between. Ricky was a pretty fit guy. His chest was broad enough for both her and Karis to lay their heads on. His stomach muscles looked as though they would be able to deflect a speeding bullet. Amelia imagined the strong, brown hands which were unfastening the final silver button of his fly doing the same for her and let out a shivery sigh. Karis gave a look of disapproval.

'Pull them down,' Karis ordered. 'Slowly.'

Ricky began to inch the jeans down over his narrow hips, revealing a pair of pristine white shorts. To the girls' delight, the shorts were already slightly tented around a hard-on at the front. Amelia noticed that Ricky's erection veered slightly to the left. Soon his jeans were by his ankles. Ricky sat back on the bed to pull them free of his feet. They were hard work, a little narrow. As he crossed one leg over the other to help him get the trousers off, Amelia had a sudden view up the right leg of his boxers. The familiar orb of a testicle peeked out from the sparkling cotton. She wanted to reach out and touch it, to feel his balls hot and heavy in the palm of her hand. But she knew she couldn't, at least not yet. This game was all about the agony of not being touched.

'And last but not least, your shorts, please, cowboy,' Karis trilled.

Ricky crossed his arms over his chest, the expression on his face now the cocky look of a guy who knows that he has what just about every girl wants. 'Now c'mon, ladies,' he protested once more. 'I really don't think that this little game of yours is fair.'

'Life isn't fair, Ricky,' Karis replied.

Amelia giggled into her hand.

'And you wouldn't want to blow your chances of being the boss later on, now, would you?'

Amelia felt for the poor underdog in front of her. That last question really was unfair. Ricky stood up one more time and took hold of his shorts.

'Are you ready for this?' he asked proudly. Karis snorted derisively in reply.

Ricky composed himself and whipped the boxers down.

'Ta daa.' Ricky waved his pants theatrically through the air.

'Whoah!' Amelia couldn't stop herself from exclaiming at the sight of Ricky's penis suddenly bursting free from its confines and springing out in front of him. It wasn't as wide as Bud's, but it was longer, smoother. His balls swung below the pink silken shaft in perfect symmetry. He hadn't been circumcised, as most American guys were, and Amelia was glad, because it would make the next part of the game a little easier for him, assuming that Karis wasn't in the habit of carrying a pot of grease in her bag.

112

Ricky stood before them, naked but proud. His hardening grey eyes challenged them to comment.

'So,' said Karis finally and as breezily as she could in the circumstances. 'Now we know the equipment is all there . . . But,' she continued, 'I would never buy a car just because I liked the colour. I go for a test drive because I like to see it in action. Don't you, Amelia?' Amelia nodded. 'So, Ricky,' she exhaled slowly. 'Let's see you in action.'

'What do you mean?' He looked hopeful. He was obviously thinking that he was going to get to try Amelia out first.

Karis smiled.

'I mean pull your pud, boy. Masturbate. Jack yourself off.'

The shock and silence in the room was palpable. What she had just asked for, he just wasn't prepared to do. No way, José. He never did that. Well, he never did that in front of a girl or in front of anyone for that matter. One of them should do it for him. He stood his ground. He refused. His dick still stuck straight out in front of him. It was obviously game even if he wasn't.

'I ain't going to touch myself for nobody!' he protested.

'He's shy,' Karis mocked.

'Very shy,' Amelia agreed.

'No,' said Karis slyly, 'perhaps he's not shy. I think he's actually just afraid that he won't be able to perform.'

'I . . . I . . .'

'Would you like some music to help get you into the mood?' Karis flicked on the television and found MTV. A slinky soul singer was extolling the virtues of anonymous sex. Amelia tapped her foot to the rhythm. Ricky stood stock-still, his eyebrows knitted together in anger.

'You're dickin' me around,' he said, reaching down to the floor to retrieve his discarded shorts. 'I ain't going to stand for this . . .'

'You could sit down for it if you wanted,' quipped Amelia.

'Go to hell.'

Karis fumbled in her handbag for a moment, then, suddenly, a very different light was thrown on the whole scene. In her hand she held something with a long, black barrel. It was covered with a handkerchief, but Ricky knew instantly that it was a gun. It was a gun and she was pointing it right at him. Right at his proud, hard, handsome dick.

Amelia was open-mouthed with horror.

'Karis,' she breathed in disbelief.

'Karis,' sobbed Ricky. His hard-on wavered, just a little.

'Shall I turn the music up?' Karis asked, 'so that nobody outside can hear what is going on?'

There was a moment of interminable stillness and silence before Ricky, shaking like a leaf from head to toe, took hold of his fast-fading dick.

'Are you ready to play the game again?'

Ricky nodded, his chin wobbling. He wrapped one hand loosely around the shaft, his other hand gently cupped his balls. Carefully and with great reverence, he pulled the foreskin back. His deep pink glans was already lubricated and shiny with pre-come. Karis settled back in her seat, the thing in her hand still aimed between Ricky's quivering legs. Amelia, white-knuckled, gripped the arms of her chair.

'Faster, Ricky. We don't have all day.'

There was no point arguing with the black-haired broad now. Gradually, Ricky began to quicken his movements. His hand slicked faster and faster back and forth. He had his eyes fixed on Karis, on the gun in her hand. How the hell was he supposed to concentrate on getting to orgasm when some madwoman might blow his balls off if he got it wrong?

'Relax,' Karis hissed, seeing Ricky struggling with a limp tool. 'You'll find it feels much better.' That was easy for her to say. He couldn't get a hard-on again while he thought about that gun. The blood was draining from his whole body, not just his dick. Karis sighed impatiently. Ricky was sure he saw her thumb shift on the veiled catch.

'Please, no,' Ricky begged. 'Please. Please.'

Karis smiled weakly. Amelia opened her mouth to implore her friend to stop the torment but her words were answered by an increase in the television volume. Ricky screwed his eyes tightly shut against the rest of the room. His only chance was to think of something else. Someone else. He tried to remember Mary-Lou, his high-school sweetheart, in the back of his first car. But all he could see in his mind's eye was the gun in Karis's hand. Where was Bud when he needed him? Perhaps they'd already drugged him and he wasn't asleep next door but in a coma. Of all the girls in Las Vegas, why did he have to run into Thelma and Louise?

'This is getting boring . . .' Karis said in a strange monotone voice even Amelia didn't recognise. Ricky heard the click of the catch. Only an orgasm stood between him and certain oblivion. Mary-Lou, Mary-Lou, he whispered beneath his breath. At last he remembered her little white lace bra. Her polka-dot pink panties. The first nipples he had ever kissed.

'Please, please,' he begged his dormant member. 'Please, please, please.' The music changed to something faster. He blocked out the room, blocked out the maniac woman with her revolver. Pulses of green and purple light flashed before his closed eyes. At last his penis began to rise majestically, though it was taking more effort than for the Ancient Egyptians to raise an obelisk to the sun.

His whole body was growing tense. The outline of his fine muscles was growing clearer. The veins in his forearms were as pumped up as the veins in his dick. Sweat glistened on his clean-shaven upper lip.

His hips bucked forward involuntarily. His eyes were closed now, he was lost to the rhythm of his own actions upon his body. Feeling the rush of steaming blood from his head to his heroic hard-on. Ricky staggered back towards the bed and collapsed down onto the orange candlewick bedspread, still stroking all the while.

He threw his head back, his mouth open in fearful ecstasy. The veins in his neck pulsed as his heartbeat raced faster, ever faster, in time with his hand. He was grimacing now, biting his bottom lip. Preparing for the climax. Enduring the final build-up of the flood before it burst through the dam.

Amelia shifted nervously in her chair. Was he aiming at her?

'Jeez!' Ricky cried, but he wasn't quite there. 'Please, please, please.' The muscles of his stomach contracted painfully, tensing harder and harder, twisting his body up. He wanted to say something but could only splutter now through his broken breathing.

'He's coming, he's coming!' said Karis excitedly, knowing that the sound of her encouraging voice might just give him the tip he needed over the edge.

Ricky strained, still pumping his dick as though he was bringing oil from the bottom of the North Sea. His eyebrows were knitted together in joyful pain. His toes scrunched. Every part of his body was crying out for this ordeal to come to an end . . .

'Oh!'
'Oh!'
'Oh!'
Karis and Amelia both jerked back in their seats

as the first ribbon of sperm shot sky-high, arcing like the jet of a fountain before it fell again and splattered, half across Ricky's thighs, half across the bed. Then another, and another, and another. Each incredible spurt going only a little less high than the one before it. Amelia was open-mouthed with amazement at the incredible volume of his ejaculation. He couldn't have come for a week or more. Ricky let go of his penis. It continued to spurt, jumping about like the end of an unattended hose. He, too, seemed amazed by the intensity of his orgasm. The look on his face suggested that he was just about to pass out.

'Oh, Jeez, no.' He fell backwards onto the bed. His dick stood proudly upright for only a moment or so longer before it began to droop slowly back onto his stomach. Amelia gave a long, low whistle and Karis ran a trembling hand through her long black hair.

When he had recovered from his exertions, Ricky sat up and looked at his mistresses. He was still alive and he had an uncertain smile on his handsome face.

'Well,' he said, looking nervously from one girl to the other in anticipation. 'I did OK, yeah?'

'OK,' Karis agreed.

'So, you two are next?'

'What?' said Karis, already getting to her feet, still pointing her weapon at his crotch as she motioned to Amelia that it was time for them to make an exit.

'We're going to get down to real business now, yeah?'

Karis spat out a spiteful laugh. 'Dream on, you jerk-off.' She picked up his cowboy hat, which had been sitting on the dresser and threw it towards him. 'Here, cover yourself up.'

And with that, they were out of the door.

Chapter Ten

'JESUS, KARIS!' AMELIA screamed when they had stopped running from the scene of their latest crime. 'What did you want to get a gun out for? He thought you were going to kill him! *I* thought you were going to kill him! We are going to be in deep shit now. What if he calls the police?'

'Calm down,' Karis told her hysterical friend. 'He loved it.'

'Loved it? Loved it? Karis, you just held a gun to a guy's dick! We could go to jail . . .'

'Here, catch!' Karis tossed the offending weapon, still wrapped in the handkerchief, across to her friend. Amelia bounced it about in her fingers.

'I don't want to get my fingerprints on it!' Amelia squealed. Karis grabbed it back from her.

'Look, stupid.' She threw away the handkerchief. 'Do you really think I would kill a man to see him beat off?' There in the palm of her hand lay, not a gun, but a shiny black and gold vibrator. Karis set it upright in her palm and switched it on. It buzzed around in a little circle.

The tension escaped Amelia's body like a sigh and she collapsed, laughing, against a car-park wall.

'So you can quit worrying now,' said Karis. 'And anyway, what do you think he's going to do, call the cops and say "Officer, officer, two broads just held me up with a dildo?" . . . Maybe we should try a bank as well.'

'Maybe we should have got Ricky to do some more,' Amelia sighed as Karis escorted her across the car-park and back through the brightly lit streets of Las Vegas to the Luxor. 'He was amazing, Karis. We should have made the most of him while we had the chance.'

'Oh, quit complaining, Amelia. You already got a screw tonight. I didn't. Besides, I was getting rather bored in there. Every second guy in California looks like him.

'Yeah, but we're in Nevada now, and I don't see us finding another one like that tonight.'

'I'm tired,' said Karis, a little irritably. 'Let's just go to bed.'

'Did you book a room somewhere?'

'I thought I'd stay with you.'

Amelia smiled. Karis wasn't tired.

'Do you mind?'

'I guess not.'

They ascended in the elevator to Amelia's room with their arms linked around each other's waists.

When the door opened at the seventh floor an old lady who was waiting to go down again smiled at them benevolently. She knew that her eyesight was getting bad but she just couldn't tell these days which one of the young couple was the boy. Karis pinched Amelia's bum as they sashayed down the corridor, forcing her to give an outraged shriek. The old lady nodded happily. Young love.

'You are unbelievable, Karis. What will that old lady think?'

'Ah, she'll be dead by the time the elevator reaches the ground floor. Do you have your keys?'

Amelia produced her keys from her pocket and jangled them for effect. Once inside the room, Karis kicked her high heels off straight away and sat down on the end of the bed to massage her toes.

'It's a hard life being a dominatrix,' she moaned.

'Can't you be a dominatrix in flat shoes?' asked Amelia.

'Don't nag me, Miss Sensible. Get me a drink and then come over here. I want you to massage my feet. You're good at it.'

'I haven't done it for a while.'

'Then you need to practise.'

Grudgingly, Amelia knelt at the bottom of the bed and took Karis's right foot in her hands. She rubbed at it fiercely to begin with, to get the circulation going, then she started to work methodically over just a little area at a time. The base of her heel, the outside edge. Karis lay back on the pillows and sighed in ecstasy.

'Do you like that?' Amelia asked.

'I'll say. Isn't that the part of the foot that's directly connected to the sexual organs . . .?'

'No,' said Amelia matter-of-factly. 'That's this bit.' She squeezed another part of Karis's sole at which Karis squealed in pain and pulled her foot quickly out of the way.

'What did you do that for?' she asked.

'Do what?'

'That hurt.'

'Well, according to the ancient art of Chinese foot-massage, that must mean there's something wrong with the corresponding part of your body.'

'Like what?' Karis asked furiously.

'Over-work?'

'You bitch!' Karis swiped at Amelia's head with one of the bright white pillows. Amelia ducked below the end of the bed and the pillow made contact with nothing but air. 'You just better retract that comment, or I'll sue.'

'You can't sue someone for telling the truth.' Amelia continued to dodge the blows.

'I only wish it were. Hell, I was practically a virgin for the whole of last year!' Karis said between swipes. 'I only slept with four or five guys. Six at the very most.'

'Yeah,' Amelia laughed, enjoying the wind-up, 'but that was just the guys. What about the girls?'

'Girls? There's been no one since you.' Out of breath, Karis abruptly gave up the fight.

123

'Really?' Amelia was suddenly serious. She crawled up from her trench at the bottom of the bed. 'You haven't slept with another girl since me?'

'I haven't slept with another girl ever, as a matter of fact. You were different. You know that.'

Amelia sat down beside her. 'Same for me too.'

'Truly?'

Amelia nodded.

The air between them had become unbearably tense. They looked at each other questioningly until Karis slung an arm around Amelia's neck and laid a friendly kiss on her forehead. Amelia returned the embrace and they stayed locked in a hug for a moment or two.

'Did you ever think about it, what happened between us, while I was away?' Amelia asked.

'Did you?' Karis carefully avoided answering her.

'Sometimes.'

'Yeah. Me too.'

Karis smoothed her hand gently up and down Amelia's back, enjoying the friction of the rough cotton against her fingertips. Amelia's head rested lightly on Karis's slim shoulder. She breathed in the perfume of shampoo and cigarette smoke that lingered in the raven curls of Karis's hair. Amelia lifted the veil of black curls out of the way and planted a delicate kiss on the white skin beneath. She thought she heard Karis murmur something in half-hearted protest, a shiver shook her dancer's body, then Amelia felt a hand squeezing her waist in consent.

'I wish you'd . . .' Amelia began.

'Let's talk about it tomorrow,' said Karis. She took Amelia's face in her hands and smoothed her long fringe out of the way. Karis's lips were cool from her iced drink and her tongue was cool too as it snaked its way into Amelia's mouth. Amelia tasted gin and lipstick, something Karis was never without. While the dark-haired girl nuzzled at Amelia's throat, Amelia flicked her own tongue quickly across her lips and gathered the taste of Karis in.

Karis, too, was relishing familiar smells, a familiar taste, as she ran her tongue up Amelia's neck to her ear. With the very tip of her tongue she circled the emerald earring in Amelia's left lobe. Amelia shivered at the sensation and clutched the back of Karis's neck suddenly with her hand. She pulled Karis back so that their lips met once again. The lipstick was almost gone now, smeared between their mouths, but Karis's lips were almost as red beneath her war-paint. Her pupils had dilated so that they seemed to fill her whole eyes. She had an animal look about her. A look of arousal that hadn't been there when they were making the hapless cowboy Ricky disport himself in his shabby hotel room. Then Karis had been playing. This time the excitement was for real.

Karis sat back on her heels while Amelia undid her tight red button-through top. She breathed in deeply as Karis's breasts were revealed, buoyed up by the luxuriously lacy bra beneath. Her nipples were already hard, poking out through the centres of a pair of lacy flowers. Amelia cupped the breasts in her hands and let her thumbs play gently over the stiff little knobs. Karis exhaled with a ripple of joy. Amelia dipped her head and placed a careful kiss where the cleavage began.

'Now you,' Karis whispered. Obediently Amelia let her sweater be pulled over her head for the second time that evening. She had lost her bra in her brief tussle with Bud and was glad to be rid of the light wool which still irritated her bare skin. But Amelia's breasts had no need for the support of a bra now. Swollen with anticipation, they hung before her like two round ripe peaches, begging to be nibbled and kissed. Her pink nipples stood out in sharp contrast against the soft white skin. Karis cupped them in an echo of Amelia's gesture and paid tribute to each nipple with a lingering kiss.

The gentle kiss that she laid on the left nipple was soon to become something deeper. Carefully, Karis sucked the stiff pink bud into her mouth, elongating it until it was between her even teeth. She nipped at it softly, not so hard as to cause pain, but hard enough to make Amelia draw in her breath sharply. Her whole body became focused around that tiny sensitised part of her which was in Karis's warm mouth. Amelia felt as though her whole being was flowing out through her nipple into Karis, like milk.

'Do it harder,' Amelia asked after a while, when

she had grown used to the rhythmic sucking and the initial strength of the sensation was beginning to die down. But Karis moved her attention to the other nipple and began the whole process again. The deserted nipple ached and throbbed as it once again found itself bare in the air-conditioned room. Karis's saliva dried and cooled there until the nipple felt almost freezing. Amelia looked down to where Karis's bobbing curly head obscured one breast from view, then at the other nipple which now looked bigger than it had ever been before.

Karis moaned quietly as she licked and sucked, drawing the hardened nipple in then letting it drag slowly, slowly out across the sharp edge of her teeth. Amelia closed her eyes and reached blindly for Karis's own breasts, still encased in their expensively lacy bra. Amelia groped around Karis's back until she found the clasp that held the bra there. She unfastened it deftly using only one hand. Karis felt her beautiful olive breasts swing heavily forward and knew that they had been freed. She let Amelia's nipple drop from her mouth and straightened herself up to discard the frivolously small black garment altogether. Now Karis and Amelia sat facing each other, naked from the waist up, as they had done four years before on another warm evening in another anonymous room.

'Should we carry on?' Amelia had asked the same question then. Karis just nodded. Amelia ducked her head and greedily took one of the breasts proffered her into her mouth. Karis's skin was so warm and so silky. The girls stretched out side by side and Amelia lay with her head on Karis's chest. She thought she could hear a heart beating, or perhaps it was the sound of her own pulse that was racing in her ears? An exploratory hand wandered lazily along the curve of Amelia's waist to the top of her jeans.

'Can I?' Karis asked as she began to unbuckle Amelia's belt. Amelia answered her question by doing the same thing herself. Soon they were lying totally naked together. Their hands roaming over corresponding curves as if they were engaged in an ancient and beautiful dance.

Karis was the braver of the two and it was her hand that found its way first between her partner's legs. Amelia gave a little gasp of surprise as she felt herself invaded by the other girl's long, thin fingers, stronger and more purposeful than she remembered.

'Open your legs a little more,' Karis instructed. Amelia drew her uppermost leg towards her so that her vagina lay more open to the gentle caress. 'You're wet already,' Karis smiled.

Her shyness almost completely overcome, Amelia decided it was time that she sought out the hidden treasure beneath Karis's curly black pubic hair but Karis quickly pushed the probing fingers away. Amelia moaned in protest, for Karis's fingers were still rubbing diligently at her clit. She wanted to return the exquisite pleasure in some way. But Karis was determined to keep

128

Amelia's hands away. For the moment, she was completely in charge.

'Lie on your back,' she instructed.

Amelia rolled over lazily, as if in a dream. Karis took a thigh in each hand and spread Amelia's legs widely apart. Then she took Amelia's arms, which lay untidily by her sides, and pulled them out to the corners of the bed until Amelia was arranged like a human star.

'Don't move,' Karis whispered. From the overnight bag she had left at the foot of the bed she flourishingly produced two gloriously bright silk scarves. Gently but firmly taking Amelia's right wrist, she bound it once as if she were binding an injury, then took the flowing loose ends of the scarf and tied them tightly around the top of the bed. Amelia only looked on in wonder, feeling no fear at the impending curtailment of her freedom. Karis repeated the manoeuvre with the other arm, and then with both of Amelia's legs, using Amelia's belt and Karis's lacy bra to tie the long limbs down. Amelia made no protest at all, sensing that Karis would never cause her harm.

'Stay there,' Karis told Amelia as she lay, now totally naked, and open-legged, across the bed. 'Well, I guess you don't really have a choice,' she added with a laugh. She bounded over to the dresser and rifled through her handbag. And returned with the infamous vibrator, whirring menacingly in her hand.

'It's a stick-up!' she giggled. Amelia writhed

deliciously in anticipation. Her instinct was to pull her legs together, to protect herself from the approach of such extreme pleasure, but it was impossible now that they were fastened with her own belt and Karis's bra to the corners of the bed.

'Oh no,' Amelia protested weakly. 'Anything but that.'

But Karis was already kneeling on the end of the bed, her eyes narrowed in an expression of mischief. The vibrator buzzed like an angry wasp, eager to give someone a sting. Amelia twisted helplessly in her bonds and closed her eyes as she felt the cold plastic make contact with her skin.

At first, Karis merely ran the quivering phallus up and down the inside of Amelia's thigh. The vibrations seemed to be travelling through Amelia's muscle to her very bones and although the vibrator was nowhere near her vagina, the resonance reached her labia as well, making them swell and part, eager for their share of the attention.

Tantalisingly, Karis moved the buzzing tool from Amelia's right inner thigh to her left, just touching Amelia's aching clit as she passed over it. From time to time, the vibrator touched a couple of her pubic hairs, which transmitted the vibrations along to their roots. Amelia bit her lower lip. Karis was going to make this moment last a lifetime.

'Karis, Karis, stop, please,' Amelia breathed in desperation as the vibrator passed from left to right again, still not touching her throbbing sex.

'This is agony.'

'I know,' Karis laughed.

Unexpectedly, Karis got up from the bed altogether and walked around it and up to where Amelia's head lay on its pillow, rolling distractedly from side to side. Karis leaned over her so that her long black curls brushed lightly against Amelia's cheek. She kissed her. Amelia responded as though Karis's mouth was a succulent ripe strawberry and she hadn't eaten for days. The vibrator still buzzed in Karis's hand, touching Amelia's ribs and making her shiver as Karis kissed her a little harder. All too soon, Karis sat up again and began to play the quivering head of her hand-held toy up and down Amelia's naked torso.

Around Amelia's nipples, Karis worked the buzzing head. The little pink buds strained upwards, reaching that point where they became so sensitive that pleasure was almost replaced by pain. Amelia bit her lower lip harder still between her straight white teeth. She didn't want to cry out, to let Karis know that she was winning and could do anything she wanted to this body tied down before her now. Karis lazily trailed the vibrator down between the breasts and across Amelia's gently curved stomach. She danced it gaily around Amelia's belly button and carried on down until, once again, she was at Amelia's pubic hair.

'No,' Amelia groaned. But no wasn't what she meant at that moment.

Karis smiled wickedly. She resumed her position between Amelia's open legs, without once breaking contact between the vibrator and her flesh. The vibrator hovered at the edge of Amelia's mound like a sacrificial dagger, waiting to plunge deep inside her and take her out of this room to somewhere altogether more exciting and ecstatic. The few seconds that the vibrator took to inch down, through the hair, towards Amelia's desperate clit seemed like a thousand lifetimes. Amelia felt as though she was holding her breath, coming up from the bottom of a deep, deep lake. Waiting, longing to exhale again.

Then, finally, it was there. The sensation exploded through Amelia's body, rushing up from her clitoris like a flame along a gunpowder trail. The vibrations, which were so frenzied and frenetic at their point of entry into her, were spreading out as far as her head like the circles which surround a stone dropped into a pool. Amelia's hands were clenched into fists, her ankles twisted in their bindings as Karis dropped the vibrator a little more again, bringing it onto the pouting lips of her vagina, finding a way between them into the narrow passage that was longing to allow her in. The vibrator slipped easily inside, sliding effortlessly in and out of the wet juices that heralded Amelia's enjoyment and desire. In the distant blur of sight and sound that the room had become, Amelia heard the flicking of a switch and felt the vibrator move up to another level of power. Karis might as well have connected her lover straight to the mains.

Amelia's hips writhed skywards until Karis had to hold her still in order to continue the torturous pleasure she wanted to inflict. Alternately plunging the vibrator into Amelia's vagina and then pulling it out to dance it over her clit, Karis laughed as she worked. Her own arousal was building inside her unfettered body. She felt supremely sensitive. She could feel the gentle brush of her black curls on her shoulders as she moved. The vibrator in her hand was sending waves up her arms so that she felt somehow plugged in to the body on the bed, sharing the experience. As Amelia panted and strained against her bindings, it finally became too much for Karis to maintain her own calm demeanour. With one hand, she held the vibrator against Amelia's clit, with the other, she sought out her own and pressed hard against the tiny throbbing nerve-head.

'Karis, Karis,' Amelia squealed.

But Karis could not hear. Though she felt close to Amelia, she was at the same time very far away, cocooned in her own pleasure. Suddenly she ripped the vibrator away from Amelia and plunged it, still wet with her friend's juices, into her own vagina. Kneeling on the bed, she drew herself up and then flopped back down again between Amelia's open legs. She curled her body up and then straightened out as the spasms began to wrack her body. Amelia, left unattended, continued to pant. She had already reached a point of no turning back and the sight of her tortureress in the throes of her own orgasm kept Amelia's climax at boiling point.

'Oh, oh, ohhh . . .' Karis screamed in ecstasy to the ceiling. Her entire body hovered momentarily in an upright position before she collapsed back on to the mattress, and from there slid, like a drowning girl going under, onto the thick cream-carpeted floor.

When all had gone quiet again, Amelia suddenly became aware that she was still bound to the bed like a beached starfish. Karis lay on the floor, motionless except for the gentle heaving of her delicate ribcage. It looked suspiciously as though she had fallen asleep.

'Karis,' Amelia called softly. 'Karis, are you asleep?'

There was no answer from the prone body on the carpet.

'Typical,' thought Amelia. 'And I thought it was just men who rolled over and fell asleep.'

Fortunately for Amelia, Karis did come round again before the bindings had completely cut off the blood supply to her feet and hands. Free to move now, Amelia stretched out an arm and turned off the light. Karis was curled into her side, her head resting on Amelia's shoulder, her raven hair spread out across Amelia's smooth white skin like a lacy veil. For a moment in the darkness they lay still in silence, but both were aware that the other was not about to go to sleep just yet.

134

'Amelia,' Karis piped up first, 'I wish you didn't have to go so soon.'

'I know,' said Amelia. 'So do I.'

But there was to be no change to Amelia's plans this time. The next afternoon she got Karis to drive her to the airport and resisted all attempts to make her extend her stay for just another day.

'Final call for flight LH042.'

Amelia glanced at her watch.

'Look, Karis, I've really got to go.' She started to get to her feet and gather up her hand luggage.

'You'll be back soon, yes?' Karis asked. 'For my wedding?'

'For your wedding! Karis, I might never come back if I wait for someone to make an honest woman of you. Besides, it's your turn to visit me.'

'Oh yeah,' groaned Karis. 'Only when London gets hot . . . or hell freezes over.'

They shared a final hug. Amelia broke away first. Karis was dabbing at the corner of one eye. 'Get going, girl,' she told her old friend, 'before my false lashes get washed off.'

'We'll be in touch again soon, Karis,' Amelia assured her, neither of them knowing that it might be much sooner than they both expected.

Chapter Eleven

AS SOON AS Amelia found her seat in the body of the plane, she rifled through the in-flight bag for the complimentary eye-mask and slipped it on. Then she lay back and made an effort to go to sleep. After her ill-timed nap, Karis had kept Amelia awake for most of the night, making love to her and talking about old times and the bright futures they were planning. Amelia was glad that Karis had managed to find her in Las Vegas. At one stage she had thought that they might never see each other again, after the embarrassment of their confused affair at college. Amelia wouldn't let their friendship lapse so far again.

Right up until the very last moment, it appeared as if Amelia was going to have her row of three seats entirely to herself. She was looking forward to spreading herself out across them soon after take-off when, to her disappointment, she was joined by a young guy who looked as though he had been running to get there on time. A·stewardess helped him to cram his bulky hand luggage into the overhead locker and fastened his seat-belt for him. He was the last person to board the plane.

'Henry,' he said in a cut-glass English accent as he offered Amelia his hand. The stewardess had asked Amelia to remove her eye-mask for the duration of the safety video.

'Amelia,' she replied, taking the proffered hand politely. Why did she always have to sit next to someone who wanted to talk when all she needed was to spend the entire flight asleep?

'Can't wait until we're allowed to smoke,' Henry said nervously. 'Calms the nerves, you know.'

'I think you'll find that this is the no-smoking section,' replied Amelia dryly.

'Oh, damn . . .' Henry swore. 'Oh, sorry, shouldn't swear in front of a lady. Sorry.'

Amelia smiled and pulled her mask down to cover her eyes again. Henry was cute, in a floppy-fringed public schoolboy kind of way. She wondered how old he was. No doubt he would let her know later.

'Flying back to London?' Henry asked.

'Unless we run out of fuel on the way.'

'Oh, yes. Stupid question, I suppose. Though you could be going on to somewhere else.'

'No,' sighed Amelia, 'I'm just flying back to London.'

'Me, too. Back to work tomorrow. Not that I'll

be able to get much done with the jet-lag I'll have and all that.'

'No, I don't suppose you will . . . Hey, listen, Henry, I really hate to sound unfriendly, but I've had a long and busy night and I really would appreciate the opportunity to get some sleep right now. Do you mind?' She raised her eye-mask to giving him a pleading look.

'Oh, I am sorry,' Henry bumbled. 'It's just that I get so nervous when I'm flying that I have to talk to take my mind off the fact that I'm sitting in a tube of metal about three hundred miles up in the sky.'

'It's safer than being in a car.'

'Yes, but you're unlikely to have a car crash over the Atlantic.'

'Oh, Jeez,' groaned Amelia, catching sight of his white-knuckled hand gripping the arm-rest between them. 'Look, you just cover yourself up with a blanket, Henry, and let me take your mind off being a mile high . . .'

Henry looked at Amelia quizzically. His big brown eyes blinked rapidly while he waited for her to explain. Amelia licked her lips. On closer inspection he was really very handsome indeed, though a little drained with fear, and perhaps not quite as young as she had at first thought.

'Cover yourself up with a blanket, Henry,' she repeated. 'They'll be turning the lights off soon so that everyone can get some sleep. And then I'll tell you a nice bedtime story.' She casually laid a hand on his knee to underline her intention. If she was going to have to talk to him she was at

138

least going to make sure she had some enjoyment as well.

The stewardesses turned out the lights and made a final journey up and down the plane to check that everyone had all they needed. Henry had unfolded his grey blanket and now it lay across his knees. Amelia was beneath hers too, but her hand had already crept up Henry's legs towards the top of his thigh. His firm thigh muscle had tensed until she was sure it must be feeling painful. Amelia chatted casually about the weather for a while to calm him down until the last stewardess had disappeared into the little staff booth. Then she leant in closely and began to whisper hotly in Henry's reddening ear.

'Are you ready?'

He nodded.

'OK. Then I'll begin. Once upon a time,' she said in a soft, sing-song voice, 'a brave Amazon set out on a journey from her village to find the source of eternal life.' Amelia tiptoed her fingers up Henry's legs beneath the blanket to represent the heroine of her story beginning her quest. 'She had a vague idea of the direction in which the source lay, but to get there she had to cover all sorts of rough and tricky terrain, encountering on her journey all kinds of trial and hardship . . .' Amelia smiled to herself as her fingers wandered blithely over Henry's stiffening member and started off down his other leg. 'But she didn't care how long it took, or what she had to do, because in the end she knew it would be worth it . . .'

Henry sighed deeply and looked at the redhead whose fingers were currently ambling down to his right knee. Their eyes met. Amelia bit her lower lip and winked at Henry in a gesture of shameless flirtation. Suddenly Henry forgot that he was in a metal tube, three hundred miles up. His fluttering heart was already flying higher than that.

'A short while into her epic journey,' Amelia continued, her fingers walking slowly up Henry's blue chambray-clad chest, 'the Amazon came to a sheer rock wall. It was incredibly high and she didn't think she would be able to scale it.' Her fingers slipped languorously down towards Henry's belt. He closed his eyes and inhaled loudly. 'But she got about halfway up by taking a long run at it . . .' Henry exhaled in disappointment as Amelia's fingers raced back up from his navel to the centre of his chest. 'However it soon became clear that there was to be no going over the top and so she had to look for a way through.' The roaming hand moved towards Henry's pearly white buttons.

The blanket was slipping down. Amelia used her free hand to pull it up towards Henry's chin.

'She had to find a way through,' Amelia recapped as she started to twist the first button out of its buttonhole. 'And, luckily for the resourceful Amazon, she was able to use her skills to open an ancient door which someone else had kindly put there before . . .' Amelia's fingers slipped inside Henry's shirt and rested on his hot

140

chest. They rose up and down slowly with his measured breathing.

'Inside the cave she had found it was very dark, and strange wiry stemmed plants grew from the hard, smooth walls.' Amelia's fingers wove their way through the soft hair which grew messily between Henry's nipples. 'Their gentle tendrils wrapped themselves around our heroine's legs and made it difficult for her to walk. She knew that she was far from her goal and by hesitating too long she might lose everything, when, suddenly,' Amelia's fingers made contact with a nipple, 'the Amazon happened upon a curious handle which grew up from the rock beneath her hand.' Amelia's stroking fingers were stiffening the nipple to a hardened point. Henry sighed and kissed Amelia's forehead through her fringe. 'Being a truly brave warrior as she was, the Amazon twisted the handle and found herself falling, falling, thousands of feet through the rock to land on a pile of the softest grass she had ever had the good fortune to fall upon.'

Amelia slid her hand right down Henry's chest and pushed her way past the waistband of his trousers to the top of his pubic hair. 'Now, she just knew that she was getting very warm indeed.'

Henry breathed in. Amelia's fingers slipped a little further beneath his belt until they struck gold. Henry's dick was already semi-hard, only his shyness at being fondled by a complete stranger in such a public setting was tempering what could be an enormously impressive hard-on. Suddenly, Amelia's other hand was beneath Henry's blanket and she was quickly unfastening his thick leather belt.

'Not much room to manoeuvre,' she explained. He looked at her with an expression of shock in his big, blinking eyes.

'I say, Amelia, I don't know if . . .'

'If I should be doing this? Lighten up, Henry. It's less frightening than thinking about flying.'

He wasn't sure about that.

'No one can see. The stewardesses certainly won't bother to come out of their cabin unless they have to. And even if they do, I assure you they've seen it all before.'

Henry gulped. Amelia took hold of the tab of his zip and pulled it down before he could protest. Now she had enough room to put her hand right inside his trousers and get beneath the elastic of his close-fitting briefs. She could imagine what they would look like, and, judging from the rest of his outfit, they would probably be in sensible navy blue.

Henry's dick twitched as the blood rushed from his body to its favourite extremity.

'That's better,' said Amelia. 'Now I can carry on.'

The guy in the seat across the aisle from Henry's let out a tremendous snore.

'See, nobody else is listening. Where was I? Oh, yes, our brave heroine knew that at long last she had come to the right place. But as she looked around her, at the proud monolith that marked the source of eternal life, she noticed that there didn't seem to be all that much life in the area. What was she to do?'

Amelia's fingers curled around the base of Henry's warm, smooth shaft.

'Thank goodness she knew that to bring the elixir from the bottom of the well, there was a great big handle that she would have to find and pull . . .'

Henry bit his lip as the hot hand moved upwards. He saw the blanket move quite discernibly.

'But not too hard, of course . . .'

Amelia's hand travelled back downwards. Henry sucked in his breath sharply and Amelia wondered briefly whether she had just caused him some pain. The anguished look on his face soon dissolved into a beatific smile however, and so she carried on. There was no need to continue with the story now. It had served its purpose and Henry was no longer listening to anything Amelia said anyway. That was a shame, Amelia thought, since she had come up with a great ending for her epic tale, with Henry playing the source of the elixir of life, of course.

As Amelia eased her hand back and forth with a smooth, fast rhythm, she felt the shaft hardening further still beneath her hand. Occasionally it would twitch upwards with impressive force, making her long for a little more leg room and a little less of an audience so that she could climb onto Henry's lap and slip his tremendous length inside. But for now that wasn't possible and so she would have to make do with witnessing his pleasure . . . Perhaps not, she smiled to herself. There was something they could do. She let go of Henry's penis suddenly and, before he had time to protest, was quickly pulling up his zip again, having first carefully tucked his turgid dick back behind his fly.

'I'm going to the loo,' she told him. 'There's no queue right now. Give me thirty seconds or so and then you can follow me up there. Knock on the door like this.' She lightly demonstrated a secret knock on the collapsible meal tray which folded down from the seat in front. 'And then I'll let you in.'

Amelia jumped up and strolled nonchalantly down the plane. She ensconced herself in a cubicle and waited. She checked her reflection in the dark mirror. She waited. She fixed her hair a little. She waited. Where was he? She'd said thirty seconds and he had been at least two minutes. The hard-on she had so carefully nurtured would probably be non-existent by now.

Just when she was about to give up hope, there came the secret knock at the door.

Amelia slid the door open just enough to let him inside.

'Where have you been?' she hissed.

'Two seconds after you got up, another passenger decided that he needed to go as well. I had to wait in my seat until there was no queue again.'

'OK. You're forgiven.' She was already unfastening his belt. She had ascertained from the outline of his trousers that all was not completely lost. Once the flies were undone, Amelia pushed Henry's trousers down over his hips to his knees. His briefs came off simultaneously. Amelia couldn't help but let out a tiny laugh when she saw that they were indeed navy blue.

When Henry was ready, his dick standing up proudly in anticipation, Amelia carefully turned around in the tiny space so that she was facing away from him. She put down the toilet seat and stood with one leg on either side of its aluminium bowl. Then she hitched up her skirt and bent over, her hands braced against the wall at the back of the cubicle. Henry's dick nudged at the rose-pink and swollen entrance of her aching sex without her having to move an inch.

'Come on then,' she told him, her voice husky with arousal. 'Give it to me.'

Away from the eyes of the other passengers, Henry was still hesitating. Amelia wondered for a second whether she was being just a little too keen for this shy English boy.

'What if we get caught?' Henry asked.

'We'll be all right as long as you don't have a cigarette afterwards. Get on with it, please, Henry.'

Henry cleared his throat. Amelia closed her eyes and waited for the first thrust. The blood rushed to her head and sent tingles through her entire body as she felt him gently nudging at her labia with his penis, trying to find a way inside. But two false starts were quite enough and soon she was impatiently guiding his shaft between her labia herself, gasping with the joy the feeling of being filled up in such a risky setting gave her.

'That's it. Push right in.'

Feeling behind her, Amelia grasped hold of one of Henry's hands and had him place it on her waist. Then she did the same to the other.

'Rock me backwards onto you,' she instructed in a hoarse whisper. 'Use my waist to pull me towards you.'

Henry did as Amelia told him and soon they were building up a satisfying rhythm with the bare minimum of movement between them. Once or twice, Henry crashed backwards into the metal folding door and Amelia had to stop herself from crying out by using one of her hands as a bit between her teeth. But it was a divine feeling. Being taken from behind was one of Amelia's favourite positions when she had all the time in the world, but here, in the bathroom of an aeroplane, with the added tension of knowing that too much noise or movement would let everyone know what was going on, Amelia didn't know if she would be able to hang on to her orgasm long enough to join Henry as he came.

Fortunately for Amelia, Henry wasn't going to be able to last out for that long either. By twisting her head slightly to the side, Amelia could see both their bodies reflected in the dark glass mirror. Henry had his head thrown back, his mouth open, letting out a small guttural grunt each time he pulled her body towards his. He was transfigured by his pleasure from a boy afraid of flying into some kind of fucking machine. He filled her so perfectly. He was so hard, and hardening ever more as his crisis approached. Amelia felt his shaft jerk upwards as it had done in her hand. His balls slapped against her body, the vibrations to her clitoris giving her so much intense pleasure that she thought her shaking knees might buckle beneath her.

'Yes, yes,' Henry was hissing. 'Yes, yes, I'm going to come.' He drew her body towards his faster and faster, more and more ferociously, so that suddenly he pulled her right away from the wall. Straightening her body up against his, Henry clasped Amelia to him, still pumping into her from behind. Amelia's arms flailed to find something to grasp hold of as their bodies began to buck, both at once. Henry groaned as his hot semen began to shoot deep, deep inside her. His spasms were echoed by the movements of Amelia's pulsating vaginal walls, squeezing and massaging his frenzied dick until the last of his come was pooling inside her and dribbling slowly down her legs.

Amelia and Henry stood locked in their position for a while. Henry breathed raggedly in her ear. She reached up to cup his face and hold his hot cheek against hers. His hands roamed lazily over her breasts.

After a minute or so, Amelia remembered where they were and slowly eased herself away from Henry's sweating loins. She pulled her skirt down hurriedly and set about straightening her hair in the mirror once again. Henry had collapsed backwards against the door where he leant with his eyes closed, still panting like the winner of a long and difficult race. Amelia gave him a playful pinch.

'Henry, Henry,' she called softly. 'Get yourself straightened up. We've got to get back to our seats. I'll go first. Don't forget to act nonchalant.'

Amelia squeezed out past Henry who still didn't seem altogether awake. A middle-aged lady was standing just outside the cubicle. She moved towards the door as Amelia slipped out and was very surprised when it locked again as she tried to get in. Amelia walked quickly back to her seat, trying not to look at the people sitting near to the loos who had probably heard everything that went on. Oh well, thought Amelia, perhaps they hadn't. Henry wasn't what you would call a screamer, she reflected. He was probably too well brought up.

'Still scared of flying?' Amelia asked when Henry finally returned to his seat beside her.

He took up her hand which lay on the arm-rest between them. 'Not at all,' he replied. 'I could make this flight twice a day . . . But I wonder if when we get back to London, you'd like to help me overcome my irrational fear of strange beds?'

'I need some sleep,' Amelia told him, then she covered herself up with a blanket again and left Henry trying to arrange his long body comfortably in his cramped seat.

*

The flight landed safely and on time, with Henry gripping Amelia's fingers until they went blue as the plane made its descent. In the customs hall, Amelia's luggage came around on the carousel first. Henry was still standing nervously beside her, obviously wanting to suggest for real that they meet again sometime but being too scared to say when and how. Amelia dragged her heavy blue suitcase off the conveyor and onto the floor. She sat on top of it while she rooted through her hand luggage for a scrap of paper and a pen.

'What's your number, Henry?' she asked.

'Oh, my number . . .' Henry didn't tell her what it was. Instead he fumbled in his jacket pocket and eventually brought out a card. 'It's on there. My mobile number. It's probably more use than giving you the one at home since I'm hardly ever in in the evenings.'

Amelia took the card from his shaking hand without reading it and thanked Henry for his pleasant company on the flight. She would ring, she promised, but for now all she wanted to do was get home. It was while Amelia was finding change for the taxi driver who dropped her off in Kentish Town that Henry's card came into her hand once again. As she waited for Richard to open the front door, Amelia fetched the card out and read it at last.

'Henry Du Pre. Mountain Music A & R.' So he was a talent spotter for Mountain. He hadn't mentioned that. Perhaps, thought Amelia, she would be ringing Henry after all.

Chapter Twelve

FOUR DAYS ALONE with Amelia's cat was enough for any man, thought Richard. Particularly when he had to come home every evening to face not only that mewling menace but a message from arch-ratbag Jamie Nettles on his answer-machine to boot. That guy sounded desperate, crazed even. What had Amelia done to him? Probably the same as she did to me, Richard reflected bitterly. The phone rang, the answerphone kicked in – Richard had set it to call-screen.

'Richard, darling, it's Amy. I'm at the airport – on my way back. If you're going to go out before I get in, could you remember to leave the key next door. I can't find mine. I missed you. See you later. Bye.' She blew kisses into the receiver. Richard's heart leapt involuntarily. She was coming back. And early.

Now she was here. Richard bounded to the door

and helped her drag her cases up the stairs. She opened her hand luggage and threw him a red baseball cap with 'Las Vegas' embroidered on it in gold thread, 'to hide his bald patch'. Richard took mock offence but was secretly thrilled she had remembered him.

'So, how was your trip?' Richard asked. 'How was the wedding? What was your bridesmaid's dress like? I bet you looked lovely.'

'The trip was tiring. The wedding was pretty much the same as the last one. The dress was Edwardian-style burnt clementine velvet with an ivory skirt and I looked like a monster.'

'You know you didn't,' Richard sighed. 'And the flight back? How was that?'

'Turbulent,' Amelia smiled. She was flipping quickly through the pile of envelopes which had accumulated during her brief absence. 'Any calls?' she asked when her rummage turned up nothing of any significance.

'Yes,' said Richard, his welcoming smile tightening. 'I didn't erase the answer-machine so you can listen to them yourself.'

'Thanks.' Amelia tripped into the lounge straightaway and flicked her messages on. At the sound of Jamie's voice Richard felt sure he saw the corners of her mouth twitch upwards.

'Amy, it's Jamie, Friday night. I've got a window in my diary, do you fancy coming out?'

'Amy, Jamie, Saturday morning. I'm not doing anything this evening so I thought you might like to come and grab a bite to eat with me.'

'Amy, Jamie, Saturday p.m. Have you gone away for the weekend? I hope not. I'm still free tonight . . .'

And so on and so on.

'I suppose I better call him,' Amelia shrugged. She dialled his number, from memory Richard noticed, and got through to the answer-machine at his home. 'Jamie, darling. Sorry, I've been indisposed. Yes, let's get together sometime soon and talk about this contract of mine. That would be nice. Can't wait to see you again.' More kisses down the telephone line.

Richard grimaced. What did that creep Nettles have that he didn't? Apart from blond hair and a great car? He took a deep breath. No point letting Amelia know he was bothered.

'So, what else did you do, apart from go to the wedding?' Richard persisted.

'I spent some time hanging round casinos, bumped into a couple of old friends from college.' Her eyes drifted faraway for a moment and her mouth lifted at the corners in a secret smile. 'Jerry was there too.'

'In Las Vegas?'

'Yes. He's in the States for work.' Amelia looked straight at Richard. He looked as if he already knew which bomb she was about to drop. 'It was a shock to see him there. I nearly scratched his eyes out when I first saw him but we've made it up. I'm getting back together with him.' Richard felt the blood draining from his cheeks, but reminded himself quickly that it wasn't his place to care.

'That's nice,' he forced himself to tell her. 'So, will you be moving out again?'

'I'm not sure . . . yet,' Amelia replied breezily. 'But as soon as I do know, rest assured you will be the first to hear.'

'Great,' said Richard. 'Thanks.'

'In fact,' Amelia continued, 'I think I'll call Jerry right now. Let him know that I had a safe flight home. What time will it be over there?'

Five minutes later, Amelia hung up the phone and dragged herself into the kitchen with the look of a dog that had just been kicked in the face. Richard was making toast. He buttered a slice and stuck it into her hand while he waited for her to decide whether or not he was going to hear about her latest disaster. He could see the tears welling in her eyes as she ate until, suddenly, she let out an almighty blub and a shower of toast crumbs spattered onto the floor.

Richard crammed the rest of his slice of toast into his mouth and rushed to put his arms around her.

'It's not fair,' she sobbed. 'He said he was coming back next week, but now he says he's not.'

'Who?'

'Jerry.'

'Oh.'

'He says he's going to be in LA for another week at the very least and then he may have to go straight from LA to New York for a project that could take months to complete. Months and months and months! What am I supposed to do, Richard? Waiting here in London all on my own?'

All on her own? Richard tried not to be offended. Didn't he and Eliza count as company any more? Amelia wailed into the shoulder of his soft green shirt. This he could do without. But how could he cheer her up? Tell her that Jerry was a rat and she should run away with him instead? That gem of enlightenment hadn't worked last time.

'Hey, cheer up,' he said helpfully after considering the matter for a long while. Then he was struck with something resembling inspiration. 'What you need is something to take your mind off this minor hiccup . . .'

'Minor hiccup?' Now Amelia was offended.

'This great disaster,' Richard continued a little more carefully.

'You're right,' said Amelia, sniffing delicately. 'I should go upstairs and write some more songs. Concentrate on my music for a bit. After all, I've got a meeting with Jamie Nettles soon. He promised me he would have a publishing contract for me by the end of this week.'

Richard pulled a strange, doubtful face.

'What are you looking at me like that for?' Amelia asked.

'Well,' Richard took a deep breath, 'I don't know whether I ought to say this, but . . .' There was never going to be a right time for what Richard was about to reveal to her next.

'But what? Go on, Richard,' Amelia snapped belligerently. 'Make my day.'

'It's just that I don't think you should bother with Jamie Nettles any more. You know that he works at the same company as me . . .'

'Go on.' Amelia was beginning to look frightening.

'Well, the other day, I was in the canteen and he happened to come and sit next to me for lunch. We have a vague acquaintanceship . . . He calls me "Dick". Anyway, we got talking about the projects he's working on at the moment and your name came up . . .'

Amelia paled. 'And?'

'And it seems that he's not really interested in your music at all, Amelia. He told me that he is just stringing you along with the promise of a contract because he's after your body.'

'No, no, no! That's just idle, jealous, gossip!' screamed Amelia, going from white to red, but the potential for the truth in Richard's words had already hit home. She started to cry again. Richard fluttered around her with a box of tissues while Amelia muttered vague death threats to the male population in general and Jamie Nettles in particular.

'Hey Amelia, calm down. Calm down. Listen, I've been invited to a party tonight. It's my cousin's engagement party actually. You should come along too. It might not be exactly your kind of scene. Plenty of maiden aunts. No hard drugs to speak of.' Amelia frowned at that aspersion.

'But we might have a really good time. There'll be lots of music and dancing!'

'Where is it?' she asked suspiciously.

'In a village just outside Oxford. I'll drive. And we can leave the minute you start to get bored.'

'OK,' she sniffed. 'Then I'll come.'

Richard was surprised that she agreed so quickly and mentally rubbed his hands together with glee. He was going to spend the evening with Amelia and at the very least that meant that he wouldn't have to put up with his grandmother asking him why he wasn't 'courting' all night.

The party sucked, as Richard knew it would, but hadn't let on to Amelia. It was held in a draughty church hall, which was festooned for the occasion with plenty of balloons printed 'Congratulations'. Amelia chatted politely with Richard's grandmother and listened to stories about his childhood. It was obvious that she thought Richard and Amelia were together, and Amelia didn't tell her otherwise, much to Richard's relief. In fact, when the DJ announced the final song of the evening, Amelia was the first to her feet, pulling Richard with his two left feet out onto the floor for the last dance.

'Richard,' Amelia whispered seductively as they swayed slowly to the rhythm. He waited with butterflies dancing madly around his stomach for her to continue. The touch of her breath on his ear and the proximity of her body in its thin, cotton jersey dress was giving him a hard-on already. 'Richard, I'm sorry about earlier on. I really am grateful for what you told me about that snake, Jamie Nettles. You're a great house mate, you know that.'

Oh well, it was better than nothing. Halfway through the song a distant cousin of Richard's strolled casually over and dragged Amelia from his arms. Richard stood at the side of the dance-floor, waiting for the song to finish, watching her drift lazily around in Mitchell's lecherous grip. Her eyes were faraway. He wondered what she was thinking about. Him? Probably not.

Richard's grandmother suddenly pulled on his sleeve.

'That's a lovely girl you've got there, Dicky,' she said.

Yes, Amelia was a lovely girl, but he hadn't got her, not yet.

Held in a church hall as it was, the party finished long before midnight. In the car-park, Amelia waited patiently while Richard warmed up his old car to the point where it would actually start. It was a balmy August night. The sky was clear and, away from the constant glow of the artificial light of London, they were actually able to see the stars.

There was a strange, spluttering sound. Richard's car had started.

'Are we driving straight back?' Amelia asked as she climbed into the passenger seat.

'If you want to.'

'Not really. It's not that late and I like being out here in the country. Is there anywhere we can go to look at the stars?'

Richard was only too happy to oblige.

Not far from the village where the party had been held stood an ancient monument known as the Rollright Stones. It was a symbolic circle of stones, nowhere near as big or impressive as Stonehenge but just as old. Legend had it that no one had ever been able to count the number of stones correctly. That every time you counted them up the number you came to would be different. Richard had even heard a story about a camera which was ripped out of its owner's hands and whipped up into the sky by a freak wind when he tried to take a photograph of this mystical place. Richard parked the car on the road between the main circle and the King Stone which stood alone in another field. He helped Amelia over the rusted iron fence.

'Wow, just feel the vibes,' Amelia laughed when she stood in the centre of the moonlit ring. She spun around, arms open like a whirling dervish. Richard sat down on the ground beside her. He picked out a juicy blade of grass and bit upon it ruminatively. The stones looked out across a vista of rolling fields which were silver and blue in the glittering moonlight. Amelia lowered herself tentatively to sit beside him.

'The grass is damp,' she explained.

'No, it's not. But you can sit on my jacket if you like.' Richard lay flat out and gazed at the sky. Using his grass as a pointer, he drew her attention to a cluster of stars.

'That's the Great Plough.'

'Is it really?'

Richard nodded solemnly. 'And that's the Milky Way. That's Pisces, that's Aries and that's Uranus.'

'Wow,' said Amelia, her mouth open in awe as she took it all in. 'How do you know all this stuff about the stars?'

'I don't,' replied Richard. 'I was making it all up.'

'You monster!' exclaimed Amelia. She leant over his body, hands on either side of his shoulders, to pull a face at him. But before she could right herself again, Richard stopped her where she was, holding her tightly just above the elbows. His eyes locked with hers provocatively. The wind rippled the grass around his head so that it looked almost as though they were lying in water.

'Kiss me,' he said.

Amelia's eyes flickered nervously across his face. Richard held his gaze steady on her soft lips. He had called her bluff, but just as he thought she would refuse and pull away, she bent her elbows and dipped gracefully down to meet his upturned mouth. And she stayed there.

They kissed softly, gently. Sometimes her lips seemed merely to graze his. Gradually, Amelia shifted her body until she lay on top of Richard, her legs either side of his legs, her toes pressing against the ground, her hands knitted together in his short, tousled hair. Richard pushed his tongue carefully between her even white teeth. She responded in kind. He traced the well-defined cupid's bow of her lips with the tip of his tongue.

Carefully, Richard rolled over so that now Amelia was on the grass and he was on top of her. She laughed up at him. Her big eyes glinted darkly with the reflected light of the full moon. He studied her reverently for a moment, as though she were a painting, until Amelia felt freaked out by his staring and insisted that he continue to kiss her, and with his eyes shut at that.

Her hands were in his hair again, caressing the back of his head, then his ears, then tracing along the stubbly line of his jaw with her fingertips. They rolled onto their sides so that Richard no longer had to support himself with his hands but could use them instead to rove all over her. Amelia had untucked his grey marl T-shirt from the waistband of his jeans and her fingers were now softly moving over his warm bare skin. She lingered on a tiny raised mole. Her touch was so light at times that it almost tickled.

Amelia was wearing a floral printed dress that fastened all the way down the front with tiny, mother of pearl buttons. Her familiar amber pendant hung from a slightly shorter chain around her throat. Richard began to fumble with the buttons nearest the scoop neck of the dress but they were fragile and he found them difficult to budge from the fabric loops into which they were hooked for fear of breaking them. Sensing his nervousness, Amelia flopped onto her back and began to help him set her free, giggling. Soon her dress was open to reveal her flimsy cotton all-in-one, which was also printed with roses. Richard sighed impatiently when he saw that he had to breach another layer of resistance before he could reach her smooth skin. Amelia meanwhile had gone straight for his fly and was manhandling his dick out through the slit in his boxer shorts.

'I don't want to take my dress off. I'll get a rash from the grass,' she told him matter-of-factly when he tried to push the dress from her shoulders.

'But how . . .?' he started to protest.

'It's got poppers,' she told him, indicating the crotch of her lacy all-in-one. He heard a faint popping sound as she undid the first one herself, then the second, and the third. Amelia wriggled the clingy material up around her hips until her venus mound was completely exposed to the glittering sky. Richard smiled. He took her hips in his hands as if they were the handles of a holy grail and brought her pelvis up to meet his descending mouth. He placed a first kiss just below her belly button and followed it with a trail of kisses winding down towards her pubic hair. Amelia shivered and let out a soft laugh at the

161

gentle sensation Richard's mouth was imparting to her skin. Unconsciously she shifted her legs apart and braced her feet against the floor to raise herself still further.

Richard sat back on his heels and supported her with a hand beneath each of her buttocks. She parted her legs a little more. Richard's dick, which was still poking out from the front of his trousers, stiffened at the sight which was opening up before him. The deep pink lips of Amelia's sex, like some rare and fragile flower, were swelling and slickening even as he watched. The world around him, the stone circle at whose centre they lay, blurred into the deepest background. All the light in the night sky seemed to be concentrating in Amelia, in her body, her sex.

'Touch me,' she begged him, as her own fingers moved instinctively towards her most vulnerable and sensitive place. Her pelvis was now straining up towards his mouth. 'Touch me, Richard.'

Slowly, reverently, Richard dipped his head to her vagina and began to caress the delicate clitoris which was calling out for his attention in the darkness of the night. First he kissed it, then cautiously he poked out his tongue to touch the most sensitive part of her with one of the most sensitive parts of him. At the moment of contact, there escaped a sigh, long and happy, from Amelia's kiss-worn mouth. Richard smiled to himself and continued with the task that he had longed for the pleasure of undertaking. As he slowly licked at her glassy smooth vulva, his fingers gently clenched her buttocks. Her fingers echoed his, tearing up handfuls of the green summer grass which grew thickly all around them. The gentle breeze that crossed the top of the hill had died down. All he could hear was her breathing, deep and measured, echoing around the ancient stones.

After a while she pushed his head away with her hands and sat up. She reached out one hand and touched his penis, which was still so hard, still straining for her attention. She wrapped her fingers around it and pumped it rhythmically while they kissed again. Richard caught his breath. She sensed that she was perhaps pushing him too far and slowed her careful manipulation of his member down a little, so that he could regain control and avoid ending this precious moment in a fountain all over the grass.

Amelia's free hand tangled in her own pubic hair again, probing the folds that Richard's tongue had left behind. She was thinking about the penis she was holding, about how nicely he could fill her, how much she wanted him to take her now, and the muscles of her vagina contracted in sympathy with her thoughts. She began to lie back down on the ground, slowly, pulling him over her as she did so, still holding his penis, guiding him towards the centre of her body. She drew her knees up and let them fall apart so that she was open to him, completely open. Their mouths never parted, they continued to kiss all the while.

As Richard's tongue penetrated her mouth, she gently swayed her pelvis up to meet his and with the gentlest of pushes on Richard's part, his penis and her vagina were also joined. Amelia wrapped her arms tightly around his body and they pulled together as hard as they could, holding the position, the moment. Just letting their bodies melt into each other, his hand twisting into her soft red hair, her hands around his back, clasping him as if her fingers would break through his skin and flow into his blood.

Then they began to move. So effortlessly in time with one another. Their bodies swaying together and apart again almost soundlessly. Richard held himself up on locked arms and gazed down at the space between them, at his penis moving in and out of Amelia's vagina. The thick rod appearing and disappearing. She watched the graceful curve of her pelvis as it moved up to meet his, the tension in her stomach muscles, and in his stomach muscles. She reached between them to pull his T-shirt up out of the way so that she could see the action better. She held his waist between her hands, enjoying the feeling of his hard flesh flexing beneath her fingers with each thrust.

Richard's face took on a look of intense concentration as he moved to bring her maximum delight. His hair flopped in sweat-soaked strands over his eyes. Amelia's hands roamed ecstatically over his body, on his bare flesh beneath his T-shirt. He was so smooth, so warm, so obviously full of love for her.

'Richard,' she murmured, as a particularly deep thrust touched her G-spot and made the stars from the sky dance for a moment in front of her eyes. He was looking right into those eyes now, his heart pleading through his gaze for her to say something more, something deeper. To say perhaps that she loved him as he loved her? But she was on the point of being lost. Her back was arching up, her throat thrown upwards to the watching sky. Her mouth parted to let forth her breath in pants and sighs as it became increasingly uncontrolled.

'Richard,' she called again as another thrust hit the mark. She gazed up at him through languorously lowered eyelids. On this grass that moved like waves in the breeze, she was like a siren, tempting him, drawing him into his doom. The blue cast that the moon gave her skin made her look as though he was seeing her through water. Water that separated them, that held them still apart even when they were so joined. Her hands slid silently over his skin. One of her bare feet rubbed against his lower leg.

'Kiss me.'

Richard kissed her again. Her lips were cooled by the breeze. He pulled away. She gave a tiny, desperate moan. He recognised the clenching of her beautiful fingers on his buttocks as she tried to force the pace to get faster. He recognised the rising pitch of her sighs. They came faster and faster, until the time between them was negligible and Amelia erupted in one long keening call of bliss.

Richard felt himself lose control at that moment too. His movements, once so smooth, were all wrong, all out of time. They came together and yet apart. Each in a separate world of desire. Feeling different feelings. Thinking different thoughts as their bodies crashed and crushed each other. Semen mixed with sweat.

Richard collapsed onto Amelia's quivering body, his face in the cool, green grass. Her chest heaved. Her breathing deafened him. Her hands had left his body and lay loosely beside her. She had let him go.

Later, they got up and drove back to London. Still jet-lagged, Amelia slept in the car.

Chapter Thirteen

TWO DAYS LATER, it was as if the night in the stone circle had never happened.

Amelia had recorded a demo tape at the studio of a friend of Jerry's. She was doing about two gigs a week now. On Tuesday she was playing at the Lamb and Flag. Richard wished her luck but this time he didn't ask to go along. He would wait until he was invited.

Before she was due to start playing, Amelia joined the promoter of the gig for a drink. He had just popped to the gents, leaving her alone at the bar, when she saw Jamie Nettles stroll in. He had no girl in tow this time but he was looking handsome as ever in a green silk shirt and black jeans. Amelia read the back of a beermat, thinking he hadn't noticed her, but it wasn't long before she heard the clatter of his cowboy boots on the floorboards behind her and a reptilian hand came to rest lightly on her bare white shoulder.

'Amelia,' he said, kissing the back of her long neck. 'You've been avoiding my calls.'

'Jamie,' she trilled falsely. She twisted out of his mouth's reach but decided there was no point in being rude. 'I haven't. I've tried to call you hundreds of times but your phone is just perpetually engaged. You must be a very popular guy.' He seemed happy enough with her answer.

'You look great tonight.'

'Thank you.' Amelia sipped her drink and waited for him to slip into the audience, but he didn't.

'What are you doing after you've played?' Jamie asked suddenly. He shifted slightly from foot to foot. 'Do you fancy going to get something to eat? We could go to that Mexican place again.'

'Thanks for asking, Jamie, but, no, I've got to get home as soon as I finish here tonight.'

'Rubbish, Amelia. Tell you what, I'll give you a lift. I'd really like to talk to you about getting a contract signed – soon. Some kind of development deal.'

'Really?' Amelia bit her lip, remembering what Richard had told her at the weekend. Was Jamie really just lying to her about her chances in the music business to get her into bed? She decided she couldn't risk the chance that he was actually being genuine. 'OK,' she told him. 'But just a quick bite, yeah?'

'Well,' said Amelia as they left the restaurant and headed for Jamie's car. 'Now that we've eaten, I really do need to be getting home. I've got a temping job in the morning,' she lied.

'But we haven't really talked about that deal yet,' Jamie protested. 'Come back to my place for a coffee.'

Amelia turned round in her seat to look him straight in the eye.

'Jamie, is there really a deal at all?'

A flicker of panic crossed his face but then he smiled broadly. 'Would I lie to you?' He reached into the glove compartment of the dashboard and brought out an envelope which he waved before her nose with a flourish. Amelia made a grab for it but he kept it just out of her reach.

'Oh, no. Don't look at it now,' he said. 'I think you really need me to go through this with you.' Jamie was already pulling his car out of the narrow road in the direction of his flat in Camden, the exact opposite direction to Amelia's home.

Amelia sat casually on Jamie's deep sofa, arms crossed, one leg crossed over the knee of the other. She thought her posture made it quite clear that she was in the mood for nothing but business. She was determined to overcome the power of the past events associated with the sofa upon which she now sat. Jamie emerged from the kitchen with two familiar balloon glasses. He had lost only a little of the self-assurance which had so charmed her the first time they met.

'Calvados,' he told her.

'Of course,' she replied. He sat down beside her. Amelia shifted across the seat so that the gap between the cushions would act as a psychological divide. She crossed her legs away from him. 'So, let's talk business.'

'In a minute,' he told her. 'Let's have a drink first. What ever is wrong with you?'

'I suppose you could say that I'm feeling a little "nettled",' she replied. Jamie laughed uneasily.

'*Pourquoi*?' he asked suavely.

'Well, dear Jamie, rumour has it that it isn't exactly my musical talent which keeps you coming back to see me play.'

'I'm sorry?' Jamie feigned ignorance.

Amelia snapped.

'I mean that you're only interested in my body, you creep.'

'Amelia, that's unfair.' Jamie racked his brain for a suitably calming come-back to her accusation. 'You know that I'm interested in your music first and foremost ... But how could any red-blooded male not be interested in the whole package, as it were? You're a beautiful woman, Amelia. I won't deny that I'd still love to see you if you had the talent of a recently deceased flea.'

'And do I?'

'Do you what?'

'Have the talent of a flea?'

'Amelia, you have the talent of the most talented ...' he struggled to find the words. 'Amelia, I struggle to find the words to express quite exactly how very talented you are.'

Her expression lightened a little.

'And I am sure that everyone at Gallagher

Records, from the MD to the receptionist, will feel the same.' He took hold of her hand and was inwardly very pleased when she didn't struggle to wrench it free. Amelia was purring inside. Jamie tickled her inner wrist with one of his fingers. He had read in some psychology book that this kind of subtle physical contact was a sure way to break down someone's defences.

'Show me the contract, Jamie,' Amelia said suddenly. She was the hard-nosed American businesswoman once again.

'Yes, sure.' Jamie popped into his bedroom and reappeared with the envelope he had shown her in the car. He sat back down beside her. She had moved across her psychological divide so that her knee now touched his thigh. She even went so far as to lean upon his shoulder. Jamie shuffled the pieces of paper inside the envelope and brought out page two.

'What about page one?' Amelia asked.

'Oh, that's got nothing interesting on it,' Jamie mumbled. Just your name and address and Gallagher Records' name and address and a load of old codswallop about the law of the land . . .'

Amelia seemed happy enough with his inexpansive explanation and so Jamie started to go through the contract from clause two. By the time he had touched upon the 'outstandingly generous' advance and royalty figures she was silly putty in his hands.

'So you mean you really think I have two albums in me already?' she asked breathlessly.

'At least,' Jamie told her, putting the final sheet back into the envelope. Amelia reached for the manila folder of her desire. 'Hang on,' said Jamie, taking it back from her hurriedly. 'You can't have this just yet. It has to go to the legal department first. I'll tell them that you're happy with all the terms and then they will send you a copy of your very own to sign.'

'Oh, thank you, Jamie, thank you,' Amelia gushed. 'I can't begin to tell you just how grateful I am.'

Jamie smiled. 'I'm sure you can.'

They had another big glass of Calvados to celebrate. The peace treaty of a contract had by now done a Berlin Wall job on the psychological divide and Amelia sprawled happily across Jamie's lap. Her head rested in his crotch and she suddenly didn't mind when she felt the familiar twitch of an awakening hard-on near her ear. He was stroking her hair. She reached up to toy with one of the buttons on his green silk shirt, commented on how nice the little piece of mother-of-pearl was and then proceeded to unfasten it. Jamie bent down to kiss her smiling lips. At last the game was back on.

Minutes later Jamie scooped Amelia up in his arms and carried her straight through to the bedroom. Since her last visit he had bought a new bed. It was made of dark wood, with beautifully sculpted bed knobs at the top and the bottom. It was piled high with pillows, covered in pure white cotton. A dream of a bed with a mattress two feet thick.

'It's lovely,' Amelia murmured. 'Really beautiful.'

'Want to help me break it in?' Jamie asked, pitching her onto its huge, soft marshmallow middle. She fell giggling from his arms and was immediately swallowed by the duvet and pillows which bounced up around her. Jamie stood at the side of the bed, pinched his nose as if he were about to jump into a swimming pool and joined her on the pillows with a dive.

They kicked off their shoes and rolled about like children, ripping off their clothes frantically in a race to get naked and beneath the luxurious covers. Amelia was pleased to see that she had not imagined how gorgeous Jamie's body really was in the light of the Calvados of their first meeting. She ran her fingers excitedly all over him, measuring his smooth brown shoulders, his firm pecs and biceps. She kissed him lightly on each nipple, bringing forth the first of many happy little groans she would hear before they had finished.

Jamie responded in kind. Amelia thrilled to his touch. So knowing, so professional even, she laughed to herself. Her nipples stiffened into little rose-pink cones beneath his fingers. As he bent forward to return the kisses she had given him, Amelia grasped his straw-blond head and hugged it tightly to her chest. She relished the rough feeling of his stubble against her delicate white skin.

'Kiss me, kiss me,' she whispered, pulling his mouth up to meet hers. He had such a sexy way of kissing, of biting her lips and nibbling at their red fullness. He tasted of Calvados and cigarette smoke. He was delicious.

Jamie's hand had already found its way between Amelia's legs. It rocked back and forth against her mound, his fingers just touching her clitoris and slightly tingling labia. As they kissed, Amelia pressed her body down against his hand to increase the sensation. She needed more pressure to satisfy the feeling that was beginning to mount inside her. Her lips were awakening, swelling gradually larger to meet his touch. It was almost as if she could feel herself opening up to him. She put her hand down between their bodies and took hold of his hand, guiding his middle finger into her velvet-lined channel.

Jamie sighed as he felt the soft, warm walls of her vagina close around his knuckle. His dick twitched upwards, longing to replace the finger and be enclosed to the hilt in her delicious wet heat.

'Your pussy feels so gorgeous,' he told her.

'You're so crude,' Amelia couldn't help laughing.

'It's the best description I could find for a girl who is as much of an animal as you are. A vixen. No, a real tiger.' He twisted a fingerful of her fluffy red pubic hair. 'And you're so wet. Wet as a swimming pool. It just makes me want to dive right in.'

'Go on then,' she challenged. She wrapped her fingers around his shaft and used it to pull him towards her. She was straddling his lap now, sitting on his upper thighs with her feet dangling over the edge of the bed. She wrapped her arms around his tanned neck and eased her body upwards so that the tip of his dick was pointing at the entrance to her vagina. Jamie took his hand away so that his glans was actually touching Amelia's labia. She rocked slowly back and forth, undulated across him so that the pinky head dragged over her smooth coral flesh, wet with longing for him. Jamie shivered.

'Dive right in,' she echoed his suggestion.

Jamie took hold of his penis and carefully began to guide it inside her. Amelia shuffled into position, easing herself down inch by inch until she felt Jamie's balls make contact with her bottom. His face and neck were flushing hotly with long anticipated rapture.

Jamie was kneeling on the bed. Amelia drew her knees up and awkwardly arranged herself so that she too was now kneeling and could move herself up and down Jamie's slippery shaft by simply bending and then straightening her knees. Her arms were still wrapped around his neck. She looked deep into his eyes. They were black with arousal. She wondered if hers looked the same. His lower lip trembled delicately as she oozed up and down.

'Stay still,' she told him when the tempo began to build and he tried to alter the pace by making movements of his own. With each downward thrust, she tightened her vaginal muscles around him as hard as she could. He seemed to be enjoying it, each squeeze eliciting a shuddering sigh, but suddenly, he grasped her around the waist and forcibly rolled her over so that she was firmly on the bottom.

'Jamie!' Amelia gasped, thrilled by his unexpected decision to take charge. Her legs shook as he began to power into her from this new position. She tried to lift her body up to meet his but he was already going much too hard, too fast. Then Jamie slid his hands beneath her buttocks to raise her slender hips up so that he could go even deeper still.

'Ow,' Amelia cried as Jamie's marble-hard shaft touched the front wall of her vagina and sent through her a peculiarly pleasurable shock.

'Did that hurt?' he asked with a grunt which was almost concerned as he continued to grind away.

'Oh, God, no,' she told him. 'Carry on, carry on.' She helped him by grasping his buttocks and moving them herself. She wanted to open up more and more and more, to let him so far inside her that he would almost split her in half. As she closed her eyes, a picture of the man in Las Vegas suddenly flashed across the movie screen of her mind. The dangerous pleasure she had felt at being totally at the mercy of a strange but attractive man. Of the terrible instant animal passion that accompanies lust rather than love.

Amelia was calling out as she had never done before. She was helpless now. Totally at the mercy of the power of her desire. She felt that she couldn't move at all and yet her whole being was buzzing, writhing inside.

Jamie grasped one of Amelia's thighs and pulled her tingling leg up towards her chest. He powered into her at an angle now. She felt open, open, open. Quaking, she tried in vain to touch her own sex, her fingers getting caught in the crush of his pelvis on hers. She was so wet. The juice of her desire for him was already running down the inside of her trembling thigh. It was shiny and clear and oh-so sticky. Her arousal was reaching its maximum. Or maybe she was about to go one further than she ever had before.

'Jamie, Jamie, stop, stop, stop!' she squealed, though the laughter in her voice and the insistence of her hands driving his buttocks told him that that was not what she actually meant this time. She felt as though every drop of blood in her body was rushing to her vagina now. Her head was light, giddy, dizzy. Bright flashes of every colour swam before her eyes.

Jamie too felt his entire body harden towards his goal. He was seconds away now. His balls ached to be free of their load. To shoot hot jets of come deep inside her.

Jamie's body reared up and twisted away from her as he began to climax violently. His face contorted. His teeth were bared, gritted together. Sperm thundered through his penis to explode into Amelia's body. Beneath him she thrashed. Her own pleasure was breaking her in two . . . Her pelvis rose automatically to meet his downward thrusts. She wrapped her legs around his, holding them together, reeling him in.

'My God!' Jamie shouted suddenly as the last of his come left him with a shudder. Amelia pressed herself against him. Her own body calming down now. The violent spasms of her orgasm becoming a vibration that was slowing to a distant and gentle hum.

Amelia clutched Jamie's exhausted body to her own. His back was slick and wet with sweat. She drew her fingers across it, stroking him until she knew he had fallen asleep.

After an hour or so of lying beside him, eyes open and wide awake, Amelia left Jamie snoring and crept out of the bedroom. Like a thief she tiptoed back into the sitting-room where the brown envelope containing the contract still lay upon the couch. She pulled it out carefully, determined to get one more look at the terms before Jamie had her own copy sent on.

Now that it was finally in her hands, she flicked over the first page, the page which Jamie had kept tucked out of the way while he showed her the important clauses. The first page of the contract which held nothing but the boring information like names and addresses and the law of the land. Names and addresses were there all right, but not one of them was hers!

In fact, the recording contract which Jamie had been showing her was not hers at all. It was made out to another artist entirely. To add insult to injury it was in the name of one of the heavy metal acts she had been supporting on the night she and Jamie first met. The words of the contract swam before Amelia's confused eyes until she shredded the flimsy pages in fury and disbelief. She had played again with Jamie Nettles and once again, she'd been stung.

Chapter Fourteen

'YOU BASTARD, JAMIE Nettles, you utter, utter bastard,' Amelia hissed at the closed door of the bedroom where he lay, oblivious to her hate. 'You are going to pay for this.'

Amelia arranged the tiny pieces of the shredded contract into a neat little pyramid while she formulated some horrifying plan for revenge. She looked around the stark designer sitting-room for inspiration. Jamie's personally engraved Zippo lighter lay with his car keys on the coffee table. Amelia glanced back at the little bonfire she had already made on the floor and sighed. Perhaps she should set fire to his beautiful flat, she thought. His expensive pale wooden floor-boards wouldn't look quite so good with a hole burnt in the middle of them . . .

'No, don't be stupid,' she chastised herself quickly. Jamie Nettles wasn't worth ending up in jail for . . . Murder and arson were right out of the question. Anyway, what this particular arsehole needed was a taste a little closer to his own brand of medicine. Amelia picked up a few pieces of the contract and let them flutter through her fingers. She chewed her lip ruminatively as she racked her brains for the perfect scenario. What Jamie Nettles needed was something which would hurt him far more deeply than physical pain.

'Humiliation,' she finally muttered. Yes, that was the word she was looking for. Humiliation.

As silently as she had left the bedroom, Amelia crept back into it and reinstalled herself at Jamie's side in the plush new bed. He was still snoring, and hadn't moved an inch so she figured he had no idea of her recent discovery. Amelia propped herself up on the pillows and surveyed the bedroom for suitable instruments of torture. As an A & R man in the music industry, constantly going to sweaty gigs to hunt out new talent, Jamie Nettles rarely had the need for a tie, but he had belts. Six or seven of them. Black and brown. Soft, smooth leather with elaborate silver buckles. Amelia could see them now, hanging up neatly in his partially open mirrored wardrobe. They would be perfect.

Amelia slid out of the bed and crept to the cupboard. Yes. The belts were just what she had in her furious mind. She picked out four and felt their satisfactory weight in her hands. How unfortunate for Jamie that he had just bought himself such an obliging new bed. She sincerely hoped that the silver buckles wouldn't leave any nasty notches in his lovingly varnished bed-posts.

'Jamie,' she whispered over his slumbering body. 'Jamie, Jamie.' Each time she spoke his name just a little louder than before. But she got no response from the body on the bed. He was out cold. Dead to the world. No way was this dream-boy waking up.

'Good.'

He was sleeping on his front. Amelia carefully took hold of his right wrist and stretched out his arm so that it reached to the corner of the bed. She fastened it to the bed-post with a belt. Jamie stirred slightly and gave a quiet moan, but he didn't wake. Amelia did the same with his other limbs until he was fastened into position, face down. Moments later, Amelia had pulled off all the sheets and his pert, firm buttocks were bared to the ceiling, but still Jamie was lost in his dreams.

Now for the pièce de résistance, Amelia grinned. In the glass vase that stood on Jamie's bedside cabinet was a bunch of long-stemmed white carnations. Amelia selected the biggest and most beautiful bloom for her purposes, but knew that she would have to complete the rest of her arrangements before she could risk placing that where it deserved to go.

Back in the sitting-room, on the coffee table next to his keys and his Zippo, Jamie's personal organiser sat quietly holding his secrets between its leather covers. Amelia knew the number she was looking for, and it was scribbled on the very first page. Jamie's office. She dialled it purpose-fully and then waited for his voice-mail box to kick in. When it did, she covered the receiver with her hand and prayed that he had a secretary who would check his messages when morning came and Jamie didn't turn up for work.

'Er . . . I'm not well, can somebody please come and collect my papers from me at home,' Amelia muttered in a suitably deep voice. She hoped that they would think any strangeness in it was due to a sore throat.

Now for the flower.

'Oh, Jamie, you're such a heavy sleeper,' Amelia sighed as she pushed the delicate stem of the crisp white bloom gently between the twin brown orbs of his bum. He didn't budge an inch. The flower stood up proudly like a tree growing between two hills. Amelia stood back and admired her handiwork. He really did have an incredible body. It was a shame he had turned out to be such a dickhead. It was also a shame, thought Amelia, that she didn't have a nettle instead of a carnation, but she was sure that, after an hour or so, the stem of that flower would be irritating enough for the poor, dear, prostrate love.

Amelia shrugged on her discarded clothes and left the hapless Jamie to await his fate. Sooner or later, someone somewhere would miss him even if the office didn't bother to send anyone to collect his papers. Perhaps that skinny girl he hung around with had a set of keys to the flat. It didn't really matter because whatever happened, Amelia felt sure that Jamie Nettles would never get the better of this girl again.

Chapter Fifteen

RICHARD WAS STILL sitting up, watching an Open University programme about physics, when Amelia got back home. That she was not in a happy mood was evident long before she opened her mouth to tell him about it. First there was the slam of the taxi door, then the slam of the front door, then the slam of her bag on the kitchen table . . .

'You were right,' she wailed as she marched into the sitting-room. 'Jamie Nettles is a total jerk!'

'There, there.' Richard took her in his arms and patted her consolingly. Whatever Jamie Nettles had done, he had just made Richard's day. 'What did he do this time to make you so furious?'

Amelia poured out the story about the contract . . . and the carnation. Richard winced and poured out some tea.

'So, do you think someone from the office will bother to go round to Jamie's house?' Amelia asked.

'I'll make sure of it,' said Richard. All of a sudden he felt that the next morning couldn't come quickly enough.

'It's late,' he said after a while. 'I'm going to turn in.'

Amelia looked at him desperately. She didn't want to be on her own. Not right now. 'Can't you stay up just a tiny bit longer?' she asked. 'I really feel like talking tonight.'

Richard was already standing up to leave. He surveyed Amelia's delicate frame curled up into a defensive ball on the sofa, her bare feet covered by her long flowing skirt. She pushed her soft red hair back with her hands and he saw that, even after the laugh they had shared about Jamie's misfortune, her green-blue eyes were bright with tears.

'OK. But I'll need some coffee,' Richard told her.

'Your wish is my command,' Amelia trilled, jumping up to run to the kitchen.

Richard sank back down into his chair with a groan. He glanced at his watch and sighed when he saw that it was almost four in the morning. Why was he bothering? He didn't want to know about the ways in which so many other men were making Amelia's life a misery when he was sure that, given the chance, he could be the one to really turn her luck around.

She must enjoy being treated badly, Richard reasoned.

Just at that moment, Amelia emerged from the

kitchen with two steaming mugs of coffee.

'Do you think I bring guys like Jamie Nettles upon myself?' she asked.

What a question! Richard bit back the temptation to say the thought had crossed his mind. Instead he gritted his teeth and assured her that guys like Jamie Nettles brought themselves upon most attractive single girls.

'I know that I could have avoided tonight in some ways, though . . . I really didn't intend to end up in bed with him but . . . Oh, I don't know, I suppose I just like sex too much. A guy like Jamie just has to sit there looking gorgeous and no matter how often I tell myself that I will hate him and me in the morning, I have to go for it . . . I have to get him into bed . . . I think I must have the highest sex drive of anybody I know,' she continued, blissfully ignorant to any pain her musings might be causing. 'And sometimes it's even better to go to bed with someone you know doesn't really give a shit . . .'

Richard looked at her sadly. He wondered if she really thought that, or whether her words were just the bravado of someone who felt she had never really been loved.

'Do you really believe that?' he asked.

'Yeah, I do,' she said blithely. 'It's much more passionate, more animal, when you can have the sex without the hassle of emotional bonds. Love can keep you warm at night but only lust can make you burn.'

'That's just sad, Amelia,' Richard told her

wearily. 'And you know that it's not even true. If it was, you wouldn't have bothered to take out your revenge on Jamie, you would have said 'Thanks very much' when you left in the morning – and you certainly wouldn't be bothered that Jerry isn't coming home from the States yet. Don't you love him?'

'Of course.'

'And he's great in bed?'

'Yes.'

'Better than me?'

'I don't want to answer that, Richard. Why ask me that?' Amelia said defensively.

'I just wondered whether you can really tell the difference between sex with love and sex with lust.'

Amelia looked away from Richard and drained her coffee mug.

The conversation had died between them now. Richard made to get up again.

'Are you angry with me?' Amelia asked.

'I just don't like to see you being used, Amelia,' Richard told her. 'Nobody likes to be used.' He began to walk towards the stairs. He heard Amelia sniff loudly behind him. It was the herald of another outburst of tears. Just what he needed at four in the morning. But this time, Richard decided, he wasn't going to be her bloody shoulder to cry on. Every time he made things better for her she would run off and ruin them with someone else the very next day. But the strangled little sobs grew more and more insistent until Richard could bear no more and, having just reached the top of the stairs, he ran all the way back down them again.

'Oh, don't cry, Amelia,' he cooed, taking her in his arms again and smoothing back her beautiful hair in his familiar way. 'I didn't mean to upset you.'

'Oh, Richard,' Amelia wailed. 'Can I stay in your room tonight? I'm just not going to be able to sleep on my own.'

'Amelia, no,' he insisted. 'No. I'll be just next door if you need me.'

'I need you now.'

'No, you don't.'

Richard struggled to keep his resolve. He managed, just, and persuaded her to sleep in her own room after all. But ten minutes of hearing her pathetic sobs and sniffs through the thin wall later, he found himself wandering in there to be with her.

'Oh, I'm sorry,' she continued to sniff. Her eyes were bright red around the rims from crying. Richard sat on the edge of the bed beside her and administered comforting banalities until he was forced by the chilliness of the room to get in under the covers. At once, Amelia's slender arms wrapped themselves around him like the tentacles of an octopus. Richard felt his heart beat increase its speed. Something sexual stirred deep inside him. It mustn't happen though, he told himself. He must not let it happen. He would be just as bad as Jamie Nettles if he let her seduce him now.

Amelia's fingers played hesitantly with the hair on his chest. He put a comforting arm around her shoulders and tried to resist becoming any more familiar than that.

'Don't,' he said when her fingers crept towards his nipple.

'Why not?' she asked. But before he had time to explain, she had silenced his protestations with a kiss.

Richard tried not to respond to her lips but it was growing increasingly impossible. When she showed no sign of giving up on him, he reluctantly folded his arms right around her and yielded to the insistence of her kiss.

'We shouldn't be doing this,' he protested when they came up for air. 'You don't really want to do this with me. You're just confused because of Jerry and Jamie Nettles.'

'Oh shut up, Richard,' Amelia said suddenly. 'Just kiss me now and let me hate you in the morning.'

She laughed at her own little joke. Richard was strangely comforted by it. And he supposed that it was she who had begged him to keep her company. He wasn't really using her if she wanted this. But, hang on, he told himself, wasn't it he who was being used?

'What if I don't want to do this?' he began. But it was too late. Amelia had her hand on the rapidly bulging front of his shorts. He had been betrayed by his body yet again. Amelia massaged him expertly so that any protest he tried to make from that moment on came out as a cross between a groan and an ecstatic sigh.

'Oh god,' he groaned as he felt himself finally going under his desire for the girl in the bed beside him. Amelia had disappeared beneath the sheets now and he could only anticipate the hot lick of her tongue on the end of his faithless knob.

'Oh shit,' Richard moaned as Amelia wriggled his dick free of his shorts and began to suck the sensitive tip. She pulled back the tightly fitting foreskin and flicked at his bared glans with her tongue. It was salty with pre-come, and smooth as a dick fashioned in molten glass.

'Amelia,' he wailed as she took his balls in one hand and gently tickled them with the long fingernails of the other. She had won him over completely now. His mind had been vanquished by the will of the twitching balls in her palm. His dick stiffened until it could have held the blankets up on its own. Richard felt the semen beginning to build within him, crowding towards the head of his dick, begging to be allowed to make its sticky escape.

'Oh no, please.' If she didn't move very quickly, he was going to have to come in her mouth.

Amelia made no effort to move away, though the jerky movements of Richard's dick to and fro inside the cavern of her mouth told her that a climax was not too far off. She continued to lick at him frantically, sucking the purple tip between her lip-covered teeth. But her fingers were still

190

massaging his balls, pulling them slightly downwards whenever she heard the pre-climactic groan, to prolong the agonising joy just a little longer.

Richard's hands were beneath the covers now, grasping at her hair, moving her head up and down, faster and faster. Almost too fast. His fingers flexed with a sudden spasm. Amelia sucked at him extra hard.

'Oh, no. I'm nearly there.'

He was there.

Amelia sucked avidly as the first of the hot semen began to spurt into her waiting mouth. She swallowed as he spurted, feeling the warm liquid oozing down the back of her throat and almost wishing that she had given him the chance to explode somewhere else. But for now, all she could do was make sure that she didn't spill a drop.

The last spasm of Richard's unwanted orgasm racked his body and left him panting on the pillows. He laid a hand on his heart, feeling it beat faster and harder than it had done after any marathon. Amelia emerged from beneath the covers, sweating with the heat of being under two blankets and wiping her sticky mouth on the back of her hand. Richard wasn't the only one who had been exerting himself. Amelia flopped onto half the pillow where Richard's head lay and gazed at his handsome, chiselled profile as he lay trying to catch his fleeting breath.

'Don't you ever, ever do that again,' said Richard.

'That I just can't promise,' said Amelia.

The morning sun poured in through the thin yellow curtains of Amelia's room and woke Richard up. For a moment, he wasn't sure where he was. Then he remembered. He gazed lovingly at the sleeping figure beside him. Her nose was whistling slightly as she breathed in and out. So, in spite of all his good intentions they had gone and done it again. How long did he have before the bubble burst this time?

The postman answered that one.

Richard trundled down the stairs to pick up the post which had been dropped through the front door. The gas bill, a Reader's Digest circular and a little package for Amelia. Jerry's personal assistant was sending her the spare keys to his flat. Jerry wouldn't be home for a while but he wanted her to move back in anyway. Though she hid it quite well, Richard knew that Amelia was pleased. The one condition was that she didn't bring back the cat.

Amelia moved her things back into Jerry's flat that very weekend.

Richard got to keep Eliza.

Chapter Sixteen

AMELIA LET HERSELF into Jerry's echoing flat and locked the door behind her. The answer-machine's alert button was flashing. She listened to the messages. Jerry's mother, three times. Jerry himself, calling to say that he was going to be delayed for just another day or so. What a surprise.

Amelia draped her coat across the back of a chair and wandered into the kitchen. She mixed herself a large gin and tonic, but found that there was no ice. Cursing, she stuck the drink in the freezer compartment to cool it down a little more. She leant against the work surface. Better get myself something to eat, I suppose, she thought. She opened a couple of barren cupboards. There was no point in cooking anything elaborate for one. A bag of cheese and onion crisps nestled between two dusty packets of dried pasta in sauce. Crisps? Pasta? She would eat the crisps while she was cooking the pasta.

The phone rang, but the caller hung up before Amelia could get across the long sitting-room to answer it. Somehow, the sudden and brief ringing of the phone made the silence seem all the more oppressive. Spooky. Amelia didn't really like being in the flat by herself any more, though she had often spent time alone there before her flight to Kentish Town. It would be better when Jerry came back, she reassured herself. She just needed company.

Jerry had a television in the kitchen. He had televisions all over the place. He subscribed to satellite and cable, because he hated to think that he might be missing something new and exciting while he was watching BBC2. Amelia flicked on the set on the breakfast bar for the comfort of the background noise while she cooked.

'And coming up later on "The Next Big Thing",' announced the wide-mouthed girl on MTV, 'an exclusive, and live, interview with London band The Dolphins who have been recording their second album here in Los Angeles. See them right after the break.'

Amelia swivelled round from the hob to look at the little screen. 'The Dolphins?' Wasn't that the name of the band Jerry was working with? Well, if he wasn't going to be coming home for a while, she could at least find out what he had been up to in Los Angeles since she left. See if he'd got this 'next-big-thing' of his playing in tune, at least. Jerry would be pleased to know that she was taking an interest in one of his projects.

The adverts flashed and flickered in a stream of mind-assaulting sound-bites. It seemed as if they were never going to end. Amelia turned the hob down to a simmering heat and opened the strongly flavoured crisps. No doubt there would be another ten minutes or so of waffle from the babe in the glasses again before they got around to the promised clip anyway.

The programme restarted. This time the presenter was pictured standing by a bar in a dingy club. Faux cobwebs hung from marble-painted pillars which were lit by purple and green coloured bulbs. The wrought iron stools were upholstered in blood red velvet.

'I'm here in the bar of The Batcave in Santa Monica, where I'm going to be joining British band The Dolphins who are in Los Angeles to record their second album . . .'

'Yeah, yeah. Get on with it,' Amelia muttered.

'The Dolphins were last here in 1992, when they toured with their multi-million-selling album "Wide Sargasso Sea". This latest album has been three years in the making but they think they're almost there. Here's how you might remember them . . .'

The programme cut to a clip from an old video. The impossibly handsome lead singer stared mournfully out over a misty bay, where two dolphins, strangely enough, turned gracefully in the air before splashing back into the grey-blue water. The picture of freedom. Amelia guessed that the creatures were probably on loan from a theme park.

Two choruses later, they were back in The Batcave. Now the presenter was slinking over to a candle-lit table. Amelia recognised the singer sitting on the right. There were four other band members at the table and two more guys who were in shadow for the moment. The presenter rattled through some names which all sounded as if they had been made up.

'And Jerry Anson,' she added finally, 'who flew all the way over from England to finish producing this album at the eleventh hour when Michael Hammerstein unexpectedly pulled out of the project after artistic differences . . .'

The camera panned to Jerry's familiar face, a cigar at the corner of his mouth. He waved his hand lazily for the audience before the presenter got back to interviewing the more aesthetically-pleasing members of the bunch.

Amelia stuck with the pretentious drivel about finding oneself as an artist for ten minutes. The camera was fixed in close-up on the singer or the drummer's face for most of that time. Then they went to another video, promising to go back to The Batcave before the show was over. Amelia turned her attention back to the pasta which was already fast congealing in the bottom of the pan. She got a fork and picked at it. Not good, but not entirely inedible. An advert for something altogether more appetising filled the screen until, as promised, they were back at The Batcave.

'Hi, I'm Samantha Dean reporting for "Next Big Thing" from Santa Monica's Batcave. With me are The Dolphins . . .'

The singer was sitting beside Samantha at the bar now, nursing a tall pink drink with a lot of silly cocktail accessories sticking out of the top of it. Some people were dancing in the background and it was to these revellers that Amelia's eye was drawn.

Instantly Amelia recognised the spasmodically jerking figure that was Jerry. He had probably learned a strange variation on a jitterbug back in the Seventies when he might have cut a slightly more svelte figure on the dance-floor. Amelia allowed herself a little chuckle. But then she thought she saw the undulations of someone else she recognised. Dancing next to Jerry. The camera irritatingly switched back to Samantha before her suspicions could be confirmed.

Amelia waited, her fork hovering in mid-air between the pan and her mouth while she concentrated on the screen. Back to the dancers. Jerry was obscured now, obscured by the tall, slim body of a young woman that had been wrapped around Amelia's own body just a couple of weeks before. The girl had her arms about Jerry's neck. She was grinding her pelvis against his generous waistline. She was even kissing the shiny top of his head.

Suddenly, it was all becoming horribly clear. The Batcave in Santa Monica. The man in the music business with the funny accent. His name wasn't Jeffrey as Karis had misheard, but Jerry. Karis had met the man of her dreams and Amelia was about to be plunged into a nightmare.

'Oh no.' Amelia killed the television immediately and put the pan she was holding down very slowly in the sink. 'It can't be true. Not again. Not Karis.'

She looked desperately at her watch. It was four in the morning. It would be just eight in the evening in LA. Amelia had at least another eight hours ahead of her before Karis would be at home and contactable, and that was assuming the unlikely event that she went back to her own home at all.

'What can I do?' Amelia moaned to herself. She paced the sitting-room. She didn't even have Eliza to hug.

Amelia's red address book lay by the phone. She started at the beginning of the alphabet and worked on through. The friends that mattered, she remembered her mother once saying, were the ones you could call up at four o'clock in the morning. She had reached the Ms before she realised that the only friends she had that really mattered were Karis and a certain boy in Kentish Town. And how could she call either of those two that night?

Chapter Seventeen

AT FIRST, RICHARD thought that the ringing of
the telephone was just part of his dream. After the
fifteenth ring, however, he was beginning to
wake up and realised that the insistent tone was
very much part of his reality.

It was probably someone calling from America
for Amelia, he thought irritably as he pulled on
his dressing gown and stumbled down the stairs.
Hadn't she let her friends know that she had
moved back into Jerry's flat again? As he grunted
'hello' into the receiver, the very last thing
Richard expected was for the person on the other
end of the line to be Amelia herself.

'Richard, it's me,' she sobbed. 'I need to come
home.'

Half an hour later, Amelia was restarting her new
life in Kentish Town. Jerry's trusty Shogun was
parked on the pavement outside Richard's house

again and he was struggling in with arms full of clothes and natural linen lampshades while Amelia made the tea.

'She's my best friend, Richard,' Amelia was wailing. 'And she's stolen my boyfriend. Again.'

'But it seems as though she doesn't know that she's doing anything to hurt you,' Richard explained patiently. 'After all, she doesn't know that her "Jeffrey" is your Jerry.'

'Yes, but he does.'

After listening to the saga for a fifth time and offering a new permutation of the same advice, Richard made his excuses and went to bed. He had to go into work the next morning, even though it was the weekend, to sort out some messy figures for a board meeting. He'd talk to her when he got back. Amelia sat up for just a little longer before she retired to her old room.

Amelia made up her bed and slipped reluctantly between the cool covers. She lay with her arms folded on the outside of the sheets and gazed up at the familiar crack in the ceiling. Her mind was racing, but she was surprised to find that she didn't feel so bad any more, just a little sad that she had cocked up once more in her choice of Mr Wonderful. She would survive all this shit. She had lived without Jerry before and she would do it again. She was young, she was talented, she had friends . . .

Amelia rolled over in bed so that she faced the wall which parted Richard's bedroom from her own. She thought she could hear him snoring. She wished that she could sleep. She could sleep much more easily if she had someone to cuddle up to. Silently, she got out of bed and crept across the landing to Richard's door. It was ajar, and she pushed it open without a squeak. When the shaft of light from the landing fell across Richard's bed, Amelia's gaze met with Richard's wide open eyes.

'I couldn't sleep,' she told him.

'Neither could I.'

'Can I come in?' she asked.

'I was hoping you would say that,' said Richard.

He lifted up the side of his duvet and let Amelia curl beneath it. Without any of the previous awkwardness between them, she snuggled in to his side and rested her head on his comfortable shoulder. He stroked her hair carefully, aware that this might be just another port in a storm for her. He would wait for her to make the first move.

Amelia lay with her head on Richard's shoulder and said nothing. Her hand rested lightly on his T-shirt-covered chest. She could feel the hair which covered it through the thin cotton. Gradually she began to move her hand, tracing out the old T-shirt's silly cartoon motif with her fingers. Richard closed his eyes and gave a heavy sigh.

'What's up?' Amelia asked.

'Oh, nothing,' Richard said.

Amelia sat up so that she could look him in the eye.

'I'm afraid I don't believe that. Do you want me to go back to my room?' she asked. She looked at him more seriously than he had ever seen her look before. 'I know what you must be thinking. That I only come back to you when everything goes wrong . . .'

'It had crossed my mind, yes.'

'Well, I must come back to you for a reason.'

Richard could hear his heart beating in his ears. But Amelia wasn't about to expand upon her explanation. Instead, she took his head in her hands and drew his mouth to her lips. This was a logic he just couldn't resist.

Forgetting all the arguments he had had with himself since Amelia had left him on his own again to go back to Jerry, Richard wrapped his arms around her in an all-forgiving and all-permitting embrace. He kissed her hungrily, like someone who thought he had already had his last chance. His tongue eagerly probed the warm interior of her sweet-tasting mouth.

Soon he felt Amelia's fingers creeping to the bottom of his T-shirt. In an instant she had it over his head and off without ever seeming to take her mouth from his lips. It was chilly in the room and Richard quickly pulled Amelia's warm body back to cover his. They fell backwards, still kissing, onto the soft pillows, their arms and legs tangled together in a lover's knot.

Eager to feel Richard's bare skin against hers, Amelia decided that she would undress herself too. She sat up astride his legs and seductively slipped one satin shoe-string strap down over her white shoulder. Then the other. The slippery red material of the delicate slip glided down her body until her breasts were completely naked. Her bare chest was heaving rapidly with the excitement. Richard sat up too to share another kiss, but Amelia suddenly jumped off the bed and stood beside it for a second, letting the nightdress slither down over her slim hips and onto the floor before she jumped back beneath the duvet.

'Oh, you're . . .' Richard searched for a compliment that would do justice to the beautiful body before him.

Amelia's hair was fanned out like a lacy shawl across her shoulders. Her long heavy fringe hid her eyes in shadow so that from time to time they glinted like gem stones discovered in the darkness. She was sitting astride him again, her hands on his waist while he reached out to touch her perfect breasts. But there was something different about her this time. It was a few moments before he realised that something was missing.

The pendant of amber, the precious pendant that Jerry had given her, was gone.

'Your pendant,' he began in a whisper.

'I don't wear that any more,' she confirmed. 'It's gone.' And in those simple words she put the seal on the past and let Richard see that she was finally free enough to build something new . . . something new with him.

'It's really over between me and Jerry this time,'

Amelia continued in a small voice. 'I never really settled at his flat again. It felt as if something was missing. As if I had left something behind when I moved from here . . . and it wasn't just my cat . . .'

Richard felt his stomach grow light and his head turn giddy.

'I missed you,' Amelia whispered. 'When I wanted to share something happy or sad, the person I wanted to share it with was you. The person I was missing all this time was you.'

The words stuck in Richard's throat and he was surprised to feel the tickly prickle of tears behind his eyes.

'Do you mean that?' he asked her.

She just nodded and kissed him. Her hands stroked his stubbly cheek with a tenderness that had been missing from their love-making until this moment. Her kisses fluttered over him, her lips grazing his nose, eyelids and chin.

'I want you so much,' she murmured. Richard couldn't find the breath to agree.

He clasped her slender body to his, big hands moulded around her delicate shoulder blades. The silky smooth feeling of her skin beneath his fingers delighted him all the more now that he felt there was something more behind her advances than pure lust.

Richard slid his hands around to the front of her body until they found her gently rounded breasts with their perfect pink nipples. First he cupped the full orbs, one in each palm, then he rolled each tiny nipple bud between his fingers.

They stiffened quickly into reddening cones. The skin on her breast-bone was glowing with her arousal.

'Richard,' she said, whispering his name like a magic word that would open his heart up to her. He looked deep into her eyes, into the blackness of her pupils. Her cheeks were burning with desire, her lips swollen and red.

Amelia's eyes flickered over his face too, taking in the gorgeous precision of his stubble-enhanced jaw. How had she not noticed his Latin beauty before? The plastic blond perfection of Jamie Nettles and the other cowboys who had passed through her life faded from her thoughts now. Richard was an oil-painting to their pencil sketches. Something other than lust emanated from him, filled the mind behind his adoring eyes. She ran her fingers through his thick dark curls.

Richard gathered up her body and laid her carefully down on the pillows. He moved until he was on top of her, protecting her from his weight with his arms. They kissed. Amelia ran her hands down his torso until they came to rest on either side of his waist. His body was so warm to the touch now that she arched her own body up to meet him, to feel her breasts against his hot, firm chest.

Amelia was already naked. Her fingers slid a little further down Richard's body until she found the waistband of his boxer shorts. The very same Mickey Mouse boxer shorts he had been wearing when she first seduced him in a fit of anger at Jerry, her ex. She made a mental note to get him something a little more suitable to the lover he was as her fingers slipped beneath the elastic and she tugged the shorts off over his bum.

Richard's dick had been hardening almost since the second she climbed into the bed beside him. When the boxer shorts were finally out of the way, it swung up between their bodies, eager for her touch. Amelia obliged quickly, her fingers expertly teasing Richard to the point where he could not wait a moment longer to have her.

Amelia's legs were already parted around his. Richard reached down to place his hand between her thighs. She sighed delightedly as his fingers gently pushed their way through her pubic hair and began to ease her hotly swollen lips apart. Amelia's pelvis rose up to meet him automatically so that her clitoris was against the heel of Richard's hand.

'That's it,' she breathed. 'Rub me there, rub me harder.'

Richard moved his fingers with tiny circular movements over the little bud that contained so much potential for pleasure. Beneath his slowly rotating hand, Amelia's body rose and fell, fluttering with the racing of her heart. She was sighing and groaning, whispering his name. Richard moved his hand from her clitoris to part her labia once more and entered the moist channel of her vagina which was aching for his attention.

She was wet, so wet. Richard entered her with only one finger at first, but soon two fingers were slipping quickly in and out of her body. Moving easily through the shiny juices of her arousal, his fingers brought her closer to the sensation she was looking for. Amelia ground her silky mound upwards against his hand, pushed against him so that, when he penetrated her, he touched the front wall of her vagina, the G-spot, sending hundreds of paralysing shivers from her womb to the farthest reaches of her body.

'Oh, god . . .' Amelia took hold of Richard's wrist as if she was going to move his hand herself. She was still holding on to his dick, furiously pumping the foreskin back and forth until she heard him catch his breath and knew that they ought to stop before it got too late.

'Make love to me,' she begged him now, dragging his penis nearer and nearer to the entrance of her trembling sex. 'I need to feel you inside me. I want to feel like you're part of me.'

Richard removed his fingers from the warm, wet vagina and allowed himself to be drawn towards her. He drew in his breath sharply as the sensitive bare glans of his penis made first contact with the wetness of her pouting labia. She was parting them with her fingers for him, clearing the way.

'Amelia,' Richard breathed as just a gentle nudge on his part let him push his way inside.

The soft velvety walls of her vagina yielded to and then closed around his shaft like a tailored glove of flesh and blood. They were joined together perfectly, made to lie like this. Amelia's mouth rounded to the feeling of exquisite pleasure, then her lips stretched out again into a beatific smile. Her vagina gently throbbed around Richard's penis, welcoming him in, welcoming him inside.

'Move slowly,' she pleaded, knowing that it would take all his will-power to prolong this instant of joy. Their bodies began to move, together and apart. Together and apart, like two halves of the same body. Richard closed his eyes tightly and cut out the world around them. He was tuned in to Amelia's body and Amelia's body alone. He was relishing the warm wetness of her vagina. The satisfying slapping sound as their bodies made contact. Wet skin upon wet skin. The deliciously slippery feel of arousal and sweat.

Amelia focused on the face above hers. Transfigured by love and desire. The smell of their bodies. Musky. Hot. The delicate scent of perfume rising up from her own heated breast. The tantalisingly soft touch of Richard's hair as his head dropped down and dark brown strands stroked her skin.

'Faster now, faster.'

Richard slipped his hands beneath her lithe hips and raised her pelvis up to him. Amelia placed her own hands firmly on his buttocks. Driving him. Guiding him. Holding him still for a second where the penetration was deepest. Their bodies glided apart, accompanied by a symphony of tiny sounds. Wet skin, soft sighs, the whispering of special names.

Richard was there. He collapsed heavily upon her, crushing her breasts beneath his chest. His pelvis continued to rock upon hers. Faster and faster and harder and harder. Amelia moved as much as she could to be with him, to make sure that this was a moment they spent together in every sense of the word.

The muscles down the side of Richard's neck tensed as he reared above her. His pelvis was locked against hers. His penis deep inside her. He was nudging at the entrance to her very womb as his dick began to spurt.

Amelia shuddered as the first sticky bullets of sperm hit their target. Her legs shook uncontrollably as she tensed them against Richard's waist, clamping him to her. Inside, the walls of her vagina trembled with the beginnings of her own orgasm. A low tremor which began in the deepest part of her, tiny spasms of desire spreading out to touch Richard as he powered into her a final time.

'Oh Richard,' she screamed as the stars danced before her eyes once more. Her head was filled simultaneously with a lightness and a blackness which threatened to take her out of this world. She clutched at his muscle-bound back with her hands, dug in her nails. She needed to hold on, hold on to him until the terrible delight which was wracking her body began to subside. Finally she felt she knew why the French call this 'the little death'.

Afterwards, they lay together, their limbs still entangled, their ragged breathing almost perfectly in time. Then, Richard slowly drew himself away from her and knelt with his feet beneath him on the bed.

'Are you OK?' he asked her. She looked as though she would never get her breath back.

'Very OK,' said Amelia.

Chapter Eighteen

'*SO YOU'RE STAYING?*' asked Richard the next morning as they lay side by side in his double bed.

Amelia nodded.

'If that's OK with you,' she added, knowing that it was, of course.

'And what will you do with yourself now that Jerry is out of the picture and Jamie Nettles' promises of a contract came to nothing? Are you still going to try to get into the music scene?'

'I don't need either of them. I can make new contacts. I'll carry on writing my songs and one day, I will get a deal.' She looked truly optimistic.

Richard smiled. 'I know you will, too.' He rolled over in the bed and gave her a happy hug. 'By the way, some guy has been phoning you here. Very posh accent. Says his name is Henry Du Pre. Is he anyone I should be jealous of?'

A broad smile spread across Amelia's face.

Things were looking up already.

'No, but he is someone who owes me a favour . . .'

Eternal Kiss

Anastasia Dubois

Prologue

A HOT, DUSTY wind swept across the plains of southern France, parching the dry land and making the leaves rattle on the vines like old bones.

Esteban stood by the window, watching the first glimmerings of dawn coming up over the sea. He was not alone, but loneliness ached within him like an empty darkness. Seven hundred years of loneliness.

The restless loneliness of the vampire.

He turned and looked at the girl in the bed. She was beautiful enough. Her golden skin seemed to shimmer against the white satin sheet which fell carelessly across her body, baring one small and perfect breast. The pink rosebud of her nipple was still pert and hard from the savagery of his kisses. As he watched, she stirred in her sleep, turning onto her side so that her long dark hair fell onto the pillow, baring the smooth sweep of her throat.

Esteban averted his eyes, suddenly ashamed. He bitterly resented the dark need which, from time to time, he was driven to satisfy. The tiny punctures on the girl's neck would have healed before the sun rose over Valazur, and she would remember nothing of their night of frenzied passion. On this occasion he had been careful, restrained even; had made sure not to drink too deeply of her sweetness. This one would live on – and so must he. But what was this life but a living death, when he must live without the only woman he had ever cared for?

The Englishwoman filled his thoughts, his dreams, each never-ending moment, with a torment so sweet that he did not even want it to end. Venetia. Venetia . . . He loved her, he hated her, he could have destroyed her and made her his for ever; but on some insane, altruistic whim he had set her free and now he must live with that folly for all eternity.

Pushing open the window, he threw back his head and closed his grey eyes, letting the hot rush of air buffet his face. Behind him, the girl sighed in her sleep, and the hunger stirred briefly within him. But he did not go to her. He would be strong. He *must* resist the darkness or it would engulf him utterly, devouring the last vestiges of his humanity.

Turning, he walked swiftly out of the room and into the cool, comforting darkness of his ancient house.

Chapter One

WITH A KICK of her heels, Venetia Fellowes cut a graceful arc through the shimmering blue water. Its coolness felt indescribably good on her skin after the blazing heat of the Mediterranean sun.

Behind her sped the muscular shape of Demetrios, the Greek graduate student who had been occupying so much of her time since she came to join a multi-national team working on a variety of archaeological projects on the island of Malta.

Oxygen hissed into her mouth from the scuba tank. She could scarcely breathe for giggling as Demetrios reached out to grab her, and she wriggled neatly out of his grasp, speeding on through the water towards the sunken ruins of the ancient settlement.

It was a strange, eerie place, thought Venetia as she swam between the broken towers of what had once been a citadel, now home to shoals of tiny, many-coloured fish. How old was it – four thousand years? Five? And what cataclysm had destroyed the settlement, plunging it beneath the warm, turquoise-blue waters? In her mind, Venetia could hear whispering voices, the voices of the people who had one lived here, worshipped here, fought and made love. Excitement made her skin tingle. There were so many secrets still to be unravelled, and she felt so good – so . . . so very alive.

Venetia had felt a powerful attraction to the project from the moment she first heard about it. Maltese history fascinated her, with its lost civilisations, its tantalising legends, its mysteries; and as an expert in deciphering ancient languages, she had been taken on immediately by the project's director, Dr Marcus Hale.

She caught sight of Demetrios out of the corner of her eye; lying in wait for her behind a broken and crumbling wall, the water between them glittering with shoals of tiny, coloured fish. This time she wasn't quick enough to escape him and his hands closed about her, drawing her close against his strong, well-muscled body.

Venetia wriggled deliciously in his embrace; not seriously wanting him to let go, only wanting to prolong the pleasure of the chase. He shook his head. No, he wasn't going to let her go, not this time. She raised her eyebrows: what, here? He understood and nodded. Yes, here. Why not here? Who's to see . . .?

Who but the ghosts?

Taking her mouthpiece from between her lips, Demetrios forced a kiss on her mouth. It was all bubbles and fumbling, the kiss half-choking her as she laughed and took in a mouthful of seawater. But it excited her to feel him forcing his passion on her, holding her very tightly as they tumbled over and over among the ruins.

The sightless eyes of fallen statues watched them play, rolling in the water like seals, their bodies sleek, perfectly matched.

At last Demetrios gave her back the mouthpiece and she sucked in the oxygen greedily, fighting to get her breath back through the laughter. Not that Demetrios was giving her a chance to recover. He was making love to her, making her pulse race with pleasurable anticipation as his hands slipped underneath the cups of her red bikini and squeezed her willing breasts.

She writhed, serpent-like in his embrace. Bad boy; bad, bad boy, she felt like purring, scratching, growling. Do it to me; do it again and again.

The thought that, at any moment, other members of the diving team might discover them only added to the thrill of the moment. With each movement of her body, the water lavished new caresses on her, sliding between her thighs, over the firm hummocks of her breasts, the generous swell of her buttocks and the secret valley between . . .

Oh yes, yes, yes. Venetia found herself instinctively responding to her Greek lover's knowing caresses. Not that she was under any illusions about their relationship: it was about raw physical attraction, and that was all there was to it. Both of them knew that, once the project was over, they would walk out of each other's lives – and that unspoken understanding made their coupling all the more intense.

Venetia's nipples were turning into hard little hazelnuts under Demetrios's caresses. He rubbed them with a circular motion, his palms moving round and round over their tips; not too hard, just enough to drive her crazy. Reflexively, her thighs parted, welcoming the intrusion of his leg, rubbing gently against her mount of Venus.

They did not need to speak or kiss. Their mutual need was powerfully expressed in their eyes, their caresses. Treading water, Venetia slid her hands down her lover's flanks, feeling the firmness of muscle beneath tanned skin. Her fingers slid down over his buttocks and thighs, then moved slowly and seductively forwards until they were grazing the swell of his balls, taut and firm beneath the tight wet fabric.

Demetrios was a work of art; like a living statue, perfectly proportioned in every way. And his manhood never failed to excite her. It rose up like some hard, ripe stamen arching above the twin, heavy seed-pods of his testicles. Savouring every moment, Venetia let her fingertip roam up along the hard swell of his dick, enjoying the answering shudder of pleasure which ran through him as she teased the bare dome of his glans, pushing its way out from under the waistband of his trunks.

Still Demetrios was one move ahead of her. Taking hold of her hand, he used it to ease his trunks down over his manhood, letting it spring free, and a dart of passion arched towards the aching need between Venetia's thighs.

His thigh worked its way a little deeper between hers now, easing and insinuating itself against the warm, pulsing softness of her sex. Her back was against a heap of broken stones, half-covered with vivid, feathery fronds of green, and the red mouths of sea anemones, opening and closing with a hunger Venetia's body echoed joyfully.

He pushed her softly against the wall, happy that she was his utterly, his to do with as he chose. And he chose to give her pleasure, his thigh moving away only to allow room for his fingers to slide down Venetia's bikini bottom.

She offered no resistance as they slid down onto her thighs, the stretchy material easily giving way so that she could part her legs still wider and admit the probing tips of Demetrios's fingers.

Venetia wanted to scream out loud, her breath halting and hoarse. She offered herself shamelessly, ravenously to her lover, opening herself up so that there could be no more secrets between them. His shaft was between her fingers, sliding wetly back and forth, the pinkish-purple of his glans like some luscious sea-creature, predatory and seductive, luring her in only to devour her.

Suddenly Demetrios seized hold of her more tightly, pulling himself against her so that she gave a muffled cry. Behind his face-mask, his eyes were sparkling with lust. She did not need words to know what was in his mind. He thrust his hips forward, and the love-dart of his penis sought out the hot, wet heart of her sex with ruthless accuracy, scything into her, embedding itself within her softness.

And in a moment they were one. Moving together, coupling like beasts possessed by the ancient, bacchanalian spirits which had once danced in festivals through these ancient, sunken streets. Around them fish wove patterns of silent wonder: groupers, amberjack, flying gurnard, scorpion fish . . .

Venetia thrilled to the sensations rippling through her as Demetrios penetrated her, his strong hips thrusting against hers, flesh against flesh, bone grinding against bone. It felt so good that she wanted it to go on for ever; and yet she knew that this electric thrill could not last long. It was too sudden, too powerful; a sword-thrust of pleasure which would depart as quickly as it had come.

Hungrily they plundered each other's bodies, pawing and clutching at willing flesh, the sweat of their lust licked away by the gently-swirling waters which enfolded them. And Venetia felt the ocean-swell of orgasm building up inside her, at first quite far away, like waves on a distant beach; then closer and closer, a white, foam-crested breaker crashing down upon her, until she was no more than a tiny presence at the heart of a great bow-wave of pleasure.

As the feelings ebbed away, Demetrios and Venetia loosened their grip on each other, but they did not part. They looked at each other, their eyes expressing what their tongues could not.

More. They wanted more. This first coupling had been nothing but a beginning, an appetising taste of the pleasures which their young and eager bodies craved.

Taking her by the hand, Demetrios kicked out and began swimming towards the surface. Venetia knew where he was leading her. Just around the headland from the expedition's headquarters lay a tiny cove, completely cut off from the rest of the island by steep cliffs, accessible only from the sea.

The sand there was pure gold, soft as a feather bed and – at this time of the morning – warm as a lover's embrace.

Venetia shivered with anticipation as they broke the surface and swam together towards the welcoming beach. She loved her work, of course she did. She also knew that at this moment, she and Demetrios were supposed to be on the road to Paola, heading out to help the team excavate a Roman temple near the hypogeum. They'd get there eventually, she told herself; the site was an important one and she was looking forward to the challenge. But some things were more important even than work.

Sometimes, the only thing that really mattered was pleasure.

'Venetia.'

Slinging a towel around her shoulders, Venetia turned round. Marcus Hale was standing in the doorway to his office, arms folded. She knew what he was thinking, and he was right. But she didn't feel guilty – well, not *very*.

'You wanted something?'

'Come inside, I want a word with you.'

He gestured her into the office and, somewhat reluctantly, she followed him inside. It was hot, stifling, despite the air-conditioning fan toiling round and round on the ceiling. Outside, the sapphire sea off Marsaxlokk sparkled and enticed, dotted with brightly-painted fishing boats and the occasional motor cruiser. This was definitely not a day for being indoors.

Marcus sat down at his desk and Venetia sat opposite, crossing her long, slim legs at the ankle.

223

She knew she looked good in shorts, but Marcus was oblivious to any charms she might or might not have, and Marcus's clean-cut, English gentleman image left her stone-cold. Right from the word go there had been a faint, unspoken antipathy between them. Venetia had often been criticised for thinking of nothing but work, but compared to Marcus she was a *Baywatch* bimbo. As far as Marcus Hale was concerned, nothing existed beyond The Project.

'Where were you this morning?' he asked coolly. Venetia noticed the slight hesitancy in his voice, as though he wasn't sure he wanted to hear the answer. It was a fair bet that he didn't. Everyone knew what a prude Marcus was.

'I drove over to Paola. You asked me to take a look at the temple inscriptions, remember?'

Marcus gave a curt nod, then fiddled with his pencil.

'And Demetrios? You took him with you?'

'He's my assistant, Marcus. What am I supposed to do, lock him in a cupboard all day?'

'Ah yes, your personal assistant.' Marcus's thin lips twitched into a half-smile, then banished it. 'It's amazing how broad a job description can be.'

A faint rush of anger quickened inside Venetia.

'What's that supposed to mean?'

'Whatever you think it means.' He leaned across the desk and fixed Venetia with a hard stare. 'Look, Venetia, you're a brilliant archaeologist, I'm not disputing that. I'm just not sure you're taking this project seriously enough.'

Venetia returned his stare with a raised eyebrow.

'You're accusing me of not doing my work?'

Hale had the decency to squirm a little. He wasn't good at people. He was better with rocks.

'Well, I didn't exactly say . . .'

'Then what, *exactly*?'

The project director cleared his throat.

'Those preliminary drawings. I need them by tomorrow at the latest.'

Venetia reached into the attaché case by her chair and took out a slim sheaf of papers. She pushed them across the desk.

'These, you mean?'

Marcus picked them up and leafed through them. Venetia could feel his disappointment. They were very thorough. Impressive even.

'Er . . . yes.'

'They're satisfactory?'

'They seem to be.'

'Good. Oh, and I prepared that report you wanted for our submission to the Maltese government.' She added it to the pile. 'Now, perhaps I can go and get some *pastizzi* and a glass of wine? I haven't eaten since breakfast.'

She half got up out of her chair, but Marcus called her back with a snap of his fingers. It really irritated her when he did that – made her feel more like a barmaid than an archaeologist.

'Is there something else?'

'Tonight's presentation.' Marcus gave a sigh and sank back into his chair. 'Let's not fight about this, Venetia. We're supposed to be on the same side. I thought you cared as much about this project as I do. That's why I was so keen to take you on.'

'Don't bullshit me, Marcus – you can't deny my commitment. I've been working eighteen hours a day to get this up and running.'

'I know, I know.' He smoothed his mid-brown hair back from his high forehead. It was moist with sweat, his hair hanging limply. Venetia thought he looked slightly pathetic. 'But we've run into trouble. Big financial trouble. The Americans have pulled out, and if we don't get more funding pretty damn quick, we won't have the cash to carry on.'

'It's really that bad?'

'Why do you think the local workers haven't been paid for a fortnight? It's hand to mouth, Venetia.'

'I'm sorry, I didn't realise.'

'You weren't supposed to. Once the vultures know we're down, they'll be in for the kill.' Marcus folded his hands and glanced out of the window, towards the quayside where a group of local labourers were cleaning and labelling artefacts raised from the sunken citadel. 'The thing is, this presentation tonight . . . it's mainly for the benefit of a guy called Gabriel Engelhart.'

Ventia shrugged.

'Never heard of him.'

'Neither had I until the day before yesterday. But it seems he's a billionaire art dealer – more money than he knows what to do with, apparently. So if we can really impress the guy, maybe – just maybe – we can persuade him to invest some of it in this project.'

'And you think I can influence him somehow?'

'You're the great communicator, Venetia, not me. I'm terrific with catacombs, but stick me in front of a roomful of monkey suits and I just dry up. I need you to impress him at the presentation tonight. *Really* impress him. Or else this whole project is on the line.'

The presentation was to take place in the grand hall of a sixteenth-century *auberge*, built to house the Knights of St John. As she glanced around at the ornate baroque architecture, the trophies, banners and arms, and the long tables littered with the remnants of a sumptuous buffet meal, Venetia wondered how much it had cost Marcus to hire the place for the night – and whether the project could afford it.

Whirling fans purred in high, ornate ceilings and waiters in perfect black and white moved silently among the invited guests, offering glasses of vintage port. Venetia smiled to herself. They were about to discover that there was no such thing as a free meal.

She hoped she looked good. At any rate, she was wearing her best dress – no, it was her *only* really good dress; the blue silk shift she'd worn to visit the casino just outside Nice, on the night she had first set eyes on Esteban . . .

She tried to shake the memory out of her head. Esteban was part of her past, a dangerous excitement that she would do well to forget. But it was as if she had breathed him in and he had become a part of the softly-woven fabric of her soul. It was so easy, too damn easy, to recall the exact sensation of his fingers sliding over her overheated skin, his kisses that started at her lips and moved slowly down the long sweep of her throat until they found the hardening crests of her nipples, pushing eagerly against the fragile, ice-blue silk.

But no. No, she told herself. I don't need you,

Esteban; I thought I did once, but I was mistaken. You have nothing to offer me. Nothing, not ever.

Passing her hand over her brow, she found it moist with a cold sweat. The dress rustled as she moved, its tight sheath opening out into a waterfall of blue silk about her ankles. Glancing to her right, she acknowledged Marcus Hale's nervous, over-formal nod; and Demetrios's suggestive wink. She knew that neither of them had ever seen her dressed like this before – on site, everyone spent all day in shorts or swimsuits – and she wondered eagerly if it turned Marcus on to see her transformed into an English ice-maiden, her breasts full and white against the pale blue silk.

She caught sight of herself in one of the mirrors which lined the sides of the room, and hardly recognised the woman who looked confidently back at her. Her tall, slim figure looked good – no, better than good – in the sophisticated evening dress, her firm, full breasts caressed by the pale blue fabric, nestling in its tight embrace, and her naturally blonde hair coiled up into a loose chignon, with a few tendrils left loose to kiss her cheeks and bare shoulders. Strange how the sight of her reflection struck a chord. The sense of déjà-vu was almost scary. She could almost believe she was back in the South of France, walking into the casino for the first time . . .

'Ladies and gentlemen,' began Marcus. The general chatter subsided a little, but didn't stop. He coughed ineffectually. 'Ladies and gentlemen, thank you for coming here this evening . . .'

The men and women seated in the audience reluctantly put down their drinks and listened. Venetia exchanged a despairing look with one of the expedition's divers. Marcus really was hopeless at this sort of thing. It was no wonder nobody wanted to invest in the project.

'As you know, we are engaged in excavating a number of important sites on the island, including a prehistoric sunken settlement. At present, our work is partly funded by the Maltese Government and the International Council for Undersea Archaeology. However, opportunities have arisen for private investment . . .'

As Marcus droned on, Venetia surveyed the faces dotted around the room. Some, she recognised. There were representatives from the Government, one or two bored-looking newspaper reporters from the *Maltese Times*, a few freeloaders in rented tuxedos. It wasn't difficult to spot who was important and who wasn't. The important ones dressed conservatively, even drably – they were so rich, they didn't need to try.

Quite suddenly, one face caught her eye. The face of a blond, broad-shouldered man in his early forties, blue-eyed and pale-skinned. It was striking rather than handsome, the nose a little crooked, the jaw a little too square. But it was a face which demanded attention. She wondered who he was – a banker perhaps? He had the coolly direct, almost quizzical gaze of a man who wants to know everything about everything.

And he was looking straight at her.

Feeling flattered and just a little flirty, Venetia turned away as she heard Marcus speak her name.

'. . . and now Dr Venetia Fellowes, our Operations Director, will explain the project to you in more detail . . .'

Venetia stepped forward, a little nervous now. It

wasn't the prospect of delivering a talk which was making her edgy – it was the blond-haired businessman with the piercing blue eyes. He hadn't stopped looking at her since she'd noticed him in the audience. And even though she wasn't looking at him, she could feel his eyes on her . . .

She began the presentation she had prepared, talking her way easily through the short video-film and slides of the many artefacts which had been raised from the citadel and the temple. It wasn't difficult to talk with real enthusiasm about the project – her work was something she felt passionate about, a real reason for existing.

'And so you see,' she concluded, 'it would be a great tragedy if work were to be halted on these vitally important sites, simply for the lack of adequate funding . . .'

A figure stood up, towering above the other diners. A few heads swivelled in his direction.

'Dr Fellowes.'

Venetia drew in breath as she met his gaze, her mouth suddenly dry. She had known it would be him, even before she turned to look at him.

'Sir?'

'Gabriel Engelhart. I'd like to ask a few questions, if I may.'

'Of course. Ask away.'

'I'd like to have a discussion with you. Outside. If Dr Hale is agreeable.'

Venetia's heart thumped. So this was the man Marcus was so keen for her to impress. He was pretty impressive himself, with his aura of authority, his broad shoulders and sweep of wavy white-blond hair. Not her type though, not her type at all . . .

'Well. I'm not sure, perhaps later. This is rather irregular . . .'

Aware of an interested buzz around her, Venetia glanced at Marcus. He looked pink-faced, sweaty and pathetic.

'Go on,' he mouthed silently. 'Go *on*!'

Excusing herself, Venetia followed Engelhart out of the conference room and into the tiled passageway outside, closing the door behind her.

'I am obliged to you,' said Engelhart, leaning up against the wall, his cream linen suit uncreased even in the sultry evening heat. 'But then, I knew you would agree. You are clearly a woman of some discernment.'

Venetia tried hard not to stare at him. Tonight was strictly business, with lust definitely not on the agenda.

'You wanted to ask me something?' Venetia was at once irritated and intrigued by Engelhart's over-confident manner.

'These excavations . . . why do you consider them so important?'

'They can provide us with a unique insight into one of the great lost civilisations of the ancient world. So little is understood about Maltese prehistory . . .'

'Very possibly,' replied Engelhart coolly. 'But why should I give a damn about the ancient world?'

VIP or not, this man had an arrogance that really got under Venetia's skin.

'I was under the impression that you are an art dealer. Surely you must have a keen interest in the past.'

Engelhart laughed. Venetia had the distinct

impression that he was enjoying himself.

'I am interested in making money.'

'And that is all?'

'Not quite,' Engelhart confessed. 'For instance, I am also interested in you.'

Venetia felt a shiver run through her body. It was impossible to be sure if it was a thrill of excitement or a shudder of repulsion. How could a man both attract and repel in such equal measure?

'I'm not sure I know what you mean,' she said slowly.

'Then allow me to explain.' Engelhart snapped his fingers at a passing waiter and took a glass of wine off his silver tray. He sipped at the chilled liquid. 'It won't take a moment. It is obvious to me that you are an intelligent woman.' He smiled. 'Intelligent as well as beautiful. And you see, Venetia, it wasn't this presentation which brought me to Malta. It was you. I knew I had to have you.'

Venetia took a step back. Was this Engelhart guy on the level, or was he some kind of weirdo out for a cheap thrill?

'Hold on a minute, Mr Engelhart, I've never met you before in my life!'

'True. But I have heard of you. Of your knowledge and your skill – and your courage. Few women would have risked their own lives to save the life of another – particularly not a worthless little airhead like your sister Cassandra . . .'

'I think you should watch what you're saying, Mr Engelhart!'

Engelhart appeared to take not the slightest notice.

'You have what I need, Venetia.'

'Which is?'

'An encyclopaedic knowledge òf ancient languages and texts – and a spirit of adventure. I want you to do a job for me.'

'I have a job already.'

'Ah, but for how long? Without funding, I understand that this project will soon be as dead as the sites you've been excavating.'

'Are you trying to blackmail me?'

'Naturally – if that's what it takes.' Engelhart drank the last of his wine and set the glass down on a small marble side-table. 'Let us simply say that if you're prepared to help me, I'm prepared to be more than generous to Dr Hale and his team.'

'What do you want me to do?'

'Tell me, have you ever heard of the *Lore of Madali*?'

An electric buzz of interest raised the hairs on the back of Venetia's neck.

'The *Lore of Madali*? Of course I've heard of it. It's a legend – it doesn't exist.'

History had spoken of an ancient collection of exquisite erotica and esoteric wisdom, but there had never been the slightest evidence that it had ever existed outside the imagination of poets and storytellers.

'Really? You're quite sure?'

'Are you telling me you know where it is?'

'Perhaps. And with your help, Venetia, I am going to possess it.'

Chapter Two

IT WAS A warm, sunny evening, and Venetia was sitting with Marcus Hale outside a waterfront café in Marsaxlokk. In the tiny harbour, brightly-painted *iuzzu* fishing boats bobbed at anchor, their shades of red, blue, green and yellow dazzling in the evening sunshine. On either side of their high prows, carved and painted Eyes of Osiris watched unblinkingly, as they had done for countless centuries.

Marcus pushed away his plate of *fenek-biz-zalza* with a grunt of annoyance. Venetia glanced up.

'What's the matter, Marcus?' she enquired coldly. 'Lost your appetite?'

'Look, Venetia,' he snapped. 'I'm the Director around here, and if I say you're not going, you're not going.'

Venetia and Marcus glared at each other across the table. Venetia took her time and chose her words with relish.

'Marcus, you can be such a bone-headed little shit. Has anybody ever told you that?' That was

234

something she'd been itching to say for ages, and it was worth it just to see the look on his face.

'Really?' replied Marcus icily. 'And have you forgotten that I'm also your employer?'

'True, but for how long?' pointed out Venetia, stabbing her fork into a cube of *gbejna* cheese.

Marcus played with his food, pushing the stewed rabbit around his plate like a sulky child.

'We'll manage without Engelhart's money,' he replied sullenly.

Venetia let out a gasp of exasperation.

'I don't get you, Marcus, really I don't. One minute you're telling me to butter this guy up, so he'll put money into the project; the next, you're practically forbidding me to have anything to do with him.' She looked at him over a forkful of salad. 'I don't suppose you'd be jealous, would you?'

'Don't be bloody stupid,' snapped Marcus, a little too hastily.

'Oh yeah?'

Venetia was beginning to see Marcus Hale in a whole new light. It had never occurred to her to think of him in *that* way before. Marcus was the kind of guy who had sexual relationships with fossils, not people. But now she noticed a look in his eyes. A look that struck a chord. She'd been in and out of enough rocky relationships to recognise the green-eyed monster when she saw it.

'It's the project I'm concerned with,' insisted Marcus. 'Not everyone is obsessed with sex,' he added darkly, no doubt with Demetrios in mind.

'Well, I'm glad to hear that,' replied Venetia breezily. 'Because it's the project I care about, too.

235

And that's why I've decided to accept Gabriel Engelhart's offer.'

'I told you . . .'

'I know what you told me, Marcus, and now it's my turn to tell you. I'm telling you that if Engelhart doesn't bail us out soon, we'll go under. You said so yourself. All he wants me to do is travel with him and help him look for this book he's so keen on. In return, he'll fund the project for another eighteen months.' She got to her feet, pushing away her plate and counting out the money for her share of the bill. 'Oh, and in case you're wondering, I'm going purely for business reasons. Pleasure doesn't come into it.'

Really? thought Marcus gloomily as he watched Venetia's endless, tanned thighs stalking angrily out of the café and off along the waterfront towards the jeep. Could have fooled me.

As luck would have it, Gabriel Engelhart was stepping onto the deck of his yacht at the precise moment when Venetia's jeep pulled up on the quayside at the exclusive resort of Sliema Creek.

He stood there for a moment, just watching her walk along the promenade towards him. She moved like a thoroughbred, her walk at once angry and graceful. Her long, blonde hair was piled in a loose knot on top of her head, baring the long, tanned curve of her neck; and he felt an insane urge to kiss it. She had a good body too, long-legged and spare without being rangy. Her full breasts bobbed free under a low-cut, sleeveless khaki T-shirt.

Jumping over the rail, he landed on the

boardwalk in front of her. She didn't turn a hair, just stood there with that seductive half-smile of hers.

'Miss Fellows. Venetia. How pleasant to see you again. Have you discussed my little proposition with your project director?'

'As a matter of face I have.'

Gabriel's face relaxed and he almost, but not quite, smiled.

'Excellent.'

'What makes you so sure I've decided to accept?'

'First, you're no fool. Second, you look angry. That leads me to believe you've just told Dr Hale something he didn't want to hear.'

'You think you know everything, don't you?'

She was beginning to wonder if she'd made the wrong decision after all. Gabriel Engelhart was such an opinionated pig of a man. But it was too late to get cold feet now. Gabriel stroked his hand down her bare shoulder.

'I know you, Venetia.'

She tried to step away, escaping his touch, but their eyes met and suddenly she felt her whole body responding to him; aroused, sensual, seductively willing. His eyes seemed both to caress and to command, taking away all her determination to keep her distance.

'I know you, Venetia; but I intend to know you much better.'

Unseen by Gabriel and Venetia, the shadowy figure of a man was watching from the quayside. As Gabriel slid his arm around Venetia's waist and drew her into a kiss, the man turned and walked quickly away, into the first rays of the sunset.

The yacht *Deliverance III* was far bigger and more luxurious than anything Venetia had ever seen before.

The nearest she had come to it was two years previously, when she had spent time in the South of France, tracking down her twin sister, Cassie. It had been there that she had her first taste of luxury villas, casinos and the champagne life-style; of sophisticated men like Bastien LeRocq . . . and Esteban.

Out here on the sunlit sea, heading out across the Mediterranean towards North Africa, Esteban seemed no more than a wild dream, a fantasy capable of existing only in darkness and shadow. Perhaps it had never existed. Perhaps Esteban himself was nothing more than the creation of her own deepest, darkest, most secret desires. And now she had left that wild, dark fantasy far behind. She was free of him now – or was she? She could never be quite free of the memory of him, or the terrible, tortured passion he had made her feel.

Standing on deck, looking out over the breathtaking blue of the sea, she allowed herself to remember what had passed between them. Esteban, the dark-haired gambler, her vampire lover, had won the price of her life and then, inexplicably, set her free. But there were some things you could never be quite free of. How could she ever forget the thrill of his tongue, lapping at the swollen pink pearl of her clitoris; the exquisite, savage danger of their coupling?

The hot sun caressed her bare shoulders. She

took the pins from her hair and let it fall in a glossy cascade down her back. It felt silky, sensual, like a lover's hand smoothing her bare flesh.

A voice behind her woke her from her reverie.

'Why don't you take it off?'

She wheeled round. Gabriel Engelhart was standing behind her, naked but for the fluffy white bathtowel tied around his waist. In the noonday sun, his pale skin seemed creamy rather than pallid; the smooth perfection of Italian marble.

'Why don't you take off your shirt?' he repeated. 'You'd be much cooler.'

She shook her head, at once very tempted and vaguely embarrassed. It still seemed incredible that she should have agreed to go on this wild goose-chase with a complete stranger. Let alone one who could make her feel lust and loathing in equal measure.

'When will we arrive?' she asked him.

Engelhart glanced at his watch.

'We should reach Tunis in about twelve hours. I have been given the name of a contact there, a man called Yusuf.' He came up behind her. He did not touch her, but Venetia found herself wishing that he would.

'And he knows where to find the book?'

'Perhaps. If not, he will know where we should look. I am told that he, like you, is knowledgeable about ancient texts.' He paused, breathing in the fresh flower-scent of Venetia's body. 'I hear he also has an eye for a pretty Englishwoman. You will doubtless be able to obtain far more information from him than I could.'

'You really believe the *Lore of Madali* exists, don't you?'

'And you don't?'

She shrugged.

'I'm a scientist. I'll believe it when I see it.'

'It is said to be very beautiful, you know. Think of it: hundreds of exquisite erotic miniatures, and all the sexual wisdom of the ancient world. Wouldn't you like to know the secrets of perpetual pleasure? I know I would.'

Venetia's mouth was dry. She could feel Gabriel very close behind her, almost but not quite touching, his breath hot on the nape of her neck.

'I suppose anyone would.'

She pretended to gaze out over the sea, but all her thoughts were concentrated on Gabriel, her body yearning for some soft caress, some touch that might satisfy the hunger within her.

His hand stroked her shoulder and she started, her whole body shuddering at the touch.

'You are very tense, Venetia. You should try to relax more.'

His strong fingers began kneading her shoulders through her filmy cotton shirt, and she leant back, offering herself to the gesture. It felt good. Too good to resist for long, and Venetia had been too long without physical comfort. How long was it since she had enjoyed Demetrios's caresses? Only two days and nights, and yet her body was strung tight as a wire, singing in the wind.

'Mmm.' Her enjoyment escaped in a soft sigh from her parted lips.

'So very tense. All your muscles are knotted. Here, let me ease them for you. Just relax.'

Gabriel's fingers were strong and supple. As

they kneaded her shoulders, Venetia yielded to the seductive strength, the smooth insistence of the caress. And it *was* a caress, there could be no doubt of that. Somewhere at the back of her mind, Venetia wondered idly how she could feel so suddenly and so strongly attracted to this man – this self-opinionated man who wasn't even her type. A man who, on their first meeting, had seemed to undress her with his eyes . . .

She could hear his breathing, soft and low. Felt him bend closer over her, caught her breath as his lips brushed lightly across the back of her neck.

'Take it off, Venetia. Who's to see?'

He's right, thought Venetia, caught in a happy haze of lazy sensuality. Who's to see? And quickly unbuttoning her Indian cotton shirt, she peeled it off and let it fall to the deck.

She was bare to the waist now, her lightly-tanned breasts a testament to the amount of time she had spent working naked on the isolated Maltese beaches.

'You have a remarkable body, Venetia,' breathed Gabriel. She looked over her shoulder at him, but he shook his head. 'No, don't turn round. Stay where you are. Let me make you feel good.'

Gabriel slid his hands round Venetia's waist. At first he made no attempt to caress her, but he pressed his body against hers, his bare chest rubbing against the top of her back, the fine wire of flaxen hairs tickling her skin. She felt his right hand move behind her, followed by the soft slithering of the bathtowel as he unfastened it and let it fall.

'Quite remarkable,' he repeated, and held her

more tightly against him. Now she could feel the strength of his desire. His penis was hardening, lengthening; nuzzling into the small of her back, its moistening tip leaving a lick of wetness on her golden skin.

'Please, Gabriel, I don't think . . .' she began. But it was all show. She and he both knew what they wanted. It was just a matter of time before the last, small resistance melted away.

'You must be uncomfortable in those shorts. Here, let me help you out of them.'

Venetia let out a giggle of protest, but Gabriel gently lifted her protesting hand away from the waistband of her shorts. His fingers were swift and adept, flicking open the fastening with a light click. Then the zipper yielded, sliding slowly down with a soft sigh of release.

'There, isn't that better? Doesn't that feel good?'

He eased down her shorts and, still facing away from him, she stepped out of them. Underneath she was wearing thin white cotton briefs, moist and semi-transparent with sweat. Gabriel's appreciative fingertip traced the dark curve marking the deep valley between her buttocks.

'You shouldn't . . . we shouldn't . . .' Venetia felt utterly stupid. Here she was, protesting like some timorous virgin, and all the time her shameless body was betraying her, her nipples hard as carved wood, her outer labia plump and swollen, her panties wet and fragrant with her need. 'You know we shouldn't . . .'

'Why not, Venetia? You're surely not afraid of pleasure?'

'It's not that. It's just . . . this is too soon . . .'

This time, Gabriel kissed her with real insistence, his lips pressing hard again and again, along the line of her back, her shoulder-blade, the soaring upward sweep of her neck. For a split second, she almost imagined she was with Esteban again, thrilling to the exquisite danger of his kiss, the fear and the pleasure so inextricably mingled.

'There's really nothing to fear, Venetia.'

'W-what makes you think I'm afraid?'

'You're shaking. Shaking all over, I can feel it.'

Gabriel's hands slid abruptly upward, smoothing over her ribcage until they met the firm, warm overhang of her breasts.

'Even your breasts are trembling. Quivering all over. It makes me want to hold them and keep them safe.'

Venetia let out a low groan of excitement as his fingers climbed higher, so so slowly, grazing the flesh with the utmost tenderness, teasing and arousing with each butterfly touch.

'Gabriel, please . . .'

Was she asking him to free her from his embrace, or to go on and on and on and never stop? She didn't want to confess the truth, even to herself. But as his fingertips closed about her breasts, forming the sweetest, softest cage of pleasure, she pressed herself more tightly into this delicious captivity.

Gabriel purred with satisfaction. Venetia was even more sensual than he had anticipated. She made his cock rear like a stallion's, made the blood pump round his body in an exhilaration of lust. He squeezed and palpated Venetia's breasts, skilfully catching the nipples between his fingers and pinching them tightly. Her gasps of excitement intensified his pleasure, made him long to be inside her.

'Do you want me?' he breathed into her ear.

Venetia let out a low answering sob, pushing out her backside so that it rubbed against the erect shaft of Gabriel's penis. Now it was his turn to gasp in excitement as the wet cotton fabric slid roughly over his exposed glans, almost provoking him to a climax.

'I want you, Venetia. I've wanted you ever since we met.' Or even longer, he thought to himself with satisfaction. Even the idea of Venetia Fellowes had seemed erotic to him, and the reality was so very much more appealing.

His fingers slid down and under the sides of Venetia's white briefs.

'You don't need these any more, do you?'

Taking his hands from her thighs, Venetia turned slowly round until she was looking him full in the face. She was smiling, breathing a little heavily.

'I can undress myself,' she murmured. 'Watch me.'

She rolled down her panties with infinite slowness, savouring the look of torment on Gabriel's face. She knew that he was a man who couldn't bear not to be in control; and here he was, forced to watch as she danced before him, slowly stripping away the last veil of her modesty.

Her honeygold pubic curls emerged, crisp and glossy in the Mediterranean sun; neatly clipped into a springy tuft which begged to be kissed.

'Venetia, you little witch, I have to have you.'

Venetia swung back her hair, and the silky curtain flew out behind her in the sea-wind. She felt strong, invulnerable.

'Then take me. Kiss me. Why don't you kiss me?'

For a moment Venetia wondered if she had made the wrong move, misjudged the game. Maybe Engelhart only liked women who were willing to play the sweet submissive. Then Gabriel's spellbound face relaxed into a grin, and he threw back his head and laughed.

'You're a shameless slut, Venetia Fellowes.'

'And you're complaining?'

'Not in the least. But of course, if you play the slut, you have to take the consequences . . .'

He gathered her up in his arms, so suddenly that she had no time to resist, even for a second. The next thing she knew, Gabriel had balanced her on the ship's rail, so that she was leaning back, half-in and half-out of the yacht.

'Gabriel . . . what the hell are you doing?' she squealed, half-terrified and half-exhilarated by his recklessness.

'I'm taking you. You wanted me to, don't you remember?'

His hands cupped her buttocks as he stood between her outspread thighs. Venetia stretched out her hands and grasped the rail on either side, hardly daring to open her eyes, caught as she was between the blazing summer sky and the fathomless glitter of the sea below.

'If you drop me, Gabriel Engelhart . . .'

'You'll just have to trust me not to, won't you?'

Trust . . . how could she trust this stranger, this mad adventurer who had simply strolled into her life and taken it over? And yet the knowledge of the very great risk she was taking only served to add extra spice to this crazy moment.

Gabriel's body was hot and hard between her thighs. She could not see him, only feel the great dark shadow he cast across her body, moving between her and the sun.

Still holding on to her with his left hand, he used his right to explore his prey.

'Such silky thighs you have, Venetia. Do you wax your thighs? I'd love to pour wine all over that creamy skin and lick it off, every drop. What do you say, shall we do that?'

Venetia tried hard not to wriggle as he stroked her inner thighs, half-caressing, half-tickling.

'Oh – oh Gabriel, don't, I'll fall . . .'

'Don't you trust me not to let you fall? Don't you? I thought you said you weren't afraid of anything.'

For a moment, he let go of her with both hands and she was balancing precariously on the narrow wooden rail, poised only seconds away from the rushing water beneath. She knew he was taunting her, and swore to herself that he would not win. By some massive effort of will, she managed not to cry out, though her heart was thumping with fear.

Tightening her thighs about Gabriel's, she forced the tremor from her voice.

'Fuck me. I want to be fucked.'

He growled with pleasure, seizing hold of her backside with one hand whilst the other explored the moist and tender heart of her sex, his fingertip drawing patterns in the sweet, wet ooze which glistened on the coral-pink folds of her inner labia.

Venetia's whole body was shaking, pulsing to

the desperate throb of her swollen clitoris. And all the time, Gabriel was torturing her with that sultry, mocking voice.

'What have we here? A pink rosebud? A juicy pink rosebud. And what's this at the very centre? It's a shiny little pearl. Let me feel how hard it is . . .'

The touch of his fingertip on her exposed clitoris was the briefest, the lightest contact imaginable, but it felt as though a huge electric shock were being passed through her body. This time she couldn't suppress the cry, which tore from her from between her parted lips.

'Bastard . . . bastard, don't do this to me!'

'But it's what you've always wanted, isn't it? The chance to live dangerously?'

Suddenly, quite without warning, he slid the tip of his penis into the welcoming entrance to her womanhood. She shuddered, writhed, moaned aloud in the torment of her own shameless lust. It was no use playing the blushing virgin now, her secret was out. She wanted this every bit as much as Gabriel did. And her hips thrust forward, inviting him deeper into the wetness of her sex.

With a second thrust he was inside her, up to the hilt. She felt the weight of his testes, full and heavy, resting in the deep valley of her sex; and the fat hardness of his shaft, the blissful, unending length of his penis as it drove into her, accepting the gift of her sexual need.

Their bodies drove together, slick and slippery with sweat. A sweet, thick ooze of juice trickled from Venetia's sex, anointing her lover's manhood, so that it glistened like smooth, polished glass.

Head hanging down and her long curtain of hair

swinging beneath her, Venetia glimpsed the white wake surging and foaming around the boat's hull. It felt as though the wild, churning waters were inside her, bubbling and fizzing in her belly. With each new thrust, Gabriel seemed deeper inside her, and his cock awoke a new world of sensations, sparkling and irresistible.

She heard laughter; her own. This reckless, foolish pleasure was carrying her beyond herself and into a realm where nothing mattered but the moment.

Tightening her thighs about Gabriel's waist, she felt his fingers clutching hard at her buttocks. His grip was tight, muscular, determined; the unforgiving caress of a man who knows what he wants – and what his lover wants also. She writhed instinctively as his pelvis ground against hers, provoking ripples of ecstasy as he brushed against the hard nubbin of her clitoris. But Gabriel did not loosen his grip. On the contrary, his fingers clenched more tightly around the soft, firm flesh of her buttocks, drawing them further apart, opening up the secret world within.

'Oh. Oh. Oh.' Her little cries escaped in little outrushes of breath, set to the rhythm of Gabriel's eager thrusts.

'Take it. Take it,' he grunted, utterly crazy for the hot, wet paradise of Venetia's sex. He had judged her to be a profoundly sensual woman, but had hardly expected her haven to be so welcoming and so deliciously tight.

'No . . . no more. I can't . . .' moaned Venetia. She felt stretched beyond capacity, her whole body filled up with the swollen hardness of Gabriel's dick. 'I really can't . . .' But she wanted more. She craved more and more and more; for each movement, each caress, brought her nearer to the top of the blissful rollercoaster . . .

She had thought there could be no more, but Gabriel had hardly begun. Releasing his grip slightly, he allowed his fingers to slide deeper into the amber furrow between Venetia's buttocks.

'Gabriel, no! Don't do that, I don't want you to . . .'

It was Gabriel who was laughing now; mocking her pretended modesty.

'My beautiful liar, are you telling me no man has ever touched you *here*?'

His fingertip slid, very lightly, along the sensitive membrane, lingering fleetingly on the tight-closed rosebud of her anus. Venetia's whole body seemed to contract in upon itself, the blossom as her anus trembled and dilated at her lover's touch. She squealed, half in outrage, half in pleasure.

'Don't fight me,' breathed Gabriel, withdrawing his penis and tantalising her aching sex, only to slide it back into her with teasing, exhilarating slowness. 'Let it happen. You know it's what you want. *I* know it's what you want.'

Venetia's heart was pounding, her head dizzy and spinning from the rush of blood to her brain. She felt dreamy and phantasmagorical, a make-believe woman in a fantastic world, weightless and unreal. Only the pleasure existed, and that was hot, and strong, and tyrannical in its relentless power.

'Do it,' she murmured. 'Do it to me.'

Gabriel needed no further persuasion. Already

his fingertip was teasing the amber rose, gently tickling and stroking the quivering petals, persuading them, little by little, to open and let him in.

When his finger slid into her behind, she shivered with a silent, private ecstasy. The double torment of his penis and his finger, toiling together inside her, left her helpless to do anything but simply allow herself to be carried on the wild wave of pleasure.

'Come for me. I want you to come. And then I want you to come again and again.'

Gabriel's voice half-coaxed, half-commanded. Something at the back of Venetia's mind wanted to resist this sensual arrogance, this man who seemed to know so much about her, but the power of pleasure was far too great. And when he pushed himself that last, blissful millimetre into the hot depths of her, her clitoris sang for joy. Its hard stalk rubbed brutally against Gabriel's pubic bone. The sensation was not sweet or gentle; it was an electric stab which transformed itself instantly into the first, unbelievably wonderful spasm of climax.

As her body relaxed into the long, delicate, dying waves of orgasm, Venetia felt Gabriel ejaculate. He remained inside her for many long moments, the only sounds around them the rhythm of their breathing and the distant thunder of the sea.

It was evening when *Deliverance III* sailed into Tunis harbour. The port was almost deserted as darkness fell; but there was one who watched, unseen, from the shadows. A creature of darkness and silence.

Gabriel Engelhart turned and called down to Venetia.

'Come up here. We're almost there.'

Slipping on a loose shirt over her bikini, Venetia climbed up the steps from the cabin and joined Gabriel on deck. She stood close to him but not touching; not feeling any urge to do any of the things that lovers do, like slipping her arm through his. It was as though they both sensed that their intimacy was not of that kind. Oddly, Venetia felt more distant from him than she had done before they had had sex.

The harbour lights glittered before them, lighting up the velvety sky.

'What will we do when we arrive?' asked Venetia.

'Tonight we will stay at a house I have in the town. Tomorrow, we will seek out Yusuf.'

'Who is he, this Yusuf?'

Gabriel shrugged.

'I know little of him, except that he is an art dealer, a bit of a rogue. But my information tells me that he will help us – if the price is right.'

They docked in the marina and Gabriel helped Venetia onto the quayside. Together they walked towards the *poste de douane*, where a group of uniformed customs officers with guns stood lounging about, smoking.

'*Passeports, m'sieur dame,*' grunted one of the *douaniers*, thrusting out a massive paw of a hand. Gabriel handed his over and it was handed back after a cursory glance. But Venetia's was passed from hand to hand.

'Is there a problem?' enquired Venetia, sud-

251

denly uneasy. She had seen the expressions on the men's faces, the knowing smiles as they passed around the passport. '*Est-ce qu'il y a un problème?*'

'*Peut-être,*' replied the senior customs officer. His hand lingered on Venetia's arm and she froze to the spot. His fingers brushed the side of her breast as he looked her up and down. '*Venez avec moi.* You must come with us for . . .' He winked. 'Questioning.'

Venetia felt panic rising inside her.

'Why? What have I done?'

A hand took her by the elbow.

'Come with us. You must come with us.'

But they had not reckoned with Gabriel Engelhart.

'Leave her alone. *Laissez! Vous m'entendez?*'

The customs officer wheeled round to look at Gabriel.

'*Quoi?*'

'I said, leave her alone.' Gabriel reached into his pocket, took out some sort of identity card and flashed it briefly. 'Unless, of course, you would like to explain this to the Chief of Police.'

Venetia was amazed by the transformation. Leers became respectful smiles, and the hand was removed from her arm as swiftly as it had grabbed hold of her.

'Everything is in order, *madame*. I hope you have an enjoyable stay.'

Pocketing her passport, Venetia followed Gabriel out of the customs house, intrigued.

'How did you do that?' she asked.

'I make it my business to know useful people.'

'Evidently.' She caught up with him. 'Thanks, anyway.'

He inclined his head towards her.

'It is of no consequence. Besides, I have to protect my investment. Tomorrow you begin work on making me my next million.'

Chapter Three

GABRIEL'S HOUSE WAS tucked away in a side-street, its façade modest and peeling, in the middle of a row of once-grand, now run-down colonial houses. Venetia blinked in disbelief.

'We are in the district of the *foundouks*,' explained Gabriel as the car manoeuvred awkwardly along the rutted road. 'These buildings were once foreign embassies, but they are now used as *oukala*, apartments for poor people.' He grinned as he added, 'The red light district begins just down there, at the end of *rue Zarkoun*.'

Gabriel opened the car door and Venetia stepped out into the street, conscious even at this late hour that eyes were watching her from all sides, a few shabby children staring wide-eyed at her from crumbling doorways.

'This is it – your house?'

Gabriel gave a throaty chuckle.

'Not quite what you expected?'

'Well . . . I mean – why *here*?'

'The great advantage of this district is that it is very secluded, very discreet. Rich tourists do not come here, they are too afraid. Come inside. I think you will be surprised.'

Gabriel's chauffeur got out and knocked on the front door. A few seconds later a grille slid open. A face peered out, dark-eyed and swarthy.

'Master!'

'Open up, Ismail. We have a guest tonight.'

The heavy door swung open, to reveal a middle-aged Arab in traditional white robes, standing in a dusty inner courtyard. Hands pressed together, he executed a small, respectful salaam.

'Ismail, this is Miss Fellowes.'

'Madame.' The dark eyes lingered, then were lowered, rather reluctantly, thought Venetia. She could feel those eyes boring into her, even after he had looked away.

'You may take our luggage up to the Balcony Room.'

'At once, master.'

Ismail led the way, Venetia following Gabriel across the dusty courtyard towards a second door, this one guarded by a very beautiful gilded gate. Once on the other side of the door, Venetia let out a gasp of astonishment.

'I told you you would be surprised,' commented Gabriel. 'You really must try to believe what I tell you.'

They were standing in a vast circular entrance hall, lined with twisted pillars of gilded marble. In the centre was a sunken pond, filled with shimmering gold and silver fish; and above arched a high domed ceiling, painted dark blue and decorated with intricate, many-coloured filigree patterns in the Islamic style.

'It's incredible!' exclaimed Venetia. So, she thought to herself, Gabriel Engelhart must be even wealthier than I thought.

'I like all my villas to be decorated in the local style,' explained Gabriel airily.

'How many do you have?'

'Oh, six – no, seven. I was forgetting the new place I'm having built in the Hollywood Hills.'

Venetia shook her head in disbelief.

'It doesn't sound as if you need the *Lore of Madali*.'

'Oh, I don't. Not for the money.' Gabriel took a stray strand of Venetia's hair, kissed it and stroked it down. 'But I *desire* it. And whatever I desire, I simply must have.' His hand rested lightly on the back of Venetia's neck. 'I have sought it for years, and soon it will be mine.'

'If we ever find it.'

'We will – no, *you* will find it for me. And when I have enjoyed owning it for a while, I shall enjoy selling it on for a very large sum of money. Now, if you are ready, we shall go to our rooms and Ismail shall serve us dinner.'

The roof garden of Gabriel's villa was illuminated by soft, rose-pink lights hidden among the tangle of greenery.

Vines twined overhead, heavy trusses of juicy fruit fragrant and glossy in the soft light. Peach, nectarine and citrus trees gave off a declicate, tangy scent which mingled with the heavier perfumes of roses, mimosa and night-scented jasmine.

Ismail arrived to serve dessert: a silver salver of sticky-sweet halva, honey-soaked *makroudh*, stuffed dates, and a pot of *té akhdar* – green tea with mint, sprinkled with pine nuts and almonds.

'All is as you wish it, master?'

'It is perfectly satisfactory. You may leave us now.'

Ismail made an obsequious bow and took his leave. Venetia felt a surge of relief. She had already decided that she did not like Gabriel's taste in servants.

Gabriel poured the mint tea into two small enamelled cups.

'Ismail is a devoted servant,' he told Venetia, his eyes caressing her, never leaving her face. 'He would quite happily die for me. Absolute loyalty is a quality I prize highly.'

'I'm . . . sure.'

'But you find him a little too . . . attentive?' Gariel searched her face.

'Perhaps.' She didn't add that, frankly, Ismail gave her the creeps, with his look of a hungry mongrel dog.

'Among his other accomplishments, Ismail is a very fine judge of women.' Gabriel leaned closer. 'Before he came to me, he was a procurer.'

'A what?'

'A procurer of beautiful girls for harems and houses of pleasure. He still has an eye for a fine-looking European woman like you. He is probably wondering what price I am intending to ask for you . . .'

The colour drained from Venetia's face. 'I hope this is some kind of joke, because if it isn't I think I'd better leave . . .'

Gabriel laid his hand on her arm. 'I am sorry, I have no desire to alarm you. You are quite safe here.' Taking her hand, he pressed it to his lips. They felt feverish and hot against her chilled flesh. 'You are perfectly free – free to stay or to go, just as you choose. Although I should remind you that you are here to help your colleagues in Malta. Without my very generous contribution . . .'

Venetia sat down and sipped her coffee. 'I don't know how to take you. I can't figure you out at all.'

'You think of me as an enigma? Really, I am flattered.'

'You're making fun of me.'

'Now, would I do that?'

She looked up at him. 'Almost certainly. It seems to me that you do just about any damn thing you feel like doing.'

Gabriel reached out and picked up a remote handset. A second later, soft Eastern music began playing, its rhythms complex and deeply sensual.

'You enjoy Syrian music, Venetia?'

'As a matter of fact I do. It's so . . . haunting. I spent time in Syria when I was an undergraduate, working on a dig.'

'I know. That is one of the reasons I chose you. You see, I have certain information . . . a rumour that what we seek has been taken to Eastern Syria.' Gabriel got up and slid onto the pile of cushions next to Venetia. 'But for now, all I want is to know more about you.'

A slight breeze ruffled the light, gauzy hangings and the lights seemed to flicker. Glancing up, Venetia could have sworn that, for a few brief seconds, shadows chased each other across the surface of the moon.

Gabriel's hand released the pins from Venetia's

hair and as it tumbled down her back he smoothed it down, as though he were stroking a cat. Venetia responded with a soft murmur of appreciation. This man truly was an enigma to her – one moment so arrogant and opinionated, the next, softly caressing.

'There's nothing to know about me. I'm just . . . ordinary.'

'Oh no, Venetia. Not ordinary at all; you must cure yourself of this false modesty. You are the most extraordinary woman I know. Extra-ordinarily attractive, certainly; but more than that. You see, I sensed the need within you the moment I first saw you.'

'The need? What need?'

'The need for pleasure. You are an animal, Venetia; a sensual animal. You need to use your body for pleasure, it is as natural an exercise for you as breathing. I'm right, aren't I?'

He stroked his hand down the inside of her arm and she trembled slightly at the unexpected intensity of sensation.

'Look, Gabriel . . . what happened on the boat . . .'

'You're not telling me that you regret it?'

'No, not exactly . . . but . . .'

'But nothing. Let go, Venetia, stop feeling guilty for once in your life. Let me liberate all this need inside you. It will be so easy.'

He was right next to her, his hand hot against her skin, the imprint of his caress unforgettable and tingling on her bare arm. Gently he took her in his arms and kissed her, his lips coaxing hers to respond. And she could not resist, for excitement was trembling through her whole body already.

As he drew away, he left her panting, her lips glistening with wetness.

'You really think you're God, don't you, Gabriel Engelhart?'

'Tonight, I'm whatever you want me to be.'

'Oh yes?' She returned his gaze defiantly, calling his bluff. 'And if I wanted you to be my helpless sex-slave?'

He chuckled. 'Ah, but you don't, do you? That's exactly what you don't want me to be. A woman like you needs to be possessed . . .'

Their lips met again, and this time, she returned the passion of Gabriel's kiss. She wanted to tell him to go to hell, but her body was whispering to her of pleasure, treacherously aching for more and still more. Parting her lips, she allowed her tongue to slide into his mouth, the taste of mint tea and sweetness mingling as they kissed.

He pushed her down gently onto the heap of embroidered cushions, and she slipped down willingly, letting him think he had the measure of her. He lay half-on, half-beside her, his thigh sliding over hers as his hands roamed over her breasts. He unfastened the top button of her shirt, then the second, revealing the pink push-up bra underneath, and the creamy swell of her cleavage.

It would have been the easiest thing in the world just to let Gabriel do whatever he wanted with her. But Venetia wanted more.

'Want me?' she murmured as he unfastened her shirt and pushed it free of her breasts.

'You know I do.'

'You promised to be whatever I want you to be.'

'Anything.'

Supple as a cat, she rolled sideways, so that

Gabriel was underneath and she was half on top of him, her thigh across his legs. Propping herself up on one elbow, she gazed down at him, her lips pouting into a self-satisfied smile. Gabriel gazed back at her, half-puzzled and half-appreciative.

'You're full of surprises tonight, my English cat,' he grinned.

'It's high time you felt my claws.'

Venetia could hardly believe she was talking like this to Gabriel Engelhart, the man Marcus Hale had marked down as the saviour of the Maltese project. The man she was supposed to be *working* for, for goodness sake. On the other hand, she could hardly believe that she had slipped so easily into a red-hot liaison with a man she knew nothing about and hardly even liked. Perhaps it was the summer sun, the wine, the warm North African night, but right here and now it felt like exactly the right thing to do.

Her fingers ran over Gabriel's face, down his cheek, the side of his neck and onto his chest; scoring the flesh lightly with her varnished nails. Then she bent to kiss the flesh she had martyred, moistening the skin with cooling saliva, darting a myriad tiny kisses from brow to the nape of Gabriel's neck. As she kissed him, her fingers worked at the buttons of his silk shirt, opening it like the wrapping on a gift, peeling it back to expose the smooth skin beneath.

'You sexy bitch,' groaned Gabriel as she ran her nails up and down his belly and chest. He was well-muscled, firm; his skin smooth and hairless, defining the contours of his powerful body. 'How do you know just what to do to drive me mad?'

Her unspoken reply was to reach down his

belly until her fingers met the buckle of his belt. She had no need of words to show him how she could give him pleasure. She slipped the buckle and slid it away from his body. The leather felt supple and smooth in her hand.

'I could tie your wrists with this,' she teased.

'You wouldn't though.' He looked at her quizzically, as though seeing her afresh. 'You're not that kind of girl.'

'Oh, but I would. And I am. What's more, you promised you'd be whatever I wanted you to be.'

'For tonight.'

'For tonight.' Venetia looked at him from under the sweep of her eyelashes. 'Tomorrow night, who knows . . .?'

Gabriel decided that he would play her at this game; it was a novelty to him – and he liked his women to provide him with a few surprises. This one was more adventurous and exciting than he had imagined. And he had already found her exceptionally stimulating, with her pretty, sub-missive face and her sensual ways.

He reached his wrists up above his head, and Venetia looped the belt around them several times, tying them comfortably, but firmly enough to hold them fast.

'Now you're mine,' she smiled. And lowering herself onto him, she kissed, licked and bit into the sweat-seasoned flesh of his nipples.

'Bitch! You outrageous bitch . . .' Gabriel's voice was more full of admiration than outrage.

He twisted and turned and wriggled, but could not escape the tyrannical pleasure of her savage little kisses. She was astride his waist, and he could feel the heat of her, soaking into him through her panties. She felt hot and moist, and he could smell her sweetness, the seductive odour which signalled her readiness for him.

And he was so, so ready for her. His manhood ached with the need of her, pushing its swollen head against the inside of his shorts. He moved his pelvis under her, pushing himself against her, thrusting between her legs; but still she went on sucking and biting his nipples, her free hand raking nail-tips down over his bare flesh. It was hell; or it was heaven? All he knew for sure was that he didn't want it to stop.

At last Venetia tired of her game, and knelt up. Her mouth was wet with her own saliva and Gabriel's sweat.

'Your nipples have gone all hard.' She stroked the flat of her hands over them, and Gabriel's body started at the exquisiteness of her touch.

'And yours?' Gabriel's sapphire-blue eyes demanded an answer. 'Are your nipples hard for me? Wouldn't you like me to suck and bite them?'

'First, I want to see you naked,' replied Venetia, running the tip of her tongue over her lips, discovering a new and insatiable thirst.

She unbuttoned Gabriel's trousers. There was no zip, just a line of beautiful mother-of-pearl buttons; old-fashioned and very, very classy. This man intrigued her. Unconventional, arrogant, exuberantly confident, he was completely different from any other lover she had ever had.

Except perhaps Esteban . . .

Banishing the fleeting memory from her thoughts, she turned attention to Gabriel's fly-buttons. There were altogether too many of them, and they were just too darn fiddly. The solution was simple.

Bending over him, she set about biting off the buttons, one by one. She felt him shiver at her touch, breathed in the acrid, spicy odour of his manhood, which still bore all the scents of their first coupling. She longed to take it into her mouth, to devour it, to drink down its elixir; but tonight she wanted to be in control. She wanted to savour these moments of unbridled power.

'Lift up your backside,' she told him. He saw no reason not to obey, and she slid down first his trousers, then his silk boxer shorts.

His penis was just a little over average length, but thick and bulbous at the tip. It reared up above large and heavy testes, the right slightly larger and lower than the left; hard and juicy within its taut seed-pod.

'Take it in your mouth,' urged Gabriel, his voice soft and mellifluous, almost hypnotic. It was a tempting prospect.

'Later.'

'I want you.'

'I know. And I'm going to make you want me more.'

Now he was naked before her, delicious in his vulnerability. Who would have thought that Gabriel Engelhart would ever allow himself to look vulnerable? It seemed only fair to even up the score.

'What to see some more, Gabriel?'

He did not answer, but he was devouring her with his eyes. Venetia slipped the shirt from her shoulders and reached round to unfasten her bra. As the catch yielded, the cups sprang away from her breasts, and she slipped the bra off, dropping it onto the ground. Gabriel motioned that he wanted to get up, to touch her, for her to untie him, but she shook her head.

'You promised, remember? Anything I want you to be. And what I want you to be is my very obedient slave.' She laughed. 'Tonight, you can be my Ismail. Lie still now, don't you dare move.'

Two lengths of scarlet silk cord held back the curtains of the canopied pergola. They were perfect for what Venetia had in mind. Swiftly she untied them.

Gabriel watched, guessing what she intended.

'You're not going to try and tie me up with those?'

'Why shouldn't I?' She smiled as she echoed Gabriel's own words. 'You know it's what you want . . .'

He made only a token resistance as Venetia slipped the red cord about his ankles and attached them to the base of the curtained pergola.

'Perfect.'

She knelt back on her haunches to appreciate the full effect of her handiwork.

'So what are you going to do to me now that you have me at your mercy?' he demanded with ironic humour.

'I'm going to take my revenge.'

'Revenge! What's that supposed to mean?'

'It means I'm going to make you feel like you made me feel this morning, when you drove me crazy. It means I'm going to take you right to the edge and keep you there until you beg for mercy.'

'I want you, Venetia.'

His voice, low and soft, awoke a trickle of

pleasure-juice between her pussy-lips, soaking into her already-wet briefs.

'I know you do.'

'I want to fuck you. Do you understand that? I want you *now*.'

'And you shall. When I've had my fun.'

'You need me. I'm the only one who really knows how to give you pleasure. Remember – on the boat . . .'

'I remember.' She laughed, deep and warm and confident. 'But I don't need a man to give me pleasure. I can do that myself.'

Standing up, she slipped her briefs down over her backside, down her hips, her thighs; the moist fabric caressing the sunkissed skin. She watched Gabriel's face, enjoying the look that passed across it as her clipped blonde triangle came into view. It wasn't as if he hadn't seen it all before, but here, now, he wanted so much to kiss and touch and fuck it, simply because it was forbidden.

She stood right over him, her thighs parted, her plump sex-lips parted in a kiss of welcome. The rose-pink light filtered through the vine-leaves, the scent of mimosa and jasmine mingling with the sweet spiciness of her blossoming sex.

'Let me show you what you're missing.' With her fingers, she opened up the soft, dewy-fresh petals of her womanhood, unveiling the secret inner beauty: the glistening well of honeydew, constantly renewed from some hidden spring; the plump, hardened stalk of her clitoris, pushing insolently out from underneath its flesh cowl. 'Do you like what you see?'

'You're a wicked, beautiful slut and I want you right now.'

Gabriel pulled hard against the straps which bound him, and almost succeeded in hauling himself into a sitting position. But Venetia stretched out her right foot – still clad in high-heeled, strappy evening shoes – and pushed him gently but firmly down again.

'You're mine for tonight. I'll tell you when you can have what you want. Now, why don't I show you what I do when I don't have a man around?'

Glancing to her left, she saw a small onyx-topped table inlaid with gold and silver flowers. On top stood many-branched candelabra, shaped like gnarled trees whose bodies took the form of beautiful men and women. Venetia took one of the unlit, red candles and ran her fingers over it. She smiled.

'It's not as big as you, of course, but I think we can still have a little fun.'

Excitement was fizzing in her veins now, the adrenaline of sexual arousal making her half-crazy. Several glasses of excellent champagne had made her head swim, and she felt liberated from the clear-headed, intellectual, ever-so-slightly boring young woman whose life revolved around tomb inscriptions and ancient texts. In the morning she might feel embarrassed about this, even frightened by her own audacity; but the wine and the exotic surroundings and the presence of this attractive, arrogant man made her feel reckless and free.

She heard Gabriel gasp as she parted her outer labia with the fingers of her left hand, and with her right rubbed the rounded end of the candle over the slippery inner folds.

'Mmm, feels good,' she purred. 'Could you

make me feel this good? I wonder.'

Without waiting for him to reply, she pushed the candle into the well of her vagina. It slid in smoothly and silently, eased in by the slickness of her secretions. Deeper and deeper ... it didn't feel at all like a man's penis; more like a robot's sex-organ, cold and mechanical, excitingly different. 'Ah. Ah yes. That feels amazing. I wish you could feel it, Gabriel. I wish you could feel how wet I am.'

Gabriel did not speak. He was fascinated by this young Englishwoman, so well-bred and so wickedly sensual. It surprised him to realise that watching her masturbate excited him almost as much as having sex with her. If only his hands were free ...

'Untie my wrists,' he begged her.

'Why? So that you can touch me?'

'So that I can touch myself. You're driving me crazy, can't you see?'

'Good. But you can get a little crazier before I untie you. Just lie still and watch.'

This unique sensation of power stimulated her like no other aphrodisiac. Suddenly she was all-powerful, all-knowing, the personification of sexual desire. The candle was her lover, her helpless male, filling her up at her whim, doing only what she commanded it to do. This was a fantasy made real ...

As she masturbated slowly and luxuriously with the candle, her right index finger sought out the white-hot pleasure-centre of her sex. It felt hard, hyper-sensitive: so sensitive that she could hardly bear to touch it. Even the merest breath seemed to send knife-blades of pleasure through her whole body.

Scooping up a little of her own moisture, she used it to lubricate her clitoris and the delicate folds which half-concealed it. With a circular motion, she began to stroke and tease, coaxing the luxury of self-pleasure from her overheated body, easing herself towards a long, self-indulgent, perfect climax.

Her eyes drank in Gabriel's discomfiture: the painful hardness of his cock, its tip dripping glittering juice onto his belly; the tautness of every muscle; the hoarse, staccato rhythm of his breathing. He couldn't take his eyes off her fingers, working like an artist's, creating a perfect sculpture in flesh. A sculpture of purest pleasure.

A familiar tension in her belly; a tingling sensation in her fingers and toes; a divine numbness which turned first to pins and needles, then to a great surging warmth beginning deep inside her . . . it was coming, coming, coming.

She threw back her head, completely uninhibited now, forgetting even that Gabriel existed. She was alone with her own need, her own quest for the summit of delight.

'Come, Venetia. Go on, do it, do it, do it.'

Gabriel's voice tore into her consciousness at the very moment when her fingers awoke the first thrill of orgasm. And seconds later she was tumbling, falling, spinning down through the sparkling, scented air; carried away on a wild spring tide.

Sweet honeydew dripped down the inside of her thigh, sparkling against her golden skin. Still dizzy with excitement, she withdrew the candle. It glistened in the rose-pink lamplight.

'Taste me,' she breathed. And she knelt over Gabriel, sliding the candle-shaft over his parted lips.

He put out his tongue and tasted. The wax had melted a little, and its redness mingled with the powerful, sweet elixir of Venetia's womanhood. He had never tasted anything more delicious in his whole life.

Venetia bent over him and kissed him, her lips now imprinted with the scent of her sex and the dripping redness of the candle. Without saying a word, she sat up, then slid herself forwards until she was kneeling directly over Gabriel's face.

She heard his indrawn breath; a desperate, blissful shudder. Then she felt his face pressing into the hot, moist space between her thighs. His tongue darted into her like a serpent's, instinctively seeking out the well-spring of her desire. Her orgasm had not sated her; it had made her still more hungry, and she moaned with delicious pleasure as Gabriel's tongue and teeth re-awakened the throb of unsatisfied desire.

'You . . . surprised me last night,' commented Gabriel. He and Venetia were sitting, side by side, in the back seat of Gabriel's chauffeur-driven Mercedes, heading into the souk quarter and the medina.

'Really? You didn't enjoy it then?'

Venetia turned away and looked out of the window at the teeming streets of the city. It was difficult to look Gabriel in the face, after what had gone on the night before. Her head ached slightly, the legacy of too many bottles of champagne; but her body was still warm with the afterglow of a long night's lovemaking.

'I didn't say that.'

Gabriel laid his hand gently on Venetia's thigh and stroked it through the thin, floaty cotton of her summer dress. She did not push him away, yet neither did she respond. She was confused about her feelings for Gabriel Engelhart. How was it possible to be sexually attracted to a man she didn't like? How could she feel so little and so much, all for the same person?

'What then?'

She forced herself to turn and look at him. He looked very Aryan and just a little frightening, with his glittering blue eyes and wavy, naturally blond hair.

'You realise I shall make you pay the price?'

He spoke the words casually, as if they were a joke, but Venetia thought she felt something else there, something dark and distant. Something she'd rather not know about.

'Do you have to talk in riddles?' she asked, with apparent playfulness.

'It is quite simple. You made a slave of me for one night,' he replied with complete frankness. 'That was our bargain, wasn't it? Well, now it's my turn. How are you going to repay me?'

Suddenly Gabriel's hand felt heavy, sticky and unpleasantly hot on her thigh. Venetia wriggled free of it, and slid a few inches away from him on the polished leather seat. She felt hot and uncomfortable in her modest, long-sleeved, long-skirted summer dress.

'Don't play games with me, Gabriel.'

'I never play games. I'm deadly serious.'

'I don't owe you anything.'

'True.' Gabriel smoothed back his blond mane, and the diamond cufflinks glittered with an unforgiving brilliance. 'But you have agreed to work for me. And Dr Hale is counting on you to save the project. You wouldn't want to let him down now, would you?'

This time she met Gabriel's gaze.

'Don't try to blackmail me, *Mister* Engelhart. I'm nobody's plaything. Just because I find a man attractive and spend a few nights with him, that doesn't mean I belong to him.'

Gabriel held his hand up, conciliatory again.

'Of course not.' His eyes were dark shadows in his pale face. 'I would never try to make you do anything you didn't want.' He smiled. 'But you do want me, don't you Venetia?'

Venetia chose to ignore Gabriel's question. She looked out of the window, at the teeming horde of colours, the meeting of East and West. They could only drive very slowly through the crowded street, and occasionally, a child's face pressed up against the car window, the mouth opening and closing on the other side of the glass, offering some gewgaw or trinket for sale.

'Where are we going?'

'Through the medina and into the *souk des libraires*. Yusuf has a shop there.' Gabriel tapped his chauffeur on the shoulder. 'Pull in over there. We will walk the rest of the way.'

Venetia stepped out of the car and into a noisy, jostling mass of men, women, children and dogs. There were even a few chickens scuttling around the market stalls.

At the very first glance it was clear that the medieval medina was very different from the modern face of Tunis. Instead of concrete tower blocks there were white domes and minarets, and tunnel-like bazaars. In between stood magnificent doorways: the doors painted blue and beige with black studs and 'Hand of Fatima' knockers, and the whole surrounded by intricately carved stone frames.

'Quaint, isn't it?' commented Gabriel.

'It's full of character.'

'Oh, it's that all right. But come here alone, after dark, and you could find a knife between your shoulderblades. That's the beauty of the place: there's always an exhilarating undercurrent of danger.' He took hold of Venetia's elbow. 'This way.'

Venetia followed, glancing to left and right. She had been in North Africa before, and expected to feel hands roaming over her body, pulling away her light scarf to touch and stroke her hair. Eyes followed her, but from a respectful distance; and it wasn't difficult to see why.

When Gabriel spoke, people got out of his way. If they were too slow, a single look had them cowering: 'Yes, master, so sorry master.' There was something at once disturbing and admirable about Gabriel Engelhart.

'You're well-known in Tunis?'

'I have had a house here for five or six years. I do quite a lot of business in North Africa. Arabs are resourceful people. They can find anything, anywhere – for the right price.'

'Which is how you found out about Yusuf?'

Gabriel shook his head.

'I heard about Yusuf when I was travelling in Tehran – a distant cousin of his was useful to me.

273

Apparently Yusuf has an Arab's eye for aesthetic beauty, and a Persian mystic's taste for the erotic arts.' Pushing a group of street urchins out of the way, he led Venetia into a narrow alleyway between a textile shop and a bread-seller's stall. 'Here we are. The *souk des libraires*.'

A plaque on the wall proclaimed in Arabic and English: 'Yusuf Akhbar, Treasures and Secrets.'

Gabriel rang the bell, and a small boy came to let them in. The shop itself was rather dark, and extremely small, lit only by a single window which looked out onto a back courtyard.

Yusuf emerged from behind a pile of antique rugs, books and furniture. About fifty years old, with a silky greying beard and embroidered cap, he came forward with a smile of welcome.

'Greetings sir, madam. You have come to buy a fine carpet, perhaps a beautiful book – or a trinket for the lady?' He cast an appreciative eye at Venetia. 'Come into the inner room and my boy will serve us coffee while we talk . . .'

Gabriel shook his head. 'There is no time for coffee. There is something we must discuss with you. Something very important.' Taking his wallet from his back pocket, Gabriel laid several high-denomination bills on the table. 'Your cousin Mukhtar sent us to you. He tells me you have information.'

'Information, sir? What manner of information? I am but a humble merchant.'

Venetia stepped forward.

'My name is Venetia Fellowes, Mr Akhbar. I am an archaeologist, an expert in ancient languages and manuscripts. My . . . colleague Mr Engelhart believes that you may know of the whereabouts of the *Lore of Madali*.'

Yusuf paled visibly, even in the twilight. Placing his finger to his lips, he shook his head.

'Please, madam. Do not speak its name here. There may be others watching, listening.' Crossing to the window, he closed the shutters then clicked on a dingy yellow electric light.

'But surely – this book – it doesn't even exist,' protested Venetia. 'I have never seen any evidence to suggest that it is more than a romantic legend.'

Yusuf and Gabriel exchanged glances. It was Gabriel who spoke first.

'In your heart, you know the book exists, Venetia. You are as driven as I am by this quest.'

Venetia cleared a spot on Yusuf's desk and perched on the edge.

'You have information, Mr Akhbar?'

Yusuf's eyes met Gabriel's for confirmation. Gabriel nodded.

'You have my word that I will make this worth your while, Mr Akhbar.' He laid more banknotes on the table. 'More than worth your while.'

Yusuf seemed uncertain for a moment, then took a key from under a heap of dusty books and disappeared into a back room. Moments later, he returned carrying a leather portfolio tied with green string. He unfastened it with extreme care, the old leather creaking in protest as he laid it flat on the table. He looked up.

'You must know, such things as these are forbidden in this country. If anyone knew that I possessed this . . .'

Gabriel offered no assurances, his blue eyes holding Yusuf prisoner. 'Show us what you have.'

Hesitantly, Yusuf opened up the portfolio.

Inside lay a single black and white photograph, yellowed with age and curled at the edges. But the image itself was crystal clear: the image of a book, laid open at a double page to display words and pictures, riotous images of beautiful men and women, mythical beasts, coupling together in a garden of breathtaking beauty within a strange and wonderful city. It was obscene and exquisite, imaginative and explicit.

Venetia was struck dumb by the beauty even of this single photograph. It was Gabriel who cried out in triumph, seizing it and examining it minutely.

'This is it,' he muttered under his breath. 'It must be, it must ... everything is as I had imagined it would be.'

Venetia looked over his shoulder, tracing the words and pictures with her fingertip; translating slowly, painstakingly.

'This page is written in medieval Latin,' she said. 'It's very corrupt, but I can just make it out. It says, "Oh my love, my flower of the citrus tree, your lips upon my penis are as the softness of the butterfly's wings ..." There are other things too, things I don't understand in a language I don't recognise. And funny symbols I've never seen before.' She traced them with her fingertip, her heart thumping with the excitement of discovery. Could this really be a page from the *Lore of Madali*?

Gabriel let the photograph fall and turned to Yusuf, seizing a fistful of his long, white jellabah. 'Where is it? Tell me, Yusuf, I will pay you anything. Anything, do you understand?'

Very afraid now, Yusuf pulled away, shaking out the creases in his robes. He took a step back. 'I have told you all I know. I have told you more than it was right or wise to tell.'

'You must know more. You *must*.'

'The picture is all I have, I swear it. Only this, and things I have heard, nothing more than rumours . . .'

'Tell me.' Gabriel's voice offered no chance of refusal.

'They say . . . it is said that the different paintings and inscriptions were found and bound together by the magician Paulus Madalinus, around the year 1590 – legend has it that the leather binding bears his sign: a star within a circle, stamped on the upper outer corner of the book.'

'But where, Yusuf? Tell me where the book is.'

Yusuf shrugged. He looked uneasy and fearful. Venetia felt uncomfortable too, torn between the desire to know more and a fear that Gabriel's obsession would drive him beyond reason.

'That is all I know.'

Venetia touched Yusuf's forearm. He jumped, as though stung.

'Please, Mr Akhbar. Tell us all you know. It is important.' Important to me, pleaded her eyes. He looked away. 'There have been rumours that the book is in Eastern Syria. Is that true?'

Yusuf turned back towards her and shook his head. 'No. Perhaps once, but not now. Not for a long time.'

'Then where?'

Yusuf hesitated, then gave a sign of resignation. 'Cairo,' he replied. 'I heard that it was seen there, not six months ago.'

When Venetia emerged from Yusuf's shop and into the *souk des libraires*, darkness had fallen. The streets, which before had been crammed full of people and noise, were now almost deserted. Only a few nameless shadows walked away into the distance, ignoring the two figures in European dress, and the shop door grating shut behind them.

'Come on. The driver will be waiting to take us back to the house. It isn't safe here after dark.'

Venetia did not move. It felt as though a cold, ethereal hand had stroked its transparent fingers down the back of her neck. She shivered.

'What is the matter with you, Venetia? Come on.'

She turned back to Gabriel, and they walked on together. But as she left the souk, she turned and looked over her shoulder, certain that she must see someone, or something, half-hidden by the darkness. A shape. A shadow . . .

And yet there was nothing there.

So why did she feel so convinced that someone was watching her, someone who had waited for her for a very long time. . .?

Chapter Four

IN THE VELVETY darkness of a North African night, Venetia was dreaming.

At first, she did not realise that she was dreaming at all. It seemed so real.

Venetia was naked; lying on soft, damp grass in the cool of a summer's evening. She was in a forest; a great, piney glade with whispering branches which arched overhead, criss-crossing to form a high canopy. Somewhere nearby, she could hear cicadas singing in the trees. The air was still, scented, clear as springwater.

It was many, many years ago, of that she was certain. How long? Her fuzzy, dreamy brain would not quite click into focus. Why was she here? And where was 'here'? And who was this lover whose kisses carpeted her body, his skin cool as sculpted stone?

She moaned as his lips traced a slow path down her belly to the soft mound of her pubic hair. He took her outer labia into his mouth, kissing and sucking them, so that the hood of her clitoris slid back and forth, provoking irresistible sensations that made her forget all the questions tumbling round and round in her head.

He did not speak, yet it was as if she could hear his every thought inside her head.

'*Toi seule, petite anglaise*. You alone . . .'

Fleetingly, she felt afraid, wanted to push him away, but he held her tightly, pressing his face into the fragrant glade of her sex, sucking and licking at her womanhood. She climaxed again and again, the pleasure seeming to go on and on, never ebbing away, only growing and swelling like her need for this man.

'Do not fear me, Venetia. Why do you fear me?'

His body slid over hers and she raked her nails down his back. She heard him growl his pleasure, then he kissed her full on the mouth, with a savage, tender passion which took her breath away. She wanted to scream, to cry, to hold him for ever and never let him go.

His lips tasted of her own sweetness, and of some far-distant, half-remembered ecstasy. At last, as he drew away and began to kiss and lick her throat, she understood.

'Esteban . . .!'

The breath escaped from her in a low, moaning cry. He hushed her again with his kisses, not speaking but holding her very tightly as his penis slid inside her. She felt the smooth stone ring which pierced his glans as it stretched the delicate, sensitive walls of her womanhood; tasted his sweat, breathed in the essence of him as their hunger joined and grew to fill the whole world.

From the velvet-dark sky above them, soft, warm rain began to fall on their joined bodies, trickling over their skin, bathing them like the world's tears.

Pleasure and pain ... there was nothing between the two, not so much as a hairsbreadth. Venetia could no longer judge between the two, no longer understood which was good, which bad. She felt Esteban climax inside her, thrilled to the twist and jerk of his penis, heard the long, low gasp as his strength became utter vulnerability; surrendering for a few, brief moments to the dominion of ecstasy.

Her own orgasm swelled within her suddenly, a chorus of pleasure rising to a scream of remorse as the last, warm ache died away and she felt Esteban pull away from her.

'No, Esteban. No, don't leave me. Come back.'

He got to his feet. She saw him in the half-darkness, his face exactly as she remembered it, only more beautiful and more sardonic. The aristocratic, aquiline profile, the mane of collar-length dark hair, the diamond-black eyes that saw into her very soul. His lips were moist with her elixir, and as he wiped them on the back of his hand Venetia remembered that this should not have happened. This was impossible, dangerous, insane. Impossible because Esteban was not like other men. Esteban was neither living nor dead.

Esteban was a vampire.

She watched him put on his armour: the chainmail tunic, the crusader's tabard that hung loosely on his tall, slim-hipped frame from broad shoulders, the sword thrust through the leather belt. And for the first time, he spoke.

'It is time. I must leave you now.'

'No, Esteban. Don't go. I need to understand . . .'

'I have no choice. You know this cannot be.'

He mounted the great, grey stallion lightly. Venetia got slowly to her feet. The first glimmerings of dawn were visible as a dark-blue haze on the horizon. An ache of longing filled her, and she heard herself cry out: 'Let me come with you.'

'Where I dwell, no mortal may follow.'

She met his eyes; such beautiful, compelling, coal-dark eyes; so often burning with anger or arrogance or contempt, now empty save for a kind of sadness.

'Stay. I don't understand. Stay . . .'

But Esteban shook his head slowly and, spurring on his horse, disappeared through the forest, into the night.

Venetia awoke confused, not certain if she was awake or still dreaming. Then she remembered. She was alone in the big carved bed in Gabriel Engelhart's guest room, a scented wind wafting in through the open window.

Opening her eyes, she blinked in astonishment, fear, perhaps just a glimmer of hope. For Esteban was standing at the foot of her bed, dressed as she had known him in Valazur: tall and rangy in his long black jacket and trousers, and embroidered silk waistcoat. Every inch the professional gambler, the mysterious figure in black.

She sat up, breathless with hope. 'Esteban. Esteban, I . . .'

'Beware, Venetia. Beware Engelhart. Trust no one . . .'

Scrabbling for the switch, she turned on the bedside lamp. Orange-yellow light filled the room; and Venetia saw how she had deceived herself. Esteban was not there. He had vanished. He had never been there at all.

A tear of disappointment escaped from the corner of her eye, and she rolled sideways, clutching at the pillow for comfort. As she did so, her fingers made contact with something soft and fragile. Propping herself up on her elbow, she picked it up and stared at it, shaking, disbelieving.

Beside her, on the pillow, lay a single thornless rose – the colour of freshly-shed blood.

Showering and dressing in a satin robe, Venetia went downstairs in search of Gabriel.

Outside, the heat would already be mounting, the North African sun sizzling the dusty mud-bricks and concrete of the city. But inside Gabriel's townhouse it was perpetual spring. The high-ceilinged, marble-lined rooms lent the house an airy, spacious feel; and the discreet air-conditioning kept the temperature cool enough for comfort, warm enough for the barest minimum of clothing.

There were flowers everywhere. Great drifts of jasmine and tropical creepers tumbled from hanging baskets and terracotta pots, forming bright-green curtains of foliage, spangled with scented flowers. Their perfume was at once fresh and heady, filling Venetia's head with dreamy thoughts of a faraway summer land, gentler by far than this harsh climate.

She walked down the broad, curving central staircase and into the entrance hall. The sunken fishpond glittered with the gold and silver shadows of fish, the water constantly rippled and renewed by a hidden underground spring which bubbled up through the polished floor.

Ismail bowed to her as she passed. Everything he did was executed with the utmost respect, and yet she could not bear to be near him. She found him creepy, too obsequious to be sincere.

'Good morning, Ismail.'

'Good morning, madam.' Ismail's head was bowed, but he was looking up, his dark eyes fixed covetously on her. Suddenly selfconscious, Venetia looked down. Her robe had fallen slightly open at the front, baring the tops of her breasts and one long, golden thigh. Small wonder Ismail looked distracted. Colouring up with embarrassment and annoyance, she adjusted her robe.

'Where is Mr Engelhart?'

'The master is . . .' Ismail coughed, as though faintly embarrassed. 'He is in the . . . er . . . kitchen.'

Venetia looked at him in surprise. Ismail explained.

'It is a fancy of the master's, madam. He does not like to be disturbed in the mornings, and so he likes to prepare his own breakfast. It is not fitting,' he added under his breath.

'Had I better not disturb him, then?'

For the first time, she thought she caught the shadow of a smile on Ismail's thin lips. A rather bitter little smile, she thought to herself.

'Madam, he shuns me, but I am quite sure he will be delighted to see *you*.'

Ismail indicated the passageway which led to the kitchens, and Venetia set off along it, wondering how many more surprises Gabriel Engelhart had in store for her.

The corridor was lined with small alcoves, each one housing a statuette, painting or mosaic. Unlike the Moslems he lived among, Gabriel was not constrained by strict religious conventions which dictated that art must never depict the human face or form. On the contrary, it was clear that Gabriel was more than appreciative of physical beauty . . .

This place was a treasure trove of artefacts from every race and time, every corner of the globe. There were carved wooden fertility statuettes from West Africa, their phalluses and breasts hugely exaggerated; fragments of a Roman mosaic pavement, depicting an orgy in which naked dancers cavorted with satyrs in an orange grove; a priceless sixteenth-century erotic miniature, 'Love's Awakening'; even an unknown Egyptian bas-relief, representing the Pharaoh as both male and female, enjoying the delights of his concubines and his serving-boys.

Venetia was beginning to understand now that money could mean very little to a man like Gabriel Engelhart. He had all the money he could ever need, and then some. No, what mattered to him now was the challenge of finding something that nobody else had got.

That must be the reason why Gabriel Engelhart was so desperately keen to get his hands on the *Lore of Madali*. And if – or when – he did, he would move on to the next challenge, hungry for another quest to bring excitement into his predictably successful life. Venetia wondered for a moment if she had been a challenge too: an acquisition he had made up his mind to have. And now he had her, what next?

Reaching the end of the corridor, she hesitated, then pushed open the door. Gabriel was sitting in the middle of the kitchen, at an enormous circular wooden table set with a jumble of fruit, meat, jugs of fruit juice, a dish of fresh *ftairs* and an unopened bottle of white wine, the chilled glass frosted with condensation.

He turned to greet her.

'Ah, Venetia. I was wondering when you would come and join me.'

Venetia stepped inside and closed the door behind her. She was standing in a large, old-fashioned kitchen with whitewashed walls and lots of carved, dark wood. From the beams above her head hung sides of cured and spiced meat, game birds, long strings of garlic and bunches of herbs. Mellow morning sunshine flooded the room from windows set high in the walls, their ornamental metal grilles casting complex patterns wherever the light fell.

'When did you wake up?' asked Venetia, accepting a glass of orange juice and sliding onto a chair at the table.

'Oh, around four.' Gabriel shrugged. 'I don't need a lot of sleep. My mind's very active.'

'Not just your mind, as I recall.' Venetia failed to suppress a smile.

'No.' Gabriel stroked her throat and she leaned back, her hair falling behind her in a long, glossy curtain. He kissed a long line from chin to breastbone, making her shiver with appreciation. 'But I don't recall you complaining.'

He turned back to the pile of food on the table.

'What would you like? I am an excellent cook.'

'And modest with it?'

'Modesty is an affectation,' replied Gabriel. 'What is the point of pretending to be any less than you are?' He picked up a physalis dipped in white chocolate, peeled back the calyx and dangled the fruit so that it was just touching Venetia's lips. She put out her tongue and licked it, and he let it slide into her waiting mouth. It tasted good; a mixture of sweet and sour, smoothness and acid juice.

He licked the juice from her lips and they kissed, his tongue exploring the last traces of juice and melted sugar glaze.

'What shall I cook you?'

'Your choice.' Venetia leaned back. 'This is luxury, having a handsome man cook breakfast for me. What do you recommend?'

Gabriel wrinkled his nose. 'Not the local food, that's for sure. *Brik à l'oeuf* is impossibly vulgar, and *draw* is just plain tasteless. How about a soufflé omelette stuffed with fresh strawberries soaked in champagne?'

'Mmm. Sounds heavenly.' She pushed back her hair, breathing in the soft scents of fruit, herbs and spices. 'You know, this is dangerous. I could get used to being spoilt.'

She watched Gabriel cooking, genuinely impressed by his confident skill as he whisked egg-whites into a featherlight fluff, and folded them into the omelette mixture. The aroma of the lightly-frying omelette was sweet and sensual. On impulse, she got to her feet and walked over to where Gabriel was standing. Standing behind him, she slid her arms about his waist.

Breakfast she could live without, thought Venetia; but she *was* hungry. A wicked little stirring in her belly reminded her that it had been – oh, hours and hours . . .

She nuzzled into the back of his neck and bit him; just gently, hardly enough to feel it. But he responded instantly, turning round and taking her into his arms, pushing his belly up against hers; proving to her that his need was every bit as great as hers.

His strong hands smoothed down her back and found the rounded curves of her backside, cupping and squeezing the firm flesh. Venetia put her hands round Gabriel's neck and pulled his face down to hers, forcing a kiss on his lips, ignoring the bristliness of his unshaven chin.

Both were panting when the kiss ended. Gabriel looked at Venetia with a lopsided grin. He nodded towards the still-sizzling frying pan, and the fluffy golden omelette.

'We'd better eat before it gets cold.'

'I guess.' A note of regret entered Venetia's voice. Their eyes met, the shared thought passing between them. Then Gabriel arranged the omelette and the strawberries onto a plate and they sat down like two civilised dinner party guests.

'Only one plate?'

Gabriel's gaze met hers.

'You object to sharing?'

'Of course not.'

He speared a strawberry on his fork and held it out for Venetia to taste. She parted her lips and took a bite from it. It was very, very cold; the sharpness of chilled champagne mingling with the sweetness of strawberry juice and the faint bite of white pepper.

As she bit into the berry, the juice sprang from the flesh and trickled down over her lips and chin.

'How very messy,' murmured Gabriel, leaning forward and licking away the clear pink trickle of juice. He chuckled. 'It makes you look like a vampire.'

For a split second, a frisson of unwelcome memory ran over Venetia's skin. No, no; she would not think about Esteban. She must not. He had belonged to a faraway time, a time before she had known who and what he was. And besides, she had never really cared for him. She was just deluding herself if she believed it had ever been more than a casual dalliance.

She forced herself back to the present, and scooped up a spoonful of omelette. Gabriel took it into his mouth, then kissed her, forcing her to share the taste and the texture.

She pulled away, gasping with laughter, wiping her hand across her sticky mouth.

'Animal,' she teased.

'Come here and say that.' His eyes sparkled with merriment. A savage pleasure which half-excited, half-frightened her.

'Come here and make me.'

He caught her and, to her surprise and alarm, picked her up in his arms. It was only now that she realised just how strong Gabriel Engelhart really was.

'Put me down.'

'You told me to make you, and so I am.'

'Put me down. I'll scream!'

'Fine, scream. No one will disturb us, not even Ismail. I'm sure he told you how much I hate to be disturbed at breakfast.'

She looked into his piercing blue eyes. He was playing with her, as a cat plays with a baby bird; taunting her, knowing only too well how much his arrogance maddened and excited her.

He tossed her over his shoulder, as though she had no more dignity than a sack of potatoes, her backside in the air and her fists drumming on his broad back.

'I suppose you think I *like* being treated like this?'

'Of course you do,' replied Gabriel smoothly. 'You're a woman. A very sexy woman,' he added, giving her bottom a hefty thwack.

She wriggled in his grasp, but both of them knew he wasn't going to let go until he was good and ready. Venetia wasn't even sure she wanted him to, though she was mad as hell with him for this act of pure machismo.

With his free hand, Gabriel found the belt which held Venetia's robe closed at the waist, and untied it, letting the silky strip slither to the tiled floor. Her robe hung loosely now, just a thin veil of pale blue satin between her flesh and his desire.

'You're a haughty bitch, Venetia Fellowes,' breathed Gabriel. 'A bitch and a prick-tease, do you know that?'

Through the satin robe, his fingers traced the deep furrow between Venetia's buttocks. She made no lucid reply, only letting out a low moan, halfway between outrage and ecstasy.

'The way you behave, it's a wonder you don't drive men mad.' Gabriel's voice became husky with excitement. 'The other night, when we first arrived here, I let you play your little game. It excited you, and it excited me too, to play along for a while. But it's high time you knew your place, my high-bred English filly.'

This time he landed a hearty slap on her backside, making it jump and quiver. It smarted, *really* smarted; and Venetia let fly with a stream of curses.

'Tut, tut, Venetia. And I was so sure you were a lady,' said Gabriel reprovingly. 'It's obvious I shall need to teach you some manners.'

Pulling up the skirt of the satin robe, Gabriel bunched it up around Venetia's waist. She was bare now; the pale golden smoothness of hips, buttocks, thighs and legs completely at his will.

Venetia had never felt so exposed in her life before. She wasn't accustomed to being treated like an object, but no matter how she kicked and wriggled Gabriel held her fast. He had the upper hand and he was obviously enjoying being in control – just as she had enjoyed her illusory feeling of power the other night, when she had tied him up with silken ropes and imagined that she had some sort of magical hold over him.

She dangled over his shoulder like one of the Sabine women, her long mass of corn-blonde hair tumbling down his back and obscuring her vision. She tried scratching at his back but he just laughed and shook her off, carrying her across the kitchen as easily as if she had been a tiny child.

The next thing she knew, Gabriel was letting go of her, and she was sliding down onto the hard, scrubbed surface of the huge circular table-top, sending pots of jam and dishes of fruit skidding in all directions. There was a tinkling sound as a serving-dish shattered on the floor, and the soft thud of a fresh-baked *pain rustique* bouncing off the tiles.

'You're good enough to eat, Venetia, do you know that?'

Gabriel's voice was low, dark and husky. Venetia, lying on her belly amid the mess of jam and squashed fruit, slewed her head round to stare up at him. His eyes glinted.

'Good enough to eat. So that's what I'm going to do.'

Venetia rolled onto her back, intending to slide off the table and walk away; but Gabriel had other ideas. He held her there, on her back, and admired what he saw. The blue satin robe was hanging open on the right side, and was soaked through in patches, rendering it almost transparent as it clung to Venetia's skin. Pink strawberry juice had soaked into it where it passed across her left breast, and the large, pink, semi-erect nipple showed clearly through the wet fabric. Lower down, cream and fragments of crushed peach spattered the gown, making it hug the contours of lower belly and thigh; her golden pubic triangle shyly peeking from underneath.

Reaching out, Gabriel plunged his bare hand into a bowl full of whipped cream, scooping up a large handful. Bending over Venetia, he let great thick gobbets of the cream fall slowly and languidly onto her body, sometimes falling onto her gown, sometimes onto the bare flesh of belly and breast.

Venetia shuddered. The cream was straight out of the refrigerator, chilled so cold that it shocked her as it touched her skin with its icy kisses. Her left nipple contracted and hardened at the first touch, half in a reflex, half because, in spite of her anger, Venetia was finding this an exciting experience.

Getting up onto the table, Gabriel knelt over her. She found his expression a little frightening. He was looking at her with such intensity, as though he was thinking not so much of pleasure or of lovemaking, but of possession.

His hands ran over her body, smearing the whipped cream over her exposed breast and belly.

'This is all the clothing you need. This must go.'

He peeled the robe from her, the last shadow of modesty remaining to her, baring the moist, firm flesh beneath. And he bent down closer, taking yet more of the whipped cream and massaging it into her skin, leaving not a millimetre uncovered.

She stopped fighting him, and began writhing at his touch. It was too intense to be entirely pleasant, too relentless. There seemed to be no escape from the sheer force of his desire. And when he dropped a cold, cold mass of cream onto the hot triangle at the base of her belly, she let out a shrill wail of fearful pleasure.

'That's it, Venetia, admit it. Admit that it excites you.'

She wanted to deny it, to look coolly up at him and spit in his face, but it was all too cruelly true. She wanted nothing more than for this to go on, to become more and more outrageous and extreme.

'I knew it instantly, Venetia. For all your cleverness you're still a slut underneath.'

His hands took hold of her and flipped her back

onto her belly, face-down amid the breakfast debris. The opened bottle of champagne toppled sideways and a pool of cool, pale-yellow liquid spread out on the table-top. Gabriel picked up the bottle and upturned it, letting the champagne fall in a cool stream over Venetia's hair, shoulders, back and backside.

She shivered, not just with cold. There was something powerful and dark about Gabriel's desire for her; something she wasn't sure that she liked very much.

Cream, fruit, more wine. Gabriel poured and smeared her flesh with anything and everything that came to hand, insinuating the slimy mess into every secret crevice, watching with satisfaction as it oozed and trickled down over her bare buttocks and tight-clenched thighs.

'Now you're ready for me,' he whispered.

She turned her face sideways, looked up at him.

'You're an arrogant bastard, Gabriel Engelhart. What makes you think I want anything to do with you?'

He laughed, running the flat of his hand over her backside, then letting the very tips of his fingers slide into the deep crease between her buttocks.

'Because I can smell you, Venetia. You stink of sex.'

He stroked her back and flank almost lovingly, and she groaned with the irresistible sweetness of it. It was no use denying the need she felt, even if she was walking a narrow tightrope between being attracted to Gabriel Engelhart and despising him.

'You smell divine, you're my finest creation, do you realise that? And now I'm going to devour you . . .'

The first touch of his tongue was a long, sweeping stroke that ran from the base of her spine right up her back to the hollow between her shoulder-blades. Instinctively Venetia arched her back, rising and falling to the rhythm of each new stroke. He licked her as a cat laps at some delicious delicacy, his tongue hollowing to scoop up the mess of sweat and cream and crushed fruit, swallowing it down then returning to caress again and again.

'Don't . . . don't do that . . .' she murmured as he slid down her back and began licking and biting her buttocks.

A chuckle of mischievous delight rumbled through Gabriel's body. 'Why not?' he taunted her. 'Not afraid, are you?'

'I told you, I'm not afraid of you. I'm not afraid of anything.'

'Not even . . . *this*?'

A sudden intrusion between her buttocks made Venetia's whole body tremble, and she tried to wriggle sideways. But Gabriel was having none of it.

'Stay still. You might enjoy it. In fact, I guarantee you'll enjoy it. Or is that what you're afraid of, my beautiful English slut?'

Gabriel's fingers took hold of Venetia's buttocks and pulled them apart. This time, there was no false gentleness in his touch. He knew what he wanted, he knew what they both wanted. Why waste time on foolish preliminaries which would only bore them both?

She was beautiful. She was insatiable. He had known she would be. The tiny, tight rosebud of her anus was a delicious shade of amber beneath the fragrant slick of cream and fruit juice. Tenderly, he licked it away, revealing its unique and secret beauty.

'Bastard,' spat Venetia, her protest muffled as her face was pressed hard against the table-top. Her fingers scrabbled at the smooth surface, but to no avail.

'Hush. Just lie still.'

Gabriel knew many tricks to give a woman pleasure, to still her doubts and dislikes, and turn her to yielding devotion in his hands. He had had many women, every one of them a beautiful, sensual creature; but none had pleased him more than this fiery, sensual Englishwoman. He intended to enjoy taming her.

His fingernails grazed and scored the sensitive membrane of her anus, and he felt her shudder and squirm. Good. That was exactly as it should be. There could be no pleasure in the thing if the girl was entirely without inhibitions. And pleasure was always at its greatest when it contained some element of the forbidden.

Bending low over her, he pressed his face between Venetia's buttocks and breathed in the intoxicating scent of her: a carnal essence of sweat and sex, mingled with the freshness of cream and fruit.

Then he put out his tongue and, ignoring Venetia's muffled curses, thrust it deep, deep, deep into the adorable softness of her backside.

Venetia felt a single tear escape from the corner of her eye. How could she express the gnawing ache which always returned to torment her, at the very height of pleasure? How could she ever escape the knowledge that no lover, no matter how skilful, how attractive, how attentive, could ever be good enough?

Because none of them was Esteban.

It was two days later when Gabriel and Venetia boarded the plane that would take them to Cairo.

Travelling first-class and incognito, Gabriel was a very different proposition to the wild beast who had possessed her so roughly and made it clear that Venetia's path to pleasure was to do exactly as she was told.

Here, sitting next to her, feeding her with red caviare on tiny savoury biscuits, Gabriel was the image of the perfect gentleman: polite, romantic, even tender. Venetia wondered what demon was inside this man, to make him change like the wind from one second to the next. And she resolved that, as soon as her work for him was concluded, she would take the next flight back to Malta and get him right out of her life.

'You are looking very attractive today.' Gabriel took off his sunglasses and slipped them into the top pocket of his Armani jacket.

'Thank you.'

Venetia dabbed at the corners of her mouth with a napkin. She had decided to play it cool, not quite sure how to react to Gabriel's change of image.

'You enjoyed the caviare?'

'It was . . . fine. Very nice. Thank you.'

Venetia resisted the urge to tell Gabriel that showing off with expensive food and wine wasn't the way to win her over. He probably wouldn't understand what she was talking about anyway. Men like Gabriel Engelhart were always convinced that they could buy anything if they were prepared to pay a high enough price.

Gabriel took hold of her chin and looked at her with interest, head on one side.

'Not still angry with me, are you? I mean, that would be absurd.'

'You think so?'

'You *are* angry with me.' Gabriel let out a gust of laughter, as though he could hardly believe that anyone could be quite so immature. 'We *have* still got a long way to go, haven't we?'

Venetia's eyes glittered a warning.

'*You* can go where you like. I'm here to work, remember?'

Gabriel put the tips of his fingers together. She hated him when he did that. He looked so calm, like a psychiatrist about to tell her that all her problems would be cured if she just did everything he told her to do.

'Yes, of course you are. I like a woman with spirit,' he added, handing the food trays to the stewardess with a nod, and snapping the tables back into the seats in front. His hand slipped sideways until it was resting on Venetia's thigh. 'That's why I like you.'

Chapter Five

IT WAS ALL very well being told that the *Lore of Madali* might be in Cairo. The problem was, knowing where to look.

Venetia had spent a frustrating day trailing all over the city in pursuit of elusive 'sightings'. She'd been to the Museum of Egyptian Antiquities, the library at the American University, even the Cairo Synagogue, all to no avail. And the book dealers on 26th July Street had simply shrugged off her questions and tried to sell her cheap editions of the *Kama Sutra*.

And so she found herself walking down Talaat Harb on a suffocatingly hot evening, so footsore and weary that she felt like a sleepwalker in somebody else's dream.

Pushing her way through the crowd, she approached one of the many stand-up juice bars which were dotted at regular intervals along the busy street. The female assistant greeted her with an apathetic '*Masa' il-kheer*' and Venetia slid her money across the counter.

'*Nus w nus, min fadlik.*'

The girl filled a paper cup with a mixture of carrot and orange juice and plonked it down with a thud.

'*Afwan.*'

Venetia silently cursed Gabriel Engelhart as she sipped the cool liquid. Why should he sit on his backside in some nice air-conditioned hotel bar, while she did all the leg-work? And did she really care enough about the Maltese project to waste so much time in a fruitless search for something that didn't even exist?

She decided to give it one more go.

'Are there any secondhand book dealers around here?' she asked the assistant. The girl glanced up.

'What?'

'Book dealers. Or antique dealers.'

The girl answered with a look that said 'stupid English tourist'. She shrugged as she turned to serve another customer.

'There is the shop of Mohammed al-Manakh. On the corner of Hoda Shaarawi, near to Felfela's Restaurant.'

'Thank you. *Shokran.*'

Just this one shop, Venetia told herself as she walked along Talaat Harb and turned the corner into Hoda Shaarawi. At first she didn't even notice the antique shop. It consisted of little more than a door and a tiny window, crammed in between a café and an airline office. A small sign above the door read simply: 'Mohammed al-Manakh'.

Venetia walked towards the shop and pressed her face against the window. A jumble of objects lay right up against the glass. As she'd expected, most of it was rubbish, designed to lure in the tourist trade. Amulets, scarab rings, 'genuine' ushabti figurines and Canopic jars lay heaped up on top of multicoloured rugs and some very obviously fake manuscripts, cooked up last week in a basement sweatshop.

She was about to give up and walk back to the hotel when the shop door opened.

'*Assalaamu aleikum*.' A very ancient-looking, dried-up grasshopper of a man beckoned to her to enter. 'Greetings, madam. You will enter the house of Mohammed al-Manakh?'

'No . . . no, I don't think so.' Venetia had already given this one up as a bad job. And besides, Mr al-Manakh was positively creepy, with his crêpy tortoise neck emerging from the gaping collar of his white shirt. She smiled politely but turned to go. 'I'm sorry, no.'

'I have many beautiful things, many jewels.'

'I'm not interested in jewellery.'

The old man came a little closer. His eyes were small and dark and glitteringly bright, the only feature of his desiccated body which really looked alive.

'What is it you seek, madam? Mohammed will find it for you, Mohammed can find anything . . . for a price.'

I bet, thought Venetia. But what had she to lose by asking?

'I am looking for a book. A collection of very old manuscripts.'

Mohammed licked his lips with an unattractive, lizard-like motion. He smiled, sensing an imminent sale. Once he had her inside his shop he would be sure to sell her something.

'Mohammed al-Manakh has many ancient books, beautiful books. If you will please to come inside . . .'

Venetia hesitated on the threshold, then followed him into the shop. It smelt of coffee and mildew, and she started as a tiny green lizard scuttled away from under her foot.

'This book . . .' she began.

'Yes, yes, beautiful books. I will show you my beautiful books.'

Mohammed rummaged in drifts of paper, pulling out book after book, tattered parchments, the odd thing of some small value, but nothing of any interest to Venetia. She cut in, interrupting his sales pitch.

'It is a collection of pictures. Very old pictures. Very . . . erotic.'

Mohammed's face cracked into a leer.

'You like dirty pictures? Mohammed have many beautiful pictures to show you, pretty lady.'

Venetia dodged Mohammed's questing hand and thrust the photograph into his face. 'Pictures like these? Pictures from the *Lore of Madali*?'

Mohammed could not have looked more shocked if he had been struck by lightning. In a split second his expression changed from lascivious interest to fear, then anger; the blood draining from his face so that its deep walnut brown faded to a jaundiced yellow.

'Leave my shop! Begone!' To Venetia's astonishment, he began pushing her away.

'The *Lore of Madali*,' she insisted. 'You know where it is, don't you?'

'There is no such book.'

'If you know something, tell me – you will be

302

paid well.'

'I will not speak of such things, *you* must not speak of such things.'

Opening the shop door, Mohammed thrust her outside. He stood inside the shop, half behind the glass door as though he feared what the Englishwoman might do to him.

'I don't understand . . .' began Venetia, but Mohammed shook his head, closing the door on her with such force that the glass almost shattered in its frame. His gnarled fingers turned the shop sign from 'open' to 'closed'.

'I know nothing. Now leave. Leave and never return. And forget that you ever spoke of the *Lore of Madali*.'

Gabriel clenched his hand into a fist and thumped it on the rail of the balcony.

'I must have it!'

Venetia poured two glasses of *asiir limoon* and carried them out onto the balcony, handing one to Gabriel.

'Here, drink this. You look like you need to cool down.'

Gabriel drank the chilled lemonade in a single draught, wiping his hand across his mouth. 'Thanks.' He paused, then, 'I guess I shouldn't be taking it out on you.'

Venetia shrugged. 'You're paying me to do a job. If I don't do it to your satisfaction, I suppose you have a right to complain.'

Gabriel searched her face, puzzled by her coolness, irritated by her lack of response. He took the glass from her hand and set it down, seizing her by the shoulders so that she was forced to look him in the face.

'You are more to me than a paycheck, Venetia, you know that.'

'Oh yes, I was forgetting.' She returned his gaze with an ironically raised eyebrow. 'I'm also your little English plaything, aren't I? That was what you said, wasn't it? *Very* romantic.'

Gabriel let out his breath in a grunt of exasperation. 'That was a game, Venetia . . .'

'If you say so.'

'Don't tell me you didn't enjoy it.' He stroked the side of her breast, very lightly, and she knew that if he chose he could have her at his mercy once again. 'I *know* you did.'

Gently but firmly, she pushed him away. It took a good deal more effort of will than she cared to admit, even to herself. 'I think we should maybe forget the sex and keep this professional, don't you?'

Gabriel followed her back into the room and took her by the arm, turning her round. 'No, since you mention it, I don't.'

Venetia saw a kind of mad hunger in his eyes. In an instant she saw what was happening. Her very rejection of him was making her ten times more exciting in his eyes. There was nothing more erotic than something you couldn't have. She prised his fingers from her arm.

'Look Gabriel, I'm not your possession, not your plaything, not *your* anything. Do you understand?'

Gabriel's eyes narrowed slightly. 'Oh, but you want to be, don't you? You want to so very much.'

She had a crazy urge to grab him and shake

304

some sense into him. How could he simply close his mind to anything he didn't want to hear?

'What is it with you? Is this some kind of massive power trip? Do you have to own everything you touch?'

'Not everything. Just the things which I consider to be truly exceptional.'

'It's a nice chat-up line, Gabriel, but forget it. It won't wash with me, not any more. In case you've forgotten, I've seen what you're really like.'

Her words seemed to evaporate into the still, burning-hot air, incapable of leaving any mark on Gabriel Engelhart.

'Your breasts, for example, are certainly exceptional,' he whispered huskily, stroking his finger down Venetia's bare forearm.

'D-don't,' she spluttered, suddenly confused. She didn't want to feel like this, like some mindless rutting beast. She wanted to tell Engelhart where he got off, wanted to push this unclean desire out of her life.

'But you want me to.' Gabriel slid his arm round her waist and drew her close, his hand roaming downwards to smooth over the swell of her buttocks.

'No.'

She pushed him away, half-heartedly. He responded by kissing her.

'Don't you?' he repeated.

And this time he held her more tightly, so that the hard swelling of his manhood pressed against the base of her belly, reinforcing his message: I want you, I want you, I want you. And like it or not, you want me too.

'Bastard.' The word escaped from her as a juddering sigh, shaking her whole body. The word that signalled her submission.

Gabriel held her close, just stroking her again and again as if she were a pet animal, soothing her with kisses on her upturned face and bare shoulders.

'Hush, hush, everything's OK. I have you now. Everything's going to be just fine,' he repeated over and over again, weaving his mesmeric web of desire about Venetia.

Eyes half-open, she returned his kiss. Pleasure surged through her body at the heat of his touch, sweat trickling between her shoulder-blades and down into the small of her back.

'How is it that you make me want you?' she murmured. 'When you know I've made up my mind to be strong?'

'Some things are meant to be,' Gabriel replied. And he gathered her up in his arms, carrying her across to his downy-soft, king-size bed.

On their arrival at the hotel, Venetia had insisted on separate rooms. She'd been determined to resist Gabriel's advances and try to get their relationship back onto a professional footing. Gabriel, of course, had easily found a way round her insistence by booking a suite of rooms with interconnecting doors and balconies, making sure that temptation was never more than a footstep away.

Up till now, Venetia had been strong. She had kept her distance, done what she had to and no more. But now she could feel every last ounce of willpower ebbing away. Lazy, luxurious, erotic thoughts took over, echoing Gabriel's persuasive words: why not? Why deny yourself pleasure? Sex is a fundamental human need: why starve yourself of it? And the need flooded her whole being, taking over, turning her half-crazy.

They fell onto the bed together, hands roaming over each other's bodies, clutching and tearing at each other's clothes. Venetia clawed at the buttons on Gabriel's Dolce & Gabbana shirt. He scarcely seemed to notice or to care as the handsewn silk tore and the shirt fell open, baring his chest. He fumbled with his trouser belt, helping her unbuckle it, not wanting anything to get in the way of instant gratification.

Venetia pulled her halter-top off over her head, letting the hot, dry air caress her bare breasts. She reached down to unbutton her shorts but Gabriel was already tearing them open, tugging them down impatiently over her hips. She responded by unzipping Gabriel's flies and slipping her hand inside; thrilling with delicious wickedness as she discovered that he was naked underneath.

His bare flesh slid so easily between her fingers, as if it was the most natural thing in the world to want to masturbate him, caressing his stone-hard shaft with short, light strokes.

Breathing heavily now, Gabriel rolled onto his side so that they were facing each other, their naked bodies lightly glistening with a sheen of sweat. Gabriel tilted his pelvis back and forth, maddened by the butterfly softness of Venetia's caresses on his dick.

'Harder,' he panted.

'Patience is a virtue,' she teased him, her eyes flashing defiance. 'Don't you know that?' And she uncurled her fingers, releasing his shaft. A brutal ache of loss tore through him. He seized hold of her hand and carried it to his lips, opening his mouth and taking her index finger inside.

She squirmed and convulsed, taken aback by the powerful sensations Gabriel provoked as he sucked, licked and nibbled at her finger. As her mind drifted and hallucinated, she imagined that she had a penis, and Gabriel was sucking it, making it swell and harden, awakening it to whole new levels of sensitivity.

'Let go, Gabriel, let go.' She giggled crazily. 'Don't! It tickles too much.'

She tried pulling her finger from between his lips, but he wasn't giving up so easily. His eyes never left hers as he let her index finger escape, slick with wetness, only to capture her middle finger, swallowing it up to the hilt.

Her pulse raced, a cold shiver of excitement running from the nerve-centre of her hostage fingertip down along her wrist and arm until it joined the burning hunger in her belly. She writhed like a snake, but it was not until she lay very still, mesmerised by pleasure, that Gabriel let her escape from his tyrannical kiss.

He ran his tongue down from the tip of her index finger to the hollow of her palm, working the tip round and round as though he were massaging her with the slick wet head of his penis.

'You see, Venetia? I told you I know what you like. All you have to do is believe me. It's so easy.'

Easy. Yes, the easiest thing in the world, thought Venetia lazily, as Gabriel covered her breasts with tiny bites and kisses. Nothing could be easier than to give in to desire and do exactly what I feel. But at the last moment, Venetia's rebellious will kicked against her submission, and she pushed her lover away.

'I'm sorry, Gabriel, but no. I told you we should keep sex out of this. This is all wrong . . .'

Gabriel's expression changed. For a moment he looked almost concerned. 'Poor Venetia, you really don't understand yourself very well, do you?'

'Don't give me that! I understand myself well enough to know . . .'

'Shh.' His mouth covered hers, precluding all possibility of protest. Her body tensed, pushed against his, then fell back. It was useless. How could she tell him she didn't want him when it wasn't remotely true? Mentally, spiritually, emotionally, she loathed him. But physically . . . her poor body needed lust, desire, pleasure. It needed Gabriel Engelhart.

He slipped his thigh between hers and rubbed it against her pubic bone – gently, but just firmly enough to excite the half-swollen rosebud of her clitoris, making her own sweet juice well up from its ever-renewing spring.

Venetia responded by grinding her belly against the muscle-hardness of Gabriel's thigh, working herself up to a peak of burning, surging heat; bringing herself ever-closer to the crisis which had simmered inside her for too, too long. It felt good to know that if nothing else, she was in control of her own pleasure. And then, very close to the point of no return, Gabriel pulled away from her.

'You've had enough, I think.'

Venetia returned his gaze with a look of pure

loathing. 'What makes you so bloody sure that you know what I want?'

Gabriel ran his tongue up the side of her neck. 'I'm *sure* that you wanted to bring yourself off.'

There was something so dark, so very serious about Gabriel's words. Her eyes followed his hand as it reached out to the bedside cabinet and slid open the drawer. There was a jumble of colourful odds and ends inside – things she hadn't even realised were there.

'What . . .?'

Gabriel reached into the drawer and lifted out something very strange – something black and heavy, that jingled curiously as his hand closed about it.

'They're so perfect for you, Venetia. I had them made with you in mind. Aren't you flattered?'

Venetia gaped at Gabriel and edged slightly away. Something told her she had jumped feet-first into trouble. 'Look, I . . .'

Gabriel smiled as he kissed her and drew her back to him. 'Don't look so afraid. What's there to be afraid of?'

'Nothing – so let me go and get dressed.'

'No, no, no. You must learn to relax, Venetia. Look at them, aren't they the most beautiful things you've ever seen?'

He placed the things in her hand. She looked down at them, an icy shiver running like a cold finger down her spine. She was looking at a pair of medieval-style manacles, made from iron painted matt black and joined by a thick black chain.

'Put them on, Venetia.'

'You're joking!' She tried to thrust them back

into Gabriel's hands, but he closed her fingers over them.

'Try them. For me. How will you ever know the pleasure if you don't even try it?'

Venetia hardly knew how it happened. One moment she was shaking her head and telling Gabriel Engelhart that he could go take a hike; the next, he was fucking her so beautifully that all she could think of was the compelling need to thrust her backside against his belly and never stop . . .

'Oh. Oh, yes, yes,' she moaned as he drove into her, grinding her belly and nipples against the rough, embroidered linen bedspread as he took her from behind. His weight made the sensations brutal and sudden, squeezing and abrading them from her, making her cry out and scrabble with her fingernails on the wooden bedhead, helpless to escape the tyranny of her own pleasure.

When at last Gabriel allowed her to climax, she arched her back and roared with ecstasy, the wetness flooding out of her to form a dark, damp stain on the coverlet. In the dizzy afterglow she felt a light caress and then heard a metallic click.

'What . . . ?'

'It's what you want. I *know* it's what you want.'

Too late, she realised that Gabriel had taken advantage of her distraction to slip the manacles about her wrists. Her arms were gently imprisoned behind her back, rendering her almost helpless. Gabriel lifted her up and cradled her in his arms.

'You look breathtaking,' he whispered.

Venetia knew that she ought to feel fear – Gabriel was talking like a madman – but all she felt at this moment was excitement. Perhaps

311

Gabriel had been right after all. Perhaps all she really did crave, subconsciously, was to be his plaything, abdicating the responsibility for her own sexual satisfaction to his capricious will.

'Such a beautiful bondage,' Gabriel repeated, running his hands over Venetia's upturned breasts, their nipples erect and hard.

For all her unease, Venetia found her body responding to Gabriel's mad desire. The orgasm he had forced upon her had left her unsatisfied, craving more. Much more.

Gabriel stroked the back of her hair, kissing her forehead and her closed eyes. 'You make an exquisite slave.'

'I'm not your slave. I'm not anybody's slave.'

'Play the game with me, Venetia. Just this once. Let me show you what you're missing.'

Reaching into the drawer again, he took out a small glass jar. He unscrewed the top, and Venetia breathed in a curious, almost sickly scent, cloyingly sweet. It seemed to be a mixture of dozens of different perfumes – almond, chocolate, jasmine, orange blossom, patchouli, musk . . . As she watched, Gabriel used the creamy-white paste to anoint his penis.

'This is a gift for you, Venetia. A gift of perfect pleasure.'

Standing up before her, Gabriel took hold of Venetia's face, quite gently. She was not quite helpless. She could have struggled, but oddly, she didn't want to. The sweet aroma of the sticky white paste made her feel dizzy, light-headed, floaty . . .

As though by some secret reflex, her lips parted and she bent to take him into her mouth. He tasted good, obscenely good. His own scent mingled with the flower-sweet aromas of the unguent, melting on her tongue. Was the pleasure as strong for Gabriel as it was for her? She knew it must be, for she could hear him softly groaning, felt his shaft harden and twitch between her lips.

And that thought filled her with a lascivious joy. For even in bondage, there could be a secret power.

This little lust-fest really would have to stop, thought Venetia as she pushed and shoved her way through the Cairo streets. She didn't even like Gabriel Engelhart, let alone like him enough to want to play the obedient little sex-slave to his Caligula.

She was still at a loss to understand what it was that made her give in so easily to Gabriel's demands. And whatever else she felt for him, she knew she couldn't ever trust him. How many lies had he told her? How could she be sure that anything about him was what it seemed to be?

A deep feeling of unease ached in the hollow of Venetia's stomach. She sensed that there were hidden depths to Gabriel Engelhart; things she'd perhaps rather not know. He seemed to be able to exert an effortless power over people, things, money – and the longer she carried on working with him, the deeper she felt she was being pulled into the murky vortex of his life.

Yes, one thing was for certain; this would have to stop.

She walked on, past the big European stores and the pavement traders. It was good to be free of Gabriel for a few hours, but this afternoon she had drawn yet another blank. Despite the bizarre incident in the antique shop, she had unearthed precisely nothing of real value since they'd arrived in Cairo. Which was not improving Gabriel's temper, she reflected grimly as she spotted a pleasant-looking restaurant and headed towards it.

It was too hot to sit outside, and she stepped into the cool, twilit interior. It was crowded, a low hubbub of conversation subsiding suddenly at her arrival, then beginning again just as suddenly.

'Table for one, madam?'

'Yes, please.'

'You will dine in the ladies' section?'

Venetia met the waiter's gaze. She hated being banished to the back room with all the other women, convention or no convention.

'No, thank you.'

'But, madam . . .'

'No, thank you. I'll be fine in here.'

She was shown with some reluctance to a table by the wall. As her eyes grew accustomed to the twilight, she saw that the restaurant was stylishly decorated, and filled to the brim with curios of every kind – Arab embroideries, wall-hangings, shelves filled with ornamental brasses, horses' bridles, and pile after pile of old books, heaped up on shelves and tables around the diners.

As she ate grilled fish with okra, Venetia let herself relax a little. This wasn't a bad place at all: good food, decent air-conditioning, interesting decor – and no Gabriel Engelhart.

Venetia's gaze wandered to the pile of books on

a nearby shelf. She never could resist books, no matter how old, tatty or worthless. Scanning them, she identified that this batch were all three. Hardly surprising really. She looked away, then glanced back again, her gaze registering something, she wasn't quite sure what.

As she turned back to the books, she felt the hollow ache of excitement deep in her belly. No. Not here, in a downtown restaurant. It couldn't be. That would be just too silly for words.

But there was no denying the symbol tooled in gold leaf on the dark, age-worn leather: an ornate star within a circle, embossed on the upper outer corner of the binding.

She got to her feet and walked towards the shelves. Hands shaking, she reached up. But just as she was about to lift the book from the shelf, her hand met another. A man's hand. They touched, for an infinitesimal moment. Then drew away.

She swung round, and the blood drained from her face. She had not seen the man sitting there before, his table half-hidden by a carved wooden screen and potted ferns. As she watched, he took off his sunglasses and slipped them into the top pocket of his long, black jacket. Now that he stood beside her, his dark eyes challenging hers, his spare, athletic frame towering over her, she wondered how she could possibly have failed to notice him. His presence seemed to fill the whole restaurant.

'Esteban!' It could be no other.

The breath shuddered from her, the shock of seeing him again making her feel hot, cold, dizzy, afraid.

'I had not thought we would meet again.' Esteban's voice was quiet and calm, the hawkish features as cruelly beautiful as ever.

Venetia's fingers tightened about the book. She must remember why she had come here, chase these dark, seductive memories from her mind. But Esteban was quicker and stronger. He lifted the book down from the shelf. Venetia's mouth was dry with tension.

'Esteban, the book. Give it back to me.'

Esteban returned her gaze impassively. 'Why should I wish to give it to you, *petite anglaise*? It is what I have been searching for and at last I have found it.'

Venetia stared at him. 'The *Lore of Madali*? A medieval book of erotica? What would you want with a book of dirty pictures, Esteban? And just out of interest, what the hell do you think you're doing here?'

Esteban chuckled drily. 'I see that you are still the same Venetia.' There was a note of something soft, almost wistful, in his voice. 'Always so impulsive, so impetuous. Whatever makes you think I would be interested in a book of erotica? This is something very different.'

'I tell you, that is the *Lore of Madali*. It has Paulus Madalinus's sign on the cover, the star within a circle. Give it to me – I'll prove it to you.'

Seizing the book from Esteban, she laid it on the table and opened it. The scent of old parchment made her sneeze, and a single, dried flower fell onto the table top in a cloud of dust.

Venetia's face fell. There were no beautiful illuminated pages here. No erotic pictures. In fact, no pictures at all. Only page after page of tiny

316

handwriting, spidery and brown with age.

'No . . .' She sighed and closed the book. 'I guess you were right. This isn't the *Lore of Madali*.'

She sat down heavily. Esteban remained standing, flicking idly through the pages. She looked up at his face. His expression had changed, his face drained of the confident anticipation which had seemed to fill him only seconds before.

'Is something wrong, Esteban?'

'This . . . is not what I was looking for.'

'And what is that?'

He shook his head.

'We agreed to part, Venetia. My existence need not concern you any further.'

His dark eyes met hers but she looked away. No, no, she pleaded in the silence of her thoughts. Don't let this happen to you again. Don't let him back inside your heart, your body, your life. He's not for you. Not for you, not ever.

She forced herself to look up at him, hating him with all the force of her being; hating him for being here, now, when she had fought so hard to forget him. 'Why are you here, Esteban? In Cairo?'

Esteban sat down opposite, pushing back the collar-length mane of his glossy, blue-black hair.

'Serendipity?' The ironic twist of his sensual mouth maddened Venetia.

'Don't bullshit me, Esteban. I want to know.'

'I have told you, I am looking for something. A book.' He ran his long, slender fingers over the dusty pages. 'But not, alas, this one.'

'You've been following me. Spying on me.'

This time, there was no irony in Esteban's

317

voice. 'Not spying on you, Venetia. Watching over you.'

'Oh yeah. Like you really expect me to believe that, do you?'

'It is for you to choose what you believe.' His fingers brushed hers, cool against her fevered skin. 'Be careful, Venetia. Be careful, he is dangerous. He is poison.'

'I don't need your advice, Esteban. I don't need anything from you. I thought I made that perfectly clear, back in Valazur.'

Suddenly afraid that she would not be as strong as she had to be, Venetia got to her feet. She shoved the old book across the table towards Esteban. 'Here, you take it. It's no bloody use to me.'

Turning away, she threw a handful of change onto the table and walked towards the door. Looking back over her shoulder, she called, 'And don't you dare follow me again. Don't even bloody well think about it.'

Yet, even as she walked out into the blazing sunshine, she could feel Esteban's cool, dark eyes on her; and the inexorable pull of need, whispering to her to fall back into his arms.

Chapter Six

VENETIA TURNED OFF the taps and swished the foaming waters with her hand, testing the temperature. Just right.

With a sigh of release she stepped into the bath and slipped into the water, luxuriating in the abundance of warm, fragrant bubbles swirling about her naked body.

Gabriel was nowhere to be seen, which was fine by Venetia. He was out somewhere making money, and at last she could relax. She reached out for her glass of chilled white wine and let a few drops linger on her tongue before savouring the frisson of delight as they slithered down her throat. Slowly the tensions began to ease out of her taut muscles, and she lay back, allowing herself to let go.

Her mind wandered. She was back in Valazur, on the pine-scented hillside above Esteban's villa. Somewhere below, she could hear the sound of surf crashing against rocks.

She lay with Esteban, her head cradled in the crook of his arm. He was whispering to her as he caressed her naked body.

'Stay, Venetia. Stay . . . it will be so easy . . .'

She let her hand skate over her own flesh, imagining it was Esteban's hand, daydreaming of the coolness of Esteban's lips as they closed over the aching, yearning crest of her nipple.

'One kiss, and life and death will have no more meaning. One kiss, and only our passion will exist. For ever . . .'

In her daydream it was dusk. In the dark-blue light she looked up and saw Esteban's eyes glow a lustrous, soft black. His hands smoothed over her body, awakening her body to a symphony of sensations. She sighed, and he bent to kiss her throat . . .

She moved in the warm bathwater, letting it explore her body, kissing the apex of her thighs, swirling about her back and legs. Rolling over onto her belly, she imagined that Esteban was stroking her back, darting cool, moist kisses from her neck to the base of her spine, floating with her in a deep-blue, tropical ocean.

Oh Esteban, she thought. Esteban, why did you follow me here? She remembered the night of their parting, when he had freed her from her obligation. She had sworn, if he helped her to rescue her twin sister, that she would repay him with the price of her soul, becoming a vampire like him, sharing his dark prison of eternity. But something in Esteban, some residue of nobility, had cared too much for her to force her to be his unwilling captive.

And so they had parted, Venetia walking away into the first pink shadows of the rising sun. Esteban had sworn that they would never meet again, yet here he was in Cairo; awakening so many memories and so many more fears and desires. Reminding her that he was the only man she had ever really cared about, enough to think of sharing eternity with him.

A sound made her open her eyes and look round. Her heart sank. Gabriel was coming into the bathroom – *her* bathroom – through the connecting door from his suite. She knew she should have locked the door.

He took off his cream linen jacket and slung it over the towel rail, then peeled off his shirt and kicked off his shoes.

'Mind if I join you?'

'Does it make any difference if I do?'

Gabriel frowned. 'Whatever's making you tense, there's no need to take it out on me.'

Unzipping his trousers and stepping out of them, he walked over to the bath and switched on the whirlpool. Bubbling, swirling eddies of warm, foamy water spurted hard against Venetia's body. It felt nice enough. But it would have felt nicer alone.

Gabriel got into the bath behind Venetia, and wound his legs around her hips. He began massaging her shoulders. She winced at the sudden raw ache.

'Mmm, you're tense, very tense. Bad day?'

'Oh, you know,' replied Venetia evasively. She had no desire to antagonise Gabriel again. 'How about you?'

'Nothing on the *Lore of Madali*. But I did a few deals, bought myself some *very* desirable Minoan curios, would you believe. They'll look fabulous in some rich idiot's penthouse. I'll charge him five

321

times what they're worth and he'll think I'm doing him a favour.'

Venetia decided that she disliked him more than ever. 'You have no principles at all, have you?'

Gabriel grinned. 'Not so's you'd notice. Principles are for people who don't mind being poor.' He gave Venetia's backside an exploratory squeeze. 'You really must drop the holier-than-thou stuff, Venetia. You're missing out on all the best things in life.'

'I get by.'

'Ah, but I could make you . . . anything you want to be.'

'And all I have to do is exactly what you tell me, right?'

'Right.'

'Dream on, Gabriel. I'll screw you for the hell of it while we're out here, but become your slave for life? No way. I have more respect for myself.'

Gabriel changed tack. His hard cock-tip nudged suggestively between Venetia's buttocks. 'I want you,' he whispered.

'So?' Venetia tried to sound cool and in control, even though her heart was thumping.

'So I usually get what I want. Especially when it happens to be what the other person wants too.'

Looking away from him, Venetia could almost, but not quite, imagine that it was Esteban in the bath with her, Esteban's hands toying with her buttocks, Esteban's beautiful pierced dick pushing its way into the deep, wet furrow of her womanhood.

Venetia did not wait for Gabriel to make his next move. She offered up herself to the invader, taking it far, far inside her, engulfing it, imposing

322

the tyranny of her own pleasure upon it.

'Mmm, that feels good. You're a clever woman, Venetia.' Gabriel slid in and out of her with long, smooth strokes. 'Tell me about your fantasies.'

'My fantasies!'

'Your erotic daydreams, your castles in the air. What do you fantasise about when you want to make yourself come?'

The word 'Esteban' almost rose to her lips, but she swallowed it down. 'Making love on the beach. In the surf, right at the edge of the sea.'

'Tell me.' Gabriel pumped in and out of her with rhythmic precision, controlling everything, making her feel pleasure she didn't want to feel.

'You know, rolling over and over on the wet, pebbly sand, with the waves breaking right over me and drenching me as I fuck.'

'And what else?'

'Screwing in a mechanic's workshop.'

Gabriel chuckled. His fingers tightened on her buttocks. 'Go on.'

'The floor's all oily and muddy, and he's wearing these really old, tatty overalls. They're torn, and I can see his body through the holes. He's so strong . . . it's obvious he takes care of his body.'

'Really, Venetia? I can't say I'm surprised. Marcus Hale said you went for the brainless, musclebound type.'

His right hand slid round Venetia's belly and down into the thickly-forested glade of her sex. She knew he was playing her like some child's toy, and hated herself for going along with it. But it felt good and in any case, she was helpless to resist.

323

He slipped a finger between Venetia's thighs, sliding into her intimacy to toy mercilessly with her clitoris. She made no sound, but her body shook with need.

'Tell me more.'

'I . . . I've come to collect my car, but I can't afford to pay for all the work he's done. He . . .' She panted, finding it hard to control her breathing as lust took over her body as well as her thoughts. 'He tells me there's another way to pay . . .

'He touches me, and he leaves oily patches all over my best blouse. It's all dirty now, I'll have to take it off. And my skirt . . . I've torn it on a rusty nail, and there are ladders in my stockings.

'He helps me to undress. I can smell the oil and the sweat on him. His hair is full of grease, and there are black smears on his cheeks. When he kisses me I can taste engine oil and two-stroke. Somewhere in the background, I can hear motorbikes revving up, and I know there are other people watching us. Other mechanics, waiting for their turn . . .'

Gabriel growled with pleasure. He had known, instinctively, that Venetia Fellowes was the woman to satisfy his every desire – and Gabriel Engelhart didn't make mistakes. He made no apologies for being insensitive, even brutal at times; but he truly believed that he knew, better than any other man, how to give this sensual creature the pleasure she craved. And that knowledge gave him the right to exercise a unique power over her.

He had imagined her in a thousand different settings. Dancing naked for him at some desert oasis, bright jewels piercing her navel and nipples. Making mad love with him in some tropical lagoon, their bodies tumbling weightlessly in the water as their mouths met and drank in the elixir of their lust. Riding bareback on a half-broken stallion, her head thrown back and her mouth open in a silent scream of joy as the rough horsehair abraded her soft intimacy, torturing her flesh to the brink of orgasm. And now this new, seductive image, so fresh in his mind . . .

His penis tingled with the onrush of pleasure. With a massive effort of self-control, he managed to prevent himself climaxing. The mental picture of Venetia offering herself to this oil-smeared mechanic with his rough hands and tattered clothes was almost too much to bear. But he wanted to hear more.

'Tell me what you do next. *All* of it.'

Venetia felt light-headed, pleasantly wicked. She had never told anyone about her fantasies before. Somehow it didn't seem to matter if Gabriel knew.

'We're undressing each other. I'm so hungry for him, my fingers are all fumbling and useless. I can't get his buttons undone. His hands are stripping off my blouse, it's sticking to my skin with all the oil. And still I'm trying to undress him. I can't think of anything but the thought of what it will be like to see and feel him naked.

'He unfastens my skirt and I step out of it. It's a hot day and I'm not wearing any panties. So I'm standing in front of him wearing nothing but my bra, white stockings and suspenders, and high-heeled shoes. He wants to take off my bra, but all I want is to get him naked.

' "Help me," I beg him, and he smiles. He rips open the front of his boiler suit and peels it away from his body. He's sooo beautiful, I knew he would be. His body's perfect, like a statue in bronze or polished stone. I run my fingers over his muscles, I can't believe they're real. I don't look down. I don't want to spoil the moment. I want to enjoy the waiting . . .

'But he wants me. He's hungry. He takes my face in his hands and kisses my eyelids, my nose, my lips, my throat. Then he tilts it downwards and makes me look.

' "I want you," he says. "I want your lips round my dick." '

'He excites me so much, I just fall to my knees and tear down his briefs with my teeth. He's unbelievable . . .'

'He's big?' murmured Gabriel, nuzzling into the back of Venetia's neck as he moved, very slowly, inside her.

'Mmm, yes. Huge . . . incredible. And I want so much to touch it and taste it.'

'My mouth waters for him, my nipples ache, my clitoris is swelling and I'm rubbing my thighs together, desperate to bring myself off. I open my mouth. He pushes forward a little, and I panic. What if it won't fit inside? I resist, but he takes me ever so gently and whispers to me: "Go on, it's all right. Trust me." Slowly I open my mouth and his cock-tip slides into me. Oh, but it tastes like heaven. So strong, so masculine, the taste and the texture and the odour of raw sex.

'He's eager, I can feel him trembling, only just managing to hold back. But I don't wait for him to take me. I take him. I open my mouth as wide as it will go, and I swallow him up, impaling myself on the beautiful spike of his manhood.

'For a few seconds I panic. I think I'm going to gag, throw up, spoil everything. But it's incredible, it's so perfect. He slides further and further into me, he's pushing against the back of my throat, he's in me into the hilt and I'm cradling his balls and they're so heavy and full of juice. I'm kneeling in a pool of filthy engine oil, but I don't care. All I can think about is pleasure . . .'

Gabriel listened to her, his heart thumping, the temperature rising. It required a superhuman effort not to come, and he could feel Venetia shaking, tense with the expectancy of orgasm. But he wanted to hold her there, keep them both on the edge just that little longer . . .

'What now, Venetia? What are you doing?'

'I'm sucking his dick. It's getting harder, I can taste a little trickle of salty liquid on my tongue. Now he's pulling out – I don't want him to, but he's sliding out from between my lips. And now he's masturbating as I suck his balls, spurting his hot white cream all over my face . . .

'And we're falling onto the filthy floor. He's still hard. I'm lying on my side and he's facing me, pushing between my thighs, burying himself inside me. He knows how close I am to orgasm.'

She shuddered, so very close now. Longing for Gabriel to press harder on her clitoris, she ground herself against his finger. But he held back, keeping her hungry, depriving her of the last, incredible explosion.

'There's someone else now,' he breathed into her ear. 'Another man, can't you feel him?'

'Feel him . . . yes . . .'

'He's behind you. He's lying on the ground and he's caressing your backside. He wants to fuck you, Venetia. He wants to fuck you as well.'

Venetia trembled as Gabriel's fingertip pushed into her. Sweat trickled down her face; she felt weak, wondered if any moment now her strength would give out and she would disappear, splashing and gasping, beneath the fragrant bathwater.

'Gabriel. Gabriel, I can't take any more!'

'Of course you can. Can you feel him? You have two lovers now, the lover who's screwing your beautiful pussy, and the lover who's pushing hard into your backside. Doesn't it feel good to be taken by two men at once? Doesn't it . . . ?'

As Gabriel's finger slid inside her to the knuckle, Venetia yielded to the power of her need. Orgasm flashed like white lightning, the first, thunderous explosion followed by wave upon wave of pleasure.

Gabriel held her tightly as she climaxed, the pleasure of his own orgasm overshadowed by the pleasure of knowing how much sensual domination he had over this young woman who believed, so wrongly, that she did not need him.

The following evening, Venetia found herself unexpectedly alone with her thoughts. Thoughts of work, of how to find a solution to the problem of Gabriel – and thoughts of Esteban.

Since their meeting in the coffee house, Venetia had tried again and again to rid herself of his memory. She cursed him in the silence of her heart – the same heart that ached for him to return and tell her that everything had been a bad dream. And she cursed herself for not being strong enough to forget him.

And what of Gabriel Engelhart? Right now, he was far more of a problem to her than Esteban. She wondered how a man she disliked so much could have such a powerful sexual hold over her. When she was away from him, she knew exactly what she was going to say, everything that she would do to distance herself from him. But as soon as he came to her, kissed her, awoke unwilling desires within her, she became his prisoner again. It made her angry, frustrated, and just a little afraid.

She picked up Gabriel's note and read it again. It was short, but concise: *Order dinner to be brought to my suite. I will join you later. G.*

At eight-thirty, dinner arrived on a trolley, accompanied by a rather handsome young waiter in a crisp white uniform. He looked around the room, puzzled.

'Dinner for two, madam?'

'It's all right, my . . . friend will be joining me shortly.' She pressed a tip into the waiter's hand and shooed him away, grateful to be on her own again. She almost dared to hope that Gabriel's business deals might keep him out so late that she would get to spend the whole night on her own. And tonight, she would remember to lock the connecting door. Tomorrow, perhaps, she would suggest to Gabriel that it would be best for her to stay somewhere else. She didn't need this luxury. All she needed was a room to sleep and work in, a telephone, simple food . . .

And I don't need you, whispered a voice in her head. A cold finger stroked down the back of

Venetia's neck as she wondered how Gabriel would react. Maybe it would be best if she cut her losses, packed her bags one day when he was out, and headed off somewhere, anywhere, to begin all over again.

The sound of a key turning in the lock brought an end to Venetia's train of thought. She looked up to see the door swinging open, and Gabriel standing in the doorway.

He looked good, there was no denying it. His golden hair, bleached whiter by the hot sun, glistened in the soft light. His tanned skin, his regular features, his blue eyes – he was the stuff of every hot-blooded woman's dreams. But he made her uneasy, with that steady gaze, that enigmatic expression which made her wonder what new 'games' he had in store for her.

'Good day?' she asked as she spooned chilled gazpacho into a fine porcelain dish.

'Very . . . instructive.'

'Did you find out anything about the book?'

'Not as such.'

Gabriel walked round behind Venetia's chair and pushed aside her hair, baring her neck. He began stroking and massaging her shoulders. 'You look tired,' he commented. 'As if you've been overdoing things.'

Venetia shrugged. 'Oh, you know. I went to that museum on the other side of Cairo, and showed them the picture. They said they'd never heard of the *Lore of Madali*, but I'm not sure I believed them. I could have sworn there was something the curator wasn't telling me.'

'Quite.' Gabriel squeezed Venetia's shoulders so hard that she winced. 'It's so difficult to know who is telling the truth.'

She slewed her head round to look up at him. 'What do you mean?'

'Just that.' Gabriel walked round to his chair and sat down. 'What did you do?'

'I went to the museum, I told you.'

'And yesterday? What did you do yesterday afternoon?'

Venetia stiffened. 'I told you.'

'Tell me again.'

'I visited practically every antiquities dealer in Cairo.'

'And?'

Venetia hesitated for a fraction of a second. 'Nothing.'

Gabriel put down his spoon, very coldly and calmly. He looked Venetia full in the face. 'You're lying.'

'Why should I lie?'

'Because you have something to hide? Another man, perhaps? A man you met in a restaurant?'

Venetia's blood froze. Esteban. He must have seen her with Esteban. But . . . 'How the hell . . .?'

'I had you followed. You could say I'm protecting my investment.'

Incensed now, Venetia got to her feet. 'I don't have to tell you every damn thing I do and everyone I speak to.'

Gabriel ignored her attack and went on talking. 'I wouldn't have thought that loser was your type, Venetia – but then again, I've known you long enough now to know that you'll screw any man if you're hot enough. That's right, isn't it? You're just a slut at heart.'

'How dare you!' She raised her hand to slap

him across the face, but he caught it in mid air.

'Did you let him fuck you?'

Venetia glared back at Gabriel, too angry to be afraid. 'You make me sick.'

'Well, did you?'

She was almost tempted to say yes, of course she had, she was a slut wasn't she? 'Go to hell!'

This time she succeeded in freeing herself from Gabriel's grip. She backed away, but he came after her. 'You're mine, Venetia. Mine. I paid for you to come here, I even paid for the dress you're wearing. You *owe* me.'

They struggled, Gabriel trying to force his lips against hers. When her eyes met Gabriel's, a peculiar, hypnotic warmth made Venetia's head swim, taking the edge off her anger, making her feel . . . sexy. Surprisingly sexy.

'I've got to have you, Venetia. Got to have you.'

'No. No, Gabriel.'

'Don't betray me. You've no right to betray me, it makes no sense, you want me, not some other man . . .'

She forced herself to look away, not to meet his gaze. He seized her by the hair and twisted it into an imprisoning rope, but as he pulled her head round, she spat in his face.

A white blob of spittle hit him on the cheek, and trickled slowly down the side of his face. As though shocked into a realisation of what he was doing, Gabriel let go of her and stood stock-still, the colour draining from his face. His lips moved, forming soundless words.

Venetia backed away, never taking her eyes off Gabriel, certain that he would make some move to drag her back. 'Don't you dare touch me, ever again,' she whispered hoarsely. 'If you lay one finger on me . . .'

Gabriel took one step forward. Venetia could not read his expression. It seemed to be caught between shock, anger and fear.

'But Venetia . . .' he began, very quietly, very calmly, reaching out his hand.

But Venetia shook her head. 'No more buts,' she replied. 'Just keep your hands off me, understand?'

And slamming the interconnecting door behind her, she locked it and threw the key onto the bed.

Chapter Seven

THE NILE CRUISER slid slowly upstream. From the banks on either side, peasant children watched amid the ruins of ancient tombs and temples.

But Venetia paid them little heed. Sitting in the saloon, she toyed half-heartedly with a gin and tonic, rolling the glass between her fingers as she pondered the mess she had made of everything.

The first mistake had been in letting Marcus Hale persuade her to have anything to do with Gabriel Engelhart. The second – and it was a big one – had been to get involved with Gabriel. What had she been thinking of? Why hadn't she just stayed on in Malta, enjoying Demetrios's uncomplicated company until the project finally ran out of money and she moved on to another job?

She took a sip of her drink. Of course, the third mistake had been to expect Gabriel to behave like a normal human being. She should have guessed that someone as obsessive as Engelhart would 'keep an eye on' her. Still, at least she had got away from him, if only for a few days; a breathing space to sort herself out.

Pushing her empty glass across the bar, she called out, 'Same again, please.'

'Certainly, madam.' The barman peered at her as he cut a thin sliver from a fresh lemon. 'You are not going ashore with the others? It is a beautiful day.'

'It sure is, honey,' cut in a rotund American matron in loud check trousers and a sun-hat. 'Say, why don't you come along with Eddie and me? We're gonna take a ride on a camel.'

Venetia couldn't suppress a smile of sympathy for the camel. 'Thank you, you're very kind, but no. I think I'll just stay here and laze about.'

Taking her drink, Venetia walked across to the window and sat down. A moment later, she became aware of someone sitting down next to her. She ignored the presence until a familiar voice cut into her thoughts.

'I warned you about him, Venetia. Gabriel Engelhart is a dangerous man. A man without honour.'

Shocked, she turned to see Esteban sitting beside her, a glass of red wine in his hand, his eyes enigmatic behind mirror shades.

'What the hell . . .?'

'Did I shock you? That was not my intention.' Esteban sipped his wine and grimaced. 'A very poor vintage. Not even adequate for American tourists.'

'How did you get here?'

'That is not important.'

'I told you not to follow me.'

'And what if I said I simply happened to be in the same place at the same time?'

'Then I'd say you were lying. So why don't you just get on with it, and tell me what you're doing here?'

'Let us just say that someone has to ensure you do not get yourself into any more trouble.'

'I told you, Esteban, I don't need this! I don't need anybody's help, and especially not yours.'

Esteban seemed perfectly unruffled. He looked immaculate as ever, thought Venetia; dressed in a loose-fitting shirt of fine white lawn and skintight black leather trousers that clung to his hips and thighs.

'How long has it been since I last saw you, *petite anglaise*? A year? Two?'

'Almost two, for what it's worth.'

Don't make me think about it, please, please, don't make me, Venetia begged silently. But it was too late. All the old feelings were flooding through her, the memories of passion and danger crowding out every other thought in her head.

'Time is a difficult concept for me,' commented Esteban. 'Days and nights . . . each one is but the tiniest stitch in the fabric of eternity.' He turned to look at her, but he did not take off his glasses. Venetia found herself wondering if his eyes betrayed more emotion than his handsome yet impassive face. 'For me, as you know, eternity is a reality. I cannot escape it.'

'Why have you followed me here?' repeated Venetia.

'To speak with you.' He paused. 'And then I will never contact you again, if that is your wish. You have my word.'

Venetia did not reply. She could not. How could she speak without betraying the tumult of conflicting emotions within her? Esteban moved closer, laying his hand lightly upon hers. It felt cool as marble, yet its touch burned like a steady flame.

'We had a bargain once. I agreed to help you to rescue your sister, and in return . . .'

Fear flashed through Venetia. She drew her hand sharply away. 'You freed me from that bargain, Esteban. The debt is paid. I owe you nothing.'

He nodded. 'I do not deny it. But you feel no regret?'

His voice was soft and warm, gentle as the breeze wafting across the river. She felt uncertain, confused, afraid of the emotions which would not go away.

'Regret?' She tried to sound incredulous. 'You gave me back my life, Esteban. Why would I regret that?'

'But immortality, Venetia. Think of it. Never to die . . .'

She looked across at him and, very deliberately, reached up and took off his sunglasses. He flinched slightly in the bright sunshine, his sensitivity to light the only outward sign that Esteban was not as other men.

'Look at me, Esteban. Look me in the eyes and tell me that you do not regret what you are. Look at me, and swear that what you suffer is not a curse.'

He did not look away, but Venetia saw the shadow of a very old, very deep wound pass across his eyes.

'Eternity is a long time. And a man may regret many things if he is alone.'

337

Their fingers met. The touch brought everything back; and for the first time in two years, Venetia admitted to herself what she had never admitted to Esteban. That she loved him. Loved with a raw, violent, enduring passion which reached out to him in spite of her determination to reject him. That she had loved him almost to the damnation of her eternal soul . . .

Esteban's lips brushed her cheek, her closed eyes, her lips; then darted kisses down her throat. Venetia felt the pain of longing, a burning ache in her belly. But as his kiss lingered on her throat a moment too long, she drew away.

'There can never be anything between us, Esteban. It was you who said so, don't you remember? That first night . . .'

That was before I lost my reason, thought Esteban. Before I met you, *petite anglaise*, before you came and showed me not what I am, but what I might have been. With deep regret, he lifted Venetia's hand to his lips, kissed it and let it go.

'What if I was not as I am now?' he said quietly.

'I don't understand.'

'What if I was as other men? Mortal, as you are?'

'That's crazy, Esteban. It's impossible, you know it is.' She turned away. 'No, never. There could never be any hope for us.'

Esteban infuriated her by smiling. 'So headstrong, *petite anglaise*. Always so very sure that you are right.'

Petite anglaise. Only Esteban had ever called her that. Had ever *dared* call her that. She felt the tiny hairs on the back of her neck bristle, making the skin tingle. 'There's no point in this, Esteban. What are you trying to do? Torment me? Drive me crazy?'

'On the contrary, Venetia. I am trying to open your mind to reality. No, not that. To possibilities.'

She looked at him sharply. 'Is this some kind of joke?'

'You should know me better than that by now.' Esteban held his wine glass up to the light. The red liquid within seemed to swirl and glow with an inner life, tantalisingly deep and distant. He snapped his fingers, and the red wine turned a pale, lustrous yellow. 'Things are not always as they seem, *petite anglaise*.'

'Don't try to trick me, Esteban. I won't let you hurt me, not again.'

'Open your mind, Venetia. That is all I ask.'

Venetia turned away, irritated and confused. Why did Esteban have to talk in riddles? Come to that, why did he have to be here at all? She turned back to tell him what she really felt: that she didn't need this, that above all she didn't need *him*.

'Esteban, you . . .'

Her voice petered out. Esteban was gone. His chair was empty, but on the seat lay something Venetia had seen before. A book, heavy and leather-bound, bearing the symbol of a golden star within a circle, embossed in the top right-hand corner.

The barman called to her across the room.

'Your friend had gone, madam? I did not see him go.'

'I . . . no.' Venetia pushed her glass across the bar counter. 'Give me another. A double.'

As the barman poured the drink, Venetia

339

reached out and stroked the leather binding of the old book. It was the one she and Esteban had almost come to blows over in the restaurant. The one she had been only too glad to let him have, once she'd realised that it wasn't the *Lore of Madali*. But what could it possibly contain that would be of interest to Esteban? He'd said himself that it wasn't the medieval grimoire he had been looking for, just some tedious old diary. And why had he brought it here. . .?'

'Your drink, madam.'

She took a sip of the cold liquid. It tasted fruity, a little acid, the iciness searing her throat as she swallowed.

Opening the book, she saw an embroidered silk ribbon marking a page. She flipped through the dusty, yellowed leaves until she reached the place. It was just another diary entry. Just another boring day in some uninteresting person's forgotten life. But there was also a note in Esteban's hand, attached to the silk bookmark:

'Read and understand, *petite anglaise*. Read and believe that all things may be possible. Esteban.'

'Rien ne va plus.'

The croupier called in the stakes, and a dozen pairs of eyes watched the roulette wheel spin, laden with their hopes and fears. Fortunes were won and lost every night in the casino at the Hotel Oasis, absolutely the most exclusive gambling club in the Nile delta.

The hotel had been built in the mid-nineteenth century, in the days of colonialism and patronage; and it still retained a certain crumbling grandeur, a golden decadence enhanced by the individualism of its patrons. Professional gamblers mingled with aristocrats, rogues and chancers, nameless adventurers passing through, never to be seen here again.

Esteban was at home here. In the centuries since vampirism had cursed him to eternal life, he had found ways and means of getting by. He lived quietly in his villa above Valazur, spending his nights in the casinos and gambling clubs, earning a good living and relieving the boredom of immortality. No one asked questions about the dark-haired, olive-skinned stranger who lived on the hill above the sea. No one questioned that a man might live from decade to decade and never change, never age. No one questioned him because he had taught them well. He had taught them to fear him.

The man to his right at the poker table – a fat Lebanese with as many gold rings as he had fingers – slapped a wad of notes down on the table, taking a self-satisfied pull on his cigar.

'Fifty.'

Esteban peeled ten notes from the roll at his side and laid them neatly on the table, pushing them towards the centre.

'I'll raise you five hundred.'

A ripple of interest ran round the table. Faces searched his, certain that they could read a clue there. Was he bluffing? Esteban's expression remained enigmatic, unfathomable. He was an excellent poker player. But then again, he had had seven hundred years in which to perfect the art.

He glanced down at the cards in his hand. The Queen of Hearts. Of course; it was as he had thought. This time he allowed himself a smile, laying down the royal flush and raking in his winnings. 'If you gentlemen will excuse me for a moment.'

A hand touched his arm, and a gruff voice interjected, 'Nobody leaves this table until I'm good and ready.'

Esteban fixed the Lebanese with a cold-eyed stare. 'Take your hands off me.'

'Sit down and play the game.'

Esteban let out an impatient sigh. He had been aware all along of the knife concealed in the man's sleeve, but had hoped to avoid this unpleasantness. The blade glinted in the Lebanese's hand. With a single, swift movement Esteban seized the knife by the blade and twisted it out of his fingers. The Lebanese winced, partly in pain, partly in astonishment that this tall, rangy loner could carry such strength in his spare frame. His eyes widened as Esteban wiped his bloody fingers on a napkin. Seconds later, the thin knife-cut had healed without trace.

Pocketing his winnings, Esteban crossed the salon and walked out into the main foyer. He felt for the card in his pocket, and walked on.

She was there, as he had known she would be, more beautiful even than he had remembered her. Her tall, slender frame was flattered by the ice-blue sheath dress, with its froth of pale silk swishing behind her on the polished parquet floor and its low-cut, décolleté bodice. A diamanté necklace sparkled at her throat, a single ruby-red drop caressing the soft valley between her breasts.

The Queen of Hearts.

He ran the tip of his tongue across his parched lips.

Venetia turned and saw him. Then walked towards him, slowly, hesitantly. Esteban greeted her almost warily, nodding his acknowledgement of her presence. 'I . . . hoped you would come.'

Venetia shook her head. 'You knew I would come.'

Esteban's grey eyes met hers and a shiver of recognition passed between them. 'Yes. Yes, you are right.' He looked at Venetia and knew that she had read the diary, every word. Knew that she had understood.

'Walk with me,' said Venetia. 'There are things I need to talk to you about, things I need to ask you . . .'

Esteban shook his head.

'We will not speak of these things now. There will be a time to talk. Tonight . . .' His eyes caressed her, running over her skin, taking in every sweet curve of her body. 'Tonight I wish to know you again. To remember the smell and the taste of you.'

They walked out into the hotel gardens: a riot of half-wild flowers and trees, tumbling down to the river's edge. The air was very still, very calm, the sky vast and starry. They walked together, very close but not quite touching. It was as though there was some invisible force which both drew and repelled them; made it as impossible for them to exist together as apart.

'Gabriel Engelhart – you and he are lovers.' It was a statement, not a question.

'What business is that of yours?' Venetia's voice quavered. She could not lie to Esteban, only

343

evade his questions.

'But you *are* lovers.'

'We were,' Venetia admitted. 'Not any more. I've left him.'

Esteban sighed.

'I warned you, *petite anglaise*. I warned you and you laughed in my face.'

She turned towards him, her face half in shadow and half in light. 'It *was* you in the dream, wasn't it?'

'Perhaps. Perhaps not.'

'There are things even you can't protect me from, Esteban. Things I have to discover for myself.'

'Even if they bring you into mortal danger?'

'What is life without danger, Esteban?'

He looked into her face and felt the huge, juggernaut force of his obsession, crushing and devouring him. Without her, time stretched before him like an empty road through a waterless desert.

'Walk with me.'

He took her arm and led her down cracked stone steps, into a secluded glade between date palms. At its centre lay an irregularly-shaped pool lined with black marble, surrounded by the broken pillars and tumbling stones of an ancient civilisation, dragged here by some well-meaning but ignorant colonial to provide 'atmosphere'. Esteban despised ignorant people – and yet hadn't he been ignorant himself, once? It was his own arrogant stupidity which had created him as he now was: a man of power, with no power over his own existence.

Stone benches were arranged about the pool.

Esteban motioned to Venetia to sit. He stood beside the water, gazing into the middle-distance, breathing in the scents and sounds of the night. His night. Letting the darkness soothe his pain.

'When you left Valazur,' he began, 'I made up my mind to despise you. I had been wrong about you. You were nothing but an empty-headed *anglaise*, just like your sister Cassie.'

'You had every right to despise me. After all, I had refused you what you wanted, and you *always* get what you want.'

He laughed, turning to look at Venetia over his shoulder. His eyes glittered in the darkness like black diamonds.

'Always so spirited, so *charmante*, so *ironique*. And you must know that I do not despise you, that I cannot despise you. That I . . .' He did not speak the word in his heart, it was not fitting. Could love exist where the heart had long since turned to hollow blackness? 'It is good to see you once more, Venetia Fellowes.'

Venetia got to her feet and walked across to join him beside the pool.

'I tried to forget you,' she whispered. 'I tried so hard. How can you come back and do this to me?'

'You are free to go, if that is what you wish. I will do nothing to hold you here.'

They stood in silence for a few moments. Venetia heard the sound of her own heart thumping in the silence, certain that Esteban must be able to hear it too, that he must feel nothing but scorn for her. And she wanted so much to hate him for forcing his way back into her life. But now, after what had happened on the Nile boat, reason seemed to have evaporated, leaving only the passion. The white-hot, searing passion which drew her to him as she had never been drawn to any man. She knew the danger, she knew the impossibility; but Esteban was like an addiction. How could she live without him, now that he had found her once again?

'But you know that I will stay. Why are you always right, Esteban?' she demanded, half-bitterly, half in humour.

'Not always. I thought you would stay with me before, remember that. I was so sure you could not resist me.'

Esteban plucked a flower and cast it onto the dark, shimmering surface of the pool. It bobbed on the surface for a few moments, swirling on the undercurrents like a whirling dancer; then was drawn into the depths and lost.

'You read the marked passages in the diary.'

'Yes.'

'Then you know that what I crave is not impossible.' He reached out and took Venetia by the wrists. His grip was vice-tight.

'You're hurting me, Esteban.'

He seemed not to notice. He was lost in her eyes, lost in his own words.

'It is *not impossible*. Do you know what that means?'

'But Esteban, you're talking about an old diary, we don't know that it's true, we don't even know if the book is authentic . . .' Venetia didn't even believe herself. She knew that Esteban could hear the excitement in her voice, knew that she dared to hope, as he did. 'Let's face it, we don't even know if Marcus Almenius existed, let alone whether this is really the diary of his travels.'

'If I were not a vampire . . .'

'Don't say it, Esteban.'

'If this curse could be torn from me, Venetia . . . I would endure any pain, any torment . . .'

No other words passed between them. Words could not express the feelings which surged through their bodies, the hunger which could only be expressed through touch, and kiss, and caress.

Esteban took Venetia in his arms, lifting her up as though she were light as a feather, holding her aloft so that she seemed to fly above him like a pale blue angel, her dress falling in soft folds about him. For a fleeting moment they were no longer joined to the earth. They were incorporeal beings, supernatural spirits tumbling and soaring in the warm darkness of the starry sky, free and powerful and unfettered.

Pulling her down towards him, Esteban crushed his lips against hers. Venetia met his kiss hungrily, her belly filled by a ravenous need to join her body to Esteban's. She knew it was crazy, knew it might even be a trick. One kiss at her throat – one small bite from those sharp teeth; the warm wetness of fresh blood, and she would be his for ever, lured into immortality as a moth is lured into the fatal brightness of the candle flame.

But in these blissful moments, Venetia cared nothing for danger. She pressed her mouth against Esteban's, tasting the coolness of his saliva mingling with hers, her tongue and his jousting, thrusting, intertwining as their bodies remembered and explored and exulted.

Leading Venetia by the hand, Esteban walked slowly down the steps which led into the pool.

The water was only waist-deep, but its coolness made Venetia shiver deliciously as it lapped about her ankles, her calves, her thighs. For a fleeting instant she thought of her dress – her one, good evening dress – it would be ruined. Then the thought faded away into insignificance. All that mattered, all that existed in the here and now, was the desire.

'Trust me.'

Esteban's words sounded in her head like the shimmer of a cymbal, a spreading vibration, echoing again and again.

One hand was behind her head, tilting it back so that he could plant more and still more kisses on her willing mouth; the other was sliding down the zipper at the back of her evening gown.

She wriggled her spine to help him, and the zipper glided down with a soft sigh, baring her back to the soft night air.

Her fingers reached out, smoothing down Esteban's back. His long, thigh-length black jacket was cut tightly to the contours of his tall, slim, almost rangy body. She felt the hardness of muscle. He wriggled out of his jacket and it slipped from him into the water, floating on the surface like a black shadow.

Underneath, Esteban was wearing a loose-fitting evening shirt, the cool, crisp cotton slightly moist with sweat. Venetia's fingers ruched up the back of his shirt, hungry for him. Despite the heat of the day his flesh felt cool and smooth.

Esteban peeled away the bodice of Venetia's evening dress and its own heaviness sent it slithering softly down her body, into the water beneath. She heard herself giggle with exhilaration, stepping out of the dress and standing before her lover in strapless ivory basque and stockings, framing tiny lace briefs which offered tantalising glimpses of golden-blonde curls.

Esteban did not unfasten the hooks at the back of Venetia's basque. Instead, he slid his hands into the cups and cradled her breasts with a sensual tenderness. She moaned softly as he stroked the flat of his thumb across her nipple, making it pout and blush with sheer pleasure.

There was a familiar sensation of wetness between Venetia's thighs. She rubbed them together, delighting in the excitement, each soft frou-frou of stockinged thigh making the hood of her clitoris slide gently back and forth, driving her to new peaks of excitement.

Her fingers fumbled with Esteban's shirt. Hunger was taking over now, making her reckless and crazy. What did she care if anyone took a walk through the hotel gardens and found them here, making uninhibited love in the middle of the ornamental pond? What did she care about anything, except having Esteban's kisses on her breasts, and his fingers so, so tenderly sliding down her panties over her willing hips?

Esteban's belt yielded easily and she unbuttoned his flies, her fingers remembering the first blissful time she had touched him. She yearned to touch and kiss him again, to rediscover the beauty of his manhood.

'Venetia. *Petite anglaise . . . Ah, que tu as le diable dans les doigts. Touche-moi, touche-moi, baise-moi avec tes doigts de feu . . .'*

Esteban closed his eyes and explored Venetia by touch alone, his whole body singing with ecstasy at the touch of her fingers on his naked penis.

Venetia sank to her knees in the water, its coldness making the breath shudder from her. Her hair floated out behind her in wet rat's-tails, but she paid it no heed. All she saw, all she cared about, was the beautiful lance of flesh cradled in her hands.

He was more beautiful even than she remembered. His penis was hard and smooth as carved stone, a marbled sabre that curved and swelled to a bulbous plum of a glans, pierced through with a ring of polished haematite. Venetia put out her tongue and tasted it, rolling it round in her mouth, sucking and biting.

Esteban cursed softly under his breath, his grip tightening on her breasts, squeezing and pinching the nipples.

'*Nom de diable* . . .'

He let out a long, low growl as Venetia took his penis into her mouth, swallowing it down with a sweet, savage reverence. Her fingers squeezed and stroked his balls, so overfull with their tribute to her loveliness that he almost spurted into her at her first touch.

With long, smooth strokes, Venetia sucked him, her lips tightening joyfully about the ramrod of his manhood. She knew that he was close to orgasm; knew that she had only to tease the stone cock-ring a little more and he would offer up the creamy bounty of his tribute, filling her mouth and throat so full that his seed would spill from between her lips, trickling down over chin and throat.

To her surprise, he withdrew from her

suddenly, gently but firmly pushing her away. She heard him panting hoarsely in the darkness.

'Not yet,' he whispered. 'I desire you, *petite anglaise*. Let me show you how I desire you.'

Tightly clasped in each other's arms, they sank together into the water. It rose up Venetia's body, lapping at her face, and she began to struggle, panicking.

'Esteban . . . Esteban . . .'

'Do not be afraid. You must not fear me, you must trust me. With trust, all things can be made possible . . .'

His words soothed her, and it seemed to Venetia that she was floating in some trance-like realm where nothing existed but the joining of her body to Esteban's; the white-hot searing of pleasure as he slid between her thighs, possessing her body and soul.

The waters washed over them again and again as they fucked, their bodies rolling and tumbling together; one unity of pleasure. She could not breathe; but she did not need to breathe. She could not speak; but words were superfluous.

For endless, precious moments, until the pure white light of orgasm summoned her back to reality, Venetia understood what it could mean to feel a passion that transcended everything.

Even the boundaries between life and death.

Chapter Eight

AS THE TAXI wove its way through the crowded streets and headed out towards the airport, Venetia took a brief look back over her shoulder.

Somewhere back there, in the teeming mass that was Cairo, Gabriel Engelhart was waiting for her to turn up and explain herself. And what was the betting that he was not pleased – not pleased at all?

Esteban was sitting beside her, engimatic once more behind the dark glasses which protected his sensitive eyes from the full glare of the sun.

'You are unsure about this?' he asked her. 'You wish to return?'

Venetia shook her head. 'I'm perfectly sure.' She paused. 'I'm just worried about Gabriel. About what he'll do when he realises I really have left him . . .'

'You don't owe him anything.'

'No, but . . .'

'And he doesn't own you.' Esteban leant towards her. 'Or does he?'

'No!' Venetia shook that thought right out of

her head. 'Nobody owns me.' Including you Esteban, she thought to herself as she looked at him, loving and hating and desiring him all at once. 'I chickened out and posted him a letter,' she explained. 'He should get it tomorrow or the next day.'

'Then that is settled.'

'Where do we go next?'

'We will take a plane to Halab in Syria, then we must travel across the desert to the oasis spoken of in the book. When we reach the mountains, we must find a guide.'

Esteban sat back in his seat. He seemed edgy to Venetia.

'Esteban . . .'

'Mmm?'

'There's something wrong, isn't there?'

Esteban gave a dry laugh. 'I always did admire your skill with the understatement, Venetia Fellowes.' His long, slender fingers fiddled with the strap of his Cartier watch. 'If I could only be certain . . .'

Venetia knew what Esteban was thinking about. She hadn't been able to get it out of her mind ever since she had read the extract from the diary they had found in the restaurant.

Despite the star and circle embossed on the binding, the book had turned out to be the diary of a man called Marcus Almenius, a medieval alchemist who had travelled widely in the Middle East. Nothing so very remarkable about that, perhaps – except for the section which had related his discovery of a settlement, high in the mountains, cut off for many years from the outside world.

353

Almenius related the story of how he arrived, half-starved and delirius with fever, at a town hewn from the mountainside. The inhabitants had taken him in and nursed him back to health; and over the weeks he spent with them, Almenius had begun to learn some of their most esoteric mysteries.

'Do you think . . .?' began Venetia.

'Do I think what?'

'Do you think the settlement still exists?'

Esteban shrugged. He gazed out of the taxi window at the dusty scrubland beyond the city. 'Who can tell?'

'I can't imagine that we'll ever be able to find it, even if we follow Almenius's directions. They're so vague. And do you really believe that these people have the power . . .?'

'That they could "cure" vampires? Remove the curse from them and restore them to life?' Esteban's whole body seemed to tense. 'You are right, Venetia. In the cold light of day it seems ridiculous. Perhaps we should turn back now.'

'No.' Venetia ran her hands over the age-smoothed leather binding of Marcus Almenius's journal.

'There could be danger ahead. Grave danger. God knows, Venetia, there is danger for you even in being with me . . .'

Esteban shuddered inwardly as, deep in the recesses of his soul, there stirred the ancient, dark hunger. For as long as that hunger endured, he could never quite trust himself, knowing how many had perished to satisfy the desire which could be suppressed but never killed. The true curse of his vampirism, the true horror and

354

punishment, lay in the fact that he loathed himself for what he had become.

'You would never hurt me.'

He shook his head slowly.

'Not willingly, that is true. But you cannot understand the darkness that overtakes me. I fear for you Venetia. As long as you are by my side, I fear for you.'

And I fear for myself, thought Venetia. But if there is even the faintest chance that Esteban can be cured, this is a risk which I must take.

The flame of need flared higher as the sun rose to its zenith in the Tunisian sky.

In the basement of his town house, Gabriel Engelhart raked his fingernails down the blonde girl's back. She arched her spine and gave a little soft hiss, unable to resist or free herself from the leather straps which bound her wrists and ankles. Gabriel smiled grimly at the sight of the white scratches, turning to raised pink welts before his eyes.

'This girl's skin is particularly sensitive,' he commented.

Ismail permitted himself a self-satisfied nod.

'I picked her out for you myself, master, on my last trip to Sweden. Her name is Jutta. I knew that she would please you.'

Gabriel gave the girl's rump a hard slap. It jumped up, quivering and reddening at the blow.

'You say she is still a virgin? I find that hard to believe.'

'It is indeed rare for a Scandinavian girl, master. But this one was taken from a convent school.' His thin, cracked lips twitched in amusement.

'Her parents wished her to become a nun.'

Gabriel laughed drily. 'I can see from her hard nipples that this one is made for a very different kind of devotion. You have done your job well, Ismail. Have her and the others prepared for my pleasure.'

Ismail's raised eyebrow was the only outward sign of his surprise. 'For your own pleasure, master? I had thought this consignment were for auction . . .'

Gabriel took a silver nipple-clamp and opened its cruel, alligator jaws. It was true that he did not normally sample the merchandise himself – particularly the virgins. That only reduced their value on the open market. But today was different. Venetia Fellowes had betrayed him and his anger and hatred and frustrated lust boiled for release. Somebody was going to have to pay . . .

The sun sat low in the sky, moving swiftly now towards twilight and the sudden, starry darkness of a Syrian night.

Venetia and Esteban sat cross-legged on a hand-woven carpet, beneath a canopy of brightly-coloured rugs. A Kurdish woman in long, dark robes and a headdress decorated with silver coins moved about the tent, serving thick, bitter coffee and sticky sweetmeats. Venetia felt a pang of guilt that she should have to wait on them, but when she tried to thank her, the woman averted her gaze. Uncomfortable in her Western clothes, Venetia drew up her knees and covered them with her floaty cotton skirt.

The nomad chief nodded and drew deeply on his hookah pipe, drawing in warm tobacco smoke sweet with honey. He was an impressive man in his middle years, powerfully built with a hooked nose and a dark beard, glossy with scented oil. There was also something in his eyes – a covetousness – which Venetia found faintly alarming.

'You say you wish to cross the desert. Why is this?'

Venetia opened her mouth to speak, but Esteban threw her a look and she shut it again. It was difficult to play the game when you didn't care for the rules, she thought to herself, and she had never been one to play second fiddle to anyone.

'We wish to cross the border and travel into the mountains,' replied Esteban.

'You are Westerners. You have visas?'

'No.'

'Crossing the border is forbidden for you without visas.'

'We know.'

The chief's eyes twinkled with quiet humour. 'There are other ways of reaching Iraq. By aeroplane. By railway, even . . .'

'Not where we wish to go,' cut in Venetia, not speaking in English but in the tribe's own dialect. The chief raised an eyebrow, clearly impressed by Venetia's knowledge of his language, but not accustomed to being addressed so directly by a woman.

'Women should learn to speak when they are spoken to,' observed the chief, more in amusement than anger. 'Lest their foolish chatter sound like the bleating of goats.'

With difficulty, Venetia controlled the urge to

357

tell him to mind his manners. She could see Esteban watching her out of the corner of her eye.

'I beg your pardon my lord,' she said. 'I did not mean to speak out of turn. But my companion and I . . . we are desperate to find the settlement of which he has spoken. We need your help.'

'And what help may we offer?'

'Your wives tell me that you and your people are soon to travel across country to the mountains.'

The chief nodded. 'This is true. We are taking my daughter to her bridegroom's village. There will be a wedding, many guests. But of what interest is this to you?'

'Would you allow us to travel with you?'

'The life is hard. And your hands are soft, a lady's hands.'

'We are ready for any hardship.'

'We share all tasks and all possessions.' His eyes met Venetia's. 'Everything. Our women also. You understand?'

Venetia looked towards Esteban. Obviously he was calm, cold even; but she could feel the anger and jealousy within him. She turned away, looking the chief straight in the eyes.

'I understand.' Her mouth was dry. 'I am willing to share . . . everything.'

The Kurdish chief's expression did not change. 'Good,' he said abruptly. 'Then you and your companion may join us on our journey. We will take you as far as the foothills. And you, my dear . . . tomorrow night you shall share my tent.'

It was dark now, the night pitch-black and cold over the watering-place. Somewhere in the

358

distance horses and camels shuffled and grunted in the blackness.

'Something is making them uneasy,' whispered Venetia, drawing very close to Esteban as they sat beside the lake. Esteban's hand tightened about hers.

'You do not have to do this,' he told her.

'You know I do,' she replied gently, almost frightened by the intensity of Esteban's kiss. 'I must spend one night with him or he will not allow us to join their caravan.'

'We will find the lost village without their help.'

'No, Esteban, the directions in the diary are too imprecise. These people know the desert and the mountains. This is the only way, you know it is true.'

'Do you desire this man?' Esteban's voice was studiedly devoid of emotion.

'No.'

'Don't lie to me, Venetia.'

'Why should I lie?' She wrapped her arms close about him, and they lay down together on the dusty earth, still warm from the heat of the sun. Esteban lay half on top of her, his thigh across hers, his hand easing open the top button of her blouse. He kissed the base of her breasts, his lips cool on her overheated flesh. Somewhere at the edge of his consciousness, a darkness was lapping like brackish water.

'If we fail . . .' he murmured.

'We will not.'

'If we fail . . . you must leave me. This must be as if it had never existed.'

'I know.' The thought entered Venetia's mind but she killed it ruthlessly. She could not afford

359

even to think of failure.

'If I were a better man, I would make you leave me now. I would never have brought you here . . .' Esteban's hand caressed her bare belly, sliding upwards to slip underneath the bottom of her bra. 'You are my weakness Venetia, my obsession . . .' But I will not allow myself to be your destruction, he told himself in the silence of his thoughts.

Venetia drew him down on top of her and his fingers sought out her left breast, freeing it from her bra, letting his tongue flick lightly across its erect crest.

'Make love to me, Esteban,' she whispered as he took her nipple into his mouth and slid up the floaty layers of her skirt. 'Make love to me and make me forget tomorrow.'

Chapter Nine

THE WHITE ARAB stallion half-trotted, half-slithered down the sandy side of the dune. The rider shaded his eyes with his hand, surveying the horizon, then dug his heels into the horse's flanks, spurring it on. A palomino pony trotted behind, its rider leading a mule laden with pots, pans and provisions.

Before them lay the Kurdish settlement, a jumble of palm trees, colourful tents and mud-brick houses dotted around a watering-place. Camels bellowed bad-temperedly as their owner roped them together and loaded them up with baskets of dates and bundles of brightly-coloured fabric. Somewhere in the distance, a young woman was coming back from the spring, balancing a huge earthenware water pot on her head. A woman whose elegant, swaying walk reminded him in some subtle, crazy way of Venetia Fellowes . . .

As he dismounted and handed the reins of his horse to a small boy, Gabriel Engelhart wondered what madness had driven him to this. But his heart thumped with the thought that she might be here, in this place . . . with what she and her lover had stolen from him.

Ismail dismounted and followed in Gabriel's wake. 'Master.'

Gabriel turned and threw Ismail and impatient look.

'What now?'

'If we find the girl, will we take her back with us?'

'Perhaps.'

'We could sell her.' Ismail licked his lips. 'Once she has been cured of her disobedience, she would fetch a good price.'

'I have not yet decided.' At any rate, Gabriel hadn't decided quite where to begin in her long and well-deserved punishment.

'And the book, master? The *Lore of Madali*? The Englishwoman has it with her?'

'I am certain of it. Assuming she has not given it to *him*.' Her lover, thought Gabriel. Esteban, Venetia's lover. It left a bitter taste of bile in his mouth.

'The air steward was very sure that they were travelling together,' Ismail continued helpfully. 'He said there was much kissing, it was very . . . sexual . . .'

'Shut up, Ismail.' Gabriel's eyes glittered.

'Yes, master.'

'We will find them together, and we will find ways of punishing them both.'

Gabriel walked on towards the centre of the encampment. At that moment, a young boy on a motorbike came roaring out from beneath the trees, kicking up a choking cloud of sand. He

362

thrust his hand into his pocket and held it out, the palm filled with the glitter of coloured stones.

'Very nice jewellery, very real. Buy it for your girlfriends, yes?'

'Go away.' Gabriel turned aside, but the youth followed, riding alongside at walking pace.

'You want girl, nice girl?'

Gabriel stopped and turned to look at the youth. Perhaps, just perhaps, he might prove useful.

'I am looking for someone,' he said. 'Two people, a man and a woman.'

The youth shrugged. 'I see nothing, I not know.'

Gabriel held out a small-denomination banknote. 'The man is a Spaniard – he has sallow skin and dark hair, and a face like an eagle. The woman . . .' Gabriel searched for the right words to describe Venetia Fellowes. 'The woman is English. She had golden hair and eyes that are blue like the summer sky . . .'

The Arab youth whistled. 'She beautiful, yes? She your woman who run away with another man?'

Bristling with vicarious indignation, Ismail raised his hand to strike the boy, but Gabriel shook his head. He added a second banknote to the one in his hand. 'You have seen them?'

'I not sure.'

'If you tell me where they are, I will give you money.'

The youth grinned, seizing the banknotes and pushing them into the pocket of his jeans. 'I see them. But they not here now.'

'Then where are they?'

'I take you to my sister.' The boy drew a perfect hour-glass figure in the air. 'She very beautiful. She make you welcome, drink tea with you. Perhaps she tell you what you want to know.'

Ismail caught Gabriel's arm. 'Master, it may be a trick, some deception the bitch has laid to trap us.'

With a look of contempt, Gabriel shook him free, patting the creases out of his shirt sleeve. 'Do you seriously believe the girl has the wit to deceive me?'

'And Esteban, master?'

Gabriel sneered and spat into the dust at his feet. 'You will speak no more of that filth.'

Suitably chastened, Ismail trailed his master across the settlement, following the boy with the motorbike. He felt uneasy, as though they were being watched. And in truth he could not understand why Gabriel should trouble himself about a girl and a book. Gabriel Engelhart had more books and more beautiful women than any man could ever want.

And then there was this inexplicable hatred of the man Esteban. Ismail had never met Esteban, but he knew that there was bad blood between him and his master – an animosity stretching back to the time before Ismail had come into Gabriel's service. Perhaps that was it then; a case of simple rivalry . . .

The youth led them to a low, square building of mud bricks, surrounded by gently swaying palms. A beaded curtain hung over the open doorway, and soft music floated out, shimmering on the heat haze of a desert noon.

'My sister very nice girl, very pretty.' The youth grinned and held out his palm. 'Very generous.'

364

Gabriel ignored his hopeful look and pushed him aside. 'Later. If she tells us what we want to know.'

Ismail ducked in front of him. 'Let me go first, master, in case it is a trap.'

'Don't be ridiculous. Stand aside.'

Ismail watched with the pain of frustrated self-sacrifice as his master stepped inside the house. It was his special, personal torment that Gabriel would never appreciate the lengths to which his manservant would go to prove his complete devotion.

Gabriel entered the house. It was initially dark, and he blinked to accustom his sight to the half-light. There was a strong scent of sweet spice on the air – cinnamon and something else he didn't quite recognise. From somewhere quite close by, a woman's voice whispered to him.

'Welcome. Enter. Do not be afraid.'

Afraid! If she had known Gabriel Engelhart, she would have understood that it was she who ought to feel fear.

The twilight resolved itself into light and shade, candle-flames dancing in a fuzzy halo about a dark shape.

The woman got to her feet. She was exotic, dark-skinned with thick black kohl outlining large and lustrous eyes. Tribal tattoos traced fine patterns over her forehead and cheeks, and ornate silver jewellery jingled in her pierced nose, ears and lips. She held out a brass goblet, filled with some cool, sticky-sweet liquid.

'You drink with me, stranger?'

Gabriel raised his hand and dashed the goblet from her hand. It fell to the ground, spilling its contents in a dark stain across the hem of her robe and the embroidered cushions at her feet.

'Please, no . . .' She backed away, but he did not give her the opportunity to escape from him. He seized the long, braided rope of her hair and twisted it back, forcing her to her knees before him.

'Now,' he smiled, the candlelight illuminating a spark of satisfaction in his cold blue eyes. 'Tell me about Esteban and his English bitch. And be sure you tell me *everything* you know.'

The wedding procession moved slowly across the desert and into the mountains, resting during the hottest part of the day and moving on when the sun sank low in the sky.

Venetia was well-nigh unrecognisable under the heavy, ankle-length robes she had been given to wear. At first she had protested against this badge of anonymity – until she realised that their value was as much practical as cosmetic. The long veils of black, filmy fabric protected her fair skin from the searing glare of the noonday sun. Naked underneath, she felt curiously sensual as a hot, dry wind blew the fabric against her bare limbs, soft as a lover's caress.

Adventures were all very well, thought Venetia – but right now, she was pining for a hot bath and a five-star hotel. She walked barefoot on the stony earth, obliged to walk with the other women while the menfolk rode on ponies and camels. She felt a twinge of sympathy for the chief's fourteen-year-old daughter, being carried half across the country to be delivered into the arms of a fifteen-year-old bridegroom she had never even met.

Glancing to her right, she saw Esteban. He had dismounted from his horse and was leading it into the whipping, sandy wind, his dark hair blowing out behind him and his clothes moulding themselves closely to the contours of his spare yet strong figure.

He seemed to sense her looking at him and turned to meet her gaze. There was something in his eyes, something dark and fiery, which frightened Venetia. She had deluded herself that she knew him so well, and yet there was so much in him that she had not even begun to understand. Was she wrong to trust him?

She moved towards him, but he shook his head, gesturing to her to keep her distance. Then he turned away and marched on, staring fixedly towards the horizon, his dark eyes screwed up against the pain of the sunlight. Whatever private demon was tormenting Esteban, she could do nothing to still the pain.

At a village in the foothills, they parted company with the wedding caravan. Venetia was not sorry to bid farewell to the Kurdish chief. Although he had not been unkind to her, she had loathed his touch on her naked skin, knew how much he craved for her to stay and become one of his concubines.

'I will leave you with A'shah.' The chief clapped his hands and a girl stepped forward. 'She will be your guide until your reach the place. You must make the rest of your journey alone.' His eyes coaxed Venetia to change her mind, to stay, but when all was said and done he was a realist. Nor was he blind. He had seen the way the Englishwoman's blue eyes caressed the dark-haired Spaniard. 'I wish you well. Perhaps you will return to me one day.'

The wedding party continued on its way into the village, and Venetia looked to Esteban. He would not – or could not – meet her gaze, and she saw that he was staring fixedly at A'shah. He was trembling, his hands clenched so tightly into fists that his knuckles shone bone-white through the flesh. And there was a look on his face that Venetia could not fail to recognise.

The agony of hunger.

The moon was full.

It hung over the mountains like a globe of frosted glass, huge and unreal, its soft, cold light chilling the night air.

Venetia and Esteban stood with A'shah at the top of the escarpment. Unveiled now, her handsome face was tilted up towards the moon, its light sculpting the curves of chin and throat.

'One more day's travel,' she announced in her husky voice. 'That will take us to the place.'

'You will come there with us?' asked Venetia, already knowing the answer.

A'shah shook her head. 'I cannot go, I must return to my tribe. And if you are wise, you too will turn back. There are stories . . . rumours. No one ever travels to that part of the mountains. Some have tried – and never returned.'

'We must go on. We have no choice. There is something we must find.'

'Then Allah go with you and shield your footsteps.' A'shah glanced at Esteban, standing a little way away. He was white and shaking, sweat pearling his brow as though he were in the grip of some fever. 'You are ill?'

He looked at her sharply, then looked away again, as though it gave him pain to see her.

'Do not concern yourself with me. I am quite well.'

Turning on his heel he walked quickly away, heading into a narrow gulley between the rocks. Venetia called after him. 'Esteban . . .'

He hesitated, then walked on, not looking back. Venetia followed him, as much by instinct as good sense. He was walking quickly away from the encampment, deeper and deeper into the darkness and shadows, a shadow within a shadow, becoming one with the comforting blackness that surrounded him.

'Esteban, why are you running away from me?'

This time, he looked back at her. 'Go back, Venetia.'

'There's something wrong. I won't leave you.'

'You must. It is – too dangerous.' His breath came in halting spasms, each drawn in with visible pain. His face seemed paler and more gaunt, his hands claw-like, his entire body tense as a sculpture in twisted wire.

Venetia took a hesitant step closer to him. 'Tell me, Esteban. Tell me what's wrong.'

'The darkness. Can't you see? It . . . overwhelms me. The hunger. I cannot control . . .'

And now Venetia understood. She had known that this moment must surely come. The hunger had returned to Esteban . . . the thirst for blood. 'Fight it, Esteban. Fight the hunger.'

He turned tortured eyes on her. Eyes that blazed with a passion beyond love, beyond death. 'I have no wish to harm you, Venetia. But I cannot protect you. It was madness to bring you here . . .'

'We had to come, you know that. It's the only chance we have.' She reached out to touch him but he shrank away, afraid of the savagery within him.

'Feed. I must feed.' A spasm of agony crossed Esteban's face and he threw back his head, letting out a long, low moan. His fingers clawed at his face, his hair, his body, as though trying to tear out and destroy the demon within him. Slowly he sank to his knees, still shaking, clawing now at the rocks around him. 'Go back. Keep away, the power is greater than my strength. I cannot control it any longer, it tears apart my very soul . . .'

For a split second Venetia caught the mad light in his eyes and almost turned and ran. But her passion for Esteban was greater than her fear. 'Give me your knife,' she said suddenly, her voice curiously matter-of-fact. He stared back at her, uncomprehending. 'Give it to me, Esteban.'

The glimmer of understanding filtered into Esteban's pain-wracked consciousness. 'No, Venetia!'

'Give it to me.' She reached down and took the hunting knife from Esteban's belt. He was too weak to resist, the dark hunger twisting and contracting his body with spasm after spasm of ravening pain. The six-inch, curving blade caught the glitter of moonlight and flashed out a danger signal. Venetia ran her finger along the edge. It was wafer-thin, and so sharp that where it had touched, a thin line of blood sprang up.

Esteban tried to look away, but he could not tear his eyes away from the sight of Venetia's blood, the fine, dark line, the plump, salty beads springing proud upon the flesh, so alluring with their seductive, coppery scent. Drawing him, drawing him, daring him to do what he despised, and what his cursed heart screamed for him to do . . .

Taking a deep breath, Venetia drew the hunting knife very quickly across the inside of her forearm. It was all done so quickly, and the blade was so sharp, that she scarcely felt any pain.

And now the blood welled up from the cut vein in a dark crimson abundance, oozing and dripping.

'Drink, Esteban,' she whispered. And she reached out to him. 'Drink . . .'

A cry of release escaped from Esteban as he caught the first, fat droplet between his parted lips. For him, this was the elixir of life – of his cursed, unending servitude. Of his passion which could never end.

He drank deeply, his tongue lapping like a cat's at Venetia's blood, his lips sucking, catching every last droplet. It was a small gift, scarcely enough to still the dark hunger; but it freed him from the agony of urgent need. Slowly his muscles began to relax, the pounding in his head stilled by the deep, ecstatic warmth which stole over him, filling him with a very different desire.

Gradually his strength returned to him; the supreme, triumphant strength that filled him whenever he had fulfilled the ancient need. Hungry now with a very different passion, his lips slid upward to meet Venetia's.

She kissed his mouth. It was sticky with blood, the metallic saltiness which would normally have made her retch with horror. Here, now, it excited her beyond belief. Maddened with need, she clawed at Esteban's belt, unfastening it, unzipping his trousers, taking out what she most desperately desired.

Tearing off her robe, she offered herself to him; and he pulled her astride his soaring prick.

'My Venetia,' he breathed. 'My queen of night. My only and my ever. My eternal one . . .'

His hands slid down her body, parting the petals of her secret flower; and he slid into her with a silent ecstasy, a sublime smoothness that took him right up to the hilt. At the first thrust his cock-tip nudged against the neck of Venetia's womb, and she felt a spasm of profoundest need ripple through her.

'I am beginning to understand,' she whispered to him. And she bent to kiss him again as their sweat-soaked bodies began slowly sliding over each other, drinking in the sweetness of purest sex.

There was a sublime electricity in their coupling; an intensity which Venetia had not experienced since that night in the garden of Esteban's villa, when he had offered her the gift – and the curse – of eternity. As his beautiful, marble-smooth penis slid between her thighs, she rubbed herself long and hard against his pubic bone, willing the pleasure to last, joining him on the very edge of pleasure and praying that they might remain there for ever.

Esteban smoothed his hands down the gentle curve of her back and slipped his index finger between her buttocks, stroking and scratching the rosebud sphincter of her anus.

'Blossom for me,' he murmured, kissing her throat with infinite gentleness as they moved together, harmonising the rhythm of their passion. 'Open yourself, give me your sweet-ness . . .'

Rolling onto his side, Esteban possessed her with long, slow thrusts, all the time kissing and licking her breasts and throat. She felt the need building up inside her, carrying her to paradise; and at last she found the strength to trust Esteban, to open herself to him utterly, to offer him her complete vulnerability.

He kissed her mouth as they climaxed together, the sweet groan of his orgasm shuddering through her as their bodies met and their essences mingled in unique alchemy.

As dawn approached, Venetia awoke and rolled onto her back. Dark smears of dried blood on her skin reminded her of what had passed. For a second she panicked, putting her hand to her throat. But he had not harmed her. She found nothing there but the memory of Esteban's gentle kiss.

Propping herself up on one elbow, she bent over him. Kissed him. His eyes opened.

With a gasp, she drew back. Esteban's eyes were no longer black and glassy as polished jet. They were yellow as a wolf's. Pushing her gently away, he sat up, sniffing the air like a wild animal.

'Esteban . . .' She drew away. 'Esteban, what is it?'

'Danger,' he murmured. 'There is danger close by.'

And a second later, before her eyes, he vanished into thin air.

Dawn was coming up over the mountains as Gabriel and Ismail toiled along the treacherous road. To the left, the rocks and scree rose up a sheer slope too dangerous for any but an expert or a mountain goat to climb. To the right, the narrow track fell away hundreds of feet to the scrubby valley below.

Gabriel dismounted from his horse and turned to confront Ismail, who was struggling to lead a pack mule up the steep ascent. He looked hot, scared and unhappy. 'Idiot,' Gabriel snapped. 'Can you do nothing right?'

'I am sorry, master.'

'And so you should be. If we do not make better progress we will lose their trail.'

'A thousand pardons, master. The road . . . it is very steep and we are very close to the edge . . .'

Gabriel's lip curled in disdain. 'To think that any servant of mine should be afraid. Afraid of heights! You are contemptible, Ismail, do you know that?'

Lashing out, he caught Ismail a glancing blow on the side of the head, causing him to stumble and fall to his hands and knees on the stony roadway. The pack mule bucked in alarm, and almost sent half of their provisions tumbling over the edge into the valley below.

'Imbecile! Will you obey me now? Will you?'

Gabriel seized Ismail by the shoulder and dragged him to his feet. But the face which looked back at him was not the sweating, cringing face of his servant Ismail. It was the face of someone who filled him with vicious rage and just a touch of fear . . .

'You know, Gabriel, you really ought to be more careful,' remarked Esteban with an ironic half-smile, detaching himself with ease from Gabriel's grasp. 'It's a long way down. You might fall.'

Gabriel took a step back, momentarily thrown off balance. 'Esteban? Esteban, my enemy,' he hissed. 'Give me back what belongs to me.'

Esteban laughed. 'And what might that be, Gabriel?' he enquired. 'Your foul and festering soul, perhaps?'

He parried the blow with ease and a strength which both astonished and enraged Gabriel.

'Give me back the book.'

'The book is not what you seek, Engelhart. It is not the *Lore of Madali*. It is an old diary, of no use or value to you.'

Gabriel drew back his lips in a sneer of contempt. 'Once again you seek to trick me.'

'I have never tricked or cheated you. I only refused you that which you had no right to demand.'

Gabriel stepped forward, his face very close to Esteban's, his handsome features contorted with hatred. 'Give me back the English girl. She is not for you, she belongs to me now . . .'

Esteban shook his head. 'She is not yours to possess, Gabriel. Nor is she mine. Venetia has made her choice, and her choice is to be as far away from you as possible.' He allowed himself a half-smile. 'But then, Venetia Fellowes is a highly intelligent woman.'

Gabriel lunged forward, enraged by Esteban's calm composure, his aristocratic disdain. But Esteban was ready for him, catching him by the throat with one powerful hand. And seconds later, he found himself dangling over a sheer drop, Esteban's stranglehold the only thing between him and oblivion.

He struggled for breath, but Esteban was not listening to his protests. 'Leave here, Engelhart,' he whispered. 'Leave here and never return. Or the next time, I may forget myself and kill you.'

When Gabriel came to his senses, he was lying in the dirt, the pack mule licking his face and Ismail standing over him, his ugly little face twisted with fear.

'Master, master, what ails you? You are sick?'

'Only of your incompetence,' replied Gabriel, rubbing his bruised throat. 'Which is why I am sending you back to Tunis, and continuing my journey alone.'

'Master! You cannot . . .'

But Gabriel was not listening. He was thinking of Esteban's arrogant threats, and the sweet revenge which had been so cruelly stolen from his grasp.

A'shah looked up in alarm when Venetia and Esteban returned to the camp together, Venetia with a bandage of ripped cloth wrapped round her forearm.

'Something bad has happened?'

'Nothing,' said Venetia hastily. 'I . . . fell and cut myself.'

'Let me look.'

Reluctantly, Venetia allowed A'shah to peel away the makeshift bandage. Her tone did not change, but her eyes registered surprise, perhaps suspicion.

'It looks more like a knife cut.'

'Does it? That's funny.'

A'shah looked from Venetia to Esteban and concluded that questions were pointless. 'I will dress it with special herbs. Wounds can turn bad very quickly in this climate. You should be more careful.'

Venetia looked at Esteban, wishing he would explain but knowing that he wouldn't. One moment he had spoken of 'danger', the next, he had vanished into thin air. Or had he? Had she imagined it all? Because when she had woken up a second time, still lying on the dusty grass in the gully, he had been there beside her, as though he had been there all night long.

They set off early, before dawn had turned into the full bloom of day, and before the furnace heat had begun to wilt the crispness of the mountain air.

Up here in the mountains was a different world, thought Venetia. Certainly very different from Valazur with its Riviera gamblers, millionaires and starlets; and more different still from the world of Gabriel Engelhart. When she thought of him she felt unsettled, uneasy; not quite certain that they had seen the last of him. And what if they returned to the 'real' world and he caught up with them, demanded to know why Venetia had suddenly upped and left him?

Her train of thought was broken by Esteban, laying his hand on her arm. 'See, Venetia. There, just ahead.'

A'shah was riding a few yards in front of them. Beyond her, Venetia made out the shape of something rocky, half-overgrown, but definitely man-made. A tense excitement tightened her stomach muscles.

'Is it . . .?'

Esteban shook his head. 'I don't know. But remember what the book said . . . about the gateway to a hidden valley . . .'

The gateway. Venetia recalled the spidery handwriting in the diary of Marcus Almenius: 'And when I was all but dead from thirst, I came upon a gateway, carved with the shapes of men and beasts in pleasures carnal and corporeal . . .'

They walked slowly forward. The passage of years had not been kind to the stonework, and some of the stones had crumbled or cracked and fallen. But the archway was still clearly visible, each yellow-grey stone richly carved with a freize depicting men, women and fantastical beasts, copulating in an orgy of sensual indulgence.

Flowers and soft grass grew at the base of the gateway, and through it Venetia could make out a steep, grassy slope dotted with trees.

'Will you come with us?'

'I can go no further,' replied A'shah. There was the ghost of fear in her face. 'This place . . . no, I cannot.'

Esteban and Venetia watched her mount her horse and ride away, glancing back only once before disappearing round a bend in the mountain road. Esteban searched Venetia's face for a sign of doubt. 'You are certain?'

'You know I am.'

'We can still turn back.'

'Things can never go back, Esteban. Only forward.'

And stepping through the gateway, they walked together down the grassy slope. Into the unknown.

378

Chapter Ten

VENETIA EXAMINED THE inscription on the gateway. It was barely discernible now after the ravages of time and weather. Esteban watched her picking out the letters painstakingly, slowly speaking the words as she translated them.

'It's in very old, very corrupt type of Latin. It says, "Alexander did not come this way, nor Gilgamesh."' She turned to Esteban. 'But what does it mean?'

Esteban shook his head. 'That, *ma petite anglaise*, I do not know. Perhaps we shall discover its meaning.'

They walked on together. The gateway had been situated in a narrow gap between two steep slopes. Once on the other side of it, they saw that the grassy earth sloped sharply away, forming a path which led round the side of the mountain. Dusty grass, stunted trees, a few pale flowers were all the vegetation here. There seemed nothing remarkable, nothing to show that this place had ever been anything but a wasteland; a staging post on the road to nowhere.

Then they turned a corner.

'Esteban, look! Just look . . .'

Esteban could hardly do anything else. He stood stock-still, gazing at the vista suddenly spread out before them.

They were standing at the head of a valley, deep and green and almost tropical in its lushness. It was the abundance of water that struck you first – the sheer moistness of this place, so incongruously placed in the heart of a rocky desert.

Gazing down through trees that swayed in a soft, warm wind, Venetia made out a broad, lazy river in the valley bottom, winding its way sinuously between green-clad banks whose leafy glades rustled with unseen life.

A shower of many-coloured brightness made her look up, and she saw a cloud of huge, iridescent butterflies, dancing above her head, wheeling and tumbling in the moist, warm air.

'This place,' murmured Esteban. 'I have seen it before . . . somewhere . . . somehow.'

Venetia looked at him sharply. 'You have been here before? But surely . . .'

He put up his hand. 'No. No, I have never been here. At least . . .' He passed a hand across his forehead. 'I believe that I have dreamed it.'

'Let's find out more about this place.'

Filled with a breathless excitement, Venetia took the initiative and stepped forward. Birds sang in leafy treetops, their clear song stirring the sleepy air. Flowers carpeted the grass at their feet. It was all unbelievably lush. A dream. Something not quite real.

Bright lianas hung across a bend in the

pathway. Venetia reached out and touched the curtain of hanging foliage, a bright-green creeper swinging lazily down the side of a rocky face. Behind it, she glimpsed craggy rocks, running with water. Hot and dusty, Venetia plunged in her hands. The water was cold and so clear, so sweet. Beyond, she found herself looking into a darkness suffused with sparks of light, and heard a soft, distant roar of thunder.

'It's a waterfall!' she exclaimed with delight, and she stepped through the leafy curtain into the wet green twilight beyond.

'Venetia, be careful . . .'

'It's all right, Esteban, it's quite safe. It's . . . it's so beautiful, I can hardly believe it.'

She stretched out her hand and, filled with misgivings, Esteban joined her. Before them a waterfall crashed down from some unseen height, the water fracturing into a million crystal drops as it thundered into the deep pool.

As they stood before the waterfall, letting the spray moisten their faces, making their clothes cling to their bodies, a red and gold parakeet scythed through the twilight, crying and shrilling as it cut through the water and emerged on the other side, a stem of coral-pink blossom on its beak.

'Look, Esteban . . . look.' She caught the blossom as it fell from the bird's beak. 'It's almost as if . . .'

'I know, Venetia. Almost as if this place is welcoming us.' So why do I feel uneasy? thought Esteban.

'There are animals here too – look, do you see?'

Esteban turned slowly. No. It couldn't be, it made no sense. Sitting on its haunches beside the

381

waterfall was an ocelot, its spotted coat dappled like leaves spotted with sunlight and shadow. An ocelot? Here, on the Syrian border? Parakeets? Butterflies as big as saucers? It was like stepping into the middle of some over-the-top dream. And yet. And yet, this was the most beautiful, the most erotic place he had ever been. He ached with the need to take Venetia in his arms and make passionate love to her.

He took Venetia's hand. 'Bathe with me.'

'Here?'

'Here, in the waterfall.' He pressed his lips against Venetia, his hot, hungry body communicating its need to her. 'You are my hunger and my thirst, Venetia. Only you can staunch the burning heat within me.'

Gently, he unwrapped the bandage from Venetia's arm, and peeled away the herbs A'shah had used as a poultice. The flesh was clean but only half-healed, still tender, and Venetia winced as he touched it.

'Be still, *ma petite*.' Esteban bent to place a kiss upon Venetia's forearm, his lips touching the wounded flesh lightly, for the briefest second. But in that second, Venetia felt a rush of icy coldness running from shoulders to fingertip, a dart of electricity, carrying away the badness and the corruption.

He straightened up. 'You are healed now.'

Venetia looked down at her arm. Before her eyes the cut was healing to a scar, and the purple of the scar fading to red, then dusky pink and white. It was disappearing even as she looked at it!

Astonished, she turned to Esteban. The look in

his eyes was soft and distant, as though clouded with some unshared pain. 'How . . .?'

'I have taken your hurt upon myself.' He silenced her protests with a kiss. 'No, no, it is nothing to me, such a small thing. Now, will you bathe with me, *ma chère*?' He laughed. 'Or must I make you do my bidding?'

She laughed with him. He was not often so light-hearted, so teasingly attractive. The darkness seemed to melt away from him, his eyes sparkling with mirth as he tore off his shirt and kicked off his black leather boots.

'Oh, I don't know. I think you should make me . . .'

Esteban stood before her, clad only in the tight black trousers which accentuated the thick, curving line of his swelling penis. Venetia felt her nipples tingle and stiffen, her sex swelling and plumping with the delicious anticipation of what must come.

He was irresistible to her, this dark, mysterious lover who was often distant, at times arrogantly self-possessed, yet so tenderly passionate. He was her lifeblood, her need, her addiction. As he gathered her up in his arms, she felt her heart soar with the adrenaline rush of delicious danger. He whispered in her ear as he bit and licked her earlobe.

'You intoxicate my senses, *petite anglaise*. What you do to me is beyond endurance . . .'

The next thing she knew, he had swept her off her feet in his strong arms. Still fully clothed, she wriggled and shrieked with mad, drunken laughter. 'Esteban, Esteban, *put me down!*'

He laughed; a warm, husky laugh which sent

shivers of need rushing through her belly, her
limbs, her willing sex.

'No,' he replied quite simply, hoisting her up so
that he could plant a kiss on her lips. 'No, I don't
think I shall.'

'Put me down, put me down!'

'You're sure that's what you want, *petite
anglaise*?'

'Yes, yes!'

'Very well . . .'

And all of a sudden he jumped, still carrying
Venetia in his arms, into the deep pool at the base
of the waterfall.

Down, down, down they sank together, their
bodies closely entwined, their mouths locked in a
kiss that seemed as if it would never end. A
wonderful, breathless, passionate, eternal kiss.

Venetia felt no need to fight for air, no need to
do anything but kiss and caress her lover. In those
fleeting moments, Esteban became her life, her
breath, her whole existence; her past and her
tomorrow. And then, just as suddenly, the greens
and cold blues and cool amber of the water
mingled and brightened, and they shot towards
the surface, exploding into light with laughter
and kisses.

'Beast!' she squealed.

'*Chère bête . . . chère petite sauvage . . .*'

She clawed at his back as they tumbled
together in the cool green water, her wet clothes
diaphanous, clinging to the contours of her body.
Her nipples were hard as stones, her pubis a
swollen mound beneath the clinging gauzy fabric.
Cool wetness soaked through her skirt and
into the warm haven of her sex, meeting the hot

384

ooze of her need, caressing her swollen clitoris with secret, lascivious fingers.

They kissed, the crystal-clear water flooding their mouths as their lips met. They drank, and the elixir filled them with an exhilarating warmth.

Venetia looked into Esteban's eyes. His dark lashes were wet with tiny, bright droplets. She wanted to kiss them away.

'I want you, *petite anglaise*,' he murmured. 'I must have you.'

His hands began tearing at Venetia's clothes. She panted with need, her body writhing as his strong fingers pulled away her shirt, baring her heavy, golden breasts. The water buoyed them up, carrying them to the surface of the water like pink-tipped lilies, offering them to the sunlight to kiss them and make them bloom.

Greenish shadows fluttered and danced across Esteban's bare torso, making him seem like some fantastical beast born out of the raw power of nature. Venetia could feel his heart pounding as he pulled her close and began massaging the firm globes of her buttocks, so closely moulded by the wet, twisted fabric of her skirt.

Their bodies locked in an embrace, they tumbled over and over in the water, splashing and laughing, blissful with a childish, carefree lust. As Esteban unfastened the button holding up her skirt, Venetia suddenly pulled away.

'If you want me, catch me . . .'

Her eyes danced with the secret light of lust. She was teasing, tantalising, revelling in the tranquil, sensual power of this place.

Esteban watched her strike out across the lake at the base of the waterfall, her skirt floating away like a pink shadow as her naked skin flashed pale gold beneath the luminous water. Throwing back his head, he laughed. Water droplets shook from his wet hair like a sparkling halo. He could not remember a time when he had felt so good. So . . . so free. Here, for at least a few, precious moments, it was as if the curse upon him had no meaning.

He followed her, his powerful body scything through the water, his arms reaching out to grab her.

She turned, laughing, her lips wet and glossy. He seized hold of her and the waters engulfed them, caressing; a soundless cocoon of greens and blues and many-coloured brightness where only their passion existed.

When they broke the surface again, they were underneath the waterfall, its power thundering about them, the water hitting the surface of the pool so hard that it sprang up again in a fine mist. Esteban took Venetia's hand and guided her through the deafening curtain of water, his strength pulling them through.

Venetia could hardly breathe, could not move against the force of the cascade. But Esteban's fingers were holding hers tightly, drawing her on, making her trust and believe and abandon herself to his will.

At last they burst through the curtain of water into the silence beyond. Venetia blinked and shook the wetness from her eyes, gasping for breath. Here, there was no sound at all save for the distant rumble of the waterfall. They were between the tumbling cascade and the sheer rock face. Tiny, scarlet-coloured birds were sipping nectar from pink and yellow flowers growing on the rocks; dragonflies with huge, shimmering, diaphanous wings skimming just above the surface of the water. The air was flower-scented, cool and clear; each indrawn breath a tiny orgasm of innocent pleasure.

A sandy bank sloped gently beneath the surface of the pool. Esteban swam towards it, leading Venetia there. Her heart pounded in her chest. She wanted him, ached for him, longed to worship his body with hands and mouth and sex.

Together they tumbled, panting, onto the wet sand. Cool water lapped at their legs as they lay there, but they paid it no heed. Esteban pulled Venetia on top of him and gently pushed the tendrils of wet hair out of her eyes.

'Here, there is no darkness,' he whispered. 'Can you feel it? All that exists is pleasure.'

He pulled her mouth down to his and kissed her. She tasted of nectar, intoxicating and sweet. And in a sudden ache of need, he rolled her onto her back.

'Take me,' she pleaded, her tongue flicking across her lips, her eyes full of need. Her fingers reached out, stroking and caressing the long, hard bulge of Esteban's penis, so tightly kissed by the wet fabric of his trousers.

Esteban's eyes closed in ecstasy at the sureness, the lightness of her touch. Only she knew the secret ways to transport him into the divine madness of inexorable desire. Gently, firmly, regretfully, he brushed her fingers away, carrying them to his lips and kissing them.

'First, I must pay my own homage, *chère sauvage*.'

Sliding down her body, he marked his progress with a long line of kisses, each one lingering and moist, a butterfly's wing brushing the skin, sipping its nectar then moving on.

At last he reached her navel. He thrust the tip of his tongue inside, slowly and languidly, like a lazy insect seeking out nectar. Venetia cried out and clutched at him, twisting handfuls of his blue-black hair about her tormented fingers. 'No . . . no, I can't bear it.'

'Patience, *ma petite. Sois tranquille . . .*'

He began licking and probing again. Venetia shivered and arched her back. The sensation was unbearable, incredibly intimate. It felt as though Esteban had searched out the very epicentre of her sex and was running it through with the finest, the most exquisite silver needles. His tongue twisted, probed, withdrew and then came back again, exploring new and undreamed-of worlds of intense sensation.

When he withdrew for the last time, Venetia was moaning helplessly, winding and twisting and gently tilting her hips.

'Oh Esteban. Esteban, no more, I can't . . .'

But Esteban was kissing the line of fine, golden hairs which led down from Venetia's navel to the luxuriant mound of her pubic hair. He breathed in her scent, his senses drunk on the fragrance of her wetness, the irresistible mixture of purest springwater and honeydew.

'You grow more beautiful by the hour, *petite anglaise*. You smell of sex. You have ensnared me with the wondrous scent of your sex . . .'

His words, low and soft, punctuated his kisses on her belly. She felt him working down, with unbearable slowness, until his lips met the wet curls cresting the swell of her pubic bone. His first kiss on her mount of Venus had the brutal intensity of an electric shock, and her backside lifted as every muscle in her body tensed, spasmed, collapsed back onto the soft, wet sand.

Esteban felt it too. He felt every shiver of ecstasy, every agonised spasm of pleasure that rippled through Venetia's body. For that was his blessing and his curse; to feel as she felt, to know her pain, to share her ecstasy.

He bent over her, softly stroking her thighs apart. 'Open for me, *ma petite*. Blossom for me.'

Her thighs relaxed and her legs parted, revealing the sex-swollen pout of her pussy-lips. He ran the tip of his index finger along the dusky pink line and she opened to him like a ripe fruit, bursting with sweet juice and soft pink flesh.

The hunger was at the back of his mind; a dark shadow looking over his shoulder; the sight of Venetia's womanhood bringing back the ache of need. It would be so simple, so blissful, to kiss her and drink her and empty her of life. To take what he longed to have, to make her his. To bring her out of the light and into the darkness – his darkness. The all-encircling darkness of the vampire.

He steadied his breathing, cursing the vile whispering in his head. *Take her, take her, she is yours now. She can be yours for ever . . .*

No. He would never yield to the darkness, not even if it cost him Venetia, the only woman he had ever truly cared for. Summoning the light to fill him, he bent to worship at her secret spring, and drank down the sweetness of her innocence.

In the haze of pleasure, Venetia abandoned herself to Esteban, banishing the fear, welcoming the kiss of his lips and tongue on the flower-stalk of her sex.

'Yes. Yes, oh yes, Esteban. Don't stop, please don't ever stop . . .'

At the point of orgasm he entered her, his penis like a rod of white-hot steel, his body feverish and hungry; their embrace so close that they were no longer two beings but one. And as their climax shuddered through them, Esteban wondered how much longer he could sustain the strength to resist his deepest, darkest passion.

That night, they pitched camp on the valley floor, in the shade of towering trees that whispered as the night wind caressed their branches.

They huddled together around the bonfire they had built from dried leaves and twigs. They had no need of the warmth it produced, but everywhere they could hear the sound of animals calling to each other.

'Do you see them?' Venetia snuggled into the crook of Esteban's arm. He held her close, his eyes scanning the darkness beyond the circle of yellow light. 'They're watching us, just waiting . . .'

'Nothing will harm you. Nothing.'

In the darkness, countless bright eyes watched and waited; a spreading circle of unwinking light, luminous in the flickering firelight.

Something moved in the darkness; a scurrying, scrabbling noise which made Venetia gasp and seize Esteban's arm. 'Something . . . did you hear it?'

'It is nothing.' Esteban concealed his own concern from his lover. He too had seen the dark shapes concealed in the dappled branches of the trees, heard the cries cutting through the air. Who could tell what might be here, waiting to prey upon them?

A small shape scurried forward.

'Esteban!'

It was a bat-eared fox, its muzzle pink and wet, its eyes large as a bush-baby's. It scurried into the encampment, darting forward on spider-thin legs to steal a piece of fruit; and then, just as quickly, it was gone.

Angry now, Esteban got to his feet. His eyes seemed to glint like polished steel in the firelight. He raised his hand to the night sky in a clenched fist.

'Begone. Creatures of the night, I command you, begone.'

At the sound of Esteban's voice the eyes blinked, darkened, then disappeared as the animals slunk away. A low howling shimmered through the still night air, then there was silence. An eerie, uneasy, unpleasant silence which Venetia longed to be broken.

Esteban turned back to Venetia. 'The beasts will obey me. They will not harm you, I swear it.'

But not all the eyes had disappeared. To Venetia, it seemed as if some were actually getting closer.

And she could have sworn they looked human.

Three days passed, and Venetia and Esteban explored the rest of the valley. They found a few small buildings, long ruined and deserted, many unknown species of flowers, fruit and insects. But no one who could help them in their quest.

'Nothing,' sighed Venetia, sinking down onto a rock.

Esteban sat down beside her, pushing back his mass of dark hair. 'We will find what we seek.'

'But Esteban, we've followed everything in the diary. Everything. To the letter. Do you think Marcus Almenius made the whole thing up?'

'We found the gateway. And this valley.'

'But nothing else. No settlement, no people, nothing. Perhaps we should turn back.'

'I at least must not give up.' Esteban's stone-black eyes rested on the middle distance, as though he could almost catch sight of something beyond mortal perception. 'I cannot, too much rests upon it. But you, Venetia . . .' He let out a long, slow current of breath. 'I cannot and will not hold you to this quest.'

She knelt beside him, her fingers stroking his thigh through his trousers. 'Where you go, I go.'

'Even if I lead you into danger?'

'I've never shunned danger, you know that.'

Esteban began massaging Venetia's shoulders, rubbing away the tension in her back and neck, caressing her as he spoke his thoughts. 'I do not understand it. The diary spoke of a settlement . . . and yet there is nothing here.'

'Could there have been a village which isn't here any more? Those ruins . . .'

'Venetia, you are the archaeologist. You have read the diary and you have seen what I have seen. There is nothing here that resembles what Almenius described, no sign that many people have ever lived here.' His hands worked gently at

Venetia's shoulders. 'But we will find the town . . . we must.'

Venetia turned to look at him over her shoulder. 'We will.' Her lips curved into a smile. 'What's the hurry anyway? Its beautiful here. It makes me . . . horny.'

Her fingers stroked up the inner surface of Esteban's thigh, reaching the hypersensitive crease between thigh and balls. He groaned with pleasure as her fingers brushed the flesh, and his hand covered hers.

'Not here . . .'

She looked up, surprised. 'Why?'

'I don't know . . . there's something . . . I can *feel* something.' He breathed in the scented air. Nothing but the perfumes of flowers and animal scents, musky and sweet. Perhaps he was imagining it. He took his hand away, and allowed Venetia to unzip his flies, taking out the glossy, ripening fruit of his cock.

'I want you, I'm so thirsty for you,' she breathed, and parting her lips she put out her tongue and began to lick.

The sound was a tiny one; scarcely more than a rustle of leaves in the undergrowth. An animal, scurrying through the leaves. Then Esteban heard it again, and this time Venetia heard it too. The sound of something . . . no, *someone*, crying out as though startled.

Venetia and Esteban turned and looked in the direction of the noise.

'Someone . . . did you see?'

Esteban nodded. With his acute vision, he had seen more than she. He had glimpsed the dark, lithe shape of a human figure, running away

393

through the undergrowth.

'Should we . . .?'

Esteban leapt to his feet, zipping his flies. 'We must follow. We have no choice.'

And they began running, scrambling, chasing through the trees and bushes, Venetia panting and gasping as she struggled to keep up with Esteban's long strides.

The shape disappeared then reappeared, a fast-moving shadow among many shadows, almost lost in the shifting patterns of sunlight among the close-packed leaves.

'There.' Esteban pointed to a gap between the trees. Venetia followed, pushing through the foliage to discover not the wooded glade she had expected, but the entrance to a cave.

'It's very dark . . .'

'Follow me.'

'I can't see . . .'

'Hold my hand. The dark holds no fears for me.'

As they stepped inside, Venetia became aware that the darkness was not quite complete. Somewhere in the far distance a muted orange light glowed, scarcely more than a soft haze in the blackness.

Venetia stumbled on loose rocks, grateful for Esteban's firm grip. She knew that she must trust him to find a safe path through the darkness.

The cave narrowed, and Esteban had to stoop, helping Venetia along, his strong hands holding her when she slipped, her fingers scrabbling helplessly on the wet rocks.

'It's too narrow, Esteban, I can't go any further.'

He held her close against him, stilling the frantic pounding of her heart with gentle kisses.

'A little further, *petite anglaise*. A little further, then no more. Trust me . . .'

Further, further, further. The orange smear of light became a haze, then a blur, and finally a glow.

'There's something . . . an opening,' gasped Venetia.

'Yes.' Esteban stopped in his tracks, his grip about her waist tightening.

'What's the matter? What can you see?'

He swore softly under his breath, Spanish curses of astonishment that came tumbling out. '*Madre de dios* . . .'

He walked slowly forward, into the light, Venetia a step behind, her hand tightly clasped in his. She gasped as she emerged from the cave and her eyes became accustomed to the soft, many-coloured glow.

'No! It can't be . . .'

At first, she could not believe it. Her eyes must be deceiving her. This was some dream, some phantasmagoria invented by a disordered mind. But beautiful, so beautiful . . .

It was a town. No, an incredible city, but from the rock walls of a gigantic chasm, driven through the heart of the mountain. It towered above and below their feet, rising hundreds of feet towards the distant sky, where huge outcrops of many-coloured quartz caught the sun and reflected it down into the city, filling it with a rainbow of light.

And there were people. People watching them from corners, eyes wide, watchful. Advancing towards them, reaching out to touch the two strangers who had stepped into the middle of this otherworldly world.

Chapter Eleven

A LOW WHISPER ran round the strange, rock-hewn city, echoing as it was reflected off the quartz-studded walls.

At first, Venetia could not see the people, though she knew they must be there, watching. Then slowly, tentatively, they began to emerge into the light, their eyes wide with curiosity.

They were a tall, handsome race; rather dark with pale olive skins that shimmered in the waterfall of many-coloured light. The men wore short tunics kilted with leather belts, and turquoise-coloured jewellery on their arms and at their throats. The woman were slightly-built, their hair cropped short in a boyish style. They dressed in filmy sarongs which left much of their bodies bare, revealing gaudy painted designs swirled over their smooth skin.

This place . . .' gasped Venetia. 'It's so much bigger than the settlement in Marcus Almenius's diary . . .'

'Many hundreds of years have passed.' Esteban surveyed the scene, shading his eyes against the shimmer of light. Eyes watched, looked back at him, spellbound, curious yet not hostile. He turned back to Venetia. 'We must not hope for too much. These people may have forgotten what they knew, if it is true that they ever knew anything at all. And once they know who and what I am, they may not be well disposed towards us.'

'I don't see what choice we have. We have to take that chance – we can't go back now.'

Esteban pursed his lips, resisting a smile. 'Your courage is equalled only by your recklessness,' he commented.

Esteban led Venetia forward, into the full glare of day. They walked slowly down a flight of steps cut into the rock, until they emerged on to a rose-pink terrace. From there, they had a clearer view over the town; and Venetia saw that it consisted of a dizzying mass of tunnels, staircases and gateways, cut into the rock. There was no way of knowing how far it extended, or what lay beyond the enigmatic, rocky façades.

Together they descended into the heart of the town. Slowly, figures came forward to greet them. Venetia tried to read their expressions, silently praying that they would be friendly. She let out a startled cry as a girl reached out to touch her hair. The girl made a strange, low purring sound like a curious animal as her long, tattooed hands smoothed over the wavy blonde mane.

Another girl, very young and pretty, reached out tentative fingers to touch Esteban, but he rounded on her, pushing her away.

'Esteban,' warned Venetia. 'Esteban, be careful . . . we mustn't offend them.'

'I will not – I cannot – tolerate their touch on my flesh. It causes me pain, it awakens the blood hunger . . .'

By now, a circle of onlookers had gathered, and Venetia decided that she must do her best to communicate with them. She placed a hand on her breast. 'Venetia. Venetia, yes?'

The eyes narrowed slightly, the heads tilting forward, listening.

'Venetia,' repeated the pretty girl who had touched Esteban. 'Ven-ee-sha.'

'Esteban.' Venetia touched Esteban's arm. 'Esteban.'

The girl's lips curved into a smile of pure lust, and she reached out to him, offering a flower from her hair.

'Esteban . . . Esteban . . .' Her voice was a silky sigh, and Venetia experienced a sudden pang of mad, possessive jealousy. She could almost have laughed at the ridiculousness of it, if it had not felt so strong, so bitter, so real. She watched as the girl pointed to herself. 'Pernette.'

Esteban took the flower from the girl's hand. For a few seconds it seemed to sparkle in his hand, as though it were made of frosted glass. But as he stroked his fingers along the stem, it dissolved into a cloud of shimmering dust which drifted to the ground about his feet. The crowd drew back with an 'ahhh' of astonishment, entranced yet uneasy.

Venetia was so preoccupied with trying to coax back the girl that she did not notice the two men approaching.

Esteban was aware of their presence long before Venetia. He raised his head, his eyes filled with a strange and troubled brightness. 'They have come for us.'

Venetia looked up to see two men pushing their way through the crowd. They were different in appearance from the other townsfolk, their bodies muscular and brown, their expressions blank and unwelcoming. They were wearing armour made from small plates of a dull, black metal, and conical helmets which reminded Venetia of Byzantine armour she had once catalogued at the British Museum. At their belts, double-edged sword-blades glittered.

Heart pounding, Venetia shrank away.

Esteban drew her to his side. 'We must go with them.'

'No, Esteban. Esteban, I'm afraid . . .'

He kissed her on her forehead and spoke softly to her.

'Welcome the fear and use it, Venetia. Fear is a power like any other.'

'I can't!'

'You can, Venetia. There is so much that you can do. Within you there is a strength you do not yet recognise or understand. Live with the fear, confront it as I have confronted it through seven long centuries.'

And together, they followed the two men out of the square, towards a small, square gateway in the rock face.

They passed through the gateway and into the first of many rooms. Despite her apprehension, Venetia found herself excited by what she saw. Each room was hewn from solid rock, yet the workmanship was exquisite, the decoration not quite like anything she had ever seen before. It

399

was European and yet not European, exotic but sometimes oddly familiar.

Crossing a third room, the walls narrowed to form a passageway; then suddenly widened again, opening into an immense hall with bright frescoes of dancing girls and animals painted on its smooth sandstone walls. Venetia looked up, and saw that there were deep shafts cut high up in the walls, flooding the hall with sunlight.

There were three people in the hall, two handsome women of perhaps thirty-five, and an older man in purple robes, with a circlet of twisted gold on his curly, oiled hair. They were sitting together on gilded chairs, raised up on a dais. Town elders perhaps, thought Venetia. The man spoke in a deep, sonorous voice.

'*Soyez les bienvenus.*'

Venetia stared, open-mouthed. French? He was speaking to them in French! Heavily-accented and archaic French, it was true, but there was no mistaking its origin.

Esteban seemed unsurprised. He inclined his head in a deferential nod.

'*Vous nous honorez, messire.*'

The Elder nodded to the two guards and clapped his hands. 'You may retire,' he said in his archaic French. Then he turned his attentions to Venetia. 'You are very striking,' he commented dispassionately.

'I . . . thank you.'

'You and your companion must also be very resourceful. Few have succeeded in finding this place since our forefathers came here, many centuries ago.'

He contemplated Venetia in silence for a few

moments, as though lost in thought. It was Venetia who broke the silence. 'Sir . . . What is this place? Who are these people?'

'I am Baudouin, Vizier of the ancient city of Tamezion.' He paused. 'My ancestors were French soldiers, pursued into these mountains by Saracen warriors. They remained and settled here, intermarrying with the natives of this place and sharing their great wisdom.' Baudouin looked from Venetia to Esteban and back again. 'Now you must tell me why you have come here.'

Esteban stepped forward. '*Messire Baudouin* . . . I am Esteban and this is my companion, Venetia. We have come to plead for your help.'

The Vizier turned his quiet brown eyes on Esteban. His expression did not change. 'I see. And why should my people wish to help you?'

Esteban felt impatience rising in his throat. 'You have helped others. Why not us?'

A flicker of interest passed across Baudouin's face, as though he had glimpsed the darkness beyond Esteban's impassive eyes. 'Tell me, *Monsieur* Esteban. And answer me truly. Are you touched by the blood curse?'

'These seven hundred years and more I have lived in torment, unable to die, unable to live as a mortal man.' His eyes glittered. 'You must help us. You cannot refuse us.'

Baudouin exchanged glances with the two women at his side. 'We do not have to do anything. On the contrary, *Monsieur* Esteban, it is for you to provide us with explanations.' He looked from Esteban to Venetia and back again. 'You and she are lovers?'

Esteban cast down his eyes, unable to meet the

401

Vizier's gaze. 'To my eternal shame and my honour's damnation.'

Baudouin continued speaking. 'You know the danger to her? If the hunger comes upon you and you cannot control it?'

Esteban turned to Venetia, his eyes filled with shame. 'I acknowledge the weakness of my flesh and spirit. My actions do me no honour.'

Venetia cut in. 'If there is any weakness of spirit, it is mine. Esteban told me we must never meet again . . . but then we found the book, and it changed everything.'

One of the female Elders leaned forward in her chair. 'Tell me of this book.'

'It is the diary of a man called Marcus Almenius, an explorer. It tells how he came here, many years ago, and saw . . .'

Her mouth dried, the words catching in her throat. Esteban took up the story.

'It told how he saw the curing of a vampire, the casting out of the blood curse.' His coal-black eyes blazed with a new intensity, the desperation of a man who has seen into the depths of the abyss.

'That was long ago,' said the second female elder. 'Many hundreds of years, when our ancestors had not long been in Tamezion, learning the ancient wisdom.'

Venetia's brain whirled. 'Will you . . . can you help us? Do you still possess the knowledge and the skill?'

The woman shook her head slowly. 'It has been many centuries . . . in the time before we began to forget the old ways . . .'

The last vestiges of colour were draining from Esteban's face. He looked waxen, ghostlike beneath the olive veneer of his skin.

'If you cannot help us,' he said flatly, 'provide us with one night's rest and we will go from this place and never return.'

The female Elder got to her feet. 'I do not say that we cannot help you,' she said. 'Only that we cannot be sure. Have patience and stay with us a while, become our guests, let us find out what can be done for you. You will be free to move about the city as you wish.' Her eyes lighted on Esteban. They seemed to see into his very soul. 'The only law here,' she added softly, 'is that you must do no harm.'

Gabriel Engelhart followed the girl along the dark tunnel. Even in the half-light from the lantern he could see that Pernette was more than attractive. Her sinuous body twisted and turned in the shadows, her snake-hips bare but for the thin, filmy sarong she wore loosely tied about her to cover her taut belly and her small, apple-hard breasts.

The darkness began to lighten, and she swung round to face him, her face almost elfin, her eyes bright with laughter. She was flirting with him. He could read her desire in those cherry-black eyes. And that suited his purposes very well. He could use an ally and a plaything in this weird, unearthly place.

'*Nous sommes presqu'arrivés,*' she told him in her light, sing-song voice. 'We shall soon be there.'

It sounded peculiar, listening to this profoundly exotic young creature speaking to him in old-fashioned French. Not that it posed many problems for Gabriel. He spoke a couple of dozen languages, all of them fluently. And by his own reckoning, he could seduce a beautiful woman in any language.

'Lead on. Show me.'

He followed close behind her, glad that he had sent Ismail away. Ismail had his uses, but here he would only get in the way, be indiscreet, ruin everything and probably get them both killed.

'Do you know where they have taken them – the two strangers?' he asked her as they paused to rest. She purred softly as he stroked her short, thick hair.

'No, *m'sieur*. But they are somewhere in the city. I saw them before the guards took them away. The woman, she is pretty. The man, he is very beautiful ...' She closed her eyes in pleasurable reminiscence, and Gabariel felt a stab of annoyance.

'Esteban,' he spat contemptuously. 'He is worthless slime, he is nothing. Nothing, do you hear?'

The girl's eyes widened with alarm, the eyes of a startled fawn. Realising he had overstepped the mark, Gabriel drew her to him and stifled her faint protests with a passionate kiss.

At first Pernette resisted him, her strong, lithe limbs pushing against him, her whole body rigid with fear or outrage or both. But Gabriel Engelhart was a skilful lover. He knew she would not long resist him. His mouth possessed hers, his tongue forcing its way between her lips and into the warm haven beyond. He thrilled to the taste of her, sweet and fresh, like her innocence. A transient taste, he told himself with satisfaction. Innocence could not long endure in the arms of

Gabriel Engelhart. He liked to destroy it before it had a chance to grow stale.

In the half-light their eyes met, and he knew Pernette was his for the taking. The mesmeric power of his blue eyes held her fast, making her yield to him. And all the time he was whispering to her of how it would be, of the pleasure she would feel as he entered her and took her for his own.

'M'sieur, je vous en prie . . . m'sieur, j'ai gran' peur . . .'

'Do not be afraid. What is there to be afraid of?' His voice, syrupy and smooth, soothed her fears like a cool hand smoothing across a fevered brow.

'I do not know, m'sieur. I do not know if this is right. Perhaps I should go, tell the Elders of the city . . .'

'Hush, hush. Be still.' The hypnotic modulations of his voice lulled her, stilled her breathing, relaxed the muscles in the hands that clutched at him, so greedy and yet so afraid.

The apprehension seemed to drain out of her face and her features relaxed. She almost smiled, her lips parting and the tip of her tongue flicking across them, leaving a slick of moisture that glistened in the lantern light.

'What is it that you desire of me, m'sieur?'

'I desire you, Pernette. I desire everything about you, my secret flower.'

His flingers slid down her back. Her sarong was moist with cooling sweat, clingy and so very fragile.

'I want you naked, my little flower. Naked as nature intended.'

Or the Devil, he thought to himself with a

frisson of malicious satisfaction.

'Non! Non, j'crois pas . . .'

She felt a return of the fear, but it was too late to change her mind. In any case, she was caught fast in the web of Gabriel's sensual intrigue. She feared him but desired him, longed for him to take her and use and devour her every bit as much as she longed for him to let her go.

Pernette's breasts rose and fell with the quickening rhythm of her breathing. Gabriel's face came closer to hers and he kissed her again, taking her breath away. Her legs felt weak, her thighs trembling and moist with the juices trickling from between her petals of her secret flower.

She felt his hands undressing her, unpinning and unwinding the loose wrap until the gauzy fabric fell away with the softest whisper and she felt the cool dampness of the air on her skin.

Together they sank to the stony bed of the cave. It was damp with trickles of brackish water, but she noticed nothing save the heat from their two bodies, mingling, kindling, flaring up into the white-hot heat of unstoppable lust.

'Such beautiful breasts,' murmured Gabriel, his thigh sliding between hers, the hardness of muscle meeting the soft springiness of her pubic mound. He took one breast in each hand, squeezing, palpating, flicking his thumbnails so that they scratched across the erect nipples.

She squealed with pleasure, writhing and bucking on the stony floor. Instinctively she thrust upwards with her pelvis, her fleshy outer labia parting as her pubic bone met Gabriel's thigh and grinding hard against it, smearing his skin with her special wetness.

He lay half-on, half-off her, his thigh between hers, his belly pressing down on hers so that the fleshy spear of his cock was trapped deliciously in a sticky prison of sweating flesh.

She was in an ecstasy of lust now, her fear forgotten, her only thought the pleasure he was giving her as he rubbed long and slow on her clitoris.

'*Je n'en puis plus, je n'en puis plus,*' she moaned as he took her to a plateau of excitement and held her there, refusing her the sweet mercy of orgasm.

'You will bear it, my love, and you will worship the cock that brings you to ecstasy.'

His voice was a caress in itself; a long, slow, sweet caress that swept over her body and made it tremble with anticipation.

'You will serve me well, my pretty one,' he smiled to himself. 'The gift of pleasure binds you to me more securely than any rope or chain. And with you to assist me, I shall soon have my revenge on Esteban and his English bitch for good and all.'

The following morning, Venetia and Esteban were summoned before the Elders once again. Guards led them down rose and amber-tinted passageways, up and down flights of steps cut into blocks of solid rose-quartz. It was all so unreal, like something out of a child's storybook. Unreal, and yet so deadly serious. For Esteban had come here to bargain for his life.

They emerged into a chamber with a high, domed ceiling made from intricately-patterned stained glass. Flickering patterns of coloured light flooded the room, dancing on the many smooth stone pillars and the mosaic floor, depicting a girl dressed in white, pursued through a forest by many-headed, fantastical beasts.

The younger of the two female Elders, Aduca, summoned them into the chamber. It was empty, save for a low dais, on which stood a simple lectern of carved wood.

'Greetings.' Aduca walked before them to the lectern, followed by a young girl Venetia recognised as Pernette, the one who had touched Esteban when they first arrived in the city. 'I have brought you here to show you something. Our Book of Ancient Wisdom. In your world, those who have looked upon it call it the *Lore of Madali* . . .'

Venetia gasped. The *Lore of Madali* – here, in this lost city?

'But . . .' she murmured.

Aduca lifted her hand to impose silence. 'This book contains all the wisdom of Tamezion,' she explained, 'gathered together in pictures and symbols, coded so that only the elect may understand our secrets. It also contains the last recorded account of a successful lifting of the blood curse.' She turned to the girl by her side. 'You may open the book, Pernette.'

'*Oui, madame.*'

The girl crossed to the lectern and opened the book, marking the page with a length of purple ribbon. Venetia stared down at it. It looked so . . . insignificant, just a collection of yellowed parchments, roughly sewn together. But just as in the photograph she had seen, the pages were filled with exquisite pictures, erotic symbols, tiny writing . . .

'You both read old Latin?'

Venetia nodded.

'Good. You will see that the relevant page has been translated.'

Her head spinning, Venetia stepped forward. Esteban did not move. Now that the moment of truth had arrived he felt paralysed, impotent. His life, his death, his torment . . . all might depend upon the turn of a dusty page.

Venetia bowed her head and read from the book. 'And the elders of the city did bring forth a holy man afflicted of the blood curse, which man was much pained by the hunger. And they bound him, for they were fearful of his strength and the darkness in his eyes . . .'

The darkness in his eyes. Venetia shivered with recognition. How many times had she seen that look in Esteban's eyes? The dark shadow, the pain, the hunger? The danger that waited patiently for her behind the innocent cloak of a kiss.

She read on, her blood chilling as she followed the course of the ritual. '. . . and after the ritual was performed he lay as if dead, and a great lamentation was heard that did shake the walls of the city, a cry that seemed to tear the moon from the sky. Great fear spread through the people, for the stars were darkened and all light was gone from this place.

'But when the holy man awoke, the curse had departed from his soul . . .'

Aduca laid her hand on Venetia's, stilling the tremor in her fingers. 'No one has performed the ritual of curing for hundreds of years,' she said. 'But the Elders have spoken, and we are willing to

409

attempt it.' She turned to Esteban. 'If *you* are willing to risk your life.'

Esteban met her gaze. 'For a vampire, there is no life. Only the darkness and hunger.'

He thought back over seven centuries, seven centuries alone; unchanging, un-ageing. Those who had made him like this had understood, far better than he, that immortality could be the ultimate curse. Immortality, and the hunger that only blood could still . . .

'And you wish to face whatever must be done?'

Taking Aduca's hand, he placed it against his lips. 'I wish to live.'

'You have your life, *Monsieur* Esteban. You have the gift of living forever.'

Esteban's expression darkened. 'All I ask is the chance to live again as other men.'

'There is great risk.'

'I have told you, I will do whatever is necessary.'

'Then you are a brave man, Esteban. Or more foolish than you know.' Aduca looked towards Venetia. 'And you, Venetia. You have read the account of the ceremony. There could be dangers, even for you. You are still willing?'

'I am willing.'

Esteban looked at Aduca sharply. 'You speak of danger – danger to Venetia?'

'She must be by your side during the ceremony. It is through her that the power must be channelled.'

'No!' Esteban pushed Aduca aside and began reading from the ancient book. He grew quiet, his face tense as though he were fighting some inner struggle. At last he looked up. 'This cannot be. I will not allow it.'

Venetia caught his arm. 'It's the only way.'

'I will not risk your life. My life is of no value, it is a living death; but you, Venetia . . . no, not you.'

'I choose to take that risk.' Her voice shook as she realised the implications of what she was saying. Doubt whispered at the back of her mind: do you really care enough? Would he do the same for you?

'And if I refuse to let you?' demanded Esteban.

'You would never refuse me.' She took his fingers and kissed them, one by one. 'Never.'

As she turned back to Aduca, she saw the girl Pernette watching her out of the corner of her eye, sly, half-smiling. No, not watching her; watching *Esteban*. Venetia saw the way her tongue-tip flicked over her lips and jealousy hit her like a kick in the guts.

And yet, what cause had she to be jealous of this half-wild girl and her childish infatuation? Venetia forced herself to look away and question Aduca. 'What must be done?'

'You must spend three days and nights apart. On the night before the ceremony you will be brought together, and that will mark the end of the preparations. The following night . . . if the heavens are willing and the omens are propitious . . .' She clapped her hands and the guards stepped forward. 'Take them away and begin the ceremony of preparation.'

As Venetia was led away, she turned to look back over her shoulder. Pernette was still standing there, that same covetous smile playing about her lips, her dark eyes fixed on Esteban, as

411

though by sheer force of will she could make him desire her as she desired him.

The next three days weighed heavily for Venetia. Forbidden to see Esteban, she found her imagination creating wild scenarios in which things went horribly wrong; scenes of treachery and betrayal; scenes in which she imagined him lying naked with the sly-faced girl Pernette . . .

With difficulty, she forced herself to think sensibly. She was afraid; well, that was only to be expected. She had been forcibly parted from Esteban, inciting her imagination to create monsters which simply didn't exist.

And she longed for Esteban, there was no doubt of that. Through the long nights she lay awake in her cool white-walled cell, gazing up at the star-painted ceiling, imagining she could hear his voice whispering to her on the night-wind: *'Toi seule, Venetia, ma reine, ma destinée . . .* You alone, my destiny, my only one . . .'

In the morning, she went out to explore the city. It quickly became apparent that it consisted of a sequence of rocky chasms, halls and valleys, connected by a maze of tunnels. In the valleys lay beautiful ornamental gardens, wooded glades, orchards and grassy meadows where animals grazed, completely unafraid of their human companions.

She walked through a grove of orange and lemon trees, breathing in the sharp tang of sun-warmed citrus. The fruits hung like luminous globes from the bending branches, reaching themselves into her hands. Everything seemed so peaceful, so perfect. It was difficult to believe that chill darkness could be so very close at hand.

A voice broke into her solitary thoughts. 'You are a difficult woman to find, Venetia Fellowes.'

Aghast, she swung round, her blood turning to ice. Gabriel Engelhart was sitting beneath an orange tree, the girl Pernette crouched in the grass at his feet, her finger stroking his thigh, her face nuzzling into his flesh like a lap-dog's muzzle.

'Gabriel! What the hell are you doing here?'

'Like I told you before, Venetia. Protecting my investment.'

'Leave me alone, I never want to speak to you again.'

'I don't think that's entirely true, Venetia. And you wouldn't want to lie to me, would you? Not after we were so . . . *intimate* together. I mean, I thought we told each other *everything* . . .'

He got to his feet, brushing Pernette aside, and walked alongside Venetia, taking her by the arm and turning her round.

'Don't touch me! Let go . . .'

'Only if you promise not to run away from me.'

'Why the hell should I promise you anything?'

'Because we had an arrangement . . .'

'And you know what you can do with your so-called arrangement.'

'. . . and because I have something very important to say to you.'

'You have nothing to say that I would ever want to hear.'

Pernette caught up with them, stepping in front of Venetia to halt her progress. '*Madame*, I would not be so sure of that.' Her sloe eyes glowed with reflected light.

Venetia looked from Pernette to Gabriel and back again. 'If you're trying to trick me you're not being very subtle about it.'

Gabriel chuckled. An unpleasant sound, thought Venetia – dark and humourless. 'Why be so suspicious, Venetia? Why think the worst of me? Has your lover Esteban made you hate all men . . .?'

'Leave Esteban out of this,' snapped Venetia. Gabriel's expression remained unchanged.

'He is using you, Venetia. He cheated on me and he will betray you too.'

Gabriel's words were like a poisoned dagger in her heart.

'No. I don't believe you, I don't believe any of it.'

Gabriel shook his head. His blond hair, backlit by sunshine, gave the illusion of a pale halo about his face. 'Very well, Venetia, if it is your choice you are free to disbelieve me. But you do so at your peril. Don't you want to know what Esteban is really like? Don't you want to know about the risks you are taking for a man who is scarcely better than a stinking, walking corpse?'

At Gabriel's sign, Pernette began to speak, laying her cool hand on Venetia's.

'*Madame*, I know nothing of Monsieur Esteban,' she began.

Liar, thought Venetia. You know enough about him to want him in your bed, you treacherous little slut.

'. . . But I have heard Baudouin and Aduca speaking of the ritual, and I know what dangers you are to undergo.'

'Listen to her,' said Gabriel, 'and listen well. Her words may save your life, my pretty one.'

414

Venetia wanted to stop her ears, make it all go away. She wanted to be far, far away from here, on some beach in the South of France, sipping chilled wine and laughing in the sunshine.

'Listen, *madame*. They have told you that the last successful lifting of the blood-curse was many centuries ago. This is true. But what they did not tell you was that there was another attempt, only a few years ago. It went wrong, terribly wrong. The cursed one lived on, but there was also a death, a painful, unspeakable death . . .'

'No . . . No, I won't listen.'

'The Elders have almost forgotten how to use the old wisdom, they scarcely know what they are doing. They will destroy you with their clumsy ignorance. Esteban knows this, but he is willing to risk your life for the chance to save his own . . .'

Venetia lashed out, striking the girl across the face, so hard that it left the imprint of her hand on the tawny features. She sprang back with a hiss of anger and pain.

'How dare you . . . how dare you strike me!'

Venetia's eyes blazed. 'And how dare you tell me these lies?'

'There is no lie . . . it is the truth.' Springing forward, Pernette spat in Venetia's face. 'Only you are too stupid to see it.'

Gabriel seized hold of Pernette and dragged her away. 'Leave her. She will not listen now, but later . . . later she will realise the truth and come running back, begging us to save her.' And later, he thought to himself, I shall have not only Venetia and the *Lore of Madali*, but my sweet, sweet revenge on Esteban.

Venetia wiped her face with an automatic hand. She felt cold, dazed, suddenly frightened. She wished Esteban were here, here to hold her in his arms and tell her that Gabriel's words were lies, vicious, evil lies.

She left Gabriel and Pernette standing in the citrus grove, and walked quickly back towards her room. But try as she might, she could not still the whispering voice in her head.

The voice that whispered darkly of betrayal.

Chapter Twelve

ON THE FOURTH night, Venetia lay in Esteban's arms once more, watching the changing patterns of moonlight play across the mosaic floor of their chamber.

'You are troubled,' he commented, his hand stroking her cheek as they lay together, his naked body strong and hard against the long curve of her backbone.

'No; no it's nothing.' Venetia fought down the fear, but she knew her voice sounded unnaturally quiet and expressionless.

'If it is nothing, why are you afraid?'

'I'm not. I . . .'

He kissed the back of her neck and she shivered, not only with pleasure.

'*Petite anglaise*, I can smell your fear. I can taste it in your sweat.' He pushed aside the thick curtain of her hair, and dotted tiny kisses between her shoulder blades and up her spine to the base of her skull.

She rolled away from him, afraid of the intensity of sensations he awoke in her. 'It's just

. . . the ritual.' She got to her feet and walked across to the window, resting her arms on the cool, carved stone of the sill.

Esteban rose on one elbow, watching her closely. In the darkness his diamond-black eyes had faded to empty shadows. 'If you are afraid to proceed . . .'

'No. No, of course not.'

'If you are afraid, you have only to say. I swore I would not try to influence you. It is not right that you should face these dangers for my sake.'

She turned round and looked at him. His body was white as sculpted marble in the moonlight. 'I gave my word.'

'And I free you from it.' The word did not come without pain. Venetia felt it shivering through him. 'Gladly.'

'If only I could be sure that that was true.'

He sat up, swinging his legs onto the floor.

'Now I understand.' The realisation hit him, full force. All at once he understood his stupidity. A black, cold feeling of unease had been with him ever since they entered the valley, but he had not been able to identify its cause. He had thought that perhaps the blood-hunger was creeping up on him again. 'It is me that you are afraid of. You don't trust me, do you?'

He took her by the shoulders.

'Please, Esteban . . .' She tried to shrug off his embrace, but he held her fast.

'All I ask is that you tell me why you fear me.'

She avoided his gaze. 'Gabriel Engelhart . . .'

Esteban let go of her, turned and walked away, pacing the room. 'He is here? How could I not have known? And yet, I sensed a darkness growing around this place . . .'

'. . . And that servant-girl, Pernette.'

'She is nothing. A creature of instinct, no more.'

'She is in love with you, I have seen it in her eyes.'

'And you believe . . .?'

'They came to me when I was walking in the orange grove. They spoke to me, told me things, terrible things . . .

Esteban shook his head angrily. 'And poisoned you against me?'

'They spoke of a vampire curing that went very wrong. But that . . . that was not what made me afraid. Gabriel spoke of betrayal. He said you were using me. He said . . . he said you had cheated him, and that in time you would betray me too.'

Esteban sank down onto the bed. 'I see. And you believe this?'

'I don't know what to believe.'

'No. I suppose not.' He looked up. 'Are you in love with Gabriel Engelhart.'

'I despise him, you know that. But . . .'

'But he has placed doubt in your mind, and you cannot drive it out.' He ran his fingers through his hair. 'What is it you wish from me, Venetia?'

'The truth. That's all I ask.'

'Gabriel Engelhart is the essence of purest evil. That, *ma petite anglaise*, is the truth.'

He saw Venetia open her mouth to speak, and hushed her with a gesture of his hand. 'But I do not expect you to believe that, and I cannot prove it to you. However, I will tell you why I hate and despise him.

'Fifteen years ago, Gabriel Engelhart had nothing. He was a penniless art student who sold his body to rich old women for the price of a meal. That is how he came to Valazur, as the companion of an elderly countess who liked to flatter herself by having a young man on her arm.

'I disliked him the first time I saw him. Two years later, when we met again, I had grown to loathe him. Engelhart had become phenomenally, inexplicably successful in those two years. He was a millionaire now, a dilettante and a seducer. A cold-eyed, ruthless wheeler-dealer whose greatest pleasures were money and the corruption of innocence. I knew the first time I looked into his eyes that I was looking upon a vision of chaos and evil.

'At that time on the Riviera, there were rumours . . . stories that Engelhart had dabbled in the black arts, that this was how he had come by such riches and success. He roused my curiosity, and I made it my business to find out more about him. The stories, Venetia . . . they were all true. Gabriel Engelhart had been playing with fire and he was about to get burned.'

Venetia hardly knew what to say or do. 'And you expect me to believe that Gabriel Engelhart is some kind of black magician?'

Esteban laughed drily. 'From you, *chère petite anglaise*, I expect nothing, except that you will listen and judge me on my words. Gabriel Engelhart was and is a fool, an amateur, a dabbler in matters he could neither understand nor control. Another, far more powerful and more malevolent, manipulated Engelhart's greed, trapped him into a bargain; Engelhart would receive all the riches a man could desire, in return for . . .'

'His soul?' enquired Venetia ironically.

'Sometimes, *ma petite*, the incredible and the ridiculous can be true. Yes, *chère anglaise*, his soul. His immortal soul, which was trapped by magic inside a mirror . . .'

'But Esteban . . .'

'Trapped within a mirror which was later shattered, and the soul lost for ever, never to be regained. Not that it troubled Gabriel Engelhart that he had become a man without a soul. It only served to make his life easier, robbed him of the tiresome inhibitions which had impeded him for so long. Now, he could do anything he desired, and never be troubled by conscience.

'But there was still one thing that Gabriel Engelhart craved. The gift of immortality. And unfortunately Engelhart had discovered the truth about me, about the curse which binds me to this earth.

'He came to me one night, begged me, pleaded with me to give him what he craved. To drink his life-blood and make him a vampire.'

'And you . . .?'

'Naturally I refused. He grew violent, trying to provoke me, blackmail me, threaten me, knowing the strength of the black hunger within me. But still I refused him. I told him in no uncertain terms that I despised him, that such a man as he was unworthy. I would not sully my lips with his filthy blood.'

He smiled in the darkness.

'And so it is that he and I became enemies. I always suspected that Gabriel Engelhart's resentment would drive him to the ends of the earth to destroy me; and as you see, he has followed me even here.'

'Surely he came here because he wants the *Lore of Madali*.'

'No doubt he would risk a great deal to own a book of such esoteric power. But he would risk everything to see me cursed to eternal damnation.'

Venetia thought she could hear Esteban's heart thumping in the silence.

'Why didn't you tell me this before?'

'It served no purpose.'

'No purpose!' Anger quickened in Venetia. 'You knew about Gabriel, and you just let me . . .'

Esteban put up his hand. 'I followed you Venetia, don't you remember? You were angry with me for knowing so much about you, for interfering in your life when I had sworn to leave it forever. But I had been watching over you, Venetia, watching over you these last two years, though always at a distance. I swore to you that I would let you have your freedom . . . but equally, I would never let any harm come to you. Never. And that is why I cannot ask you to risk your life for me.'

He reached out and drew her to him. She felt the coolness of his breath on her cheek, yearned for him, felt her passion opening up to him. And she knew that, despite her fear, despite Engelhart's talk of betrayal, she believed him. That she would risk anything for a chance to be with him.

'You don't have to ask me.' She kissed him, her passion taking over, guiding her lips and her hands. She smoothed her fingers over the sharp contours of his face, the long sweep of neck and back, the hardness of buttock and thigh.

They sank down together to their knees, facing

each other on the cool mosaic floor. Esteban murmured to her as his fingers caressed the upturned points of her breasts. '*Ma reine, ma reine de la nuit* . . . my queen of darkness, you excite me, you rouse me to sweet madness . . .'

As they rolled on the floor, their limbs entwined, they breathed in the sweet, musky fragrance of damask roses.

'You are my temptation, my obsession . . .'

Venetia scarcely knew if she was really hearing Esteban's words, or if she was listening to his thoughts. She felt as though she had entered the secret rhythm of his being, his hunger joining hers and making her mad for him, animal-hungry for his body.

He lay behind her, the throbbing lance of his manhood pulsing as it pushed into the valley between her buttocks. She had to have him, could not wait any longer, had to feel him inside her.

'Take me,' she gasped. And she thrust back with a single flex of her hips, opening herself, taking the tip of his cock and swallowing it up in the haven of her sex.

Esteban responded with a long thrust. Venetia cried out as she felt his thick cock-ring distending the walls of her pussy, driving deep into her, seeking out the supersensitive G-spot at the front of her vagina and caressing it with a brutal tenderness.

'Oh yes, Esteban, oh yes . . .' She held apart her buttocks, urging him deeper, and he pushed hard into her until his heavy seed-sacs were slapping against the juicy split fig of her sex.

They coupled with the madness of lovers who know there may not be much more time; lovers who live for the moment, for the exquisite power of the passion which drives them on.

Moving her hips, Venetia drove back again and again onto Esteban's prick. He slid one hand onto her breast, the other down into the soft dark tangle of her maidenhair, winding his fingers about the honeyblonde curls, letting a fingertip stray lower, to the pout of her labia, to the tingling, juice-filled flowerstalk within.

It could not last long; it was too powerful, a meeting not only of bodies but of spirits. A lightning-flash of pleasure; a short, savage spasm that tore through him, and then it was gone, leaving them exhausted, spent, their bodies tangled in the warm, sweat-scented aftermath of pleasure.

Esteban stroked the side of Venetia's face as she slept in the crook of his arm. He had expressed his passion towards her, but he could not express the fear. The fear that he had brought her into his own private nightmare, into a world which might yet destroy them both.

Silently, he lay down beside her and watched the sky grow light. Waiting for the day to begin.

As the sun set once more over Tamezion, and darkness crept down over the mountains, a strange, expectant silence fell over the city.

Esteban and Venetia, dressed in high-collared ceremonial robes of unbleached linen, were led along a narrow, winding passageway towards the distant glow of flickering flame.

They emerged into a high-walled courtyard lined with polished black stone, the floor strewn ankle-deep with great drifts of white lilies and orchids. Bonfires in iron braziers stood at each corner, their flames licking with yellow and red tongues at the heavy, blue-black darkness, and the air was heavy with the scent of incense and fragrant woods. High above hung the round, yellow disc of the full moon.

Aduca stepped forward. 'You are willing?'

'We are willing.'

'Then the ritual may begin.'

Somewhere in the distance, Venetia heard the slow thump, thump, thump of a hundred drums, beating in unison. Her heart raced in double time, skipping beats; her mouth dry, her throat hoarse. The low hum of a distant, mumbled chant filled her head, making her dizzy and disorientated. She looked at Esteban. His face was expressionless, but his skin felt clammy and cold.

'Let darkness fall.'

At the word from Aduca, the bonfires were extinguished, one by one; scented smoke filled the courtyard as water sizzled on the embers. As darkness crept over them, Venetia heard Esteban's voice in her head: 'You alone, *petite anglaise*. You alone.'

Her last glimpse was of a face in the crowd. A face she loathed, despised and feared. The face of Gabriel Engelhart, smiling at her as if he knew some obscene secret . . .

She put Gabriel's face out of her mind. Perhaps he had been there, perhaps not. She might easily have imagined his evil smile, creeping into her consciousness to destroy her. She must remember what she had been told, the precise order of the ceremonial.

In the darkness, she felt unseen hands

stripping her, unfastening and peeling away the robe. The night air felt cold on her bare skin. Then something cold, wet; soft sable brushes painting her body with secret signs, signs so powerful that they could only be drawn in darkness, where none but the eye of heaven could see them. That was what Aduca had said. Venetia wondered, with a frisson of fear, if any of this was real, true; if Gabriel Engelhart could even have been right . . .

The hands slipped away and the drums began to quicken; the beat faster, faster, louder until it became a blur of sound.

They knew what they must do now.

Venetia and Esteban drew together, nakedness meeting nakedness in the darkness. The scents of sweet unguents dripped and melted from their bodies as they embraced. Closer, closer, closer. And kissed.

As their mouths met the whole world seemed to tremble. From somewhere nearby – or was it a thousand miles away? – Venetia heard a shrill cry, then silence.

Closer, closer, tighter; two becoming one, the passion growing, the hunger shared and burning.

Until at last, a bright light burst in the sky above them, showering down upon them, glowing with a furnace-heat which descended to earth, enshrouding and enveloping them.

Hiding them from human sight.

Esteban stirred. He groaned with pain as he opened his eyes; his whole body felt bruised and painfully sensitive.

It was daylight, and reflexively he narrowed his

eyes, waiting for the sear of discomfort; but it did not come. His body welcomed the brightness, the warmth, the daylight. His heart thumped. A change had come upon him, he felt . . . different. Could it be true? Or was he dreaming it all, only to awaken in some other place at some other time, to discover that he was still Esteban? Esteban the vampire.

Slowly and dizzily he sat up, and took a look around him. He saw that he was no longer in the black courtyard, not even in Tamezion. He was back in the wooded valley he and Venetia had explored, close by the gateway to the city.

Venetia. Where was Venetia? Panic grabbed at his guts. She was there, he could see her; but she was lying sprawled face-down on the earth, her honeygold hair spreading out around her in damp, disarrayed tendrils. She was not moving.

He tried to stand, but felt much too weak, all his accustomed strength drained from him, fear invading him as it had not for over seven hundred years. He stretched out his hand to touch her.

'Venetia . . . His voice was scarcely more than a dry croak. Still Venetia did not move; she just lay there, pallid, unmoving, her skin deathly cold.

Mocking laughter rang out behind Esteban. He turned to see Gabriel Engelhart, arms folded, head thrown back in vicious merriment.

'I have waited too long for this moment, Esteban,' he smirked. 'You were fools to trust the people of the city and their pathetic "wisdom". And I fear you have underestimated me. It was obvious to me from the beginning that the Englishwoman was the only thing you have ever

427

cared about, beyond yourself. And it was simplicity itself to seduce Pernette and have her alter the words of the ancient ritual so that your precious Venetia would be destroyed. Now the *Lore of Madali* is mine, the English bitch is dead, and you and I are equals.' He chuckled to himself. 'Though I scarcely see you as my equal, Esteban; poor, feeble, half-dead creature that you are.'

Esteban snarled his defiance, but his weakened body would not obey him, and as he lunged in rage towards Gabriel, his old enemy kicked out, catching him in the belly and sending him spinning to the ground, sick and helpless. Engelhart stood over Esteban, the smile never leaving his lips.

'What is it, my old friend? Are you too much of a coward to fight me now that your powers have left you?'

Panting, struggling for breath, Esteban looked up at Gabriel through eyes that swore vengeance. 'You are the devil incarnate.'

'And you, my dear Esteban, are a pathetic fool. For only a fool would choose mortality over eternal life.' His boot slid over Esteban's outstretched hand, and exerted pressure slowly and deliciously, crushing it into the dusty earth. 'How do you like your new life, Esteban? Such a pity that it will be so brief. But I shall do what I can to give you an interesting death . . .'

As Esteban's face contorted in helpless pain, his half-closed eyes made out a sudden shape . . . a lithe and savage thing that leaped and sprang. A creature of claws and teeth, that growled and hissed as it dragged Engelhart away and flung him to the ground.

428

'Venetia . . .' gasped Esteban, as Gabriel Engelhart fell away from him with a curse of pain, blood springing crimson from his bitten throat. 'Venetia, *petite anglaise*, what curse have I inflicted upon your sweet flesh?'

It was much later, and Venetia was sitting, cross-legged, upon the ground. Night had fallen in the valley, and a sweet languor had fallen over everything, the perfumed air soft and gentle, and quiet with the soft whisperings of a thousand night-creatures. Death had no place here, and yet Gabriel Engelhart was very dead.

Esteban lay beside her, his sleeping face pale in the moonlight; his dark hair falling across his cheek in a sweat-moistened strand. Tenderly she brushed it aside. He stirred briefly in his dream but she willed him not to wake, and he slumbered on, the darkness cradling him in its warm embrace.

When dawn broke, they would head back through the mountains together, leaving Engelhart's body sprawled on the ground beside the stolen book which had brought nothing but destruction; and before the gateway to the city of Tamezion. The gateway, which by some mystery had closed forever, reduced to a few ancient and meaningless carvings on a sheer rock face.

She knew it had gone for all eternity. Like her own mortality.

Venetia looked down at Esteban, her passion for him both savage and tender. Her life for his, it had seemed a small price to pay, but after all, she had not died. She had taken his darkness upon her and lived on, cursed as he had been cursed. A vampire now, as Esteban had been before.

She stroked her long, slender fingers over his neck and shoulder. He was beautiful. She longed to nuzzle against his throat and sip the elixir of his life-blood. But she could never harm him. She adored him with a passion that transcended simple hunger.

And so she would sit beside him through the night, and guard him. And in the morning they would travel on together. Into the unknown.

Epilogue

THE MEDITERRANEAN SURF crashed on the beach, far below.

In the grounds of Esteban's villa, high above the sea, two figures walked amid the orange trees.

'I have betrayed you, *petite anglaise*,' said Esteban, gazing out to sea, watching the pinks and apricots of dawn slowly blooming in the royal-blue sky.

'It was my choice to take the risk. You know that, Esteban.'

He turned to look at her, the old fire burning deep in his glittering dark eyes.

'If I had known. If I had known that this might happen, I would not have permitted it . . .'

Venetia flicked back her long mane of blonde hair. 'You could not have known, nobody could.'

'And Engelhart's treachery . . .'

She looked him in the eyes.

'Gabriel Engelhart is dead.'

'Yes.'

'Can you forgive me?'

'For saving me? For taking his foul and useless

life? There is nothing to forgive, Venetia.' He took her hand. 'If not for you, I would be dead.'

Venetia returned his gaze, her blue eyes bright. 'I don't regret what has happened to me, and neither must you.'

He laughed bitterly. 'But I have placed a curse upon you. A terrible hunger, a darkness that will abide with you for ever . . .'

'Eternity is a long time, Esteban. There will be other chances, we will find other ways to make things right. I am content. Or at least, I am patient. I can wait.'

Esteban took both her hands in his.

'We might both be content, *petite anglaise*,' he whispered. 'There could be a way . . .'

Venetia shivered, suddenly cold. She knew what he was thinking. Hadn't she thought it herself, a thousand times these last weeks?

'No, Esteban . . .'

'You have the power, Venetia. It is within you now. Will you deny me what I once offered you?'

'Esteban, you're crazy. I won't do it . . .'

He hushed her with a kiss, his warmth and urgency melting the fear that lapped at the edges of her mind. She felt his heart thumping against her chest, felt the tremor of excitement pass through him. And his excitement aroused her, the tang of his sweat, the animal warmth making her hunger for him in a hundred dark and dangerous ways. She let out a low moan of longing.

'Venetia. Listen to me. Once, long ago, I offered you immortality. Now I am asking you to bestow the same upon me.'

She stared back at him, at once incredulous and excited. 'You're asking me . . . you want to

432

become a vampire again? After all these hundreds of years of searching . . .? Esteban, you are mortal again, you have what you wanted . . .'

'I do not have you.'

'Leave, Esteban. Leave Valazur, you can go anywhere now, be anything, love any mortal woman . . .'

'It is you I want, Venetia.'

'If you stay with me, there is such danger. You, of all men, know the darkness and the hunger . . .'

His eyes met hers, their gaze steady and strong. 'Can it be danger if it is something I truly crave?'

They walked on through the trees, the lawns gradually sloping down to the cliff edge. Behind them, the stone turrets of the villa rose up to puncture the lightening sky, letting in the sun. Beneath them, the distant surf crashed down on the beach, spray framing a lone figure walking along the margin of the sea, picking up driftwood.

'It will soon be light, Venetia.'

'I know.'

'It should be now.' He took her hand and drew her down beside him on the dew-fresh grass, scented, cool and moist. 'Now, Venetia. Kiss me now.'

Their lips met, their hands roaming over each other's bodies, the old hunger meeting the new, the darkness battling the light. Venetia pulled away.

'No, Esteban. I can't do this . . .'

'For me, Venetia. Do this because you hunger for me, as I hunger for you.'

Venetia closed her eyes. A red mist cloaked her vision, her pulse raced, a black hunger filling her, overtaking her, mingling passion and tenderness

433

and savage need.

And her lips brushed Esteban's throat. He tasted salty, appetising, the blood pulsing softly in a fat vein, just beneath the skin.

'For ever, Esteban. You are sure?'

'For ever.'

'Venetia . . . aah . . .'

Esteban let out the softest sigh of orgasm as her teeth broke the skin of his throat. Venetia drank deeply, a strange exhilaration filling her as their passion joined and pleasure refreshed her insatiable, immortal, incorruptible body.

Afterwards, she laid him down tenderly on the grass, in the shade of tall pines, and lay beside him, curling around and about him, her face snuggled into the crook of his neck and her lips still moist with the taste of him.

Death would claim him for a few hours, no more. And when night came and he awoke, they would be together again.

Together for all eternity.

Shopping Around

Mariah Greene

Chapter One

WITH A STEADY flicker, the dim night lights gave way to the burning fluorescent of day. Lights designed to be brighter than day itself. Display cabinets lit up, instantly recognisable logos illuminated and goods were displayed. Spot lights, strategically positioned, would guide eyes in precise directions, towards desirable commodities, things that had to be had. Under a layer of total silence, the brightness changed. The shop was stirring.

Karen Taylor sighed with contentment as the cock entered her. She enjoyed sex first thing in the morning, while most people were still sleeping. The best way to wake up. He was pressing hard against her, pushing himself in with a forceful enthusiasm. It was the third time they had made love since entering the bed the night before. Karen's favourite pattern. Once when she got in. Once in the middle of the night. Best of all, one final time in the morning. She raised her knees higher, pulling the duvet so it came off his shoulders, revealing his back, long and shapely. She lifted her head and peered over his shoulders, watching his back ripple and undulate, like a wave spreading out from his rear-end and diminishing at his shoulders.

Staff began to arrive. Some together. Some alone. Some friends, some lovers and some enemies. Through their own special entrance they filed, into the infrastructure of the building. The brighter sparks shouted things cheerily at the less cheerful. A network of people too vast for everyone to want to know everyone else. Into the brightness of a new day, they immersed themselves.

He mumbled something against her ear, but Karen could not tell what it was. He obviously enjoyed it in the morning as well. Her pussy was warm and relaxed, comfortable and accommodating to the speed and depth of him inside of her as she gripped him tightly, both with her pussy and with her arms. His flesh was hot from the bed and his brow was developing the finest mist of morning sweat, like dew. A drop fell from him and landed on her collar bone, gathering in the cleft of skin and bone. Karen placed her hands on his sides, feeling the outer edge of his ribcage, so close to the surface and the skin so smooth and taut, his whole torso moving in her hands.

In the basement, a small army of good-looking men, all in their twenties, fussed around. They dressed and undressed mannequins, folded and re-folded garments that were displayed on tables and adjusted racks and racks of suits and jackets, discreetly tucking the price tags in. It was an expansive area hollowed out to a single level, the roof-supporting joists integrated into the decor of the room. The air-conditioning silently pumped an artificially cool atmosphere into the dungeon-like space, the only public entrance to which was a large and elaborate stone stairway, rough and granite-like. There was banter, in-jokes and gossip as the basement was preened and primped, the whole room dressed and ready for another day of being slowly undressed and tousled.

Her body was now fully awake to the passion it was experiencing. She had drifted through the light veil of sleep that had still shrouded her when she initiated sex and she was now fully cognisant, using all of her senses to their fullest potential. His weight was on her, compressing her into the mattress as each thrust pushed her against the sheet. In the early morning quiet of the room, what sounds there were became amplified. Her breathing, his breathing, the movement of the bed and the rub of the bed linen.

In the café, three of the four men who worked behind the counter were robed identically in white shirts, black trousers and a white apron, crisp and pressed. The espresso machine warmed up and the smell of coffee was in the air. Pastries were delivered from the store's bakery and set out in glass display cabinets. Fresh oranges, grapefruits, strawberries and cranberries were juiced and placed into large glass jugs while cups and saucers, plates and glasses were checked and stacked. Bar tops and the few small tables were given a final polish, condiments laid out in a precise fashion. In the back, the cook warmed the griddle and waited for the first rush to start.

Inside her, his cock was solid. It was a definite part of him that had planted itself inside a definite part of her. He had stopped thrusting for a moment and was resting his body against hers, his chest against her breasts, their hips still joined. As she lay, she felt him quiver and pulse his cock inside her and was conscious of its shape, the head so large and imploring when it had entered her the first time, a whole night ago. His pubic hair was weaved with her own and they were a mixture of sweat and juices, ready to pump on and bring them both to an elongated and painfully pleasurable orgasm.

On shelves of glass, the detailed and delicate china and glassware shimmered in the light and juddered almost imperceptibly from the movement of traffic outside and people around it. Cut crystal absorbed the light into its own pattern and refracted it with a brilliance and complexity that the lighting alone could never have achieved. In the aisles around the shelves, deep pile carpets in Wedgwood blue smoothed the path, carefully vacuumed each night. The whole area seemed fragile, easily shattered by even the slightest sudden movement. With the delicacy and care of archaeologists or museum curators, men and women polished the surfaces of glass.

His rhythm picking up where it had left off, Karen lent him encouragement by grabbing handfuls of his slinky behind and pulling him deep into her, squeezing his buttocks and raking them with her nails as she did so. She reached a hand over and down his crack, tickling his balls where they rested on her, making him yelp like a puppy. He was using his knees to lever himself and make his rush on her that much faster as his cock shafted her pussy with increasing speed, making Karen tingle and ache at the same time. She yearned for her orgasm but wanted to relish the sex some more, feel him over her and on her, in her and out of her. She wanted to hear him yell as he spilled into her, jerking and thrashing around on the bed, shattering the quiet of the dawn.

Down the centre of the department, suspended from a high point near the ceiling, ran a long and narrow catwalk. Mannequins were frozen in poses that both mimicked and mocked the supermodels who would ordinarily inhabit such a space. On the mannequins were the finest couture names, both new and old, clothes that were outrageous or conservative, bright or discreet. All, however, were expensive and lush, able to make even the plastic dummies appear casual and stylish, as though a moment from a Paris show had been frozen in time. The windows in the whole department were masked, as if by sunglasses, affording only a glimpse of the natural light outside.

Faster and faster he went into her and Karen could sense he was as close as she was, but not quite. She clung on to him, continuing to move in time with him, and readied herself.

The front doors opened and the first customers trickled through, regulars making their way to familiar destinations within the store.

The light of the new day filled Karen. As she came,

she was illuminated by it, the glow flowing through her and radiating from her. She was bathed in pleasure, burnishing her like the golden sun. Karen had coaxed herself from the dark of the night into the dawn of sex and now the sun rose gloriously in her, the steady and certain throb of her climax suspending her momentarily, freezing her in time before launching her. She exhaled heavily, the breath coming from deep inside her, and felt herself open out anew.

A new day had begun.

Chapter Two

KAREN TAYLOR ENTERED Sloane Square at ten-thirty, feeling and looking every inch the maverick. Her metallic Richard Tyler jacket practically screamed off of her, smothering the casual classic look of her Hermès trousers and Paul Smith shirt. She had been thirty for six months and relished every moment of it. She didn't know if she was in her prime, but she certainly felt better than she ever had and hoped the feeling would go on getting better and better.

She darted quickly over the zebra crossing, ignoring whatever the driver in the passing cab had said, and made her way to Hamiltons, the department store where she worked. Karen loved London, especially at this time of the day, when people had already started work and were into their routines. Sloane Square was always lively, a mix of cars and people frantically vying for any available space to occupy.

Switching her briefcase to her left hand, she ran a finger over each eyebrow, making herself feel in order. She was wearing her hair shorter than it had been for some time, and had applied mousse to make it fall in a gently tangled and tousled way that went just over her ears, while the fringe fell short of her eyebrows. The hair accentuated her look which was sensuous and soft. Her skin was smooth and even, nose slightly snubby, even cute, and her eyes were grey-blue, seeming to darken slightly at the rim of each iris.

Karen's face was the most striking thing about her and she had been told many times that she would not be out of place modelling cosmetics – the kind of advertisement where the face says it all. Somehow, she could never quite see herself shot through gauze and voiced-over by an out-of-work actress with a baritone and body hair. She was more proud of her body because she had worked at it, whereas her looks were a given. She pounded the metal at her health club and the result was a body pleasingly firm, displaying her most feminine aspects to their fullest – her long, shapely legs, tight stomach and well-formed rear. Her breasts were round and pert, barely needing the support of a bra.

People would have noticed her, whatever. She knew that. Even if she had not been as attractive, she would still have made herself noticed. That was the sort of woman she was.

From her favourite piece of the pavement, she eyed Hamiltons. It was a cross between a castle and the Bank of England. A white fortress with small turrets on either side, it took up most of one side of Sloane Square. Five floors and a basement, housing men's and women's clothing, perfumes, home wares, furniture, a bookshop and its own café. It was not the broadest mix but nor was it a paltry one. By virtue of being there in the first instance and because of its concerted attempts to win over customers, Hamiltons had survived.

In the years prior to her joining, the shop had gone through a slump and it had been rumoured for a time that it might be sold or even closed. When Karen heard via a friend that Hamiltons were looking for someone to manage promotions in the store, her interest was sparked. They were looking for someone who would run special campaigns to promote particular products or product lines, to pull people back into the shop. More than that, they wanted innovation and provocation, something that would give them a reputation for flair, a shop not afraid to be daring. She knew she should have the job.

In a little more than three years, Hamiltons had shifted its axis from a slightly stuffy shop that most people thought sold haberdashery to old ladies on coach trips, to a store that was known for its daring and as a fun place to shop. For a whole month, she made everyone in the perfume department wear identical pairs of Revo sunglasses all day, on the instruction that they were not to answer any questions as to why they were wearing them. The store was written up in the evening newspapers and even got a mention on one of the London news programmes. More than just the sale of sunglasses jumped. Whatever Karen felt it took, she did. She loved her job and the freedom it gave her.

Today, a warm Wednesday in July, she was about to start the next phase of Hamiltons newest venture – a unisex skin scent. Hamiltons had entered into an arrangement with a medium-sized cosmetics company which was to be the perfect marriage of their production technology and Hamiltons' style and marketability. The marketing campaign was something of a double coup for Karen. Firstly, she had convinced Hamiltons owner Daniel Avendon that they should handle the concept side of the marketing themselves and, secondly, she had managed to secure Linda Cole, a cult photographer who shrewdly functioned on the borders of art and commerce, to do a shoot with Maxwell, the latest up-and-coming boy supermodel. Maxwell was perfect for it, an androgynous man-child, as ambiguous as the fragrance itself. Karen had been at college with Linda, so it was easy enough to arrange. With Linda attached to the project, getting Maxwell had been simple.

She looked up at the sky, smiling because she could see that the sun would be perfect by noon. With some careful negotiating and by taking Linda there, Karen had convinced everyone that the roof of Hamiltons would be the perfect place for the shoot. Linda had balked at first, but once she was up there, she too had agreed that it was a good location and that it would give the campaign continuity if all three publicity shots were done there.

As she entered the large brass door, the doorman, dressed impeccably in full livery, made a peace sign at her. She smiled and entered Hamiltons.

'Karen! Jesus, where've you been?'

It was David, her personal assistant. A nervous shiftiness and a shock of black curly hair were two of the three things that defined David for Karen. The other was that he was good at his job of looking after her and completely trustworthy. She could have told him what she had *really* been doing all morning, but David was beyond shock by now, so it would have been a wasted effort.

'Nice jacket,' he said, his concentration lapsing momentarily. He snapped back to attention. 'I've been calling you . . .'

'And leaving hang-ups on the machine. I knew it would be you. I suppose I can expect to find another five on my mobile messaging service?' She was even in her tone, not testy.

'Daniel's been looking for you. He wants to talk to you about this afternoon.'

'I thought he would,' she said. 'What did you say to him?'

'That everything would be fine.'

'And is everything fine?'

'No.' He looked at her and then at the floor.

'Did Linda arrive yet?' she asked, looking at him.

'She's been here since seven this morning, according to security. She's on the roof setting up. The bird handlers arrived an hour ago.'

'It sounds to me like everything's under control. Why so worried?'

'Daniel,' he said, using the word carefully.

Karen drew breath and looked around. The ground

445

floor housed the men's and women's fragrances as well as a gift shop. It had the noise and commotion of a train station at most times and now was little exception.

'Do we have a problem?' she asked.

'Yes.'

'David,' she said, touching his hand lightly, 'I'm going up to the café and I'll get us both a coffee, then you can relax and we can talk. First, I want to have a walk through the shop. See you up there in ten minutes.'

She walked away from him and his exasperated look, picking her way through the perfume girls, all yielding tester bottles as though they were Mace, and the aftershave boys all giving off the right degree of attitude. They all smiled at her, but she thought they would have smiled even if they were blindfolded and locked in a darkened room. It was their way. One day she would dress them all as rabbits who would stop the customers and ask if they could test the perfume on the humans.

While she stood on the escalator that took her to the second floor, she surveyed Hamiltons from the vantage point the height afforded. There was a buzz. Something she could never quite pin down or identify. It was like trying to see air. The shop was organic, a living thing that grew and had a life of its own that was over and above the simple sum of its parts. Daniel Avendon, the store's owner, liked to talk of it as a communal energy or Gestalt. To Karen it simply felt as though there was an air of expectation, the anticipation of someone arriving or having just arrived. Hamiltons' secret was making the customer feel like *they* were the one who had arrived. Each floor occupied several thousand square feet and the spaces were light and airy; chandeliers on the ground floor made it stately, while the clothes departments were fitted out in a more modern style. Each of the departments had its own decorative style and identity, but there was an overall theme of sumptuousness. Karen felt there was a wickedness in the air.

The smell of coffee from the third-floor café wafted through the air as the escalator neared its destination. She felt as though she were home, as though the shop were a part of her and she a part of it. Hamiltons had always been in the hands of the Avendon clan, but it had a tempestuous history. It had opened in the early Fifties and was carried along by a post-war optimism and the spending power of a class for whom it would have taken more than a war to spoil their shopping. In fact, Hamiltons was the outcome of a more specific war. A war between two families, the Avendons and the Foxtons.

Daniel Avendon's father Lawrence was the founder of Hamiltons and he had been in bitter competition with Dick Foxton, the owner of a nearby store. It was this rivalry that had kept Hamiltons sharp and sassy in the early days. According to Daniel, things turned sour when his mother Mary entered the fray and there was a battle between the two men over *her*. Karen had not properly established how the story ended, but in the space of a few years, Mary had married and divorced the both of them.

Her shoes bumped the top of the escalator and she turned her mind to more practical matters. She settled at the coffee bar and ordered two double espressos. David was there instantly – had probably been stalking her through the shop. He had a clipboard in his hand, on which would be written a schedule and a list of things to do. David's nose twitched and his cheek ticked nervously. He took it on himself to do all of Karen's worrying in addition to his own, all at the tender age of twenty-six.

'Tell me what's the matter,' she said, her eyes fixed on the waiter and his careful procedure for producing the coffee.

'It's the nudity. Daniel thinks we may be exposed.'

She laughed at his choice of words.

'*We* certainly won't be. Do you think he means the reputation of the shop or that the shoot itself may cause a problem?'

David shrugged and raised his eyebrows. She sipped at the coffee.

'Okay,' she said to herself. 'Where's Daniel now – he's not up there interfering, is he?'

David shook his head.

'When we've had coffee,' she continued, 'I'm going up on the roof to have a word with Linda. Give me about ten or fifteen minutes and then bring Daniel up. I'll introduce him.'

'Supposing he won't come up?'

'David, please. Daniel won't be able to resist. That's probably why he's kicking up a fuss. We should have let him meet Linda sooner. Trust me.'

She had drunk half of her coffee before she spoke again.

'Remember, David, only necessary people out there today. I don't want all the nellies from the dungeon up here ogling Maxwell.'

'It's taken care of. Hardly anyone knows we're doing it today and I've arranged for security to have a couple of people on the door to the roof.'

'Linda wants to shoot through lunch to make the most of the light. You did arrange for lunch to be sent?' she asked.

'They're sending it from here, around one-thirty.'

'Fine. I'd better get going. Take my case for me and head off Daniel for ten minutes,' she said, swallowing the last of the coffee and standing.

When she went out on to the roof, it was alive with activity. Linda was ordering two assistants to move things around and they scurried obediently while on a quiet corner of the roof, two middle-aged women tended to a dozen or so bird cages. A small plinth had been set up and flash units with umbrellas behind them were positioned at various heights. To one side was a large silver board that Karen had seen other photographers use to reflect the sun. Linda turned around and her face lit up when she saw Karen.

'Hi,' she said, rushing over and kissing Karen on the cheek. Linda was dressed in tight black ski pants with a similarly snug Lycra top over which was a looser black cotton vest. Her reddish blonde hair was pushed into a black baseball hat, her normally long earrings replaced by sleepers.

'I don't think I've ever seen you dressed for work before,' Karen said, stepping back and looking at her old college friend.

'If I look like a complete bitch,' Linda said, 'people will basically do as I tell them and then leave me alone. It works for me.'

'We might have a small hitch,' Karen said.

Linda's features remained neutral.

'My boss is getting a bit jumpy about the shoot. The nudity to be precise.'

'Karen, it's not going to work if he's wearing clothes. That's not the point of it, you know that. We've discussed it enough times.'

'I agree completely,' Karen said, nodding.

A tall wiry figure came through the door, went past them and made his way to the bird handlers.

'So what does this add up to, Karen?'

'Nothing, I hope. He'll be coming up here in a few minutes. He knows who you are and if you could just lay it on a bit, I'm sure things will be fine. He's a fan of your work.'

Karen looked over at the boy talking to the bird people. He was familiar. He bent to look into one of the cages and turned his face up to one of the women and said something. In her mind it clicked and Karen had to double-take, before whispering to Linda, 'Is that him?'

'Maxwell? Yes,' said Linda. 'He's absolutely fascinated by birds. Loves them. Let me have a quick word with him and then I'll introduce you.'

Karen watched as Linda leaned a hand on his

shoulder and bent to talk to him. He listened to her intently and nodded before straightening up. Linda smiled over at Karen and she took it as her cue.

'Max, this is Karen Taylor. She runs special promotions here. And she's an old friend of mine, so don't be rude to her.'

Karen was surprised by Linda's familiarity with him. It started to dawn on her why it may have been so easy to get him for the job.

'Nice to meet you, Karen,' he said, extending a hand.

His palm was wide and flat, the fingers long and spindly. The gesture of a handshake had an awkward formality to it. He was tall and skinny, dressed in jeans that were baggy on him but would have been tight on most other people. Long lank arms connected to narrow shoulders that barely supported his clothes. He wore a grey woollen polo shirt with a white T-shirt underneath.

Somewhere between sandy blond and red ginger, his hair was swept over his head in a centre parting which caused the two points of the fringe to rest just above his dark eyebrows. The brows contrasted with the hair enough to make Karen think it might have been dyed or, more likely, sun-bleached. The boy's jaw and cheekbone were almost at right angles and they reached a delicate point at a chin that protruded only slightly.

The general impression was an angular face that sat on a thin, white-skinned neck. He flicked his hair from his clear green eyes, revealing the famous tiny scar on the corner of the right one.

'I'm really looking forward to the pictures,' he said.

His tongue protruded slightly at the beginning of the sentence and he squinted and seemed to push all of his features forward as he spoke, to give the words more trajectory. The right side of his mouth lifted in a faint smile when he spoke, as though he were privately amused at something. Maxwell's mouth remained open, the tongue protruding through his lips for a second before disappearing into his mouth. He pushed his bottom teeth on to his top lip. His nose was puggish and cute, his ears jugged. He's flirty, thought Karen.

'My, it's blowy up here,' a voice boomed from behind them.

It was Daniel Avendon. Dapper and a well-kept fifty-two, he would stand out of a crowd big enough to fill a football stadium as the most powerful and richest person there. It hasn't been ten minutes, Karen thought, annoyed at David who was nowhere to be seen.

'Daniel, this is my friend, the photographer Linda Cole.'

'Delighted,' he said. 'I saw some of your work at ICP Midtown in New York. Marvellous.'

Daniel was a stream of one-word adjectives.

'And is this the lad who'll be in the pictures?' he asked, turning imperiously to Maxwell and sounding like Mr Bumble from Oliver Twist.

'Yes, sir,' said Maxwell, holding out his hand. 'I'm Maxwell and I'm pleased to meet you.'

A wind picked up and Maxwell folded his arms, cradling an elbow in each hand and pulling his shoulders in frailly. The doves in the cages fluttered and the sound of their wings beating the air was syncopated against the backdrop of the wind and the strains of the London traffic. Maxwell turned round to look at the birds.

'Do you like birds?' Avendon asked Maxwell.

'Oh yes,' he said, the tongue protruding slightly. 'I love them. Look at this,' he finished, squatting eye-level with the cage. Avendon joined him and soon they were in a conversation.

Over their heads, Linda winked to Karen and they moved away.

'Max's father kept pigeons,' Linda said to Karen.

'How do you know so much about him?' she asked coyly.

'Karen, he's one of my favourite models. He's to die for in front of a camera. Wait and see.'

'If we get to see. If Daniel decides to get stubborn, we may not see anything,' Karen said.

'Surely he won't disappoint a famous photographer like me?' Linda said in an exaggerated tone. 'He's seen my work. At ICP. Midtown,' she left large and deliberate gaps between her words in an imitation of Daniel's grandeur. 'Just let Max turn on the charm.'

Karen looked at the two of them squatting and pointing at the birds, like father and son. The roof of Hamiltons gave a spectacular view of the London skyline from an angle and direction that few people got to see.

A few minutes later, Daniel Avendon walked past them.

'I look forward to seeing the photographs,' he said.

'Let's go to work,' said Linda. She turned to Karen. 'We'll be about an hour finishing the set-ups and stuff. Why don't you come back then?'

Karen could take a hint, and left the roof, filling the hour in her office, making calls and checking her mail.

When she returned, it looked like not much had changed, except that Maxwell now wore a white towelling robe, his chest just visible through the opening in it. Karen watched silently and after ten minutes of make-up and hair, Maxwell was ready. He sat in a chair, patiently waiting while Linda checked a few final things.

'Ready for you, Max,' she shouted.

With a complete lack of self-consciousness, as Karen would normally have understood the term, Maxwell stood and dropped his robe to the floor.

Naked, the skinny boy with pale skin was an absolute delight to look at. His hair dropped forward into his eyes and his large mouth was already poised, as if in anticipation of a kiss. His torso was slim and bony with hardly any muscle to see save for the faintest definition around his chest. The nipples were red, encircled by the odd hair, and pert in the brisk air on the roof.

He stood on the plinth and Karen let her eyes run over him a number of times. His legs, like the rest of him, were fairly skinny and hairless. His cock was long but perfectly in proportion to him, his pubic hair a downy brown.

On the roof, Karen, the bird handlers, Max's stylist, Linda's two assistants and even Linda stood in silence. Despite the sunlight, it was windy on the roof. They were high enough not to be seen by too many windows, although a few people would be able to see. Karen had already cleared it with the local police in case they got any calls wondering what was happening on Hamiltons' roof.

The initial shot was the most involved and was being done first as it would be the hardest to get right or repeat. If they lost the light, they could do the other two another day.

'Max, let's practise a few times the way we said,' Linda instructed him.

He nodded and squatted down on the plinth, his hands on the floor in front of his feet and his chin resting on his knees. Karen looked at his hunched figure, balls dangling from beneath him despite the briskness of the wind. He held the squatting pose for a few seconds and then stood quickly, raising his arms to either side of him.

'Try and keep your head straighter towards the camera and not look up so much. Movement's good, though, nice and fluid,' Linda said to him.

Karen looked on. Several times he went through the movements, looking like a flower blooming as he went from a scrunched-up position to standing proud with his arms out to the side. After Linda's first instruction, his head came up level with the camera every time. Linda was taking some shots with a small instant camera and said things to her assistants who bustled around.

'Let's have the doves,' called Linda.

Maxwell squatted and held his position for twenty minutes. Karen looked at his lithe body and could see why he was one of the most successful male models in years. He had it. As with Hamiltons itself, it was not possible to locate precisely what *it* was, but Maxwell had it. She wanted to mother him, to be his sister, to be his friend and to be his lover who would fuck him senseless, all in one simple look. She felt envious of Linda if she really had captured him on more than just film.

Karen knew that the shot was a success. The doves had been positioned carefully all around his feet and then some behind him and in front of him, below the level of the plinth. Even more carefully, a dozen or so were placed on him, his shoulders, knees and head. At that point, he looked absurd, like Nelson on top of the column, but when he stood on Linda's cue, his movement was one of sheer liquid flexibility and Karen could see in her mind a photograph of Maxwell bursting forth from a sea of doves, his hands held out by his sides, face etching itself into the camera and the grain of the London skyline behind him. Linda's cameras had been clicking frantically and Karen looked forward to going through the contact sheets with her.

The rest of the afternoon slipped by. While the bird handlers recovered the doves, Linda took Maxwell off to one of the turrets where they would do a shot not involving birds. His stylist fussed over him, fixing his hair and spraying it. Linda said something to the stylist and she went off to get something. He slipped his robe back on and they talked to each other. Karen observed, not wanting to get too much in the way of Linda but fascinated to see if she could discern any sort of relationship between them.

She suddenly became aware that David was by her side, cradling his clipboard.

'How's it going?' he asked her.

'Fine,' she responded, still looking at Linda and Maxwell.

'Daniel's happy then?'

'Very, as he would say. Any calls for me?'

'A few, but nothing I couldn't handle. You just concentrate on up here,' he said to her, surveying the ever present clipboard. Some people in the shop laughed at his clipboard, Karen knew, but she did not tell David.

'He's quite stunning, isn't he?' David remarked.

Karen turned to look at David, surprised.

'He must be to rouse your interest,' she said, a friendly mocking in her tone.

'You know what I mean.'

'I do. I do,' she said, realising that she was practically sighing. David left her to it.

Like a small and perfectly pretty gargoyle, Maxwell sat on the turret wall and Linda shot him from behind, looking out on London. He wore a pair of angel's wings held tightly on to him by leather straps. His head was hung slightly and the hair pushed forward and held by whatever industrial-strength concoction the stylist had recently applied.

'I think I'll call this one "Forlorn Angel",' Linda confided to Karen during a break.

'When do we get to choose which pictures are best?' Karen said gleefully, wondering if it were moral to enjoy her work so much.

'Monday or Tuesday next week. I'll call you.'

'Are you getting enough good stuff?' Karen asked.

'Plenty. We'll have trouble choosing. I always do with him.'

Maxwell was back where he was happiest for the last shot, on a plinth. Again he was naked except for a large leather gauntlet covering his right hand and on which was perched a peregrine falcon. Instead of the bird, it was Maxwell who wore a leather hood. Karen looked on as the afternoon light faded, studying his naked body, drinking every inch of it in, her eyes soaking him up like the film in Linda's camera. His image made her feel restless, desire sparking in her.

She pulled her mobile phone out and dialled Hamiltons' switchboard. After a few moments, she was put through.

Chapter Three

KAREN TOOK THE lift up to her sixth-floor apartment.
Most days she would walk, but today she was tired. It
had been a successful day and with most of it spent
looking at a nude boy supermodel, it had been a sexy
one too. She was ready to unwind. While the plush lift
carried her, she shook off the silver jacket and hung it
over her shoulder. Casually she sauntered along the
hallway to her door, opened it and entered.

Keeping a flat on Sloane Street, midway between
Knightsbridge and Sloane Square, was a minor
indulgence on Karen's part, but she loved the place
and its location. She would not have considered
herself to have come from money, certainly not in the
scale of the Daniel Avendons of the world, but her
family were comfortable and the flat was the only
thing for which she partly relied on them. She could
walk to Hamiltons in just over five minutes and, in the
other direction, she could reach Harvey Nichols and
Harrods in the same amount of time. In terms of her
universe, she felt her apartment placed her very much
at the centre of it.

The flat itself consisted of five rooms on one
level; living room, dining room, a study and two
bedrooms. As was common for the area, the ceilings
were high and the rooms large and square. Mostly
furnished when she moved in, it was decorated in
neutral shades of white, green and blue throughout. In

her living room she had two identical black leather sofas that were overstuffed and oversized, like hotel furniture. A small shelf of books and a few racks of compact discs were her main source of entertainment, the TV large and largely unwatched in a corner. The living and dining area both had bird's eye maple floors with expensive rugs and the other rooms were lushly carpeted.

Karen went to the bedroom and kicked off her shoes, throwing the jacket on to the bed at the same time. She removed the bracelet that went with the outfit and placed it on the teak dressing table along with her earrings. She sat and looked at herself in the mirror briefly, picking up the brush and running it through her hair several times. Over the shoulder of her reflection, the bed loomed large and low, the mattress set on a plinth that was about six inches wider than the mattress itself. The sheets and covers were pure linen and she looked forward to sinking between them. Standing, she wriggled out of her tights and put them into her wicker laundry basket.

In the kitchen, she fished a bottle of mineral water from the fridge, the rubberised tiles of the floor warm on her bare feet. The units were a light ash and the work surfaces marbled. It reminded her of a display kitchen she had seen in the window of Heals.

In the living room she put a compact disc into the machine and sank into one of the sofas, drinking her water from the bottle and feeling cradled by the triumph of mood-lighting the strategically placed lamps always managed to achieve. When the buzzer rang, she almost did not want to get up. Then she thought of the cool and crisp linen sheets that awaited her in the bedroom.

'Hello,' she said on the entry phone.

'It's me,' his voice came back, crackled but confident.

She smiled and pushed the button on the wall unit.

'Very nice,' she said, pulling on his waistcoat as he

stood in the doorway.

'It's Dries Van Noten,' he said.

'All of it? The whole outfit is Dries? Surely not?'

'No, the shirt's Comme des Garçons.'

'And the trousers, let me guess,' she said, tugging at one of the pockets, 'are Armani?'

'Wrong,' he said, deepening his voice at the end of the word. 'They're Rykeil Homme. And my boxers are . . .'

'Shush,' she said, putting a finger to his mouth, 'I'll find that out soon enough.'

She studied him. Richard Fraser was twenty-five and would have looked more comfortable modelling most of the clothes he sold for Hamiltons. He had been working in the menswear basement for seven months and Karen had spotted him early on. She had assumed that, like most of the men down there in what the women at Hamiltons referred to as The Dungeon, Richard would be a boy who liked boys. The discovery that he was not sent a minor ripple of excitement through many women at Hamiltons, giving Richard some instant celebrity status and a rarity value if nothing else.

He was model-good-looking, she thought to herself. His mane of hair, mid-brown and not light enough for him to be considered blond, was pushed back over his head in a way that was meant to imply a careless hand had ploughed a rough furrow into it. In truth, Karen knew that many hours of grooming and chemical additives had gone into giving it the fake-casual look. This calculated devil-may-care coiffure gave him the demeanour of a good boy who wanted to turn bad. In truth, his features were too angelic for that and he was sensible enough to realise it, dressing himself carefully in a relaxed way. To Karen he was the product of a thousand labels.

The post-choir boy, post-public schoolboy face made Karen want to grab for him almost continually. His eyes were a quiet blue-grey and his mouth delicate and formed from well proportioned lips. The jaw and cheekbones had the angles that would hurtle aerodynamically down a catwalk if required, and she had seen him mould his features into a smoulder on more than one occasion, his rich golden colouring promising hot days in the sun and hotter nights in bed.

'So are you going to tell me why you were such a bitch to me today?' he said to her over his shoulder as they went to the living room.

She ignored him and went to the fridge to get another water for herself and one for him.

'It was a difficult time,' she said, returning. 'We were in the middle of the photo shoot and I was down in my office for a quick break and to return a few calls. Plus, Alan Saxton was there breathing down my neck. I can't just stop and chat away like some bimbo. I'll look like one of the Saturday girls, gabbing away to her friend about the weekend while she's serving someone.'

'What did he want anyway? Is the old fart sniffing around you?'

'Richard, please. He's old enough to be my, well your, father. I'm not in that market. He was checking on one of the items on the budget for the underwear promotion we're doing in the basement.'

'I'm sorry. I know it's hard. Big power woman and the humble shop boy. We're like a fairy-tale cartoon,' he smiled.

'You are so cheeky, sometimes.'

She went and sat next to him on the sofa. In profile, his features were sculpted and he was very pretty, his lips pouting away from the solid line of his jaw. She explored the material on the waistcoat's shoulder with her hands and then on up through his hair.

'Careful!' he said to her as she moved his hair about in her fingers.

'Don't be so vain,' she said to him, cupping the back of his head in her hand and pulling him towards her so she could kiss him. She enjoyed homing in on his even complexion, the skin unblemished and soft, ready for her caress. She wanted to blow on it gently and watch it twitch under her breath.

Karen leaned up on the sofa and pushed him back into it as they kissed, using his shoulders for support, the linen of his waistcoat delicate under her fingers and reminiscent of the bed sheets she had eyed so longingly before Richard arrived. Soon, she was sitting astride him and she kissed him in long and deep repetition, tasting him and smelling the waft of his aftershave, still sweet in the early evening heat. Her skirt had ridden up to reveal the tops of her thighs, bare without her tights, and his hands rubbed them, leaving goose bumps in their wake.

Sitting back and resting her weight on Richard's legs, his cock pushing at her behind, she took the waistcoat off him, and he leaned forward to allow her to lift it from his back and on over his head like a jumper. It was the first small stage towards nudity and she relished the journey. She enjoyed removing, one by one, Richard's collection of labels, leaving him bare before her with only his own label to show. Devoid of his clothes, of the symbols and tag and mark of another, he had never disappointed her so far. His body was supple, with only a faint tendency towards muscularity, mostly around his chest and stomach muscles. Working out at the gym, Karen could appreciate a good body when she saw one. At that moment, she wanted more than anything to see one. His.

When the buttons at the front of his shirt were undone to the waistband of his trousers, she tugged it open as though he were Superman rushing towards a phone box. She lifted and moulded his chest muscles in her hands, her thumbs flicking at the small hard nipples which had a trace of dark hair around them. The rest of his torso was hairless apart from the line of hair that began under his navel and which she knew journeyed down to his mat of pubic hair but was at that moment stopped abruptly by his trouser line.

461

Karen leaned closer to him and kissed him again, darting her tongue out and letting it catch the underside of his top lip to feel the sharpness of his teeth. Between her legs her pussy was coming to life and she shifted herself on him to calm its stirring. She held each of his hands in turn while she undid the cuff and gauntlet buttons on the white cotton shirt and then that too, in the same way as the waistcoat, came off. His body was a gentle V shape from shoulder to waistline, his navel protruding a quarter of an inch and the muscles of his stomach a tight palette of six even sections.

Concentrating fully and completely on her task at hand, she dropped to her knees on the floor and worked on his belt, slithering it slowly through the loops on his trousers, watching it unfurl from around him. The button at the top of his trousers came undone easily and she unzipped his fly, splaying it open at the top.

'Ah,' she said, 'so the underwear was Armani. I thought there would be some somewhere.'

He grinned at her and shifted restlessly on the sofa.

Removing his shoes and socks, amazed at how the gold of his skin extended to every extremity, she reached up and pulled off his trousers. He was left on the sofa in only a pair of white boxer shorts with a large white label on the front of the waistband like real boxer's shorts. The underwear was stark and white against the black leather on the sofa and the golden glow of his skin.

She used his hips for support and kissed at his chest, concentrating on one nipple at a time, the flesh pink and solid in her lips. She stood up, towering over him as he sat spread on the sofa. In a slow and confident manner, Karen removed all of her clothing. Shirt, the Hermès trousers, bra and pants, all came way from her body in a swift and practised routine which she knew would excite him. It excited her. She lifted her breasts and stretched her back, feeling herself loosen and spring free in the twilight breeze of her living room while Richard looked on. For a few seconds she toyed at her pussy, dipping her finger to a shallow depth, parting the lips slightly and nudging her clitoris.

Again she kneeled and this time she stroked him through his underwear. The shorts were pulled high, accentuating the length of his legs, his thighs taut and the flesh so inviting. Up the side of his leg she ran her hands, and when they found the white cotton of the boxers, she pressed into his flesh, feeling the density of his body. She pushed her fingers into the leg of the boxer shorts and felt the side of his buttock, raking her nails over the flesh. The elastic of the waistband stretched under her fingers when she gripped it at either side, ready to slip it down over his long legs, pausing briefly to allow him to remove his cock. She tugged at the shorts.

His underwear removed, she studied his cock intently. As she moved closer, she felt its heat rise to her face and caught the light manly musk in her nostrils. His left ball hung lower than the right and was fuller in his sac, which she reached out and compressed with her hand, causing him to sigh. The skin of his scrotum looked like a well worn material and was lightly covered in hair with a thin wrinkle of flesh running up its centre, almost as though it were dissecting a line which his balls hung either side of. Where the base of his cock began, the skin around his balls was heavily wrinkled and the lines shifted as his growing ardour caused the testicles to sway of their own accord. The sac seemed to tighten and the balls draw into him.

The beginnings of an erection had lengthened his cock as she watched it, like a timelapse camera showing the growth of a flower over a period of months. The tumescence had pulled back his foreskin and revealed the red phallus which was seeping a clear fluid in the smallest drop, an outward sign of his inner desire. The skin on the shaft of his cock was darker than the rest of him, not as golden, and criss-crossed with a map of blue veins. As he stiffened, the cushion his skin gave to the veins thinned and they came to the surface, as if the skin were translucent.

Karen held the shaft and drew Richard's foreskin back over the head of his cock, watching the loose skin gather under the top of his glans, wrinkling in the same pattern as his ball sac. The phallus was wide at the glans and rounded at the tip in a way that would make the penetration into her so pleasurable as it pushed at her lips and then opened her vagina and found its way into her.

But she did not want that right there and then, she realised. There would be time for that. First, she wanted to taste him and to swallow him and to have him do the same to her. She held his hands and pulled him to the floor, pushing him over on to his back, his hair falling loosely about him.

Karen sat astride his chest, a knee under each of his armpits. She thrust her hips at him, displaying her pussy, then pulled away again. He started to rub the fronts of her thighs but she slapped his hand away.

'I can do that myself,' she said, leaning forward and lowering herself into his face before he could say anything.

Richard's whole mouth worked on her, his tongue driving into her, wet and hot at the opening of her vagina. Her juices ran and he took them eagerly, his face muscles contracting and relaxing while he tongued her. Bit by bit, the muscles between her legs loosened and she became elastic and slick, relishing the noises she heard him make on her, the feel of his nose grazing her pubic hair.

With the intensity and speed of a lash, his tongue thrashed her clitoris, which was inflated and heaving from its own fullness. Her head was in a spin, heat rising around her face, and she felt flushed with emotion as he toyed with her. She was leaning over and resting her hands on the floor, knees open wide

464

and breasts dangling free and weighty, two pendulous mounds. His hands were all over her lower back and behind, kneading and pressing the flesh, occasionally parting the cheeks; sometimes a finger ran under and touched the base of her pussy.

She wrenched herself from him before it was too late, not wanting to let herself spill into orgasm just yet. She wanted him to carry on feeding from her pussy, but she wanted to taste him too, to feed from him. Karen got off him and rolled him over on to his side. She lay facing him on her side also, but with her head in his crotch.

Immediately, he was at her again, barely pausing for breath. She felt his head move closer and he shuffled around on the living room rug, making himself comfortable. One side of his face rested on her leg and he hitched her other leg over the side of his head, so that he was completely buried in her. She waited and enjoyed the feeling he was giving her before turning her attention to him.

The cock which she had examined with such interest earlier had grown and pumped itself until it was almost unrecognisable. Seen from this angle, Richard *was* the good boy turned bad as his flaming cock hung inches from her face, pressing towards her. She followed the line from his balls under to the cheeks of his behind, the skin darker and less gold, a secret place exposed to her close examination. She wondered how many women had seen him this way, such a basic part of him, writhing and moving.

Karen pulled on his thigh and used it as a pillow. She took his cock and quickly put it in her mouth, not lingering, but eager to get the taste and heat of him in her mouth. Their sixty-nine position meant that his cock was upside down, and she savoured the inversion, sensing the difference as his glans was in the roof of her mouth and the ridge of his phallus against her tongue. It was tart, the small warm emission from the head of his penis, and Karen let it sit on her tongue, the bitterness giving way as his flavour was diluted by her mouth. She was assimilating him into herself. The rest of his shaft filled her mouth with both its size and its heat, and she forced her lips wide apart to insert as much of him into her mouth as she could.

The feel of him in there was delightful, the skin of his shaft supple against the curve and contour of her mouth, the head of his cock rubbing against her. She closed her mouth and sucked hard, as though on a straw, but instead if drawing in air, it was his member which she closed around tightly and gulped further into her mouth. The shape of it was pronounced, the skin on the inside of Karen's cheeks drawing through her teeth and touching the side of Richard's shaft.

Down below, in her pussy, she was assailed by him and his tongue which felt as though it must have been stretching painfully to its root to burrow into her in the way it was at that moment. Her legs trembled from their position and from her passion and she wanted to come but also wanted him to come. She set to work on his cock in earnest.

It was a question of finding the right timbre with him, of moving in a way that was just right or at least close enough. He was unable to give her any verbal direction as his face was attached firmly to her crotch, so she made what she thought would be the most excruciating and exciting movements with her mouth and tongue. It seemed to be working, she thought, as he wriggled and began to pump with his groin. His legs were long and muscular and Karen enjoyed running her hands over the back of his thighs, the hairs tickling her palm.

She took the base of his cock with one hand and used the other to hold on his hips. She bobbed and ducked her head, his cock making her lips tingle. It was coated in her spittle, shining as the light from the lamps caught him as though he were lit for a take in a movie. As she manipulated him with her mouth, her

466

abrasions against him fell into time with her breathing and she opened her mouth to allow some air in. Momentarily, she took him from her mouth and masturbated him, enjoying the sight of just his cock, knowing he was up there somewhere, feeling him inside her, his tongue toiling on her clitoris.

Karen closed her eyes and her mouth practically fell back on to his cock as she sucked wildly. She felt her orgasm, the one she had delayed earlier, come back to haunt her like the ghost of an old friend. It murmured deep within her, communicating a deep and arcane feeling that spilled into her consciousness and made her shut her eyes even tighter and give out small squealing sounds which were blocked by Richard's cock. She straightened her back, almost slipping her pussy away from his face and he followed her movement, quickly clamping himself back on to her.

In order to cry out, to let the fury of her passion loose in the room, she took his cock from her mouth and worked on it with her hand, partly to stimulate him and mostly to hold on to something, anything, for fear that she would slip away into her orgasm and be swallowed by it. She clung to him and came. It was like ice melting from heat in one sudden and powerful blast, as if from a furnace. She was a combination of hot and cold, the two sensations working in her and playing off each other, resulting only in ecstasy.

Her body contorted and bucked, but all the time Richard held her and kept his face in her, his tongue less insistent, merely fooling with her in a way that prolonged the giddy peak she had just reached and was enjoying the fall away from. She still held him in her hand and was sheathing him back and forth more from the movement of her whole body than from her arm. It had become like a beacon for her, the one thing she was clinging on to and she had almost forgotten her real purpose for grabbing him in the way she did.

He cried out in desperation and then in sudden and definite resignation. Her eyes were still closed and she was dizzy and in a dream-like state halfway between the worlds of awake and asleep. The first heavy drop of his come caught her on her right cheek and the shock of it made her open her eyes. She saw the eye in the head of his penis open and push forth another spurt of thick white semen. It landed on her chin and its distinctive odour rose to her nostrils. When the next jet sprang from him, she had firm hold of him and it landed on her tongue, splashing up onto the roof of her mouth. She could tell he was watching her now, looking down to see what she was doing. He ejaculated several more times and she moved him around, splashing her face with him.

They held on to each other, still in their inverted position, wanting to simply cling on to flesh and feel its warmth and texture, the pulse of life through it.

And they hadn't even made it into the linen of her bed.

Yet.

Chapter Four

'HERE'S TO ANOTHER success,' said Alan Saxton, gently clinking his large brandy glass against Karen's.

'How many times have we toasted it now?' She smiled. 'From the water, the wine, the champagne, of course, but even the coffee and now the brandy. Let's wait until we see the pictures.'

'I wish we could have toasted it yesterday,' he said, 'on the day it happened. While it was still hot off the presses, as it were.'

'I know. I'm sorry, Alan. I had a family thing to do that had been planned for ages. You know what families are like, they set things up months in advance, you say yes, completely forget about it and then suddenly realise it clashes horribly with something.' She felt she had gone on for too long, overcompensating her lie to the point where it was obvious. She sat and felt as if there were a sign around her neck saying 'I was with Richard last night.'

'I understand. I don't expect either of us to be at the call of the other,' he answered.

They had shared a long and relaxed meal together. Alan had brought her some flowers, ordered champagne and chatted easily with her. That simple. What Karen would normally have called the full works. With Alan, though, he was not trying to impress her. She knew this was how he would be with anyone he was attracted to. Like the restaurant itself, he was smooth, efficient and comfortable. Another part of him was too sheltered and sweet to try any bravado.

An inch over six feet and a year under fifty, Alan Saxton headed the finance division of Hamiltons. He oversaw all the shop's financial affairs and his influence was wide. He was a knowledgable and powerful man and he conveyed it in his physical presence and in the quiet but confident manner of his speech. Outside of Daniel Avendon, he knew more about Hamiltons than anyone.

Karen would not have said fifty if she was asked how old she thought Alan was. He was not young, but nor did he look his age. His shoulders were broad and she had been surprised at how well his body was kept. His hair was a wave of black for at least eighty per cent and the rest was grey in streaks that made him distinguished without looking stuffy. Karen thought he was sexy and forceful in a cabinet-minister sort of way. He was mature and had a charisma that could fill a room, in a sedate fashion, like a soft glow. She had noticed him many times when she first started work at Hamiltons but never dreamed she would end up sitting across the table from him at a romantic dinner for two.

'I think its nice to toast whenever possible,' Alan continued, oblivious to her train of thought. 'You so rarely get a chance to these days. I prefer intimate toasts between two people, not like wedding rabble.'

He looked at her as he spoke.

She reached and lighted her hand on his, where it cradled the brandy glass. His fingers were full and powerful. She brushed his knuckles lightly with her fingertips and looked at his hand. With her eyes she trailed up his arm and came to rest on his face. He was still looking at her, but shifting his gaze slightly, as though the intimacy was making him jittery. She gently removed her hand.

'What's next for you?' he asked.

'Oh, there's the sports promotion. They want to run

it in the Autumn to try and boost sales. It would be a change to do something that had more of a life expectancy. The campaigns come and go,' she said.

'I thought you would enjoy that. It seems in keeping with you.' He smiled.

'An unfocused flirt?' she chided him.

'Of course not. Just that you don't seem the sort of person who would want to be tied down to a single thing.'

'It depends on the thing. And the underwear promotion before the Autumn sports. A bit of a rush, but I'll slot it in.'

'How will you promote underwear? It seems a bit of a need-it-or-you-don't product to me.'

'Do you mean don't need as in don't wear any?'

He reddened almost imperceptibly, the skin around his mouth quivering slightly.

'No. No, I meant, you either have enough or you don't.'

'I bet you've never once gone anywhere without underwear, have you, Alan?' she asked him.

'Probably not since I was a small lad.'

'I'll sort you out some nice boxer shorts from the promotion, promise,' she said, recalling that on their two previous encounters, he had been in Y-fronts.

'Thank you – no,' he said to her in an exaggerated way.

He gave off the soft glow again. It was the same when he had first asked her out, six weeks earlier. He had met her in a corridor. She thought they had bumped into each other casually, but on reflection she realised he must have planned it. He was nervous and shifted his expensive shoes around on the polished floor.

Instantly, from the look on his face, she knew that he was going to ask her out. He acted like a schoolboy, mumbling – and at the same time he was asking her out, he was telling her she probably wasn't interested. In fact, he *was* just a schoolboy, she thought. Karen,

471

like most people at Hamiltons, had heard he was recently separated from his wife Margaret and that it had been painful. They had been together since they were at university. Karen knew she was most likely the first woman he had asked out since then, so his chances to practise his chat-up skills would have been limited. She was both flattered and interested enough to say yes.

She had only one regret and that was not telling Richard about it and, similarly, not telling Alan about Richard. If they had both worked somewhere other than with her at Hamiltons, she would have, but something about the situation felt difficult, as though she was caught in a crossfire of feelings for the two of them and from the two of them. Predictably, as time rolled on, it had become hard to the point of impossible to tell one about the other.

For the first three weeks, they saw each other once a week. Very proper with minimal physical contact, apart from the occasional half-accidental brush and an obligatory goodnight peck. She was careful to keep the subject of his wife out of the conversation. He did not mention her very often and did not, on the surface at least, seem terribly upset. Karen sensed, however, that deeper in him something was working itself through and she was not sure how it would make itself known.

In the fourth week and after as many dates, they went to bed together. He was careful and considerate, certainly not as reserved as he was in public, but not an animal. The power that was there in his everyday life, bristling just below the surface, remained there also when they were in bed together. She wondered if she could coax him out of himself. She puzzled as to what might be a hot button for him, what would turn him on. He was nice to her, she found him attractive and she found the idea of pushing down his sexual barriers a challenge. So, six weeks later, as she sat in an expensive restaurant in Fulham, she found herself, gently and unwisely, falling for him.

There wasn't even just the single reason of Richard, telling her why she should not get involved. On the contrary, there were a few other good reasons. He was older. He was still married. He worked in the same place as her. They had different friends and interests. The list rolled through her mind like the credits for *War and Peace*. Still, as she watched Alan settle the bill and then look up at her with an expectant lift of the eyebrows, she felt herself free-fall a fraction further. She checked herself mentally, wondering if rather than falling for him, it was her job to let him down. Gently and soon. Now, perhaps?

'Will we go back to my house?' he asked her.

'I'd love to,' she said.

Alan's house was, like the restaurant, also in Fulham. In the expensive part, naturally. Two storeys high and a basement down below, he and Margaret had occupied it all. Karen wondered how the two of them had managed to fill out its expanse. Padding through it on his own must be hard, she thought.

Karen felt the buzz of the wine and champagne. She had not drunk too much but just enough had been consumed to give her the feeling that she blended perfectly with everything around her. It heightened her senses of touch, taste and smell but slowed her reactions just enough to enable the amplified feelings to linger in her. She was relaxed and she felt safe.

She sat on the sofa in the drawing room. It was just after eleven-thirty and the house was quiet. Karen could sense its size around her. He came back from hanging his coat and stood in front of her. She looked up at him and he held his hands out to her. She looked quickly at his trousers and saw they were pushing out at the front. He moved his fingers slightly in front of her face, giving a sense of urgency to his need, his desire for her to take his hands. She reached out and put her hands in his. He closed his palms and pulled her up firmly from the sofa.

As she reached her feet, so their mouths met in a kiss. He was taller than her by several inches and she tiptoed to give herself added height. In turn, he craned his neck down to make contact easier. Their mouths moved over each other, looking for a pattern that worked. The rhythm of their kiss was syncopated and they both gasped for breath after a few moments.

'That was nice,' she said to him.

'Very,' he replied, raising his eyebrows, eyes widening as he did so.

'Do you want to take me to bed, Alan?'

He nodded.

She touched the woollen material that covered his crotch, finding the shape of his cock and pushing to one side. It was firm. Gently she played her fingers over the material of his trousers, in much the same way as she had done to his fingers in the restaurant earlier. He gave an urgent gasp. Karen stepped an inch closer to him, coming fully into his space. She felt overpowered by it. The small step she had taken, just an inch, perhaps less, changed all of her feelings. His strong arms encircled her and she felt drenched by his presence, any previous doubts eradicated.

'Take me to bed, please,' she said.

What had a few moments earlier been a question now became a plea which she delivered hoarsely. He led her by the hand.

They fell on to the bed together, still fully clothed. As they kissed, she kicked off her shoes. Karen was wearing one of her favourite outfits, a suit by Romeo Gigli in a heavy brown stripe. Now Alan was pushing the high single-breasted jacket off her shoulders. He knelt up on the bed and lifted her shoulders, pushing the jacket further down her back. It was crumpled under her and she frantically wriggled her arms free as his hands quickly undid the belt on her trousers. These were round her ankles and off before she had time to move her legs. With hardly a moment for titillation, Alan removed her stockings and suspender belt. Karen

474

pulled the jacket out from under her and discarded it, not bothering to look where it landed.

On the large double bed, Karen lay wearing only her knickers, blouse and bra. She felt half undone. Alan did not remove any of his own clothes. She looked at him as he leaned over her and kissed her. His eyes were alight and his hair fell forward. The calm exterior, the brooding power, had been replaced by a fervour. She relaxed as he swiftly unbuttoned her blouse. Her body wanted his touch. So far he had been undressing her with a ruthless speed but he had not touched her skin. She wanted him to caress her and touch her breasts. To rub his hand against the softness of her stomach and down on into the soft mound between her legs.

In seconds, she was nude. He was up on his knees, kneeling over her naked form. He bent and kissed her. As he did, she felt his hand between her breasts, the side of his little finger between the cleft. Her skin was warm and she felt a trace of moisture. A thumb circled under one of her breasts and came to its apex, pressing her nipple, pushing it back into her. He allowed it to pop out again and then she felt him circle its tip with his thumb. Her nipple stood proud and under his touch it became for a moment the most sensitive part of her body. Even as he kissed her and began to probe her mouth with his tongue, her nipple sang out.

When he broke the connection of the kiss, Karen leaned up on her elbows and brought her knees up, feet sliding up the bed as she did so. She dropped her knees wide, displaying herself to him. She saw his eyes run from the top to the bottom of her tight body. As they tracked over her body time and again, his look took on the feeling of a touch and she shuddered under it. Over her face, down her neck and on to her chest, where her breasts hung weightily, the heavy and delicious feeling of sex. The same feeling of sex ran along her taut stomach, the navel, and down into the cavern she had created with the position of her legs. Her juices drizzled slowly and she felt them lubricate the slit of her pussy. She was gripped by the temptation to rub herself with her own hands, but she resisted.

She looked at Alan. His cock seemed to fill the whole front of his trousers. Karen wanted to spring him free and massage him. Hold him in her hand and in her mouth. And then inside of herself, moving the both of them closer towards release.

He touched her pussy and she closed her eyes slowly, placing herself in a white-grey world. She had blocked her vision and was going to use her pussy as the only point of focus. His finger, the middle one, made a small line up and down her pussy lips. It went up towards her clitoris, just near enough to give her a shudder.

He introduced it into her quickly and determinedly and she cried out. She was thrown into tumult by the hard and harsh invasion and she relished it. Her juices helped smooth its way as she writhed on his finger, letting it play inside her and push its way deeper. His sturdy digit was in her to the second knuckle and his thumb was resting near her clitoris, as though it was waiting for her to go to him. She flicked her head about and heard the sound her movements made against the bedclothes, noises that were absorbed by the insulation of the whole house. Again she felt the size of the house looming large around her and how small she was inside of it.

The juices flowed from her as she became more pliant and she wondered where it was all coming from. She was overrun by him and his invasion into the narrow passage between her legs. He overpowered her as he deliberately swivelled his finger inside her, causing her to try and move with it. Its rhythm was so different from that which she would have used on herself that it increased the intensity of the experience. That and the fact that at that moment she found Alan himself to be so different from how she knew him. The reserve had gone. It had given way to an energy that both enthralled and frightened her. She was afraid she would lose herself in him even though she desperately wanted to.

He stopped just when she was moments short of an orgasm. Her breathing was irregular and she gasped the air into her lungs and forced it out again as quickly as she could. She opened her eyes and saw him removing his clothes. He threw them carelessly about the floor, unlike their previous two encounters when they had been neatly folded on the chair beside the bed.

Planting his knees between her legs, he stretched himself over her and she put her hands on the back of his shoulders. The bone was surrounded by well-toned muscle and she moved it gently with her hand. His cock hung heavily from him as though it could barely support its own weight. With one hand she gripped it halfway down his shaft and tentatively sheathed the foreskin back and forth. He let out a groan. His cock was dense and just a little longer than was average, in Karen's experience. The second time they had made love, she had noticed how his cock was just too long and just too wide. Inside her, it ploughed a certain and delicious line between agony and ecstasy.

The heat of his body warmed her as she masturbated him. His shaft swelled and swam in her grip and he moved his body in time with her hand. Karen drew his foreskin back completely and rubbed the head of his cock on her stomach. Alan leaned in closer and she guided his tip down to where she wanted him. Later, she would touch him all over and have him do the same to her. She would mould both their bodies into unusual positions and stimulate him until he shouted. Now, her aim was simple. She wanted him to enter her and fill her with himself.

For a minute or so, she held his shaft and worked his phallus against her pussy lips, up and down them and then in a circular pattern. She waited for the moment, the one she cherished the most. The moment when they would really connect. From two undulating areas of flesh, they would suddenly make one. Their movements would find a harmony and they would be joined. She could never tell exactly when it happened, but the noise she made was usually the best guide.

'Oh!' she cried, elongating the sound and raising the pitch as he entered her.

On into her it went, the long and wide penis. Even as it opened and stretched her, she knew it would also penetrate deeply into her. A two-way stretch. Her juices were both a lubricant and an adhesive. She felt them smooth his path into her vagina but she also felt that it was these which bound them together.

'My God!' she cried when he was fully inside her.

Karen tightened her legs around him and he began to move up and down, back and forth, slowly rocking his cock in and out of her. The beat and pulse of his movements were almost calming, as though they would send her into an ecstatic sleep, carrying her off on the wave of an orgasm. She gripped his body with her hands, his skin mature and worn by time. She thought of his years of marriage and the number of times he must have made love to his wife in that time and the way he was changing this experience into something different for her benefit. How different he was now compared with his demeanour in the shop – the gentle romance in the restaurant and now this.

His shoulders were close to hers, his arms either side of her where he supported himself on his elbows. She felt very close to him, both physically and mentally. Like a mirror image, similar areas of their bodies touched and, like a puzzle, the bits that were not similar fitted together perfectly.

She ran her hands through his hair and kissed him. He increased his motion and the gentle movements gave way to thrusts. In and out of her he went and she gripped him, feeling the walls of her vagina where he touched them with the outside of his cock, which was stony hard, the shape of it prominent in her softness. She pulled him tightly into her and squeezed with her legs as he continued to pump at her. She felt in a daze as he fucked her with a precision and a passion.

His hands moved and he scooped them under her shoulder blades, lifting her a fraction from the bed. As he pulled her tightly, she felt her flesh move with his, a sheen of sweat covering them. There was a light draft under her back where it was now separated from the bed and Karen put her elbows out behind and supported herself. The mattress moved under their exertions and it was the only noise in the room. Locked deep in the cavernous house, it might as well have been the only noise in the world.

The position of Karen's back was now at a slight angle in relation to the bed and it made Alan's cock enter her in a different way. Even though he was on top of her, smothering her almost, it gave her the sense of riding him or clinging to the front of him as though trying to scale him in some fashion. He had reared back, supporting himself on his hands, and she could see down to where they were joined. The lunges he made at her made a sound, barely discernible, but there nonetheless. It was the collection of subtleties that made sex so good for Karen. Over and above the obvious things that were there, the cut and thrust of simple fucking. Beneath it lay a whole realm of tiny movements and sounds that were the real grist of it. These all added up to something much larger than simply fucking with someone.

'Is this all right?' he asked her.

'Very,' she said, mimicking his earlier conduct in the restaurant. She wondered if he and Margaret ever talked dirty?

'Fuck me harder, Alan,' she whispered into his ear.

With a groan he began to increase his efforts. She let herself fall back on to the bed and splayed her arms out at the side of her, letting him make the pace. She felt her orgasm close by and concentrated on holding and

479

nurturing it, making it ready to flower.

Deeply, she breathed the hot vapour they had generated and felt it turn to liquid as it touched their bodies. They were moving hard and fast, both pushing towards the same goal. She could hear how close he was to coming, the desperation and pleading in the sounds he made. She felt herself coming.

In her mind's eye, she saw it. It was a distant spot on the horizon at first, barely visible against the heated landscape of her passion. It moved into view, slowly and assuredly. The image took hold of her and she was inserted into the picture as surely as if she were there. An image that had been with her for as long as she could remember, for as long as she had been sexual. A powerful and muscled white horse galloped over the rocky landscape, brilliantly defined against the harsh background. With long and steady strides it approached her. As it neared, so she trembled and quivered, watching it and waiting for the moment when it would be with her.

It arrived and she was swept up by it. She rode it and felt it drive between her legs, the muscles pulsing and swelling with its movements. She felt the gathering speed and the rush of it against her body, the feeling of complete and absolute freedom and disconnection from everything. A single focus on a point of pure and utter pleasure. The landscape, the fire of it, the speed, everything was assimilated.

'Alan!' she cried out, holding him tightly and opening her eyes to look at him. She shook with the last vestiges of her orgasm and felt him releasing inside her.

He yelled her name into the empty silence of the room and his cock throbbed in her, the semen heavy and viscous inside her.

When they were both done, they lay and he whispered in her ear, his breath warm against it.

It was over an hour later when she jolted awake. He was there beside her, sleeping soundly and looking comfortable in his own house. His sleep had the serenity of recent sex. She lay thinking about him, about Richard and about Hamiltons.

Karen rose from the bed. She went to her attaché case. From it she took a pad and a pen and made her way quietly downstairs. She went into the large kitchen which was on the basement level and switched on the lights. She enjoyed being naked in a strange house at the dead of night. A bowl of fruit was the centre-piece of the table and Karen reached for a green apple. She went to the sink and washed it under the cold tap. She turned and was about to take a bite when she caught a glimpse of herself in the large patio door, her image shimmering like a ghost. As the reflection came back at her, naked and about to take a bite of the apple, she muttered under her breath, 'All I need now is a fig leaf.'

She went back to the table, her mind racing.

With the blank sheet of paper in front of her, the ideas began to flow. She jotted things down, doodled and made little charts here and there.

After half an hour or so, she had come up with an idea.

Chapter Five

'*OH MY GOD*, he's even more adorable on paper,' Karen said into the receiver, which was held on to her ear by the pressure of her shoulder, enabling her to leaf through the contact sheets of Maxwell and talk to Linda at the same time.

'I thought you'd be impressed,' came Linda's voice back down the line. 'That's why I printed a few shots as well, just to give you an idea.'

Any small doubt that had been in Karen's mind regarding the choices of photographer, model and location were now allayed. The three had combined wonderfully. Maxwell and the roof looked suitably intense, the bird imagery graceful and soft. Karen knew it had been a good choice and was pleased with the results.

'How come they're back so quickly?' Karen asked Linda.

'I was anxious to see what they looked like. Excited even. Maybe.' Linda was halting with her words.

'Has Maxwell seen them?'

'He loves them too,' Linda replied breezily.

Karen was unused to such a light tone from Linda, normally more prone to seriousness, and was about to remark at it when she flicked through to a picture of Maxwell emerging from the sea of doves, arms raised, and she thought better of it. She could see why Linda was so captivated.

'I can't wait to show them to Daniel,' Karen said, looking up from the photographs and out of the window of her fifth-floor office, at Sloane Square going about its business.

'Has he said anything more about the nudity?'

'No,' Karen answered. 'But if we have to, we can avoid full frontal, right?' she continued, with heavy accent on the word can.

'There's one where a dove is covering his modesty,' Linda responded unenthusiastically, 'but I think it spoils it if you go with that approach.'

'I'm hoping we won't have to, but you were wise to cover us, Linda.'

During the shoot with the falcon, Linda had taken the planned shot and some side-on shots. As Karen held them in her hands, she realised the fact his cock was not on view was almost as exciting as the full-frontal shots themselves.

'Are you going to show him all the shots, including the cover-ups?' Linda asked.

'Linda, I think the phrase cover-up is somewhat emotive.'

She heard Linda laugh down the other end of the line before she said, 'You know what I mean.'

'I know perfectly. I'm going to keep the cover-ups in reserve in case I need them. I think Daniel will be swayed. He seemed charmed by Maxwell,' Karen said.

'Everyone is. Everyone is.'

'Linda, when I've shown Daniel the prints, I'll give you a call and you should come in for lunch, okay?'

They said their goodbyes.

Karen sat and squinted at the contact sheets, wishing she had one of those small magnifying glasses she had seen professional photographers using, before turning back to the full-size prints Linda had made for her. It was Linda's not terribly subtle way of suggesting which shots they should go with. Karen trusted Linda's eye and expected her to want some feeling of control, particularly as she was used to being in complete control when it came to artistic showings of her work.

What would be the best way to approach Daniel, she wondered? Since the night at Alan's when she had so frantically begun scribbling ideas on paper, she had been thinking of the best way to communicate them to Daniel Avendon. Now she had the opportunity of showing him the photographs and if they set him in a good frame of mind, she would push ahead with her idea. If he did not like the pictures, she'd delay pitching the idea until another day. She buzzed for David. Hamiltons' offices all had old-fashioned buzzers for summoning secretaries and assistants and Karen thought they worked well, although David was not necessarily in agreement.

David entered, clipboard in hand.

'Were they the pictures?' he asked her, sitting down on the chair in front of her desk.

'Yes,' she said, handing them to him. 'I want you to look at them and then I'll ask you something.'

She studied his face as it in turn studied the images before it. She watched his eyes focus, the occasional twitch of his mouth that would give way to a smile. David was handsome in his own way and she held a great affection for him, realising at that moment that the only way she could have someone like David as her assistant was if he was gay. David closed his eyes in mock beatification before looking at Karen.

'I'm speechless,' he said.

'Now. Imagine you are Daniel Avendon. Do you like them?'

'Yes,' he said, without hesitating.

'What makes you like them?'

'They're artistic and sexy both at once. He's androgynous enough to sell the idea of the scent. It's got everything.'

'That's what I thought,' Karen said.

'Do you? Or do you think he won't like them?' David asked.

'I've got a meeting with him at twelve-thirty and I want to show him these but I also want to discuss something else with him,' Karen confided.

'So show him the pictures and if he has a wobbly, don't say anything else. You know how to handle Avendon better than me. Why ask my opinion all of a sudden?'

'I mostly wanted your take on the photos. They are gorgeous, aren't they?'

'I might have to take this one and have it done in easy-wipe formica laminate,' David said, swooping up a picture of Maxwell with the falcon gripping the gauntlet, the bird seeming to stare at the leather hood Maxwell wore.

'Sometimes, David . . .' she said in a warning tone.

He placed the picture back on her desk and looked at his clipboard, switching into business mode.

'Avendon at twelve-thirty, like you say,' he said to her. 'This afternoon we should go down to The Dungeon and finalise what's going to happen with the underwear promotion. They want the boxers out of the stock-room next weekend, not the weekend after, and want us to roll forward.'

'Fine. We've done no advertising for it, but what the hell?'

'Alan Saxton called for you while you were on the phone. No message. A woman called and wouldn't leave her name or a message. I tried to wheedle one out of her, but she said she'd call back.'

'Young, old?' Karen asked him.

'Sounded young, a bit mousy. I'm not good on ages even if they're standing in front of me. On the phone . . .' he raised his shoulders indicating the difficulty this would add.

'That everything?'

'Almost,' he answered. 'I booked you Virgin Upper Class to New York on the flight you wanted. The return's for the Thursday but I can extend it if you want. Four days doesn't seem like long.'

'It is, believe me,' she told him.

Three or four times a year, Karen went to New York to look at potential campaigns she could run. Most of Hamiltons' more successful of these normally involved the States. Several European-themed promotions and two from Africa had worked well, but none as well as America. America sells, was one of Daniel's favourite sayings. Avendon loved America, New York in particular, and Karen quickly caught on that it was a good way to stay on his best side. While there, she would visit three or four of her usual contacts, gathering ideas and leaving the ultimate legwork to the buyers at Hamiltons. She hoped to be able to put the trip to good use, especially if her meeting with Avendon went well at twelve-thirty.

'I'll be around the shop for the next hour or so if you need me,' she told him. 'My pager will be on, just like a doctor on call . . .'

Karen went around to the other side of the fifth floor and into Alan Saxton's office, the door of which was ajar. Alan sat there, leaning back in his chair with his chin supported by his strong hand. He was deep in thought and Karen knew that he hadn't noticed her enter. His office seemed more old-fashioned and musty than her own, dating him slightly although he was still far from stuffy. His desk was a picture of order and efficiency, a blotter and a pen set with a marble base, the usual paper clips and bulldog clips dotted around. There was no picture of his ex-wife in evidence and Karen wondered if there had been one on the other times she had been in his office. She racked her brain but could not remember.

It was only when Karen closed the door that his concentration broke. He looked at her and she saw his expression lift, going from one of serious thought to pleasure at the sight of her.

'You look light years away, not just a million miles,' she said to him, her voice light. 'Are you okay?'

'I'm fine, really,' he said, getting to his feet and

coming round the desk to plant a short kiss on her cheek. He seemed to have a problem with the sort of middle-distance intimacy where they were not in public but not having sex.

'David said you called.'

'Oh yes, I did,' he replied, as though that had jogged his memory. 'I've got something for you.'

He reached into the drawer of his desk and produced a book. He handed it to her. Karen looked at it. It was by one of her favourite authors.

'I didn't know this was out yet,' she said to him.

'It isn't,' he responded, looking pleased with himself. 'I have a friend who works at her publisher's in the States. She sent it over for me. It won't be out over there for another month. I know you like her and I thought you could read it on the plane.'

She grinned at him and looked at the book. 'It comes all the way over here only for me to take it back again. How indulgent.'

'I'm supposed to say you're worth it, or some such phrase at this point, I assume?'

'It's not mandatory, Alan.'

'Will I see you before you go?'

'It might be difficult. We're going to do the boxer shorts promo a week earlier, which is a bit of a pain. I'll let you know.'

He looked at her and she felt a twinge of guilt go through her. She told herself to stop it. Alan was an adult and so was she. They knew what they were doing. However, he did not know what she was doing with Richard. She was about to ask him why he had been so rapt when she first walked in but was interrupted by her pager.

'I have to go. Thanks for the book,' she said, clutching it to her. He smiled at her.

Dispatching David quickly, she filled the time in between her meeting with Avendon by wandering through the store and talking to the staff, doing what she called her woman-of-the-people bit. It was more than just a PR stunt for Karen. She loved Hamiltons and enjoyed simply walking through it, soaking it up. Just before she was due to see Daniel, she returned to her office and looked through the photographs of Maxwell once more. She now felt confident they would please Avendon and put him in a good frame of mind.

Daniel Avendon's corner office on the fifth floor was breathtaking. It could be seen from Sloane Square, protruding slightly from one side behind the turret like a small glass extension to the building. With two walls made from nothing but glass, it let the light flood in. The furniture was lush, an eclectic mixture that he had collected on his travels, bringing it all together in his office and making each piece fit with the other. Just like he did with everything, the overseer of all the pieces on the board.

'What's the essence of Hamiltons?' he asked her as soon as she had entered, not even giving her the chance to say hello or sit down. She made her way to her usual chair.

'Ambiguity. Fun. Eccentricity. Class. Choice.'

'And the fragrance will convey all this?'

'And vice versa, Daniel. It conveys us and we convey it.'

He seemed satisfied. She watched the way he would suddenly develop a nagging feeling about something that he would make someone else allay for him. Then he would change tack completely, the thought apparently buried.

'Do we have much of an agenda today?' he asked her.

We certainly do, she thought.

'Linda Cole sent the contact sheets and a few prints she had made.'

She handed them to him, not committing herself to an opinion in advance of his.

'Fine. Excellent,' he said as he took the envelope.

Karen tried to read his face, to get a sense from his

expression of what was going on in his mind as he surveyed the images before him. His eyebrows were intense and his whole brow furrowed while his eyes dragged over the picture. Whatever he decided would hold sway. That was the way of things. She was thankful that he had an interest in photography and would no doubt be evaluating the shots seriously, with the eye of a collector.

'Linda Cole. Wonderful. She has such an excellent eye and the composition of the shots is delightful. The boy will sell this. Which order do you plan to use the three shots in?'

'Originally, I thought it would be good to use the one with the doves first. But now I think it would be nice to start with the hooded picture, where you can't see it's him, and then use the over-the-shoulder angel shot and finish with the doves. Slowly revealing him. What do you think?' she asked him.

'The doves would be a nice climax. Good. It sounds fine.' He appeared happy.

'And you like the shots?' she asked, not sure if she should push him too much.

'Yes. Have you scheduled New York?'

'I go out on Sunday. I've been in touch with Madeleine and also with George. They're both available to meet. I think a New England style clothes thing would go over well in the Autumn. We've never really done that whole L L Bean, J Crew thing.'

'It's not too Ralph Lauren?' he asked her.

'I don't think we'd do it in quite that way, Daniel,' she told him.

'True. We'd have to do more than just clothes, though.'

'Sure. There'd be a whole lifestyle concept to it, the usual sort of thing. We could run advertorials, food promotions. There's mileage in it.'

'And you would like to do this in the Autumn, or should I say Fall?'

'That's the most obvious time to do it, although I've

been thinking about something else as well, perhaps a little more permanent.'

'Permanent?' he asked, raising an eyebrow.

She went into it.

'It's a high concept kind of idea. It's aimed at women and I think it's something they'd all appreciate.'

'Which is?'

'Eden without the Adam.'

She continued while the previous sentence was still nesting itself in his mind.

'Shopping for women only. A department catering specifically to their, our, needs and wants. A fun place to shop where you'd come with a group of friends. We could call it The Garden, as in Eden.'

'Interesting.'

'Specially selected products and staff. A well thought-out shopping experience from beginning to end. Not just where they offer you a coffee or mineral water. Something more committed and, well, honest.'

Avendon was about to say something when his intercom buzzer went. Karen was annoyed that her flow had been broken. Avendon would not normally let himself be disturbed. He leaned over and pushed the button.

'Yes?'

'Gabrielle is here, Mr Avendon.'

'Tell her I'll be with her as soon as I can.'

'She's insisting that she sees you now, Mr Avendon.'

'I will only be another ten or fifteen minutes, Jane. Tell her to wait.' Avendon was becoming irked.

'But, sir . . .'

The intercom went abruptly dead, as though Jane had been strangled or stabbed. The door to Avendon's office swung open. Karen decided not to turn her head when the door opened. She remained seated and tried to relax and fight the angry feeling that was taking her over. It was the first time in all of her meetings with Daniel that his secretary had even dared to buzz him. She gripped the side of the chair, her knuckles whitening, before her survival instincts kicked in more consciously and her face assumed a relaxed mask that wore a gentle smile.

Into her field of vision came a woman in her mid- to late-fifties who would once, Karen thought, have been glamorous. Now she looked as though her life story was sculpted into her features and engraved on to her skin, an outward sign of some inner turmoil, quite what Karen could not wonder, being more concerned with exactly *who* she was. She wore a sweeping blue dress that would have been more at home at a party or even on a panto dame and Karen pondered whether this was a studied eccentricity along the lines of Vivienne Westwood or simply bad taste, her gut reaction veering towards the latter assumption.

'Karen, this is my sister, Gabrielle.' Avendon was on his feet and Karen followed, looking at the sister and trying to see the resemblance.

'He means half-sister,' the woman said, not extending a hand, 'but that always leads to some nasty remark from him. I'm glad to see he's learned.'

'Pleased to meet you, Gabrielle. I'm Karen Taylor.' She put her hand out and continued. 'I run the promotions . . .'

Karen got no further. The woman had turned from her and went to look out of the window.

'The view doesn't change much,' she said, speaking to the glass rather than to anyone in the room. 'Very little does, here.'

'Gabrielle worked in the shop for a time, in the late Sixties,' Avendon said to Karen with an apologetic look on his face.

'Worked in the shop?' she said, turning, emphasising the questioning nature of her statement. 'You make it sound like I did make-overs. I owned, still do, fifteen per cent of the stock. The unsilent partner, you used to refer to me as.'

'It was noisy partner. Actually,' Avendon responded, scratching his forehead and squinting, as though

491

used to such verbal jousting with his half-sister.

'Should I come back later, Daniel?' Karen asked him.

'Please, don't let me interrupt. I'll return to my window view and you can carry on,' Gabrielle said to Daniel as though Karen had not even spoken.

'Daniel, I'd rather talk about it when you have more time.'

Karen looked at the woman and thought about giving her a quick shove through the glass.

'Please. Do finish, Karen. It sounded exciting and I'm sure Gabrielle would not mind waiting outside.'

Gabrielle had gone back to her window view as she said she would and did not appear about to go anywhere. Karen licked her lips, which felt dry, and tried to think on her feet, willing for David to page her at that precise second.

'Daniel. I have to go. I'll talk to you later.' She was firm and precise in her tone and nodded at him as though the physical movement of her head would lodge the meaning of her words into him. As she did so, Gabrielle turned and gave a smile which was small, barely discernible but triumphant nonetheless.

Karen left quickly and closed the door, heading straight for Alan Saxton's office.

'Alan, who the fuck is Gabrielle?' she practically shouted at him.

'You've met her then?'

'Met her? She crashed a meeting with Daniel, right in the middle of something. His half-sister?' She raised her arms as she spoke.

'I'll close the door,' he said, standing and crossing the room.

He returned and sat in his chair with a resigned sigh. Karen saw him gather his thoughts and take a breath.

'Daniel has told you the old Dick Foxton story? I've been there when he has, I think?' he asked.

'Yes, I've heard it only once and as an anecdote. All that old-fashioned bitter rivalry between his father and another store owner. It sounds like an Ealing comedy.'

'Gabrielle and Daniel have the same mother, Mary. Mary was married to Daniel's father Lawrence and to Dick Foxton, Gabrielle's father.'

'What happened to Dick Foxton?' she questioned.

'He was killed in a motor racing accident. Fast cars were a passion for him. Mary was married to him at the time and Gabrielle was only four years old. Only eight months after Dick Foxton died, she married Lawrence Avendon and a year later, Daniel was born. I think a lot of people thought that Mary must have been having an affair with Lawrence Avendon long before Dick Foxton died.'

'How does all of that result in Gabrielle having a fifteen per cent stake in Hamiltons?'

'Daniel never says very much, but I think Lawrence and Mary had an absolutely horrible time of a marriage. They separated when he was only five. Lawrence kept custody of Daniel and I suspect the buy-off was a stake in Hamiltons for Gabrielle. At the time Dick Foxton died, his store was in bad shape and closed not long after his death, so there was no real money for Mary or Gabrielle to fall back on.'

'And did Mary get any benefit from this?'

'She was looked after. Daniel made some alteration to her trust fund in the late Sixties and I administered it up until she died in nineteen-eighty.' Alan's tone was even.

'God. I thought we were just a small, well-respected department store with a reputation for eccentricity. We're in the wrong business. We should be making a soap opera. What does her fifteen per cent add up to?'

'In sheer commercial terms, not a lot. The deal was structured to enable her type of share capital to give her a good income and little real involvement. Lawrence Avendon was a bastard and made sure that Dick Foxton's offspring wouldn't get any piece of his beloved Hamiltons. In practice, however, I think she can make life awkward, especially as she has hooks into Daniel.'

493

'This is going to fuck things up, I can tell.'

'What do you mean?' he asked her.

She shook her head, exhaling through her nose. 'Nothing. Thanks for filling me in on all of this. And thank you again for that book.'

Karen sat in her office for half an hour, staring at nothing, thinking of nothing in particular, having instructed David not to disturb her under any circumstances. 'Not even for Daniel?' he had asked her. 'Especially not if it's Daniel,' had been her reply.

Picking up the receiver she called Daniel and was put through to him instantly.

'I've been trying to reach you,' he said 'but I was told you were not to be interrupted. Are you that mad at me?'

'Did you like the idea?' she asked, ignoring his attempt to be winsome.

'I think it will sell. This is a big project. You should produce a proposal of some sort. When you have a rough draft, talk to Alan about costings and we'll schedule a meeting after you are back from New York. I think that, providing the cost analysis works, you'll have your Eden without Adam.'

'Thank you,' she said, wondering if it was really going to be that simple.

She finished her day by taking a last look at Maxwell and then going out on to the roof, watching the light change over London. She stooped and from the gravel retrieved a single white dove feather. She put it in her pocket and left.

Chapter Six

AS KAREN STEPPED into the taxi, Richard had his head in the front window, giving the driver an address in North London. She settled back on to the black leather of the seat, which had been worn shiny and looked not far from splitting. She saw the driver's eyes in the mirror, flicking up and then trying to peer down and get a view of her legs. She pulled the dress down, not because of the driver, but to cover what she had on underneath, not wanting Richard to see. The dress was a short slip in a lamé that was almost pewter in colour, hanging from her shoulders by the thinnest of straps. The nipples of her bare breasts pointed out with a sexy prominence and the shortness of the skirt showed off the muscular shapeliness of her legs to its fullest.

Richard joined her, placing his jacket carefully on the seat next to him. Not wanting to risk Alan seeing them and needing to change in any case, Karen had made him pick her up from her flat. She had pushed her short hair back as much as she could with the help of some mousse and she had kept the lines of her make-up thin, giving her the same metallic look as the dress. She wore no jewellery and the impression, almost correct, was that with one small cut to each of the straps, she would be completely naked except for the silver stilettos. There was still her underwear, of course, but it was a long ride to North London.

'You look like a little rocket girl,' Richard said to her.

'How do you mean?'

'Like something from the Jetsons or even the Flintstones. Sort of wild. Don't walk near any magnets.'

He beamed at her, pushing at his hair, and she felt a quiver run through her, forgetting that she was in a taxi.

'You look quite harsh yourself,' she said, rubbing the leg of his grey trousers.

'This is meant to be a soft line. Like a blunt blade.'

'I see. Is it one of ours?'

'We just started stocking them. Krizia.'

'Is this the long narrow line in suits I keep reading about?' she asked him sarcastically.

'Everyone wants a long suit at the moment. All we did was pull the trousers up on the mannequins to make the jackets look longer, and it works. This is a proper long suit, of course.'

'Of course.'

'Nice, huh?'

'Yes,' she said, almost biting at the word. It would be her last chance to see him before she flew to New York at the weekend and already the four days she would be there felt a long time to be away. From Hamiltons, from The Garden, from Richard and from Alan. For the moment, she concentrated only on Richard in the taxi beside her.

A grey waistcoat matched the trousers and the jacket so neatly folded on the seat; a three-piece suit underpinned by a white T-shirt. It was loose around him, revealing different angles and aspects of him as he moved. Very London in late Summer. They were both deliberately dressed up, ready for a night of dancing and posing at the opening of a new jazz club in Islington. Karen wanted to blow off steam and had already been to the gym early that morning, releasing a lot of pressure, but some partying and some sex with Richard would finish things off nicely. When she came back from New York, she would be ready to give Daniel a full, uninterrupted pitch for The Garden, without any gatecrashers.

Karen turned her mind to Richard, wanting to enjoy him while she had him. She knew he would ask the question eventually. She waited and a minute passed, but he did not disappoint her.

'Are you wearing knickers under there?' he asked lasciviously, gripping her thigh and squeezing it. She slapped his hand away playfully.

'I've got you a present,' she said to him.

'Where? Not in that little Chanel bag?' he asked, motioning towards it at the same time.

'No.'

'Where then?'

She hitched one side of her skirt up and revealed the leg of a soft pure cotton boxer short and then pushed it back down again.

'John Smedley underwear from Harrods. Contraband,' she said huskily.

Karen glanced up and met the eyes of the taxi driver in his rear-view mirror; his gaze quickly averted as their eyes met in glass. Richard, meanwhile, gawped at her and then laughed.

'You are so naughty,' he said to her.

'It's the most gorgeous soft natural cotton. You wouldn't know you were wearing them,' she purred at him. 'Maybe I won't be, soon. Feel how soft.' She raised the side of her skirt again, positioning her leg so it was easier for him to touch, but not making her movements too obvious to the driver, who she knew was watching everything.

Against the side of her leg, his fingers brushed the skin and then came to the border of the boxer shorts. Richard popped his index finger under the hem and into the ridge of muscle on her outer thigh, letting his digit travel up until it was at the top of her leg. She turned her head and looked at him as the taxi made its way through the traffic, the sounds of the evening simmered by the heat of the waning sun. They looked at each other, both resisting the urge to kiss, and he removed his finger, letting his whole hand move

497

around to drop between her legs, resting on the seat in front of her crotch. The outside of his hand was against her inner thighs, close to her pussy, which was beginning to moisten. His finger lighted on the material where it covered her sex and then the hand was gone.

She leaned over and whispered to him, 'There's a slit right down the front of these.' She let her words sink in. 'And I've left the fly button undone.'

In the mirror, the driver's eyes were darting wildly about in their sockets as if he were trying to follow a fly. Karen moved her rear forward on the seat by several inches and leaned back, positioning her legs just provocatively enough. Richard picked up his jacket, pretended to look through it for something and then when he had finished, placed it on her lap. The wool was surprisingly gentle against her legs. The motion of the vehicle shifted her from side to side, a rocking action that was soothing and sexual at once; the feeling of her nudity under the metal-coloured dress, only the boxer shorts holding her in check. Inside them, her pussy was damp and ready for him.

Casually, Richard's right hand made its way across the seat, as though it had a life all its own, a force he could not control. As the hand moved, he simply looked ahead or out of the side window, seemingly unaware of what his hand was up to. Its journey was agonisingly slow, like a snake stalking its prey, the movement agile and unhurried and his little finger twitching from time to time. She stared at it as though it were disembodied from him, nothing to do with him as it made its way closer. It disappeared under the portion of the jacket that hung off the side of her left leg on to the seat. She waited for his touch but it did not come. The taxi seemed silent and she turned and frowned at him. He smiled at her, teasingly.

She jolted when he touched the side of her leg, an involuntary spasm seizing her. One finger quickly turned into two and then three and before long his whole hand was resting on her leg, feeling a degree cooler than her own flesh, which had taken on a feverish heat. A few circular motions on her leg above the knee and then his hand was off, journeying under the jacket on her lap, up the front of the top half of her leg and under the rim of the skirt. It made contact with the velvety cotton of the underwear and he brought it to rest on the curve of her inner thigh, close to her crotch. And then nothing but the same smile.

Karen sat in the taxi with the jacket on her lap and Richard's hand up her skirt. That was the exterior. On the inside, she felt herself boiling with desire, the shorts getting damper by the second. Like they were playing a game of poker, they both sat still, moved only by the motion of the taxi. Karen was confident she would hold out longer than he could. Richard was a novice tease. She set her face into a relaxed expression, as if enjoying a pleasant ride in the countryside, gazing out of the window.

The hand spread out over her pussy like a shadow casting itself across her. It cupped her, fitting easily with the shape of her body, cradling her. He had found one of the small white buttons that should have held the fly of the shorts in check and he was twirling it between his fingers. Karen felt her pubic hair sprouting from the slit in the front and the static tickle of Richard's fingers as they grazed it. The heat between her legs was intense and her rear felt glued to the seat of the cab. His attention turned from the button to *her* as his fingers scratched at her hair, the soft puffy mons beneath it, which he pushed his fingers into. As he delicately caressed his fingers against her pubic hair, the fly on the shorts opened wider and her sex was bared beneath the dress.

Richard's movements were discreet and careful, as if he were performing microsurgery or defusing a bomb. The jacket on her lap barely moved, bobbing up and then down again only occasionally, as he worked delicately at her with the fingers of his right hand.

Karen alternated glances between Richard, the jacket and the rear-view mirror of the driver, his eyes seemingly never far from it. The track made by his fingers increased, spreading out over her crotch, both up, down and across it, running themselves over the available surface area, gliding over her but never entering, merely tormenting her.

In a first outward display, Karen inhaled deeply through her nose, the oxygen filling her head and clearing it, her senses becoming more attuned to Richard and to his hand. He seemed to take the breath as a sign and he cautiously poked a finger between the wet lips of her pussy, which accommodated him with ease and eagerness. She was well lubricated and pliant to his precise touch. Her clitoris swelled and Richard caressed it briefly, trailing his hand along the slit made by her lips. When his fingers were at the bottom of the fly hole, she felt him reach and grip the material of the boxer shorts and then pull them upwards from between her legs, the fabric tightening around her rear and gathering up in a tight stretch on her sex.

She smothered her cry by placing her hand to her face and holding her breath in, her legs quivering as Richard continued to pull the underwear up into the crack of her pussy, gathering a steady rhythm that echoed its way through her. As he coyly tugged the cloth up and down between her legs, she let the passion swell in her, all the time maintaining a cool exterior, not forgetting that she was in the back of a taxi riding through London in the evening rush-hour. The cloth was soft and damp against her, the nap of it maddeningly stimulating.

Richard released his grip on the boxers and placed his finger through the slit and into her pussy, his palm close to her clitoris. Karen let her legs droop apart as his finger slipped into her, a slick and experienced probe that explored her depths. He positioned his hand so that it formed a cage over her crotch that could remain still while only the middle finger, inside her, did its work, like a tiny piston reaming her pussy. She wondered if the position of his hand, cramped over her, was painful for him, although the speed and fluidity of his finger gave no indication that it was.

No words had passed between them and Karen stared at the jacket on her lap as though mesmerised by it, waiting for it to move. But it did not. She could feel him fingering her but that was all. Neither of them gave any apparent sign of what they were doing. She continued to watch the jacket, Richard's arm across the seat and his hand buried under it, clawed over her pussy with his middle finger pushing in and out of her. Other cars passed them or the cab overtook someone; people on the pavements wandering or rushing about; everyone oblivious to them and what they were doing; except for the driver. He knew what they were up to and had been observing them in his mirror since she had first got into the taxi. Karen could see enjoyment in the intensity of his eyes.

Her breathing became short, intense but quiet pants escaping her. Richard had increased the speed at which his finger was moving in her and had changed the direction of the pressure, pushing more upwards to the underside of her clitoris. She reached across and briefly stroked the back of his neck, the hair slightly bristly like a brush. Returning both hands to her sides, she concentrated on herself and the feelings that were stoking up in her, needing release.

The back of a taxi was, she supposed, an unusual place to feel such passion, but in that single moment it seemed perfect. She was in contrast to her surroundings – the inside of the car, the traffic and the frantic rush of London itself. With the movements of his finger, Richard had at first created a frenetic pace in her but now she was ready to let that break into a long and delightful release, like a high diver free-falling through the air before finally hitting the water.

A twitch in her legs was the first sign. Her rear tightened and it lifted her up in the seat. Richard's finger was now massaging her vagina and clitoris deeply, roving between them and spreading her, making her squirm away from it and towards it by turns. Her hands gripped the edge of the black leather seat and her body tensed itself as though contracting towards some invisible centre.

She gritted her teeth as she came, her vagina rippling and her eyelids falling heavily shut. She fought the urge to clench her whole face and wail, instead forcing her eyes open and glimpsing the driver's eyes in the mirror, on hers the whole time. She kept her eyes open and locked them on the driver's as her body made very tiny convulsions, a brake on her orgasm that filtered it out slowly. It felt as though the orgasm had gushed into her from nowhere and she was now filled to the brim with it, forcing it out with high pressure through the very small actions she had permitted herself.

Richard's finger slowed and finally stopped, slipping itself out of her and from under the dress and jacket. Karen saw sweat on the back of the driver's neck and also on Richard's brow.

Carefully and quickly, she raised her bottom and pulled off the boxer shorts, damp and sweaty from her juices, knowing exactly what they would leave the driver as a tip.

Chapter Seven

HAVING FREE RUN of a large and well-furnished apartment in Greenwich Village was a luxury Karen planned to make full use of. Not that she had managed to yet. She had been in New York for a day and a half, her time split between the obvious places in the garment district around West 34th Street and several irregular hours spent in bed beating the jet lag. The next day, she planned to spend some time venturing to Queens or the other way to New Jersey. She would not have considered herself a well-seasoned Manhattanite, but she had been enough times to feel comfortable and to enjoy herself. Now she wanted to take in her immediate surroundings.

The apartment belonged to Jake, a friend who was a video director with his own successful production company. Jake was attempting to make the jump from music videos and advertisements into movies, the reason his apartment was empty while he was in Los Angeles. She had stayed with him once before, but in a different apartment on Central Park West. Jake obviously felt the Village was the place to be, in addition to Los Angeles. Jake left the key with the doorman who had played deliberately hard to convince when she arrived, but soon succumbed. Karen knew she was expected but he had enjoyed stringing her along and she enjoyed playing the game.

Karen sat in the main room of the apartment, nibbling on blue corn tortilla chips. With Jake not there, she felt like a burglar with an invitation, certain the police would rush in on her at any moment and accuse her of something. Even the silence in a strange house sounded different. Fresh from a post-shopping-trip shower, she wore a thick blue towelling robe that had been laid out on the guest bed when she arrived. From her grocery bag, yet to be unpacked, she pulled a diet cherry soda.

The time away from Hamiltons was helping to get her thoughts in order. Away from the bustle of the shop she was able to think clearly about what she wanted The Garden to be like, how it would look and feel. It gave her the chance to visualise it unhampered. At other moments, she had thought about Richard and about Alan. The distance between her and them was not as helpful in giving her a clear picture. Whenever she thought of one, the other popped up too, as though they were inseparable in her mind and she was unable to have one without the other. Unless she had neither. Karen put her thoughts on hold.

She found her way up the main stairwell, on the opposite side to the one that led to the guest's wing. The apartment was particularly well designed for guests, with a suitable number of bathrooms and spare bedrooms. Jake enjoyed hosting people, she knew, even *in absentia*. The robe that had been laid out when she arrived had a long note left on top explaining where everything was and that she should help herself to anything she needed.

She wandered past the main bedroom, to a door at the end of the landing. It was unlike the other doors in the house, Karen could tell, as it seemed set into the frame in the way a sauna door would be. On the floor outside it, tucked close to the door and almost obscured by shadow, was a remote control with a Post-It note stuck on it. Karen picked it up and read it.

K, once inside the room, use the remote and go through the numbers sequentially. It's the only way – and a teaser. Have fun, J.

Karen looked at the remote control unit in her hand. The buttons on it were numbered from one to five plus a red button on the top right. The controller had nothing else on it but the five numbered black buttons and the one red. She smiled, flicked the light switch on the wall outside and opened the door of the room. It was heavy and swung inwards with a precision and weight that suggested well-oiled hinges or hydraulics. Harsh fluorescent light flickered, giving a strobe effect to the room, making it impossible to tell what was in there. Karen stood in the doorway until the light finally clicked into full brightness.

The whole room was banked with televisions, from floor to ceiling. As Karen turned to close the door, she was amazed to see that it had three television monitors down it, accounting for the weight. She pushed it to and was surrounded by screens, all with red standby lights beaconing silently from them. The room was small, but not claustrophobic – about twelve feet square.

'Oh boy,' she muttered. 'This is like science fiction.'

Under her bare feet the maroon carpet was made up of carpet tiles, a foot square and with a deep luxurious pile to them. The light was glaring and unforgiving, like the lights over a dentist's chair or some of the lighting they experimented with at the shop. Alone in the room, the screens lifeless and waiting, the silence broken only by the whistle of air-conditioning, she felt a stirring in her groin, not unlike one she had resisted earlier, in the shower.

Looking down at the controller, she studied its simplistic design. It was a TV remote control with five large channel change buttons. There were no controls for volume or brightness. She pushed the red standby button, wondering where to aim it. She just held it above her head, realising as she looked up that even the ceiling had monitors embedded into it.

Slowly and with no particular order, the red lights disappeared, replaced by green dots. The room lights, which ran around the point where walls met ceiling, dimmed down to a much more accommodating and friendly glow. There were a few audible clicks and then the hiss and crackle of static as the screens came to life. All the red standby lights had now extinguished but the screens merely showed black. The lights remained at the same level.

Karen pushed the button numbered one on the control pad, as that seemed to be the most logical thing to do. Gradually music started to fade in. Each of the four walls and the ceiling acted as a single screen, showing a video. Karen recognised it as a popular boy band, one of the many that had spawned from the clubs and into the bedrooms of millions of young girls via Saturday morning television. There was a digital clock on the bottom right corner spinning with the precision required for video editing. Karen wondered if Jake had actually directed this one. It was not a song she particularly cared for although the band members more than made up for that. She liked to look at their flesh, and it had been edited in a way just titillating enough to make her feel the pulse of herself against the robe. Fast cutting shots showed glimpses of torso, smiles and camaraderie. Karen wished she was Jake, able to play with these images however he chose in the editing room.

The walls rhythmically changed so that each of them split into four, quadrupling the images at once. Then they switched to each single monitor with the same image on them, making the size of the pictures in front of her eyes vary in time with the music and choreography.

The screens went abruptly blank. Karen could hear her quickened heart in the closeted atmosphere of the room. She looked down at the remote and pushed button number one again to get the images back.

Nothing happened. She thought about Jake's note and the need to press the buttons in sequence. Karen pushed button three – again, nothing. Jake was a teaser. When she touched button two, she heard the speakers come back to life, a faint sound of breathing on them.

On the screen the black gave way as the image faded up. It was the boy band again. One of them at least, one of the backing singers – a shot of the side of his face and shoulders. He was lying on his back, on a bed, grimacing and sweating, turning his head from side to side every now and then. As the camera pulled back, it revealed a woman astride him and they fucked with the familiar, practised motion of lovers, their bodies rolling in similar directions as their movements quickened and complemented each other.

Karen stood and stared with her mouth open, gawping at the tight sinewy flesh and failing to believe what was in front of her eyes. The wall was one single image of the two of them fucking away furiously and wordlessly. Then the bank of monitors split into two halves, on the horizontal, the top half preserving the view of the bed, the bottom half a close-up of a cock entering a pussy, mercilessly back and forth, the vagina expanding as it did so. The timing between the two images was perfect, a unison of thrusting.

Like a window, the wall went into four squares, the two figures thrashing on the bed and the close-up of the pussy remaining on the top two. They were joined at the bottom by a close in shot of the backing singer's head pushing itself into the pillow. On the final quarter, the video of the band's latest single played. As the song approached its climax, so did the couple on the bed. Karen saw the contortion on the face, the cock sliding out of the quivering pussy and the singer sitting up abruptly. His body rigid, the singer came into mid-air, the video freeze-framing, back-tracking and repeating the ejaculation in a sequence that seemed endless. Threads of come forming on the taut bronze flesh of his stomach, his cries just audible as the music began to fade.

And then blackness again.

This time, the silence was broken by Karen's panting. Through all of it she had been rubbing at herself with the robe, not certain her eyes were telling the truth. She felt under the robe and was wet and swollen, the lips of her pussy covered in fluid. She gathered some on a fingertip and licked it. She wished she had made the most of the video while it had been there, instead of just gawping. Knowing it was pointless, Karen tried to restore the image using the controller. It was time to move on. She undid the robe, dropped it to the floor and sat on it, legs crossed, her sex alive and heavy in between them, waiting to see what button number three held in store.

A bass drum started, insistent and thudding, one, two, three, four. The music had a dirty, masturbatory rhythm to it.

If she had gawped before, now her mouth almost fell like a lead weight. On the screen, to the music, a single solitary male figure was lying on a bed, stroking and caressing himself. Hands running over the delicate body, tweaking at his own nipples and cupping his balls in his hands. Through all of the movements, the hands eventually came back to concentrate on the large erect penis that glistened as though from the application of an oil. All of that would have been enough to send Karen off into a fantasy from which the only outcome would be orgasm.

But, there was more.

The image that had haunted her for the last two weeks, that had been there when she made love with Richard and with Alan, was there before her on the screen in a raw and explicit way that even her subconscious had been unable to process adequately in her dreams. This was her dream made electric and twelve feet high and she was both dwarfed by its size and smothered by its expanse. She drowned in the image.

It was Maxwell.

Lazily and unhurriedly, he lay on a large oval bed, his body against a background of crisp white cotton, masturbating himself. Karen watched his hand and the rhythm that seemed so accustomed to the pace of his own desire as he beat himself. His torso moved slightly, indicating the flurry of movement that she hoped would follow shortly. The drum beat on, going through her. His dainty, thin hands and body were the perfect counterpoint to the sharp picture of ecstasy he wore on his face, his nose scrunched up and his teeth showing.

It was a different sort of arousal to that she had felt previously, watching the band member fucking. This image generated a heat in her that permeated her skin from the inside to the out, making its slowest journey on her face, where her cheeks were red and flushed.

Karen slowly worked a finger into herself, feeling the outline and shape of her sex around her digit. She lay back and raised her knees higher to make herself more open and round. As the finger slid into the second knuckle, she let out a gasp and closed her eyes. Straining her arm further forward and down between her legs, she moved her finger in deep enough to feel as though she held herself in the palm of her hand. She kept her position and then opened her eyes and looked at Maxwell on the ceiling monitors, massaging himself in keeping with his hunger. All the while his cock quivered and pulsated. Karen worked at her clitoris, her pussy feeling closer and closer to her own face as her body bent to allow her finger entry. She closed her eyes again, holding Maxwell in her mind, wanting to edit him in her head.

When next she opened her eyes, ready to flood her sight with him and push herself to orgasm, the image had gone and the music was dwindling. She continued to work on herself, not knowing if she should release herself now or wait in case there were yet more images to come for her and carry her off. She wanted to come, but more than that she wanted to push buttons four and five. Karen gritted her teeth and removed her finger as she sat upright, blinking at the empty banks of screens in front of her.

Perhaps she had imagined it, her aching desire for Maxwell and her feverish imagination combining and ending up displayed on the screen, as though the image up there was a reflection of the one in her mind. That would have been pure bliss, she thought, to have been able to make her mental images appear on the screen, although she could not tell exactly what they would be.

She pushed button four, but not before giving button three a quick try to see if she could retrieve Maxwell from wherever he was stored.

This time it was much more conventional. A melange of different images danced before her eyes. On each screen a different fantasy. A man entering a woman from behind, the both of them making strained faces from the exertions of sex. Three people stood in a line, a woman in the middle of two men throwing her head back and letting her tongue protrude. A woman standing on tip-toe gripped handles high on a wall whilst a tall man gently gripped her hips and entered her with his large phallus.

Karen's finger was back inside herself and she concentrated on her clitoris. She rolled around on the floor to see different walls and what they showed. She lay on her side, then on her back. She crouched and looked in front of her. All around, a frenzy of sexual activity. She felt lifted by the static energy and the rush of all the sensory input, as if she were running a small charge through her own body. Her pussy was humming, needing to be filled. She concentrated on her clitoris, rubbing it harder and faster, the strokes getting shorter. Now she was on her knees, sweat running down the bridge of her nose, and she was about to come. She rolled over to her left side and her elbow, furious from the force of masturbation, banged the controller. She was shocked when a small door in the floor opened.

Scuttling back, she was startled by the way the carpet tile had suddenly shifted to one side, revealing a small mirror less than a foot or so square. She peered at it like a cat that had been scared, her sweaty reflection looking back at her.

On the walls, people were at each other madly. They were licking, sucking, rubbing and penetrating each other, using their own bodies and the bodies of others in a desperate frenzy. Her senses were overloaded with stimuli. Somewhere between her tight clitoris and her slowly widening vagina, she was gripped by a force that held her in a precarious balance.

Karen stood and squatted over the mirror, looking at her pussy in it, the trail of her buttocks and then her hand. Her face became a scowl as she explored herself and watched the whole process in the mirror.

Glancing down at her image and then up on to the screens, she ran her fingers over the lips of her pussy, stroking her clitoris. Karen chose to focus on one particular image on a monitor. It happened to be the screen that was easiest for her to see in her current position, but she also found the image exciting. A woman was suspended from silken scarves, wrists bound to ankles, hanging like a pendulum. A man stood, his thick cock deep inside the hanging figure, and rocked her back and forth on to his member. The woman in the sling threw her head back with pleasure as though on a swing.

Karen turned her attention to the mirror for a few moments and when she looked back up at the screen, the woman in the sling was gone. On the outside screens, forming a border around the central section, countless images were cut together, impossible to focus on but subliminally exciting. In the centre, on four screens, was a pussy that was filmed from beneath. Karen halted her own movements to watch the screen, removing her hand from herself.

The figure on the television stopped also, the hand there disappearing.

Karen put her hand under herself and her own hand came into view on the screen. Tentatively, she manipulated herself, all the time watching the identical image on the screen.

Focusing on two things, the screen with the picture of her pussy and her pussy itself, Karen touched herself harder and faster, the backs of her thighs banging on to her sweaty calf muscles, back arched and clitoris crying out between her fingers. She expelled her breaths sharply and made a desperate squeaking sound as she did so, feeling the dirty and delicious nature of her own hand. She speeded up and enjoyed the feeling.

On screen and in the mirror, she was able to watch her own hand as it massaged her clitoris and thrust a finger into her vagina. She was overcome by images of herself and what she was doing. The muscles in her body caved in to the inevitable and she let the first wave of her orgasm rise in her, feeling herself coming and watching herself too.

Her muscles stiffened and she felt her pussy tighten its grip. She stopped moving up and down on it and the only remaining motion was her hand on her clitoris. The room was quiet except for her own groans and whines.

The fluorescent lights reactivated just as the first tremble of her orgasm readied itself and she contracted tightly. She convulsed and shouted out as she came in powerful bursts.

She was demolished by her orgasm. Her desire had created a most delicate and intense construction, full of detail, each peculiarity her own, and now it was being torn down as the raw physical nature of the orgasm shook her to her foundations. In the rush of feelings she had lost her sense of time, her sense of place, even her sense of self. Karen writhed and jolted about, the light burning into her sweaty eyes.

Her breathing returned only gradually to its normal rhythm. She picked up the controller and pressed button number one, the lights dimming as she did so.

Chapter Eight

KAREN FELT EYES on them from every quarter. The stares were not, however, for her. She was having dinner at New York's Gotham Bar and Grill with Jake and a friend of his. It was the fact that the friend was one of the hottest post-Brat Pack actors that was drawing the collective furtive stare.

Chris Nichol, at twenty-seven, had been in several reasonably successful movies, commercially and artistically, and the world seemed poised for his leap to stardom. It would have been pointless to describe him as movie star handsome because that was precisely what he was, but he had none of the menace common to his generation of actors. Instead, he oozed a wholesomeness and down-home politeness and charm, particularly cute when he seemed embarrassed by the attention he was getting.

'You will be in the gossip columns tomorrow, Karen,' Jake said. 'Chris Nichol and mystery date seen on the town with up-and-coming video-maker Jake Summer.'

The contrast between Chris and Jake was so marked, Karen thought. If somebody had asked Karen the question, what is the first thing that springs to mind when someone mentions an English video director living in America, she would have responded, lots of black clothing, and long hair, prematurely greying and tied in a ponytail. Features that were heavy and rubber-like, eyes that were grey and glassy. That was what she would have answered to such a question and that was also what described Jake.

Chris Nichol was at the opposite end of the spectrum and had yet to make the journey Jake wore so obviously in his demeanour. Chris had the collegiate look, a sophomore rather than a freshman, just knowing enough, but not quite spoiled by the knowledge. His hair was short and black, shaped neatly, and his nose was grand, giving him the slightly regal East Coast look he had milked so well in his movies. When he smiled, his face was filled by it, his teeth naturally perfect and his head dropping slightly as though trying to win her over to a point of view or apologising for coming home drunk the night before. He made her feel like they had known each other for a long time.

'This isn't really a glitzy Hollywood place, is it? I've never thought so,' Karen said.

'Glitzy?' Chris repeated. 'I like that word.' He continued to pick away at his dessert, moving impishly, as though he were Karen and Jake's errant son out for his graduation dinner with them. He looked up at her suddenly.

'So Karen,' he asked her, 'do you have a boyfriend back in England?'

'If I remember Karen correctly,' Jake interrupted, 'she will have several. All chasing her and wooing her madly and she just taking her pick.'

'Please. I hardly need to speak with you singing my praises. I'm seeing someone on and off,' she said, directing her last sentence towards Chris.

'More off or more on?' he said.

'Fifty-fifty, I'd say.'

'Hmm,' he grunted, considering this before reconsidering the fruit concoction in front of him.

Jake had privately told Karen that he was wooing Chris Nichol with the hope of attaching him to a film project his production company had in development.

515

With Chris Nichol attached, the project may just break out of development-hell and get picked up by a studio. Jake had directed several videos for one of Chris's favourite English bands and they had met on the set of one. The two of them seemed to get on well enough and, as far as was possible, lacked the kind of falsity in their friendship Karen would have expected in the movie business.

'Are you seeing anyone back in LA?' she asked, turning his question back at him.

'More off than on. Thirty/seventy, I'd say.' He beamed at her, pleased with himself. If he hadn't been so damn nice, she'd have cut him dead there and then. But she wanted to play a while.

'An ageing starlet?' she asked, raising her brow.

'Over twenty is ageing out there. I make it a rule to try and not fuck actresses,' he said.

'Try and make it a rule. Do you try and succeed?'

'Most of the time,' he replied, chewing on fruit. 'You never jump the customers, I guess, so it's the same, right?'

'Don't assume anything!' Jake interjected loudly. 'Karen could tell you stories and I'm sure she will.'

'Actually Chris, Karen could tell you a lot of stories about Jake,' she said, enjoying referring to herself in third person, 'but I'm sure he wouldn't want me to any more than I would want him to about me.' She shot Jake a glare and he merely smiled, his eyes the colour of smoke.

'I'll get the check,' Jake said eventually, obviously enjoying the repartee. 'But first I have to use the bathroom.' He got up and left.

'He's hoping I'll do this movie for him or just sound like I want to enough to convince a studio to buy it. You know Jake better than I do – what do you think?'

'Well, his videos are wonderful and he's a lovely man to work with once you get past the bullshit. We used him for an in-store video that we showed as a promo and it went over well.'

'I guess, but selling perfume is different to directing a movie. We'll see.'

He looked at her and Karen was aware of him consciously switching on his charisma. She felt it from across the table as though the whole place were suddenly deserted and it was just the two of them. It's just like a movie, she thought, desire rising in her as she looked at him and felt the warmth he exuded. He cracked the smallest of smiles at her and she saw him signal with his eyes. He was not arrogant or even particularly confident, licking his lips slightly as if he wanted to ask her something. Inside, her better judgement tried to win out but she was having little trouble beating it down into a poor second place.

The taxi ride back to Jake's was filled with tension and anticipation for Karen. If Jake had not been there, she wondered if the journey would have ended in a similar way to her last taxi ride in London with Richard. Jake kept the conversation going and everyone joined in the banter, but Chris was interested only in her, she could tell. Jake had not picked up on it and as he burbled on, laughing at himself, Chris would keep his attention on her with a different look in his eyes.

He held her arm to help her out of the taxi and she felt confidence in his grip, their eyes meeting for a frozen moment as she stepped on to the sidewalk, an acknowledgement from each of them of what they wanted. Jake, still unaware, was paying the driver.

The three of them sat in Jake's living-room, sipping wine and mineral water. It was just after eleven-thirty in the evening and Karen was still not in sync with the time-zone, her mind racing and her body following not far behind it. Chris sat on an armchair, legs crossed, and they chatted and laughed. Jake had put on some low music, very jazzy and tasteful and typically Jake.

'So do you go and see many films?' Karen asked Chris.

'Premieres mostly. When I was a kid, I'd cut classes

and go all the time. It was why I wanted to be an actor. Or I went because I knew deep down I wanted to act. I'm not sure which and both sound pretty hokey. You see many movies?'

'Just the big ones or the obscure ones that get recommended. It's a time thing. Jake's probably seen enough films for all of us,' Karen said.

'I have a very filmic imagination, always have,' said Jake. 'Chris, don't you think Karen's pretty enough to have made it in the movies?'

'Of course,' he answered without hesitation. 'Cast her in your movie and you'd have my signature,' he said and Karen saw Jake eye him as though to ask if he were serious. She knew Jake would stop at nothing for that break.

'Would you do a love scene, Karen?' Jake asked her.

Karen felt her temperature rise in the most pleasurable way she knew.

'For the camera you mean? With the right person and the right director, I suppose. Chris must know more about this than either of us,' she said, looking at him.

'It's just like everyone says, really unerotic, lots of people around, lights, worrying about shadows and are you moving in the right way.'

'Would you direct a love scene, Jake?' Karen asked him.

'Of course,' he answered.

'How would you start it?' Chris asked him.

'Two good-looking people in a living room in an apartment in Greenwich Village. They've not really known each other long, but they want to enjoy the sex enough not to just go at it hell for leather the first time. They both want it.'

Jake stood and went to the chair by the small bar in the corner and sat on it, surveying the room in front of him. He casually took a sip from his wine glass and looked at the two of them sitting opposite each other. Karen watched his eyes roving over them like a camera, zooming and focusing. He spoke and his words sounded like the only thing in the room.

'He gets up from his chair and approaches her, very deliberately and carefully, not like he's stalking prey exactly but something close to it, a definite precision to the act. For a moment he stands, towering over her, and she looks up at him. It is a moment of tension but also of the first release of the tension and the transformation of it into something else much more powerful. He crouches and looks at her, their eyes meeting, and he leans over and kisses her passionately.'

Chris's lips were wandering over hers and Karen reciprocated, tasting the wine on his mouth and flicking her tongue at his, the two meeting and touching before darting back. His hair was soft to the touch and bristled on the back of his neck, the muscles there powerful and firm. He pulled away from her and they looked at each other, she taking in the fresh face from the new distance, enjoying the intimacy of it. He licked his lips, the way he had in the restaurant, and she wanted to grab him and crush him into her.

'After they break the first kiss, he feels a little confused, not sure where the desire came from and just a bit afraid of where it might lead him. But he is not in control of himself, because he wants her so badly. She sees this and knows that she is in charge of the situation and can lead it wherever she wants. She can tell him to go away now and he will, or, she can tell him to undress because she wants to see him naked.'

'Undress,' Karen said to him. 'Let me see you.'

Chris stood obediently and began to unbutton his crisp white shirt. Karen saw his long fingers easily untwist the buttons and the shirt come apart from the top down. It was open to the waistband of his trousers and he left it tucked in as he bent down to remove his shoes. Karen saw the hair that covered his chest and ran into a sprinkle over his stomach. The zipper of his trousers sounded loud in the room as he pulled it down, the sound quickly followed by that of his belt undoing. He stepped out of his trousers and discarded them, the white shirt now hanging on him like a nightshirt, held in check by one last button at the bottom which he undid before peeling off the shirt. He stood before her in just jersey grey Calvin Klein boxer shorts, his physique well proportioned and naturally shaped, not too hard and not too soft. He stared at her and then made a face that seemed to say 'what the hell' and put his thumbs in either side of the waistband of the shorts and pushed them over hips, down his legs and off.

'Naked in front of her, he now feels better than he did, like he has nothing to hide from her. This is him. He touches himself, releasing himself and letting his cock hang freely, slowly getting tumescent. He is just going to stand there now and let her make the next move, which she does.'

Karen took in his naked body, the curve and contour of it, the simple manliness of his outline and the gentle hairiness which caught the light and threw strange shadows about him. She sat forward and placed her hands on his hips, cupping him and squeezing lightly to feel the bone beneath. She looked up at him and he was gazing at her, loose in her grip and ready to go wherever she wanted. She slid her hand around and held his behind, which was tight, and then she stood and kissed him with more force than he just had, opening her mouth and allowing him into her. She placed her arms around him and hugged him, almost like he was an old friend she was meeting at a train station. She pulled him tightly, his skin against her clothes, and it excited her and made her want to be naked as well, so that she could get closer to him.

'He is enjoying her touch and the safety it gives him. He can tell that she wants to be undressed as well by the look on her face. He removes himself from the embrace and takes her in, enjoying the vision and the expectation of her nudity, imagining all the while what her body will look like. He sees it in his mind as lithe and hard in all the right places. He will lift her breasts in his hands, weigh up the cheeks of her ass and toy with her pussy, opening it and ravishing it with all he has to offer. But first, he must undress her. He does this silently and with care.'

Karen had long since kicked off her shoes and now stood in her stockinged feet. Chris went down on his haunches and reached up under her dress, pulling off her tights and then quickly following it with her panties. She was surprised that he had gone for them so quickly, imagining that he would leave her in her underwear for a moment in the same way he had been in front of her earlier on. He undid her skirt – the button in the back and the zipper – and it fell to the floor, a pile around her ankles. Karen instantly felt naked even though her top half was still fully clothed. She knew that her blouse was covering her sex so that Chris could not see it, but she still felt as though she were on show. With the buttons on her blouse, he took longer, and when they were undone he pushed the material over her shoulders and let it fall down her back. He turned her around, not even glancing downwards, and unclasped her bra, easing it down her arms with a slinky, dirty motion.

'Now that she's naked and has her back to him, he moves in behind her and lets his cock rest against her behind. He touches her stomach, impressed by the taut flatness of it, and spreads his palms out on her pelvis, pushing her further into him. He leans down and bites her shoulder, making her jump like an electrical current has run through her body. His hand tickles at the nap of her pubic hair and a finger traces down to find the opening, which is moist, hinting at a deeper and more profound wetness. With prudence, he pushes a finger in, barely disturbing the lips but already finding the wetness he knew would be there.'

Just at the opening of her sex, Chris's finger was only the beginning as Karen felt it push in lightly, awakening her inner muscles which had started to jar and jump with excitement. Her breath escaped in long pants and she felt his breath on her shoulder as hot as her own. His cock was nestled against her buttocks and she could feel it expanding, the weight and the heat of it betraying his growing desire to penetrate her with it. She reached around and gripped him, running the head of his cock over the cheeks of her behind and then in between them, he adjusting the position of his legs to allow for maximum stimulation. Her anus trembled as the head of his cock passed over it and she felt her desire take a different direction, one she had seldom charted and now realised she wanted to.

She leaned her head back and pulled his forward, nuzzling his ear and whispering into it. 'Fuck me, please.'

'Waiting for him, she kneels on the sofa and bends forward so that her behind is presented to him in such a way that will make it easy for him to fuck her there. The deep bend of her position on the sofa has spread the cheeks of her behind and just visible is her anus, tight and puckered, but ready to yield to touch and entry. He returns and kneels, kissing her rear and removing the lid from a large jar. He takes a dollop of the clear gel-like substance on one finger and rubs it in the general area of her anus, a prelude to the long and tantalisingly languorous fingering he will give her to ready her for the size of his cock.'

The cream was cold in the first instant it touched her, but Karen soon felt it warm up as the long fingers massaged it around her opening, not venturing in but merely making her ready for the first tentative digit to enter her. The cream made a squelching sound as it was applied to her and the attention she was receiving in this area served to amplify the feeling in her pussy and made her wonder whether she needed to be penetrated there or if she simply needed to be penetrated.

The muscles of her anus were tight around the tip of

his finger as she felt it probe perhaps a half an inch, the sensation more of widening her than entering her. The skin on his finger was lined and she was sure she could feel the outline of his fingerprints against the slicked and smooth skin of her anal passage. A tiny mound of cream was placed directly over her entrance and then his finger suddenly pushed into her, taking the cream with it as it went up into her. As quickly as it had been there, so the finger was withdrawn. Karen fidgeted with her knees while all the time her behind cried out for more attention now that it had been inflamed by the gentlest of touches.

'For a while, he just stops and looks at her crouched on the sofa and on show for him. He thinks about the restaurant earlier and the way he had desired her then, wondering if he would be able to fuck her. Now, he can't believe his luck. Here she is, pushing her ass up in the air and asking him to fuck it. Her body turns him on, the position of it. His cock is hard and painful and soon he will slick it up with the same gel he has been using on her and they will become one.'

The first stage of the fingering was very coy, shy almost, and Karen could imagine it as an extension of the persona Chris had exuded in the restaurant. The innocence and the freshness, the naivety and the willingness to learn. He was a fast learner. Soon he had two fingers pushed into her, all the way up to the knuckles, and he worked away at her with a gradually increasing speed. He stopped and slopped an enormous amount of the lubricant on to her, as though she were being flooded, and this time she felt him go to work with a third finger slowly entering the fray. He began by just using the two, which her anus had now relaxed and expanded enough to accommodate, and then she felt the third finger push at her as the two came out and made the downward plunge. He slowed the fingering and decreased its depth, concentrating more on getting the third finger into her. They pushed against her anus and she relished the feeling, the way she would comply with his intrusion only for him to increase its scale. Karen relaxed herself, pushed back on to his hand and, with a slippery shove, he had three fingers inside her.

'He has three fingers in her now and can feel her warming up and becoming loose enough for him to be able to fuck her. He thinks about putting in his little finger as well and then resting his thumb on her ass while the rest of his hand casually fucks her brains out, but he thinks better of it. Instead, he'll keep on at her for a while longer, getting her ready for him and ready to accept him into her. He listens to the sound of her breathing and the noises she is making, wondering if she is even aware of her own sounds or if she is utterly lost, astray in her own passion.'

Empty of his fingers, Karen gaped and puckered, her rear end a warm and greasy combination of tension and relaxation, ready to be pushed further. She heard him work the gel on to himself and looked behind her to watch him, his face a study of concentration which made him look even prettier and cuter. Here he was, the college boy adorning the walls of teenage bedrooms, about to take her from behind. She quivered at the prospect and played her fingers over her clitoris, shocked by the wetness there and the sensitivity of her bud. She heard him approach her.

It was much wider than even his three fingers. The fingers had been more moveable and free in her, whereas his cock was wide and solid, able only to plough a single furrow into her without by or leave. The advance of it into her was relentless as it forged a path into her well-prepared rear. Just when she thought she was full, so Chris eased himself still further, holding the cheeks of her behind and splaying them. His balls came to rest against her oiled buttocks and she was glad that this part of it was over.

'He's deep inside her now, feeling a part of her and feeling not a part of her. Both alien and native. He enjoys the feel of her ass against his pubic hair and the way his cock looks stuffed into her, the ring of her anus holding on to his shaft. He reaches down and pushes a finger on the top of his shaft and manages to get it into her a short way, making her cry out. He likes the feel the finger makes on his own cock and leaves it there for a while. His balls feel heavy with come and his cock stifled by the blood that has gushed into it in the preceding moments. What he wants now, at this moment, is very simple, despite the deeper complexities of sex. He wants simply to fuck her.'

Karen's whole rear moved with the motion of his thrusts. Where the fingering had been a preparatory and teasing experience, this was a definite and concentrated effort that she felt was designed to bring both of them off as quickly as possible. The depth, speed and intensity of his drives into her all indicated this. She was pushed into the soft cushions of the sofa by his energy and his hands were on her hips, using them like handles with which to control the speed of something that would ultimately become uncontrollable. His hips made a slapping sound as they made contact with her behind, finishing with a thud as his cock rammed home.

The pace was now frantic and Chris was murmuring and mumbling to himself although Karen could not tell what he was saying. It sounded like he was coaxing and egging himself on, wanting to continue fucking her for as long as possible but unable to resist the urge to let it spill over and end. Carefully, Karen massaged her clitoris and used the feelings of her rear as a focal point for the pleasure that was about to soak through her. The whole region below, both her pussy and her anus, were alive and involved in the heat of the fucking.

He gasped and his legs seemed to tremble and his whole body spin out of control, like a fighter plane that had been shot down and was in a frantic tailspin. The act of fucking her which had been initiated by him seemed to have become bigger than him and was now in control of him rather than the other way around. His passion built and swelled like a wave in Karen and she was ready to ride it. As he shouted and she felt his cock pulsate, she came in brief and throbbing spasms, the walls of her vagina rippling around nothing, the muscle of her anus echoing its motions and finding the thick cock there. Warm shots of semen filled her and she slumped forward on the sofa, her face twisted by the exertion of her orgasm. She shook and convulsed, grinding her rear on to him and squeezing his cock with it as it gushed forth into her.

With cries and gasps of almost identical pitch and length, they were finished.

'Cut.'

Chapter Nine

NEW YORK HAD gone, and felt, like a dream.

As far as going like a dream, Karen had met with several people, her usual contacts and some they had in turn introduced her to, and these meetings produced useful discussions about Hamiltons in general and The Garden in particular. She had picked up some ideas and was formulating them into her original thoughts, ready to pitch it at Avendon properly. She would call on Alan for help, giving the proposal a firm and solid foundation, and also getting his tacit approval for The Garden as it would help convince Avendon. Karen was not certain Avendon was behind the idea. She believed he may have been paying her some clumsy lip service as a way of apologising for his half-sister's behaviour, although that would have been an unusually magnanimous gesture from him.

New York felt like a dream for quite different reasons, most of them to do with Jake. She was not now sure if she had really seen Maxwell on the video screens in Jake's apartment or if she had simply imagined him as a way of fulfilling a wish deep inside her. Perhaps she had imagined the whole room. She had not mentioned it to Jake nor he to her, so she could not be sure. Chris Nichol, she had not imagined. That was an experience that would remain vivid in her memory for a long time to come, along with the filmic record of what they had done afterwards.

The taxi she had jumped in at Heathrow made the right turn into Sloane Street and she looked through the window, feeling at home and glad to be there, the friendly yellow glow from the shop fronts of Harvey Nichols and YSL Rive Gauche seeming somehow more English than the shop windows of New York, despite the similarity in style between the countries. She was wearing a simple, short Betty Jackson dress with chiffon arms, something she had picked up in Bergdorf Goodman, unable to resist. She had topped it off with a purchase at Saks, a Sonia Rykiel jacket, black with a velour collar and round gold buttons. She had also been through the doors of, and exited with bags from, Henri Bendel, Lord & Taylor and Bloomingdale's. As ever, Macy's was simply too overwhelming to make a purchase there and she had instead wandered around it for almost three hours, still feeling as if she had only scratched the surface.

She paid the driver, tipping and getting a receipt, and gathered her luggage, which had increased considerably since her departure four days earlier. It was just after four in the afternoon and she approached the entrance to her building, looking forward to a shower and some sleep.

'Karen,' said a small mousy voice from behind her.

She knew, as soon as she heard the voice, who it was and was surprised that when David had mentioned the phone messages from the person with the mousy voice a week ago, she had not realised who it would be.

'Caroline,' she said, turning.

'Hi,' said Caroline, her facial muscles weakening and looking ready to break into a sob at any moment.

Karen hugged her and kissed her.

'How have you been? It's been ages. Three months? Six?' Karen asked, the surprise still in her voice.

'Oh, six I think. You know,' she replied, shrugging and widening her eyes at the same time. 'It's been the usual, only worse.'

'Gareth?'

'Oh Karen,' Caroline said, rushing back to hug her again, a small sob going through her.

'You'd better come in,' said Karen.

'So when did you find out?' Karen asked her.

'A month ago, really. He said he had to go away on business for two weeks in Hong Kong. I offered to go visit him, but he told me there wouldn't be any time, meetings everyday and that it wouldn't look good if he took his girlfriend out there.'

Caroline was speaking quickly, sniffling and sipping from a cup of tea.

Karen had known Caroline since they were in the same halls of residence at university. They were the same age, but Caroline could have been her mother or her little sister, depending on how life was choosing to treat her at any given moment. Right now, it was dealing her a pretty lousy hand. Karen had only met Gareth twice. Once had been enough, but she had stretched to a second time for the sake of her friend. He was exactly what Karen imagined when someone used the word prat. A loud, obvious, overgrown and brash rugby-playing boor would have been another description.

'But didn't you suspect something before that?' Karen asked.

'Sort of. Not really. Yes. I thought he was just busy at work, which was why I saw so little of him and that when I did, he was too tired from all the work. And I thought a bit of the shine went out when I moved in with him and that it would probably get better. Just that the idea of living with someone scared him – the commitment, you know.'

'I thought Gareth's idea of commitment was talking to you after he'd come,' Karen said, regretting it as soon as the words were out.

'Karen, I know you thought he was an arsehole, but

529

I loved him. I still do,' she snivelled again, hiding it in the cup of tea.

Karen sighed. What was she supposed to say? You could never be honest with your friends about their choice of partners while they were still with them – that would be dangerous. She looked at Caroline and thought of some of the bastards she had hooked up with at university – the evenings Caroline had spent fretting about them, the days Caroline had been depressed, and all for someone Karen would not have bothered even to give the brush-off to. Not a lot had changed for Caroline, she thought.

Caroline could only be described as almost. For as long as Karen had known her, Caroline's hair was almost right, her dress sense almost right and her personality almost right. But not quite. It frustrated Karen that Caroline was so close to being an attractive and interesting person but seemed incapable of the short journey to the point where she actually was. Karen had tried to drag her there on numerous occasions, offering to help her with clothes, to fix her hair and just to push herself a bit more. None of this had ever worked and Caroline seemed to drift from job to job, flat to flat and man to man, never quite settling. Almost, but never quite.

Karen had thought that Gareth had changed that. Caroline had been seeing him for nearly a year and he had suggested to her that she move in. Caroline had been excited at the time and Karen tried to share it, but she had diminished her contact with Caroline mostly because of Gareth. She was suspicious about him and his motives concerning Caroline. When she was first introduced to him, Karen felt his eyes rove over her lasciviously and she knew instantly the sort of man he would be. Certainly not the sort for Caroline. After that, she had seen Caroline alone for girls' nights out, but Gareth on only one other occasion and then he had been frosty to her.

Caroline sat on the sofa, sipping tea, pushing her

hand through her dirty blonde hair and frowning through her clumsy make-up. Karen knew that she should offer to let her stay and was prepared to, but was not sure if she wanted to do the guardian angel bit right at that moment, particularly with the work The Garden would involve in the coming weeks. Caroline had regained her composure and now seemed to be a bit angry at Gareth, which made the tale more lucid.

'She's some cow he used to see at work. She left the company and went to work for a competitor. Her name's Marilyn. He actually called me it once and tried to make me think I hadn't heard him properly and that he'd really said Caroline.' She shook her head, recalling her past foolishness. Karen smiled sympathetically.

'How did you find out exactly?'

'She sent him this card, a crude one about a pussy eating a cock, and I found it. Gareth just thought I wouldn't find it. He can be so stupid. Or perhaps he wanted me to find it, I don't know. Perhaps. When I did find it, I went mad. He told me she was pestering him, tried to paint it like *Fatal Attraction* or something.'

'When did all this happen?' Karen asked her friend.

'Three weeks ago, just before this supposed Hong Kong trip. He'd been telling me about this trip for two months and there was no way he wasn't going to go, just because of me. That's what he told me, like it was my fault. I found the name of her company and called her last week. She's away on holiday for three weeks. Then I called Gareth's company, using a funny voice – I must be mad. He's away on holiday. Not business, but a holiday.' She sniffed.

'Have you left him?'

'As good as. I'm going to sort a place out while he's away and then move my stuff into it. I've left the temping job I was doing and I hope I can just put him out of my mind and my life by the time he gets back.'

Mentally, Karen ran a hand through her own hair and shrugged and sighed; it was so like Caroline to give up her temporary job just when she would most need her independence.

'You know you can stay here if you need to. There's room. When is he due back?'

'A week next Tuesday. Are you sure it's not a pain? You're the best person I could think of.'

'Borrow some of my clothes for tonight and tomorrow night we'll go and pick up your stuff and store it here. I'd do it now, but I just got back from a trip and I'm exhausted,' Karen said, suddenly feeling weary.

'Your assistant told me you were in New York. He got quite stroppy about me not leaving my name.'

'You've been haunting him for the last three weeks,' Karen said. 'He wants to find out who you are.'

'You can tell him he's got a very sexy voice,' Caroline said, brightening a little.

'I hate to be the one to tell you but . . .'

'Gay?' Caroline interjected before Karen could finish the sentence.

Karen nodded solemnly and they both burst into laughter that they held on to and let subside into a few moments of silence.

'Karen, I'm so rude. How are you? I haven't even asked.'

'Same as I ever was. Busy.'

'What exciting promotions have you done lately? I keep an eye out for advertisements.'

'The current one is a bit different,' Karen said. 'Hamiltons are launching a unisex fragrance and I convinced them that I could handle the creative side of the advertising campaign.'

'That was clever.'

'Thank you. There's minimal risk as the launch is quite low-key. We're not looking to shift a million units in the first month. Linda Cole is doing the photography for us.'

'Linda? I haven't spoken to her in ages. How is she?'

'She's doing great as far as I can tell. She's become

532

more of a business acquaintance these days,' Karen told her.

'You two were so close at college. The bad girls.'

'She's still bad. She's seeing a model. Maxwell – do you know who I mean?'

Caroline pondered the name for a moment. 'The boy who was in that advert for mineral water?'

'Yes,' Karen said, having partly forgotten the commercial.

'That sounds like Linda.'

'We're using him as a model for the campaign. He's adorable. I could use him for a few things,' she said.

'How's Daniel? Still oddball?'

'Very,' she said. 'Some half-sister of his has crawled out of the woodwork and there are rumours flying around the shop about why she's here. She has a stake in the shop and could cause trouble. She used to work in the shop and I've already heard a story about her poking her nose into something. We'll see.'

'Are you seeing anyone?' Caroline asked, a glint in her eye.

'More than just one. Two, actually and it's getting very awkward.'

'Karen! Who?'

'They both work at Hamiltons. One's younger than me and the other one's older – quite a bit older in fact.'

'Do they know about each other?'

'No! That's why it's getting difficult, being in two places at once.'

'Do you have a favourite? The older one, I bet?'

'You know me, I've never really weighed or measured those sort of things, but now it seems like I have to. Stringing them both along doesn't seem to be a choice.'

'What would happen if you came clean with them?'

'The younger one, Richard, would be all right about it, I know that. We're pretty free with each other. The older one is more difficult. He's just been through a bad divorce. I don't want him to think I've let him down.'

'And I bet you're still getting into the odd tussle, aren't you?' Caroline said.

The word tussle had become a kind of code for them to signify Karen's occasional forays, her seizing of opportunities.

'One or two,' she replied modestly.

'You're still searching, Karen, aren't you? I thought I'd stopped and that the search was over with Gareth. Turns out I was just off the scent for a while.'

'Like he was a hunt saboteur, you mean?' Karen said.

'Something like that.'

They wiled away almost two hours, remembering their times at university, friends and enemies, things they would have done differently, things they were glad they had done. Karen realised that she had missed Caroline without noticing it consciously and she was glad to see her again. Somewhere during the conversation she put on a record she had not heard for ages and for a while was transported, regressing almost, as she and Caroline shamelessly reminisced about who they used to be. Eventually the jet-lag got the better of Karen and she had a quick shower and showed Caroline where things were before she turned in, just before nine. She called Richard and arranged to see him in the shop first thing in the morning, knowing she would be up early. As she drifted off to sleep, she made a mental note to try and find Caroline some work at Hamiltons.

In her own bed, between the pure linen sheets, she drifted through multiple video images of doves and falcons, hooded in the sunset and coming to transport her to the garden.

Chapter Ten

KAREN ENTERED HAMILTONS through the special side entrance, exchanging pleasantries with the guard as she signed in. It was ten minutes before seven in the morning. Richard had signed in fifteen minutes earlier and she knew exactly where she would find him.

The menswear department was described by everyone in Hamiltons as The Dungeon. The room was square and the main access, certainly as far as customers were concerned, was down a wide and dramatic staircase that felt like a descent into Hell. The stairs were a granite material with heavy welts and scars cut into them. The air-conditioning was fabulous and the area always had a slight chill to it. With its menswear, unlike the womens', Hamiltons went for the younger, high-spending and fashion-conscious end of the market. There were no good old trusty names in the dungeon. No Chester Barrie, Aquascutum or Jaeger. One such designer had once actually persuaded Daniel Avendon to model one of his suits. Daniel beamed out and beneath him a caption read, 'When it comes to menswear, even he has to go elsewhere.'

The department was laid out in a way that tried to fuse styles. Rather than have areas dedicated to a single designer, ranges would be blended in an attempt to create a look. Karen always had trouble every time they ran a promotion connected with menswear. They were successful promotions but setting them up was difficult as it meant trying to deal with the primadonnas who staffed the area. The most recent promotion for boxer shorts had gone better than anyone expected, but the dungeon staff still thought they could do it better than her.

Gently, she took the steps one at a time, hardly making a sound. She smiled when she saw Richard, unaware of her and trying on a jacket, turning and looking at himself, flicking his hair out of his eyes and jutting his chin forward. Karen found him vain in the sweetest possible way, his adorable face, even with his squarish nose, making her forgive whatever he did. He took the jacket off, replacing it on the hanger and preening it before returning it to the rail, then picking another, much more garish one. The bright yellow check set against his honey-coloured skin and this time he let his hair fall forward into his eyes. Becoming aware of her presence, he turned, completely unflustered and unembarrassed, and launched a smile that grew over his face with disarming rapidity. Karen realised that she had missed him while she was in New York.

'How long were you watching me?' he asked her.

'Oh, ages and ages. Me and all the guards on the cameras I expect.' She scooped his face up in her hands and kissed him directly on the mouth, comforted by the familiarity and intimacy.

'I've missed you, I really have,' she said to him warmly.

'You sound surprised. This is nice,' he said, looking at her outfit. 'It's not like you to wear Gucci.'

'Show-off,' she said.

'How was New York? Did they have the new Calvin Klein yet?'

From her pocket, in a well prepared and practised motion, she produced a bottle of eau de toilette from the new Calvin Klein range, not due for launch in the UK for another six months. He scrabbled the cellophane off, tore the box open and quickly sprayed it into the air. A flowery smell soon rose in the dungeon.

'It's brilliant. Did you pay full price for it?'

'Of course not. What have you been up to while I was away?'

'Nothing much. Same old same old. You know.'

'I was going to call but I was busy,' she said, wishing she had phoned him after she had called Alan on the second evening.

'How do I look in this?' he asked her, shrugging his shoulders and allowing the jacket to fall and move around his broad frame.

'Not as good as you'd look out of it,' she said to him.

'Is this why we're here so early?'

'I was too tired last night and I really wanted to see you. Do you mind if we go up to the furniture department?'

'You want to do it in the furniture department? The guards will enjoy that.'

'No, it's business. I wanted to look at it before anyone arrived. Then we can go to my office or even to the flat. No security cameras there,' she said.

'I wonder if they bug your office?'

'I hope so.'

They went up the granite steps and took the ground-floor lift to the fourth floor. The furniture department occupied several thousand square feet. Karen tried to visualise The Garden fitting somewhere into it. There had been talk of contracting the space the furniture section occupied for some time. It was Hamiltons' least profitable line of business and took up too much space relative to the profit it generated, staying largely because no one knew what to put in its place. Karen hoped she had found the solution to that problem.

'Are you looking at anything in particular?' Richard asked her.

'No. I just wanted to see something. Come here,

you,' she said, pulling him towards her and then spinning him so his back was against a large and ornate fitted wardrobe. Here she repeated the earlier kiss, but with a greater depth and intensity. They were in a quiet corner away from the prying eyes of the store cameras, of which there were less in the furniture department, stealing being that much more difficult.

Richard's hair was tousled and falling over his forehead in spindly strands as she pushed and pulled at him, unsure of exactly what she wanted to do with him. She was just roughing him up a little, running her hands over his trousers – which he had already told her were Bill Blass – gripping the bits of him that protruded, feeling her way round his body, reintroducing herself to him and his essence, the smell, touch and taste of him. He was responding in kind, his hands inside her jacket and then on her hips. He was erect and his cock pushed against her. She shoved him harder against the wardrobe, feeling the dull thud his body made.

'I still owe you for that taxi ride,' she said.

'More of a joy ride, wasn't it?' he said naughtily.

Karen fumbled at the zip of his trousers, and the slow tearing sound it made as she pulled it down sent a shiver through her. His underwear pushed out of the fly from the pressure of his cock. He had placed his hands on her shoulders, surrendering all control to her, and she reached down and carefully removed him from the fly, slipping it through a similar fly in his boxer shorts. As he stood, fully clothed but with his long and erect cock sticking out of his trousers, Karen wanted practically to attack him, barely knowing where to start first, her passion for him multiplied by her absence of just a few days.

Dropping to her knees, she smothered him with her mouth, her lips quickly coming against the fabric of his trousers. They had never really had sex in the morning as much as she would have liked and Karen was pleased to discover that he was a morning person as well as a night-time one. With her tongue, she sent signals to him, flicking herself against his shaft and over the head, skilfully rolling over the ridge of his phallus and then under to the glans which she burrowed into. Richard's hands stayed on her shoulders but his grip tightened, the beginnings of movement stirring in his groin, Karen's mouth relaxing and stretching to accommodate all of him that was on offer through the small gap in his fly.

Pulling him from her mouth, Karen licked frantically at his shaft, smearing him before swallowing him up again, the acid of his fluid on her tongue. She placed both hands on his hips and increased the speed with which she took him in and out of her mouth and he sighed, his hands roving over her shoulders and into the hair at the back of her neck.

'. . . do something about this area here.'

Karen stopped, thinking Richard had said something, but unsure through the wet noises she had been making on him with her mouth. She felt his body stiffen and she looked up at him.

'Someone's coming,' he whispered harshly.

'We could move some of the beds out, open the floor up a bit,' a voice was saying.

Karen stood up quickly, the voices almost upon them, sounding about to round the corner into their no longer so private cranny. As quickly as she could whilst being silent, Karen opened the door of the wardrobe and pushed Richard into it, following him then closing it.

In the darkness, she could hear him panting, sucking in lots of air and trying to regulate and silence himself. Karen was a mix of arousal and adrenalin. They were completely in the dark, the tight space of the wardrobe allowing no light in. Karen listened, but the voices were muffled, the wardrobe affording a reasonable degree of soundproofing.

'What should we do?' he whispered, his body pressed up behind her.

Karen reached behind and found what she was looking for. In the warm darkness of the wardrobe, beneath the sounds of muffled voices from outside, she manipulated Richard's cock until the blood began to flow back into it and the shaft became stiff in her hand.

'Not in here?' he said, a slight tremble in his voice.

Richard's cock was hard and with her hand behind her and firmly on him, she moved it up and down, masturbating him awkwardly but effectively nonetheless. Carefully and with his arms gently knocking the wardrobe, he hitched up her skirt and pushed her knickers down as far as he could given his restricted movement. With her panties around her knees, she released her hold on his cock and allowed him to explore her crotch under the front of her dress.

His hands roamed, stroking and brushing her skin in the sensitive area of her groin, the palms of his hands slightly coarse on the satiny skin it explored. Karen left him to it, happy for him to forage around in the darkness of the wardrobe and the darker depths of her. He circled the tops of her thighs, drawing nearer to the tops of her legs and the crevice between them, his fingers imploring and her pussy equally willing.

Despite the darkness, Karen still clenched her eyes tightly shut when he dipped a finger into her, the flat of his hand on her pubic hair and his digit confident and driving. She caught her breath, savouring the feel of his finger in her and his cock driving against her behind. Moving her legs, she felt the constriction of her knickers around her knees, preventing what little movement the walls of the wardrobe would have afforded. She realised that she would have to make her pleasure with what was available, moving her body in the small space around her, manipulating the both of them with care. She pressed herself against one of the side walls, the muffled voices on the outside long-forgotten, and arched her backside to him, making the angle of her pussy more sheer. He followed her movement with a deft one from his hand and increased the depth of his intrusion into her, his breath feverish against her neck.

While he continued to finger her, she made herself ready, manoeuvring herself into exactly the right position, communicating her desire to him through her actions alone, unable to see him, this presence in the darkness that fingered her with a relentlessness both brutal and compassionate. Her juices coursed around his fingers, a sucking sound coming from the combination of hand and pussy. She bent forward, almost sitting in his lap as he craned his arms around her and continued to push into her and flick at her clit with his thumb.

Karen moved away from him and reached around to find his member. It was hot in her hand, the flesh slightly damp from the heat their bodies had generated in the confines of the wardrobe. She squeezed it, feeling the way the shaft gave way ever so slightly under her hand, and imagined it buried inside her, rending her pussy-lips apart and filling her. He had stopped fingering her and lifted her skirt up, exposing her behind. Karen guided his cock and rubbed the head of it over the cheeks of her rear, feeling the sticky come glazing over her buttocks. His hand was on hers, gently pushing it off his cock so that he could do the work for her. She put her hands up to allow him free rein and she found the rail that ran across the top of the wardrobe. She gripped on to it, the metal cold under her hands, and suspended herself there as Richard continued to explore her with the tip of his cock.

Along the join of her buttocks and down to the opening of her pussy, Richard investigated her, his cock rigid against her, pushing into the sensitive area between her anus and her pussy, tickling her with a light touch and then returning for a heavier stroke, an indication of what was to come. Karen was still wet from the fingering he had given her and she was ready for him to enter her, to take her carefully from behind in the unlit interior of a wardrobe as she clung, hands above head, to a metal rail. It was as though her whole body had been blindfolded, the remaining senses accentuated – the smell, touch, sound and taste they created between them all flooding through and making up for the loss of vision.

Cautiously and precisely, Karen felt Richard guide his cock into her pussy, nudging at the folds of skin that protected her before they slowly yielded to the thrust and accepted him. The opening of her vagina enlarged with him, expanding to accept his size but holding him tightly enough to make the sensation a precious cross between pain and pleasure. Their posture made it hard for him to get very far into her but Karen found it all the more enticing: once again the space was dictating how they would make their pleasure and she was determined to make the most of it. She let a hand drop from the rail, feeling behind herself, finding where he was in her. She began to move.

Karen rocked tenderly back and forth on to his cock, a gentle and tantalising rhythm, feeling it open and close her and stretch her with each partial entrance. They made few movements, the smell of their bodies all around them and the secret noises of passion amplified and echoing around the tiny cavern. She held on to the rail again, her arms above her head as she backed on to him, feeling the lap of his trousers contacting with her bottom and the rumpled skirt in the small of her back. The end of his cock continued to nudge at the opening of her sex, and Karen arched her back, pushing her pussy out at him to allow his shaft to stab at her clitoris.

The heat of the wardrobe seemed to swell her clitoris and she felt about to erupt into orgasm, hanging off the rail and impaling herself on his unseen rod. He brought his hand around and pressed at her clit, but she needed little stimulation and savoured the closeness of her climax as she continued to keep the same pace to her movements. She was not going to allow herself, or Richard, the luxury of a fast and furious orgasm. She was controlling her movements in order to coax the biggest response she could, from him and her.

'Oh my God,' she heard him whisper, his clutch on her tightening.

His body bobbed up slightly behind her, sending his cock up at her slightly further, and he shuddered.

'Hold it for just a little longer,' she said before dropping her head down.

Still she continued with the relentless and steady movement of her body on to his cock. The first spasm went off between her legs and she drooped, her weight hanging from the rail. As the second wave took hold, she pulled herself back up, the physical reaction now taut rather than loose. In a steady stream of pulsations in time with the methodical movements, she came, the force of it sending the blood rushing around her body. She forgot where she was – the darkness, the heat and the musky odour – as she rode Richard's cock. She was enjoying rearing on to it in the dark as it discharged into her, this stiff cock poking through the fly of his trousers.

For several moments, she clung to the rail. He moved and allowed his cock to slip from her, reaching down and pulling her knickers back up. She heard him do up his fly and then the sound of him running his hands through his hair. She pushed the door a fraction and it clicked open. She listened through the crack and heard nothing.

'I'll go first. You wait for a minute,' she said, deciding to take the chance.

She pushed the door open and walked into the light, blinking and rubbing her eyes as though she had entered another world.

Chapter Eleven

IN THE MEDIUM-SIZED meeting room on the fifth floor of Hamiltons sat Daniel Avendon, his half-sister Gabrielle, Alan Saxton and Karen. The room had two doors, one that led from the corridor outside and the other which was attached to Daniel Avendon's office, causing him to refer to it as his 'en suite' meeting room. Avendon and Gabrielle had just arrived and there was an awkward silence in the air, brought on by Gabrielle's presence.

Fifteen minutes earlier, Karen had been in Alan's office discussing the proposal she had put together for The Garden. Alan had been extremely helpful and Karen was confident that Avendon would be sufficiently impressed to give the go-ahead. Alan had assured her that there was no way Daniel would bring Gabrielle along to the meeting. Obviously, Alan had been wrong and Karen looked across at him, he returning the gaze with an expression that said little. Part of her had been ready for it. David had given her the full story about how Gabrielle had tried to stop one of the buyers in the china department making a routine purchase and the drama that had followed. The management at Hamiltons were awaiting some kind of announcement regarding Gabrielle. What her role in Hamiltons was to be, if any. Based on her first interaction with her in Daniel's office and on the stories that were going round, Karen knew full well that Gabrielle would be attending the meeting. Karen even had four copies of the proposal prepared in case it happened. She was not going to change her basic pitch, whatever the circumstances, because she believed in it and in its ability to sell itself.

They exchanged some pleasantries, Gabrielle as distant and aloof as she had been the first time Karen met her, and then they got down to the purpose of the meeting – to discuss The Garden. Karen handed each of them a copy of the proposal, which was bound in a clear plastic cover, the image of a snake slithering across the bottom right corner of the title page. She watched Daniel's face as he scanned the proposal, leafing through. Gabrielle did not even pick it up. Alan studied it courteously, having already seen it at least a dozen times in the preparation stage.

'Tell me more,' Avendon said, dropping the proposal on the table and fixing her with a stare.

'A shopping paradise for women,' Karen began. 'An Eden without Adam and a place where no fruit is forbidden. There are,' she continued, 'four levels to The Garden.'

'It's going to be on four floors?' Gabrielle cut in.

Karen gave her the briefest and sharpest look of disdain she felt she could get away with and continued, refusing to let her stride be broken.

'Theory, concept, environment and product. Four levels. Simple.' The last word was directed mainly at Gabrielle.

Avendon nodded thoughtfully, the high-concept stuff appealing to him, and Karen took it as a sign to continue.

'The key to The Garden is choice. It is about women making choices, and it's fun and satisfying. The high theory, if you like, is choice or the freedom to choose.' Karen looked at Gabrielle and Alan, neither of whom seemed entirely convinced. She knew Alan had a predilection for numbers and had heard a lot of this before, so Karen was not surprised by his non-committal look but she wondered where Gabrielle's mind was. Daniel, by contrast, looked keen, his smart features all standing to attention, and appeared interested.

'Concept is the next level. What particular concepts are important?' she asked rhetorically and followed quickly with an answer in case Gabrielle had some stupid comment to make. 'Atmosphere, space and privacy. Hamiltons already has such a wonderful atmosphere and it will be an extension of that. A sub-set dedicated to women. We already get a mix of customers, but The Garden will be for the female. The space needs to be carefully constructed. Practically, we'll locate it in a small area and this will create privacy and comfort.'

Alan was raising his eyebrow and looking interested, as was Avendon. Gabrielle was looking around the room, appearing to study some of the art that adorned its walls.

'The environment. This has specifics.' Karen was even and relaxed in her tone, confident but not over-rehearsed. 'Music but not muzak. Decor should be entertaining, but still tasteful. It's not going to look like one of those tacky gift stores in Oxford Street. Naturally, it will be verdant and garden-like, but in a sexy and earthy way. Service. This is a case of finding the right people, and notice I say *people*, not women or men. There needs to be a definite *type* of person, not the usual Saturday crowd. I want people who are educated and personable.

'All of this,' she continued towards the final point, 'theory, concept and environment, has to play out into one thing. It has to facilitate product. It's a conduit. We're not making any bold statements about femininity here. Hamiltons is not political in that way. We pick a few product lines and put them exclusively in The Garden. Clothes, beauty and accessories form the core – a favourite trinity – and we populate from there with whatever we think fits best. There are a number of suggestions in the proposal.

'It's simple and it's straightforward,' she finished. 'From theory, through concept and environment and on ultimately to product. The basic philosophy of shopping for women only. The Eden without the Adam.'

Karen had finished.

'It will never work.'

It was Gabrielle, suddenly focused in on the conversation and looking directly at Daniel Avendon when she spoke, the now familiar triumphal smile on her face. She was wearing a gown of crushed velvet, a kind of deep mauve colour, that was far too tight for her. Her stomach pressed on the dress and Karen thought she looked like an aubergine. If only her rinse had been a shade more green.

'I will make it work,' Karen said, looking at her and then Avendon. 'What makes you think it won't work?'

'The cost will be far too high,' Gabrielle replied.

'Alan and I have produced detailed costings and see a payback period of just nine months. This is based on a very modest assumption of turnover increase. This is not going to be expensive.' Karen saw Gabrielle take the words in and then ignore them. It must have been obvious to her that Karen knew what she was talking about. Perhaps she wasn't expecting that, Karen thought.

'But who would come to such a department?' Gabrielle said, appearing to change her direction away from the financial aspects. 'Feminists? Lesbians?'

Karen sighed. 'Women will come. Women who already come to Hamiltons and women who have never been to Hamiltons. Women who come for one specific thing will use The Garden to buy others. It's a long-standing promotion, basically.'

'How long would it take to be up and running?' This was Avendon.

'Two months,' Karen replied immediately. 'We can use the back half of the furniture department, sealed off and accessible by a single lift.'

'Two months!' Gabrielle interjected, snorting as she did so.

'I don't know how much Daniel has told you, Gabrielle,' Karen said, turning on her, 'but I have been responsible for some of the most successful promotions this store has ever run. In all its long history. It can be open in two months and after six we will know whether or not it is going to pay off.'

'Alan, what do you think?' Avendon asked.

Alan had been looking at Gabrielle and jumped to attention when Daniel spoke. He paused briefly, in a way familiar to Karen, before embarking on a considered answer.

'Well Daniel, financially it is sound. All we are doing in effect is re-modelling the way we offer some of our products and giving it a different approach. What Karen just called a conduit. The main expense is environmental, but Karen has looked into all of that quite thoroughly and the costs listed here have some leeway.'

'What do you think of it commercially?' Avendon asked him.

'It's not really my field, but I like it. I can see something in it.'

'Don't you think it's a little, well, insulting?' Gabrielle asked. 'Defining us by clothes and lipsticks?'

Karen was about to ask when Gabrielle had suddenly joined the sisterhood but held her tongue.

'There's no statement,' she said instead. 'I've already said that. Hamiltons has always left that up to its customers. They'll take what they want from it.'

'But men will feel excluded,' Gabrielle said, sounding childish.

'Probably,' Karen replied.

'Karen, how many people will it need?' asked Daniel.

'Alan and I think twenty-five to thirty staff, including five supervisors over teams of four. Every team should have full knowledge of the product-offering in The Garden. We can re-deploy at least ten people from in-house and the rest we could take on temp to perm six-month contracts.'

Karen looked over at Alan and he gave her an encouraging smile with one side of his mouth.

'Advertising?' said Avendon.

'We restrict it to a few good magazines – *Vanity Fair*, *Tatler*, *Cosmo* and maybe *Marie Claire*, but no lower than that,' Karen said.

'Talk me through The Garden,' Avendon said dreamily. 'I am a woman and I've just arrived at Hamiltons.'

'You will be able to get to it only by a lift from the ground floor,' said Karen. 'One or two people will act as greeters on the ground floor. The inside of the lift will have pictures of famous women, some of the Hamiltons library ones from the Fifties where they're actually in the store. Elizabeth Taylor, Lauren Bacall, Joan Fontaine, Vivien Leigh. A few notable quotes. Some announcements in the lift about what to expect in The Garden, the need to ask if you want assistance, that sort of thing.

'When the lift arrives and the doors open, your world will change. It will knock you over. The lighting will be artificial, creating a perpetual but gentle daylight and the surroundings will be lush and green with foliage but it will not be like a jungle or a greenhouse. The atmosphere will be pleasantly cool, a sound of water in the background. The colouring will be differing shades of green, very relaxing. No more greeters. You'll be on your own from there. People will be on hand to help if you ask, but you won't be mugged like when you walk into Gap.'

'You'll be able to wander freely around a select range of cosmetics, the new Hamiltons fragrance at centre stage. Lingerie, hats, clothes, bags and shoes. All the best of Hamiltons will be distilled and captured and it will be there for you. A bar will serve complimentary juices and there will be plenty of sofas for you to relax on and read the various magazines.

'From start to finish, the experience should be easy and lacking in pressure. And, importantly, all the other customers will be women and the whole concept will be aimed at you as a woman. The male staff will, I'm afraid, have to be gorgeous. Either Rob Lowe or Mel Gibson, a whole range of ages. The women more classic, like the elevator pictures. The whole of the staff should feel like a familiar ensemble cast that people will come back to see again and again. But classy – this is not a burger joint. Theory, concept, environment and product. On all four levels The Garden works.'

'This sounds like a fantasy,' Gabrielle said in a goading manner.

'Exactly,' Karen responded. 'Which is why it will work. Daniel?'

'Two months?'

Karen nodded.

'Alan. The costings?' Avendon asked.

'They look fine.'

'This heyday, the Fifties and Sixties you pine on about,' Gabrielle said to her. 'What do you know about them? I suspect of the four people in this room you know the least.'

'It's not just about that, which is why I can make it work. Look at the profiling we've done on our customer base. They don't remember it either, what Hamiltons was like. They don't want to remember, they just want to buy an idea of it. That's what I can sell to them. We can't sell the real thing. It's gone.' Karen breathed deeply at the end of her speech.

'Daniel, remember?' his half-sister said to him. 'They were such times.'

Gabrielle's eyes glazed and she looked as though she were time-travelling. Karen gave Avendon a frustrated look but he took no notice of her. Karen feared he might be about to jump on the same bus as Gabrielle and disappear off down memory lane. Alan seemed faintly embarrassed by Gabrielle's antics.

'Daniel,' Karen said firmly. 'What do you think?'

'Yes. I like it. Very much.'

'Thank you.'

'But—' he paused.

'But?' Karen said.

'I think Gabrielle has a point. I like this retrospective angle. I'm not saying make it a museum, but the original glamour of Hamiltons was something spectacular. Work with Gabrielle on that aspect.'

Karen looked at Gabrielle, who was staring off and looked as though she was about to stand and waltz with a non-existent partner. Karen wished she could smell Gabrielle's breath. She was hoping she was just drunk rather than senile.

'I'd love to help, really I would,' Gabrielle purred, suddenly switching from the wicked witch to Dorothy in the blink of an eye.

'Settled,' said Avendon. 'Good.'

Uncertain whether to feel victorious or defeated, Karen gathered her papers. Gabrielle stood and so did Alan.

'Let's arrange to meet,' Gabrielle said, sweeping out.

Karen stood.

'Wait behind a moment, Karen,' Avendon said, nodding to Alan to leave.

When the door was closed and they were alone, the silence touched all the surfaces in the room. Karen did not know what to say. She was not quite de-railed, more re-routed, but it would still be difficult for her to work with Gabrielle. Eventually, Avendon broke the silence.

'I'm sorry that this has to be so hard for you. Really I am.'

'What do you mean?' she asked.

'Gabrielle has me in a delicate spot. My father saw to it that she remained a very token gesture in the great scheme of the Hamiltons world. By the time he was gone, Gabrielle hated all of us and there was no way to make that better. She can cause a lot of trouble if she wishes.'

'Will she? Why should she?'

'She's had a lawyer look over the structure of her deal with regard to the shop. She has a fifteen per cent stake, but her voting rights were limited and this lawyer thinks a certain part of the contract that regulates it may be unfair. If they challenge it in court and win, she could suddenly be a lot more than just a fifteen per cent pain in the rear. Alan and I have long been aware that the position was somewhat gentle. If she mobilises now, we may have a problem. Despite everything she feels toward me, her holding has always effectively been an Avendon family holding. If she lets it go, we are diluted.'

'How is her helping me going to stop that?' Karen asked him, already resigned to Gabrielle's involvement and realising that this situation had more nuances to it than she first thought.

'She is right, you know. The heyday. I know she can seem ridiculous.' Avendon was looking out of the window. 'She was here and a part of it, until she left. She looks at you and I think she's jealous. She knows she gave up her chance and now she wants it again.'

'Are you saying I should humour her?'

'Perhaps I'm saying you should humour me.'

'And she has no power of veto? I just use her as an advisory resource, like a consultant?' Karen was asking questions, but also laying down some rules.

'It's not something I would ordinarily ask you to do, but it is an unfortunate collision of circumstances and timing. I will be grateful. It's a favour,' he said to her.

'Can I ask you a favour,' she replied. 'Something I wouldn't ordinarily ask?'

'I'm listening.'

'I have a friend who could use a job.'

Chapter Twelve

KAREN TURNED FROM David and reached behind her, picking the phone from her desk.

'Karen Taylor.'

'Karen, it's Linda. How are you?'

'I'm fine,' Karen said, politely motioning for David to leave.

'Thanks for the letter. I'm glad the pictures went down so well,' Linda said, 'and I'm looking forward to seeing them on display myself. Do I get a bottle of the fragrance?'

'I'll ask David my assistant to send you one. I thought we had already, unless it was just to Maxwell. Guess who's staying with me?'

'Give up,' Linda responded instantly.

'Caroline.'

'Caroline Sayer, from college? Dreary Caroline?'

Karen knew that Linda had little time for Caroline and her antics. At college Karen had maintained a discreet kind of Chinese wall between the two friends. Karen supposed she was closer to Caroline, but that was because Caroline was ultimately easier to get closer to. Linda liked a little distance between herself and people and that had never bothered Karen.

'We should try and get together, the three of us,' Karen said.

'Maybe,' Linda responded with little or no enthusiasm. 'I have something to ask you, Karen.'

'Go ahead.'

'It's sort of a favour, but I think you'll like it.'

'I'm still here,' Karen said.

'It's Maxwell.'

'What about him?'

'You have a fan there, Karen. He's burbled on about you for the last four weeks now.'

Karen felt a flush run through her, the sort where she was excited and apprehensive all at once, like a near hit in a car or a drop down a water slide. She had mentioned the video room in Jake's house to no one, having convinced herself that it was simply someone who looked like Maxwell that she had seen up on the screen. Maxwell was talking about her to Linda? She pulled open her desk drawer and retrieved the dove feather she had found on the roof shortly after the shoot, twirling it in her fingers.

'It must be my maternal side coming out,' Karen said to her.

'Some of the things he's been saying about you haven't been very, well, familial.' Linda chuckled dirtily. 'He'd like to meet with you, for a date.'

'I thought you and Maxwell were, well . . .'

'We do, but we're not glued together. He's an attractive boy and I like to think I can still hold my own. We go our own ways. He asked me to call you. He's been on at me about it all week. You must say yes, Karen, or I'll have to contend with a Maxwell tantrum.'

The doves. The hood. The wings. Karen recalled the shoot on the rooftop, his lissom body and the studied way he carried himself. The prospect was inviting. Very inviting. A gift to herself for getting The Garden through. Like a new dress or a special meal. She would treat herself to Maxwell and perhaps she would make it a treat for him as well.

'Are you sure about this, Linda?'

'Come on, Karen, it won't be the first time we've trodden the same ground. Remember Erik the Viking?'

Karen sniggered.

'When would he like to meet?' Karen asked, visions racing through her mind.

'Tonight?' Linda asked her tentatively.

'Tonight.' Karen looked at her diary, knowing already that she had promised to go to dinner with Alan. She could put him off, but he had seemed so excited about taking her out. She chewed her bottom lip on its right side, ruminating. 'I think I can make tonight. Where would he like to go on this date?'

'Just your house, probably, but you can do something else if you want. Before.'

'Christ, say what you mean, Linda. Why don't I just run over there and do him now?'

'Take him for a walk in Hyde Park. He loves it there, the ducks and all the birds. I'm sure he was a bird in a past life.'

'Can he meet me outside the shop, around five?'

'I'm sure he can. I'll call you if not,' said Linda.

'You've got my mobile number, it's on my card.'

'And Karen?'

'Yes?'

'I want to hear all about it.'

'I thought you'd hear that from him.'

'Oh I will,' Linda said, 'but I'd like your opinion as well. Another perspective.'

'I see.' Karen smirked, remembering the way they had compared scores over Erik the Viking at college.

'He likes someone else to take the lead. Don't be shy with him. I haven't found anything he won't do yet.'

'That's a scary thought, Linda,' Karen said.

'Call me tomorrow, okay?'

'Promise.'

Karen replaced the receiver. She picked it straight back up and dialled three digits.

'Alan Saxton.'

'Hi,' she said, breezily.

'Hello,' he said, uncertainty already in his voice. Karen knew he could tell she was about to let him down.

'I've got a problem on tonight,' she said.

'Oh?'

'My friend Caroline, the one I told you about. She wants me to go and help move the last of her stuff tonight. Her boyfriend is back and she wants to get it over here, but doesn't want to face him alone. He's such a pig. Can we reschedule?' Karen always went on too long when she was lying and she wondered when Alan would realise it.

'Of course,' he said, sounding as though he were trying to put a brave face on it.

'Tomorrow?'

'That would be awkward for me. Friday would be good. I could get us theatre tickets, bring the car in,' he said.

'That sounds wonderful. We'll make a night of it. I'm sorry about tonight, Alan. Definitely Friday.'

'You have to help your friends,' he said to her and she cringed, wishing he hadn't said it.

'Thanks for being so understanding. I'll pop round and see you later. Bye.'

Karen sat and stared at the phone. She looked at her watch. It was one-fifteen. She called her flat and spoke to Caroline, telling her she had changed her plans and wouldn't be at Alan's but would be having different company later on at the flat. She also told Caroline to let the machine pick up any calls if she was there when the phone rang. Karen wondered why she made her life so complicated but thought of Maxwell and then it seemed worth it.

Her mind reeling with the expectation of her evening, tempered by some feelings of culpability at putting Alan off, she felt the need to escape her office and Hamiltons so she could both prepare herself for the evening and rid herself of the complications. There was one place she could do both.

'I'm going to the gym,' she said, passing David on her way out. 'I'll probably be back around three-thirty. Leave messages on my mobile or page me if you need to.'

She changed quickly and in a practised fashion. Karen was something of a gym veteran and had been working out since before she was at college. It had paid dividends and she was happy with the shape she had moulded herself into. The gym was through a small doorway just off Knightsbridge and the sort of place where women made up *before* they went to work out. Karen scrutinised herself in the mirror, glad and proud that her skin tone, eye colour and bone structure made make-up an optional extra for her. She wore a tight blue Lycra body suit that supported her breasts and a half-cut jersey grey T-shirt over the top. She carried her New Balance workout shoes by her side and made her way to the stretch area.

At one-forty, the lunchtime crush was starting to ease. Karen preferred to frequent the club at off-peak times, using it purely for the purposes of exercise and never involving herself in the social aspects. Hamiltons paid for her membership and she used it to its fullest, always finding time to exercise at least three times a week. There were only ten or so people in the gym, mostly women, and all the equipment Karen preferred to use was more or less free.

She sat on the mat and looked at herself in the mirror, pulling her feet together and towards her crotch as she dipped her head and felt the stretch in her hips. She leaned deeper into it and then released. She pulled her right foot under her left thigh and leaned forward to elongate her hamstrings, enjoying the relaxing feeling that spread through her leg. Gradually, like a whole flower bed blossoming, she worked through her body, stretching it and letting the elasticity of it take over as she came to a standing position and ended finally by stretching her neck muscles. When she had finished, her muscles were glowing warm and she laced her shoes up.

With the Stairmaster set to a mid level and for a

short time, she did a slow and casual warm up on the machine, her mind already becoming a blank, the images of MTV permeating it and taking hold. The effort required started to increase and she felt her blood begin to flow and her heart speed up, her breathing deeper and much more directed to the simple task of inhaling and expelling air from her lungs. Sweat started to break on her brow and Karen was stepping fast and hard to keep pace with the machine, the red digital readout taunting her with the exertions still to come. She pushed a few buttons to check her effort levels and then looked at the heart monitor attached to her wrist. Karen loved the technology of workouts and on her other wrist was a watch with pre-set times programmed in order to maximise her time and energy in the gym.

Via the Cybex cycle, Karen made her way towards the weights, a mixture of Nautilus machines and free weights. Her current programme had been designed for her by a fearsome South American woman called Dominique and she had used her as a personal trainer for the first two months while she became absolutely familiar with her routine. Karen had been emphatic with Dominique about wanting to cut her physique to a fine and pleasing line and not to stack it up with muscle. She told Dominique that as soon as her body started to look like Madonna's, she wanted to slow it down. That had seemed like an acceptable and amusing goal to Dominique, who looked like she could kill with her bare hands.

Karen worked her major muscle groups on several Nautilus machines and used the free weights for some more specific areas on her arms and back, her breathing steady and regulated and her form and balance in handling the weights perfect. Karen knew that it was too easy to come along to a gym and throw a weight around. Any fool could do that. For her, the workout was more about mind than body. It was an intellectual process where she brought her body into harmony with something external to it and then controlled it. It was only her mind that enabled her to do it. Her demeanour and her attitude. By the end of her session with the weights, she was on another plane completely, glad of the timer on her wrist beeping her out of her reverie. Finally she returned to the mats and did her previous stretching routine but in a much deeper and longer way, her body tired but relaxed, the correct balance between taut and slack.

After a quick shower, Karen sat in the sauna, her thoughts returning to her, but now she had the benefit of seeing them from a different perspective. She poured more water on to the coals and let her body drink steam through its pores, the sensual feel of clean and pure sweat covering her body like a mist. The Garden seemed so clear and so easy to her. Even Gabrielle could be fitted into her plans with little or no disruption and that would do her no damage with Avendon. It had already helped her get Caroline a job, which she hoped would not backfire on her. Tomorrow she would see Alan and talk to him about The Garden, about Gabrielle and about the two of them. She also knew that she had to make some time for Richard in the midst of it all and the thought of his lithe body made her decide that it should be sooner, not later. Slowly, most of her thoughts turned to Maxwell. Something about it seemed so right. She had not realised she had sparked in him something similar to what he had started in her, but obviously she had. A walk in the park, she thought to herself.

Karen spent twenty minutes in the sauna before taking a plunge and a final long and revitalising shower. By the time she was dressed, she felt an incredible calm and serenity. It was four o'clock, somewhat later than she had intended, but then she was a free agent. No one would be looking for her. She went to the bar and ordered a cranberry juice, calling in on her mobile service to David. Nothing major was occurring. She decided to wait in the bar and then wander along to Hamiltons to meet Maxwell at five. She would stow her gym bag in her locker at the club and leave her kit for the laundry service. For forty minutes, she sat and leafed through several papers for work, a couple of magazines and watched the occasional video on MTV. At four forty-five she left, ready for Maxwell.

At first glance, she did not realise it was him. From a distance she saw an unkempt-looking youth in a cobalt blue suit, hair everywhere, and for a moment Karen thought he would ask her for money. By the time she had neared and he was saying hello to her, she realised it was Maxwell. The sandy red hair, the cartoon caricature-like angles of his face and the scar over the right eye all added up to Maxwell. She gripped his hand tightly, holding his thin fingers and feeling the soft cushion of his palm.

'Hello, Karen,' he said, an impish grin spreading a wave of charm which she let ebb pleasantly over her.

'Hi,' she said. 'Do you prefer Maxwell or Max or Maxy?'

He smiled at her. 'Max is nicest. Maxwell was my dad's name and it makes me feel old. My publicity lady doesn't like me to be called Max.'

The solid blue suit was single-breasted and under it he wore a lighter, sky-blue Fred Perry shirt with a red trim, the three buttons all undone to reveal a glimpse of collarbone. His shoes looked as though they had been bought in a charity shop – clumpy black brogues held together by thick laces – and the trousers of the suit were just too long, resting on them as he stood there in Hamiltons' doorway. Despite his scruffy appearance, there was nothing shabby about him. Under the slipshod façade, he was well scrubbed and groomed, the blaze of hair carefully washed and styled and the sweet smell of a recent shower and cologne rising from him. He looked at her, his head held down at an angle as though about to be photographed, and she felt ready to grab him there and then. Why wait, she thought? You are only here to have sex with him, nothing more or less.

'Linda said we should go for a walk in the park,' Maxwell was saying to her, rousing her from her pleasant thoughts.

It would be nice to wait, she thought. To prolong it and tease herself with him.

'That would be nice.'

They were halfway down Sloane Street en route to Knightsbridge, walking side by side and chatting about nothing in particular, when she felt his hand very gently and tentatively slide itself into hers and squeeze.

'Is that all right?' he asked her, looking in front of him, like a marching soldier.

She did not reply but simply exerted some pressure on his hand and continued to look straight ahead. People looked at them but Karen was not sure why. Some may have recognised him or have been troubled because they were sure they knew him from somewhere but couldn't remember where. He exuded a sense of celebrity and presence, his shambolic image a poor disguise for it.

'How did you end up being a model?' she asked him.

'My dad was a film producer and my mum was an actress. Not a very famous one, but she was in a few films. At first, she didn't want me to act or be involved in films or anything. Then she would change her mind and I'd be off doing auditions and things and then she'd change her mind back. One of her friends said to her that they needed someone to model for jeans and that I would be good. It took off from there.'

'What do your parents think about it now?'

He scrunched up his lips and his small slits of eyes, which gave him his asexuality, narrowed impossibly tighter as he considered a reply. Karen traced her thumb over the palm of his hand as it swung gently by their sides.

'My dad died when I was a boy, so I don't know what

he thinks. My mum likes it, I think. My agent is the daughter of an old friend of hers, so she knows I'm looked after and I can do most things I want. She says it's like the next generation of people coming along. Me and the children of all her friends.'

'Do you enjoy it, being photographed?'

'Most of the time. Sometimes I see the pictures, on billboards or in magazines, and it's not me. It's like I'm an actor anyway, even though my mum didn't want me to be. I'm Max down here but up there I'm Maxwell. I enjoy being both.'

Karen listened to him intently, surprised at how level-headed he seemed, clearly having given some thought to the process of his fame. They entered the park and strolled towards the lake, he taking her case from her, having insisted he carry it. She was touched enough by the genuine nature of the gesture to accept. Karen studied his profile, seeing the perfectly constructed features from a different angle – the snub of his nose and the pout of his lips and the way his brow furrowed into a moody shape. Through the images she had seen of him, those features had been moulded and trained, giving off different messages at different times. Seeing him in the flesh, watching him as he spoke, she was witnessing him in full flow, the expressiveness of his face running in time with his words, often saying more than the words themselves.

They came to rest on a bench by the lake, people hurrying around them as they made their various ways home. In the midst of the hubbub, Karen felt relaxed, still glowing from her session at the gym, enjoying Maxwell and anticipating the prospect of an interesting evening. He sat sideways on the bench so he could face her and stared at her intently, deeply interested in her.

'Linda says you're really good at your job,' he said to her.

'I suspect you would say that. And her too,' Karen laughed.

He laughed as well. 'Honestly, she did,' he said persuasively, his eyes scanning the bench and quickly running over her before averting their gaze.

'I am good at what I do. They give me enough room to be, that's the important thing.'

'You've known her since college?' Maxwell asked.

'Linda? She was one of my best friends there. We had some good times.'

'I like Linda,' Maxwell said. 'She's a challenge sometimes.'

'You don't have to tell me that. I've had some horrible rows with her because she's so wilful.' She looked at him as she spoke, her mouth saying one thing, her mind in a million other places, recalling the photo shoot, the video room at Jake's, Maxwell and Max himself.

'I bet you're just as stubborn as her,' he said to her.

'I don't know. I hate the way women are always called stubborn or bitchy if they have some, any, kind of power.'

'Can I kiss you?' he asked her nervously.

'Do you want to?'

'I wouldn't ask unless I did.'

She leaned towards him, pushing her face and, by extension, her lips, forward. He was there to meet them and their mouths were joined, the air between them suddenly becoming common, and she tightly locked herself in a gesture of tenderness with someone she barely knew. Karen pouted and twisted her lips, her hand coming up to cradle the back of his head as he craned further forward to get at her. Karen leaned further sidewards and brought her other hand into his jacket and ran it along his side, the roughness of the Fred Perry shirt against her skin. Her hand wandered down and then up the shirt, feeling his hip where it touched the waistband of his trousers. She was ready to take him home.

They wandered back, Karen keeping her desire under control and Maxwell looking at pigeons and ducks, even talking to them occasionally. The birdboy of Alcatraz, Karen thought to herself. Where they had said much on the way there, the walk back was punctuated by only the occasional comment, the silence one of anticipation more than nerves. When they were in the lift on the way up to her apartment, he spoke in a low tone.

'I want you to do me,' he said, pushing into her with his groin as though his libido had suddenly gone up a gear.

'What do you want me to do?' she asked.

'Anything you want. Everything you want. Did Linda tell you I'll try anything?'

When he moved against her again, coyly coaxing her with his body, she felt the hardness in his groin.

'What does Linda do with you?' she asked, intrigued and excited at the thought of them together.

'All sorts.' He was whispering dirtily in her ear. 'She ties me up, hits me, sticks things in me. I love it. Feel.'

He grabbed her hand and pushed it into his crotch. She gripped his cock through the blue material and it grew even in the brief seconds that she held it. He looked at her the whole time she was on him. The lift bumped to a halt and she released him, composing herself before the door opened.

'Where's the bedroom?' he asked her as she put the key in her front door.

'Third on the left. You're keen,' she said, opening the door.

'I loved you in New York, by the way,' he said as he ran past her, laughing and heading for the bedroom door.

'Max!' she shouted after him, pausing to close the door.

When she reached the bedroom, he had already kicked off the beaten-up black brogues and removed his socks. He looked up at her, his head dropped in the familiar posing manner, an expectant and dirty look on his face as though he had suddenly gone from Jekyll to Hyde.

'Do you want me dressed or undressed?' he asked her.

'I want to know what you mean about New York,' she said to him, a confused anger simmering in her.

'At Jake's house,' he said, casually sitting down on her bed and staring up at her.

'You know Jake?'

'Friend of the family. Of my mother's, actually.'

'Does your mother know what you do for Jake?'

He laughed at her. 'You sound more like my mother than she does. Does yours know what *you* do there?'

'When did you see me there?'

'When you were in the monitor room. I watched you on a video tape where you were watching me on a video. And I saw the video of you and Chris Nichol. Very nice.'

'You weren't actually there at the time?' Karen asked, feeling spooked retrospectively.

'No, don't be silly. I saw it afterwards.'

'I talked to Jake about you, just to test the water. He didn't say he knew you,' Karen challenged.

'We keep our friendship very private. Do you want me dressed or undressed?'

Karen was angry and excited, the mix a potent one. She would have words with Jake later, but right at that moment, Maxwell was the nearest thing to hand and she was prepared to take it out on him.

'Get undressed,' she said snappily, a small satisfied smile on her face as he quickly complied.

She stared at his nude form, scrutinising in the flesh and up close what she had seen in person, on paper and in film in the previous weeks. The agile and hairless figure was appetising to behold. She held him in her silent scrutiny, waiting until he would start to feel nervous in her presence. Her examination was cool, long and unforgiving, revealing nothing to him about her thoughts. As he shifted from foot to foot, his hand touching his stiff cock, she knew she had reached the uncomfortable stage for him. So she continued to appraise him, wondering how it felt for him, someone so used to being looked at by millions of people, to stand and be looked at by only one. He gave a loud and tight swallow. Karen had locked him to the spot with the power of her gaze and she felt his timidity as surely as if she could have reached out and touched it. She decided it was time to release him from it.

'Lie face down on the bed,' she said to him.

While he did so, Karen slipped out of her own clothes, all the time observing the naked form on her bed, the curve of his rear barely perceptible, the shoulder blades bony and the arms thin extensions from the slight torso. She went to her case and retrieved the feather.

Kneeling next him on the bed, Karen traced the feather down from between his shoulders into the small of his back and airily over his buttocks, sweeping a circle around his rear before lighting the feather along the rift where his cheeks met. He quivered and shuddered under the touch, the feather able to cause movements far out of proportion to its exquisite graze. Between her legs, Karen felt a moistness and a longing, her earlier anger forgotten and replaced by the urge she had for him.

Down the backs of his legs and over the soles of his feet she whisked the feather, making him giggle and fidget on the mattress, his whole torso wiggling at her teasing touch. She played it against the nape of his neck, pushing it under his hair and watching it emerge from beneath the thatch. He turned his head to one side and she stroked his cheek with it, moving her body closer to his, the feeling of skin on skin. She tickled under his arms and he cried out, telling her it was not fair. She then flicked it where she knew he wanted it most.

Karen knelt between his open legs and brushed the underside of his balls with the feather. He let out a long and low groan that reverberated around the room and through the mattress. Opening his legs further he raised himself up, reaching to push his balls further down under himself so they were on display for Karen. She skimmed the surface of his ball sac, watching the wrinkled skin move under her caress, occasionally running the feather up the crack of his taut bottom.

'Turn over, Max,' she said.

Instantly he was on his back, his hand grabbing at his cock.

'Leave that alone until I tell you,' she said and it was instantly let go, slapping against the bottom of his stomach with a satisfying crack. She would get to his cock eventually, but it was her turn now.

Straddling his chest first, Karen wriggled her way up until she was over his face, her knees planted either side of his head. Her bottom touched his chest lightly and as she reared up, her pussy was suspended several inches from his pretty face, his hands stuck close to his sides. The view of his face from her position consisted mostly of the top half, his nose just visible and his green eyes glassy. She toyed at herself with the feather, stroking it lightly against her pussy-lips. Behind them, she felt herself swell and fill with juices that sprang from the very centre of herself, a tangible expression of the seething hunger that was gripping her like a vice. The feather was agonising as it whistled against her lips, rustling her dark pubic hair as she felt the gush of her juices held back by her like a dam.

When she was ready to burst, she discarded the feather, reached down and gently opened her lips with two fingers. A small droplet, like the first sign of rain, escaped her and tumbled onto Maxwell's high cheekbone, his eyes widening from their slit-like shape as it did so. Karen moved herself back so that she was more directly over his mouth.

'Keep your mouth closed until I tell you to open it,' she ordered him. He nodded.

She opened herself wider, and put her hand on her clitoris, feeling the gentle rush of breath through Max's nose. She pressed into herself, her fingers indenting the soft area around the peak of her desire, signals transmitting through her whole body as a light shiver ran up her back. She looked down at his face, wet with her and she spoke.

'Open your mouth.'

He licked around his lips, his tongue long and pointed, taking her juices and tasting them. She dipped lower, bringing her pussy perilously close to the lashing tongue, playfully pulling away as it neared her, allowing it to catch her once or twice. His arms were still pressed against his side, held in check by Karen's legs. She retrieved the feather and deftly spun around, her rear resting on his chest. As she did so, Maxwell freed his arms and she soon felt his hands smoothing over her cheeks.

Karen looked at his cock. Long, quite thin, very stiff and a large wide head. His pubic hair was the same light sandy colour as that on his head. Raising her backside and leaning forward, she began to work at his cock with the feather, listening to his cries as she did so. She was determined to prolong the agony for as long as she could, wondering if she could eventually bring him to orgasm with the feather. It seemed a likely a prospect, judging by the jerking movements his member was making. The skin that sheathed the shaft seemed barely able to keep it in check as it burst forth from him, seeming out of scale to his frame.

There was a flurry of movement from Max and then Karen felt the rough wetness of a tongue skimming the sensitive area of skin that marked the pathway between her pussy and her anus. His hands were opening her cheeks and Karen could feel him flecking away at her, the tongue leaving small spots of wetness as evidence of its presence. His tongue made a journey further upward and she gasped as it moistened her anus, the wrinkled pucker feeling suddenly more elastic from his licking. Maxwell's cock momentarily forgotten, Karen placed her hands on his stomach, just under his ribs, and raised herself more upright, allowing him to burrow his tongue lightly into her anus. As he did so, she gripped him, feeling his ribs under her palms. For several long moments she allowed him to probe her, to enter his long pointed tongue into her behind.

From far inside of her a guttural cry escaped, a desperate whimper of passion, and she was off his tongue, rushing down his body to get at his cock. With her back still to him, she straddled him and roughly shoved his cock inside her, he crying out from the painfully upright angle at which she held him and she from the feel of such a rough and delightfully quick penetration. The angle of their bodies made only a very short penetrative depth possible, but it was sharp and ruthless enough for Karen and concentrated much of the sensation on her clitoris. She supported herself on one hand and writhed her body quickly, shifting Max's cock in and out of her pussy with a vengeance.

Moistening a finger with her own juices, Karen reached under Max's legs and down between the cleft of his rear, and he moved his legs helpfully. He whimpered contentedly as she fingered him, massaging him in time with her lunges on to his body. His anus was tight and her finger was held tightly by it.

He called out to her, telling her he was about to come. Karen speeded her movements up, both her finger and her whole body, pushing herself to get where she had been aiming since they had met that first afternoon on the roof. Unable to see him, only to feel his cock in her and her finger in him, she closed her eyes and let the images of him from the previous weeks engulf her. It was not the doves nor the falcon nor the leather hood which finally pushed her into flight. It was what Linda had described as the Forlorn Angel picture where he had been sitting wearing small wings held to his body by leather straps and had sadly surveyed the London skyline. He had looked so vulnerable, ready to leap off and take flight at any moment. Karen formulated the image in her mind and forced it to stay there as long as possible before her orgasm would rip it from her mind and spread it all over her body, translating images into feelings.

With broken and desperate cries, she relinquished him to her whole body, the forlorn angel now shaking throughout her, her pussy undulating from the deep intensity of the orgasm. Around her finger, Max's anus tightened and he grunted. Karen slowed the movements of her pussy on his cock but kept the same relentless rhythm inside him, making him cry out and beg her to stop. She did not. All the way through his orgasm, as he throbbed into her and contracted around her digit, she continued to finger at him, trying to imagine the agony and the pleasure she was giving him as he ejaculated long and hard into her pussy.

When they were done, she released him. She turned and lay back on the bed, out of breath and covered in a sheen of sweat. Maxwell put an arm over her and nuzzled himself under her arm, his head resting on her shoulder and his still-quivering cock touching her side. She pulled him to her and he squeezed her. As she rested her face into his sandy hair, the cologne still sweet to her nostrils, she stroked the skin on his shoulders and kissed at his forehead. He was wordless and seemed anxious to get close to her and be intimate, as though it was all he had left to give.

In the warmth and the closeness of their bodies, her arms wrapped around him like wings, they slept.

Chapter Thirteen

HAVING NEGOTIATED THE central London traffic late on a Friday night, Karen and Alan were on the west side of London heading out to his other house in Berkshire.

'I've had such a nice evening,' he said to her, concentrating on the road and steering the large car round a bend with ease.

'Me too. Thank you.'

As he had promised, Alan had booked theatre tickets and they had been to a play at the National Theatre and then on to dinner. Just the two of them, as always. Karen had gone home after work and changed into a dramatic Claude Montana opera coat with a fine wool crew neck and light silk skirt underneath. The cloth moved in a theatrical fashion and she liked the feel of it around her. At the end of a hectic Friday spent on the phone and in meetings, all connected with The Garden, she was tired enough to have just dropped straight into bed when she got home, but was glad she had decided to see Alan. She felt she had neglected him in general over the past several weeks and she still felt guilty for putting him off two days earlier, when she had seen Maxwell. He had been so helpful with The Garden and for that reason alone she did not want to do anything that might hurt him.

The play had engaged her and the dinner had

relaxed her. They shared easy and familiar conversation, laughing and giggling, and Karen was conscious of the ways in which they were becoming comfortable with each other. Still, Alan's suggestion that they travel to the house in Berkshire had caught her off-guard. Karen knew he had a house there, but did not expect to be invited to it, such an invitation seeming to signal a progression to a further stage in their friendship. Since Karen was not entirely sure she wanted to enter such a stage, she had hesitated, but it was a Friday and she was curious to see it.

'Which house did you have first? The one out here or the one in Fulham?' she asked him, not mentioning his recently ex-wife.

'The one out here. Fulham came quite a bit later, once we'd settled on not having any family.'

Karen listened to his voice in the dim light of the car, wondering if he was happy to talk to her about it. 'Why did you settle on the idea of no family? Couldn't you?'

'We could have, but didn't. We lived in a lot of places around London to be near Hamiltons and the Inns of Court, but the house out here was a stable weekend retreat. It was fun because we could always pick odd or off-the-wall kinds of places to live in London, like we were still students.'

'Do you wish you had children?'

He hesitated, staring ahead at the road, not speaking. She was about to ask the question again.

'I do wish that, yes.'

'You met Margaret at Cambridge, didn't you?'

'Yes. She was all those sorts of things people mention when they go glassy-eyed and talk in clichés. Funny, clever, attractive, sharp and forthright. She was all of those, much more than I could have been.'

'And still is?'

'Probably. Sorry, I know I shouldn't talk about her in the past tense, as though she were dead. If she were dead, I wouldn't be able to use the present tense.' He glanced over at her and smiled at the mock evil in his tone.

'You don't really wish that, do you?'

'Only sometimes, and never as bad as I used to.'

'Was it hard to get divorced after all that time?'

'Yes. Very hard. Never divorce a lawyer,' he laughed with a trace of bitter-sweet. 'That's not fair actually. I did well. Both houses, but then she hated both of them.'

'You're lucky to have two houses,' Karen said to him.

'Hamiltons has been good to me. Anyway, your flat sounds nice. Convenient. I look forward to seeing it sometime.'

'Hint taken,' she said.

They had left the motorway and were on a small lane, narrow, unlit and bending, the beams of the headlights illuminating the road far ahead, insects lit by the beacons of light.

'Here we are,' Alan said, turning into a driveway, the solid sound of the road giving way to the crunch of gravel.

A security light lit the front of the house as they approached it. Long and low with a double front, a garden that seemed to be well-kept even in the darkness, the house was very countrified, particularly to Karen's urban gaze. As she stepped from the car, gown flowing, her breath was visible in the chill midnight air.

Inside, it was a rural version of Alan. All the city things that she associated with his house in Fulham, the art nouveau antiques and the slightly jazzy decoration, were toned and refined to an air of sedate and expensive taste. Karen could tell it was his house as soon as she entered it. He gave her a quick tour, showing her around upstairs first and then the downstairs, which had been extended off either end of the house to yield a large kitchen and a small studio.

'Margaret liked, sorry, likes, to paint. We built this

eight, no, nine years ago. She used to come out here and paint.'

The air in the studio smelled of white spirit and all the surfaces were perfectly clean, no trace of paint anywhere. Karen wondered if Alan had scrubbed it down after she had left.

'Do you have any pictures of her?' Karen asked him.

'Somewhere. You don't really want to see them, do you?'

'Only if you don't mind. I'm curious to see her, that's all. If it's too awkward for you . . .'

'Of course not,' he said to her. 'Let's go to the drawing-room and I'll fix us a nightcap and dig out an album or two.'

Sipping brandy from a huge glass, Karen sat on a sofa in the drawing-room – a mixture of greens and whites and dark oak furniture. She had casually discarded the opera coat and was enjoying the new freedom of movement afforded by its absence, while Alan sat next to her and flicked through an old book of photographs. Margaret was very striking, although she did not say so to Alan. Her eyes were piercing, black almost, and she glared at the camera in almost every photograph as though extremely angry with the photographer.

'She's not what I expected,' Karen managed finally.

'She had all but stopped attending any of the Hamiltons functions by the time you arrived, otherwise you would have got to meet her.'

'You don't think she'll be a customer at The Garden, then?'

'Not Margaret, I'm afraid. A few years ago, possibly, but not now.'

'Is she involved with anyone else at the moment?' Karen asked.

'Another lawyer,' was his short and simple reply.

'At the same firm?'

'No, she wouldn't do that. Not like us,' he answered.

'Does she know we're seeing each other?'

'Karen, I don't think anyone knows we're seeing each other, it's been such a state secret.'

'That's the best way though Alan, really.

'Who's that?' she asked, pointing to a colour snap of a boy, a typical first-of-school photograph. A brave smile on a presumably cold September morning.

'Oh, that,' Alan said, his mind appearing to fumble. 'His name is John. A nephew of Margaret's. Good-looking boy.'

Karen looked at the boy and could see that he would have grown up to be quite cute.

'When was this taken?' she laughed. 'He might be worth meeting.'

'Oh, I don't think so,' he said quietly, and Karen thought he seemed upset by her comment, jealous almost.

'I was only teasing, darling, really,' she said, never having called him darling before.

She let her hand drop on to his arm and he closed the book.

'I know you were. How are you getting on with Gabrielle?' he asked.

'It's not as bad as I thought it would be. She's more like noise in the background, interference. She doesn't seem to have any agenda that relates to me, so it's not so hard.'

'Her agenda,' he said, placing emphasis on the word agenda and showing it as one he would not normally use, 'is very much related to Daniel.'

'There must be such a bad history between them.'

'Yes, but it's none of their doing. It all happened because of their parents and they were caught up in it, Gabrielle especially. Daniel was more protected. I think his father saw to that.'

'What was Lawrence Avendon like?'

'He was a bastard. Not even a fair bastard, just a bastard. I may have joked about wanting to kill Margaret, but when Lawrence died, Daniel felt such a mixture of emotions. I don't think he ever recovered.'

The conversation had come to a natural conclusion. In the silence that ensued between them, Karen listened to the sound of the room and the whole house around her. A clock ticked in the background, metronomic and precise, and she felt the presence of the past, the history of Alan and of Hamiltons. It was strange to be involved in something that had so much of a past, the true story of which she was certain she did not know. Deep down, she wondered if part of her logic for getting involved with Alan in the first place was to try and connect to some of the legend and myth of Hamiltons, to make her feel a part of it. That may have been true, she thought, but at that moment she wanted nothing more than to connect with Alan in a very basic and physical way, regardless of the reasons or the implications.

Karen felt a tingle of excitement as her desire for Alan slowly worked its way through her, obliterating all her other feelings, and she let the sensation wash away at her, smothering any doubts she had about their relationship. Reaching out across the small distance between them, she rested her hand on his knee, feeling the power of even such a simple connection. Still there were no words, only the sense of touch, her hand on the material of his trousers. Carefully, Alan set the photograph album to rest on the floor along with the other one and when he had done so, he placed his hand over hers. Karen could sense that he was thinking about speaking and she could almost hear his thoughts, which were the same as her own. 'This won't work. We're too different. Our ages. Our positions at Hamiltons.' Karen had other, supplementary thoughts of her own about Richard and about The Garden and she hoped that Alan was not aware of those. But, despite all the unspoken words between them, the thoughts and reservations, the power of feeling was too strong. Karen moved her hand higher, resting it on his thigh, taking his hand with hers.

Alan led her by the hand up into a bedroom that was very floral in a Laura Ashley way. The bed was large, king-sized, with a heavy brass bedstead. For a long silent moment they faced each other at one side of the bed, the atmosphere heavy with the expectation of sex. Alan lifted her crew-neck over her head and as it was removed she shook her head a fraction, letting her short hair swing as freely as it could. Alan's face was concentrating closely on his task as he removed her bra, unzipped her skirt and then unclipped her stockings. Her knickers and suspender belt followed immediately, as though Alan was not interested in the titillation of her underwear, wanting only her. He had not rushed in his undressing of her, but nor had he lingered, his need for her seeming to have found a speed which was comfortable for them both. With a similar pace, he removed his own clothes while Karen looked on.

As she stood, he reached out and rubbed at her hip bones, his thumbs gently pressuring the trim flesh that led towards her pubic hair. His hands spread themselves and roved around her hips and made a cupping shape on her behind, squeezing it gently before his strong fingers delicately splayed and ran up her sides, the lightness of the touch tickling like a feather. Karen breathed heavily as he fondled her breasts, pressing at the soft flesh and pulling on her nipples, holding each between a finger and thumb. With each pinch, she closed her eyes and felt gravity change around her and her head become light. With his hands back on her hips, he kissed her and carefully steered her on to the bed.

Where he had used his hands when she stood, now, as she lay on the bed, he replaced them with the brush of his lips, nibbling at her hips where they pointed through the skin and nuzzling at the border of her pubic hair. His mouth made her nipples wet, causing them to stand out still further, the sensitive nerve-endings of her lust on display for him. He bit carefully at them and rolled them about in his teeth, alternating from one breast to the other, never lingering too long on either. He kissed her throat and the skin under her jaw and then the jaw-line itself, finishing up back on her mouth. Karen held his head and stroked his hair.

Alan produced a small bottle of massage oil and unhurriedly removed its top. The aroma of spicy orange pervaded the atmosphere around the bed. Karen lay, a warm and slack feeling all over her. He began with her shins and the tops of her feet, spreading a fine film of oil over them and moving his hands fluidly back and forth. His hand felt large as it moved around over her inner thighs, grazing closely over the top of her pussy and then pulling back, retracting itself to give her tightly muscled leg a squeeze. Karen enjoyed the pressure he exerted on her stomach as he covered it in a veneer of oil, his hands making a sound just discernible as they moved about her. On her breasts, he used more than elsewhere and they were soon slippery in his hands, occasionally escaping his attempts to squeeze them.

After he had oiled her arms, he gently turned her over and finished off the bottom of her feet and the backs of her legs. Karen felt the oil pouring on to her behind and then Alan's hands kneaded her buttocks, squeezing and pushing them together, the side of his hand occasionally in the cleft. Finally, he concentrated long and hard on her back and shoulders and she felt the knots of the day undo themselves as he pushed his fingers expertly into her flesh. Karen wondered if he had ever been trained to massage, since his touch was so firm and relaxing. When he was done, she turned on to her back and looked at him as he gazed silently down at her.

Needing no oil, Alan worked his hand at Karen's pussy. As he leaned over her, one hand supporting himself, his cock hung from him in a swollen erection. He toyed with her as though deliberately holding back as long as possible both on her and himself. Karen opened her outspread legs an inch or two further and Alan continued to push his middle finger in and out of her, stopping only to apply pressure to the area around her clitoris. He had worked over her whole body, preparing her, and had now come to rest on this single area. His pace was steady and continuous and Karen felt the results of his earlier lengthy preparation approaching as she shifted herself on the bed and closed her eyes.

Karen made barely a sound as she came, communicating her pleasure to him through movement alone. She arched her back off the bed and pulled at her nipples, which were slippery to the touch. Several times in short succession she lifted herself from the bed using her feet and shoulders as pivots. Her head flicked back rhythmically, a deep contraction in her neck forcing it regardless of her will. Dropping back on to the bed she closed her legs, feeling oily foot on oily foot, and gripped Alan's hand, pushing it harder into her. Her vagina swelled around his finger and her movements subsided as she passed the peak of her orgasm. Squeezing his hand and removing it from her, she gripped it and lay on the bed, letting her breathing regulate.

When she opened her eyes, he was kneeling there and gazing at her intensely, his cock still looking painfully hard. The grey eyes feasted on her and his hair hung carelessly over his forehead, the streaks of grey caught by the lamp looking like small forks of lightning. She pulled herself upright using his hand and took the oil bottle from the foot of the bed where it rested against the bedstead. Pouring a large helping into her palm, she transferred it to his cock, beginning at the base near his balls and working up over the tip. The noises her hand made were liquid and she squeezed his shaft, enjoying the way it slipped and slid about as though trying to escape her. The movement of her hand was easy, the lubricant effect of the oil allowing her to trace a path over him, both her hands working on him at the same time, passing each other but never meeting. She clutched him hard and then released him, watching the way the blood pulsed and he swelled, the oil making his cock shine in the soft light of the room. Circling her finger tightly around the base of his cock, she studied it for a moment before she took it back in her whole hand, clenching it tightly, and lying back down on the bed, bringing him over her at the same time.

Alan reached his hand above her head and pulled a pillow from under the bed-cover. Knowing what he wanted to do, Karen raised her behind so he could place it on the bed, but not before he had doubled it over to maximise the height it would give her. Karen felt her body tilted back into the bed and she drew her legs up, which made them feel heavier and as though they were trying to gravitate towards her head. Partially giving in to the sensation, she allowed her knees to fall sideways towards the bed and her feet to hang inwards. As Alan leaned over her, so she felt that the angle of their bodies was perfectly aligned and that she was ready to be penetrated by him.

The penetration was silent and precise. She whimpered as his oiled cock slid between her lips and into her upraised pussy. Holding her legs behind the knees and pulling them back further, she allowed Alan's weighty cock the access it needed. In what seemed a very short space of time, he had entered her and his pubic hair was against her own, their bodies joined at the groin. Karen's shoulders were pushed back into the mattress by the position of her body on the bed with the pillow underneath her.

With a beat and speed that was similar to the way his finger had been earlier, Alan began to move himself in and out of her. Like all of their sex so far that night, he started in a relaxed and unhurried manner. This gradual and careful pace allowed Karen to focus on the very precise nature of their coupling, the way her vagina moulded itself to him and the way his cock stimulated her both inside and out. She pushed her head back and stretched the muscles in her neck and down the whole of her back. Her body was still nicely oiled from the massage and her muscles were warm. Feeling completely at ease, Karen moved her head from side to side on the bed, running her hands through her hair as she did so and making little noises of pleasure.

Inside her Alan's cock felt firmly planted and as it became more engorged, so it expanded Karen around him. He was pulling out as far as he could before making a determined drive back into her and Karen admired his control, sensing he could easily go over the edge, as she had earlier and was now ready to do again. For several seconds, she opened her eyes and rejoined him, watching his hair flick from his exertion and his face change as the tenor of his passion for her grew. Karen reached up and touched his sides, the slight contour of his biceps there, and she moved her hands down a little further and used them to make encouraging movements in time with his own, coaxing him to go faster into her.

When his speed had built up and his face contorted further, Karen closed her eyes and concentrated on herself, leaving the work to Alan. The darkness of her closed eyes seemed to become lighter and she felt herself drift around in her head, as though weightless and roaming free in there, not bounded by specific thoughts but once again guided only by sensation. Alan's increasingly frantic movements pushed her against the mattress, but after a while she became less conscious of the specifics of his movement and what became important was the impression it left on her thoughts. Even the sounds he made became less audible to Karen and all her feelings wove themselves together as she felt her orgasm stir.

It was an amplified version of her earlier peak, when Alan had been using only his finger. This time, however, Karen released all the feelings that had been building in her since they had arrived at the house and let them flow through into a long and loud cry. The thrusting became more erratic and Karen felt warmth flow into her with sharp jets, his cries mingling with her own. Karen's body snapped with whip-like motions as the orgasm brought her to attention and against this rigidity Alan thrashed at her, spilling wildly into her.

While Alan slept, his breathing getting deeper and more rhythmic as the minutes passed, Karen lay staring into the darkness, making out unfamiliar shapes in a strange room.

Earlier, her feelings had led her down the path to sex, ignoring the words that she knew should have passed between them and would possibly have held her back – perhaps held the both of them back. As she drifted into sleep, Karen wondered how long it would be before she could find the words that would lead her down the other path. The path that led away from Alan.

Chapter Fourteen

KAREN LOOKED OVER at Caroline as they went through the doors of Hamiltons. Caroline was tugging at the tweed suit by Isaac Mizrahi, the one Karen had loaned her that morning. Formal and double-breasted, it made the best of her shoulders and tapered in at her hips. Caroline insisted on trying to pull the skirt down until it was almost like a hipster in order to give it more length.

'Stop it,' Karen said to her, slapping her on the arm at the same time.

'Sorry!' Caroline replied. 'I'm nervous.'

'Everything will be fine.'

'I've never got a job without even having to interview before. It's worse than having the interview.'

'Caroline, it's only a temporary job. I told you that.'

'I know, but working for Daniel Avendon. You must have pulled strings.'

Karen smiled and did not reply for a moment, waiting until they were in the store and, as was her practice, riding the escalator.

'Believe me, my strings are being pulled substantially more than his,' she said, frowning as Caroline fingered the hem of the skirt.

Karen herself wore a stone grey outfit by Jil Sander – a short dress with a vest-like top whose round and low neck-line stopped just short of her cleavage. Her nipples showed through the material and the perilously short skirt was redeemed by a marginally longer one of identical colour and material that flowed from underneath it. A loosely constructed top finished off the outfit, which was cool and easy to move in. She wore discreet earrings that were Chanel, a present from a former flame, and she had sprayed herself in Coco, matching fragrance to accessories. As they made their slow ascent, she said hello to several people.

'Does everyone here know you?' Caroline asked her.

'More or less.'

'When do I get to see the two lovers then?'

'Caroline, discretion please. Here we are.' Karen led her through the door marked 'Private' and into the office area on the fifth floor.

Karen introduced Caroline to Avendon's secretary. She had been worried that getting her this assignment would have upset Daniel's full-time PA, but it had not. They went in to meet Daniel, who was in the middle of punching a number into the telephone. When he saw them, he stopped, smiled and placed the receiver down, standing to greet them. Karen forgot occasionally how charming and charismatic Avendon could be, not unlike Alan but with the benefit of several million more pounds. He moved across the floor as though wearing dancing shoes, gliding over French chalk.

'Karen, hello. This is Caroline?' Avendon said, bathing her in his full attention.

'Pleased to meet you. I'm Caroline,' she said extending her hand, the other playing at the skirt. Karen wanted to kick her, but resisted.

'Excellent. Fine,' Avendon said.

'Thank you for giving me the chance to help out,' Caroline was saying.

'I'm sure you won't thank me. This filing project rolls around every six or so months and I won't have Jane do it any more. She's my PA. You met her on the way in, presumably. She can show you what needs doing.'

'Caroline, as I said, Daniel, is a very experienced office worker in a number of contexts. She'll have no problems, I'm sure,' Karen said.

'If she does, I'll just hold you responsible,' Avendon said, holding the silence at the end of his sentence for a second before booming out a laugh. Karen saw the relief spread over Caroline's face as her hands ferreted away at the Isaac Mizrahi and she wondered if this had been such a good idea.

'I'll introduce Caroline to Jane properly,' Karen said, grabbing her up and jockeying her out, 'and then if you have a moment, I'd like to pop back?'

'Certainly.'

'That wasn't so bad, was it?' Karen asked. 'Except for when you nearly ripped the skirt off. I think he thought you were a strip-o-gram I'd hired for a joke.'

'It's too short,' Caroline said.

'Never for Daniel,' she replied. 'Jane, can you show Caroline what she needs to do?'

She left Caroline, imagining how a mother feels when her child starts school, and went back to Daniel's office.

'How are things in The Garden? Rosy?' Avendon asked when she returned.

'Very. I have a meeting with Gabrielle on the floor in about ten minutes,' Karen said.

'I know. She has been here and went down there a half hour ago. She was surprised, I think, at how well advanced things were.'

'We agreed, Daniel, that she would have some consultative input into this. That doesn't mean she gets to design the thing from ground up. It wouldn't have been appropriate to involve her too deeply before now.'

'I agree. I'm not questioning.' He clenched his hands and rolled his thumbs around each other as he spoke. 'Simply reporting. I do appreciate her having this outlet. The launch of the fragrance and The Garden will still be on schedule?'

'Definitely, unless there's a catastrophe of some sort.'

'Wonderful.'

'I wanted to say thank you again for letting Caroline help out. She's had a bad time lately.'

'Glad to. A bit of back-scratching. She seems lively enough – a bit fidgety, perhaps.' Avendon grinned.

'I'll come by and take her out for a long lunch a bit later. See how she's coping. See if she's found anything incriminating in all that filing.'

'My dear, Jane shreds that long before it gets to this stage. And the real scandal?' He tapped his head, 'Is all in here.'

Before going to meet Gabrielle, she conferred with David, he reading items off his clipboard, ticking as he went. He had been helpful in humouring Gabrielle when she was trying to contact Karen over the previous weeks, and she was sure that Gabrielle had taken a liking to him, something she had teased him about. 'I'd be like one of those dancing boys Eartha Kitt has on stage,' he had said to her in horror.

'How was your friend?' he asked.

'As well as can be. I'll take you to lunch with her some time and you can meet her for yourself. She's capable once she gets going, it's just that initial kick.'

David sniffed before beginning his next sentence and Karen braced herself at this signal of a gripe to come. 'Richard Fraser was up here looking for you Friday night, after you'd left. He was rude to me as usual. Could you ask him not to be? Tell him just because he's *fucking* my boss, that doesn't *make* him my boss.'

'David!' she said in surprise. 'Who says I'm fucking him?'

'The list of who doesn't would be shorter,' he trilled.

Karen, even after her considerable time there, was still surprised at how completely impossible it was to keep a lid on anything at Hamiltons. She wondered if Alan knew. He would probably say something to her if she did.

'Do you think Daniel or anyone like that knows?' she asked him, trying to make the question sound general.

'No, I don't think Alan knows,' he said, intoning heavily. 'And don't worry, I think I'm the only one who knows you're fucking Alan.'

She looked at him, wanting to laugh and wanting to slap him at the same time.

'David, sometimes.'

'Any chance of Richard coming our way when you're done with him?' David asked, a fragment of genuine hope in his voice.

'More chance of Alan coming your way, I think. Thanks for letting me know, David. And thanks for keeping it quiet. I need to sort it out,' she told him.

'Choices, choices,' he said to her. 'Bane of my life.'

The area set aside for The Garden was at the back half of the furniture department on the fourth floor. It was certainly the most logical area of the shop in which to house her project both commercially and architecturally. A number of false walls had been taken down, including some offices at the very back, and a huge expanse had opened up in their wake. With the wide open space there, a new false wall was erected, floor to ceiling, completely sealing off the space that would become The Garden. A number of the display sofas from the old department had been retrieved and were off being re-covered for use in The Garden.

Cabinets and display areas had already been planned by a specialist retail agency and a group of shopfitters were currently working on them plus the lighting, which was being done by a contract firm. Following this, what Karen referred to as 'the green people' would arrive. It was a plant and flower hire company that would make The Garden into the lush and verdant paradise Karen imagined it to be.

As she walked through the door that bore the sign

apologising for the inconvenience, it was difficult to imagine the ambience and how it would really be. Still, this was halfway towards the realisation of what had been nothing more than a notion only seven weeks ago. A feeling of satisfaction swept over Karen at the way she would be able to make The Garden real. Several workmen were ambling around, carrying or shifting building materials. When the department was open, the door through which she had just entered would be sealed off to the public, their only access being the lift that ran up the back of the building. Karen made her way over to it, to appreciate how the customer would first see The Garden, and as she neared, she heard the strains of an argument.

'What seems to be the problem?' Karen asked, planting herself between Gabrielle and the foreman.

'This man will not listen,' Gabrielle said petulantly.

Karen turned to Malcolm, the foreman, and looked at him apologetically.

'Malcolm, I'll come speak with you in a moment,' she said in an even and friendly way, using her eyes to indicate whose side she was on.

Disgruntled, he turned and was gone.

'What's the matter, Gabrielle?' she asked.

'I told him that we would not need all this space in the entrance. That we should put a cabinet or two there.'

'The space is meant to let the customer catch a breath, rather than the whole thing jumping on them in one go. It should almost be like foreplay,' Karen said, wondering if foreplay was a good word to use with Gabrielle. She tried to steer her away from the topic. 'How are we going with the photographs for the lift?' she asked her.

'I have some delightful ones. I went through the ones in the album here and I have some of my own, all the way up until I left. There's one of me with Lauren Bacall, poor love. The book's over there, we'll look in a moment. I still don't understand this empty space and foreplay.'

'There will be the pictures we shot for the new Hamiltons fragrance, blown up to beyond life-size.

They should dominate the eye as you walk out of the lift. Imagine you're just coming out of the doors,' Karen said, turning with her back to them.

The plan was to have a blank space, almost like a waiting room, that restricted the overall view of The Garden until the customer rounded the corner and was faced with the whole thing, spread out before her. To Karen, it had to feel like entering an exhibition at an art gallery, passing through a small and minimal space and into something much bigger. It would create a sense of anticipation.

'So,' she said to Gabrielle, placing a hand on her shoulder, getting her first feel of the now familiar crushed velvet, today's colour being green, 'you come through the door, big picture of Maxwell and the doves curving over this low dome ceiling and the other two pictures on the side. Then you go through and you see a whole range of fragrances. It's familiar, because we don't want to shock or turn people off. It's what they would expect to see.'

She led Gabrielle into the empty space, trying to create for her the image of what was to come.

'You come through the entrance hall and there's a long red carpet held down by brass runners with potted palms at the side. Along either side, counters. Here,' she pointed to her right, 'will be shoes and hats and over there on the other side, lingerie. Through here, the next section, will be a range of select designers. Donna Karan, Chanel, Vivienne Westwood, Versace and some others, preferably English and perhaps just starting up. We'll switch them around every few months. There'll be plants along some of the walkways and in corners and in high hanging baskets. This is where the fountain and bar will be.' They had reached the central point.

'Over there, the juice bar,' she pointed to it, already constructed around the plumbing for the fountain which protruded from a plinth. 'Over that side, on those counters will be some jewellery and other

589

accessories. As you pass the bar and fountain, there is space for more women's wear. And there on the back wall,' she pointed dramatically, 'will be a high wall with water cascading down it very discreetly. Like the Trump Plaza in New York, but not as garish. The water wall will gently cascade and the gantry you see up there will be open too, allowing you to go up and be near the flow of water and to see The Garden from an ariel perspective. Sofas are going to be spread about, staff able to assist if you need it. Don't you think this will be a wonderful place to come and shop?'

'Perhaps. I really think there should be something more outside the lift,' Gabrielle said, as though all Karen had just said to her was meaningless. 'Some people to greet the customers? Handsome men or something?'

'Definitely not. Cliché. That was discussed at the original meeting and subsequently with Daniel. The photographs will be enough. The green marble on the floor, the gold trim around the edges. It will all carry itself off. Why don't you show me those pictures now?'

Karen spent half an hour looking through the Hamiltons collection and Gabrielle's personal collection of photographs. She may not have particularly liked her, but the pictures were interesting and she felt a little sorry for the woman, her collection of memories mounted in a book and yellowing slowly around the edges.

'Is that Alan?' Karen exclaimed at one point.

'Oh yes. Quite the looker wasn't he? A very popular man with the staff in his younger days, especially the young ladies. Look, this is a ball we had in the Christmas of nineteen-sixty-seven. Alan would have been, oh, twenty-two. Only just joined and Daniel too, his father still here. Look, that's Lawrence Avendon.'

'He'd divorced your mother by then?'

'Oh yes! They had not been together for over fifteen years by then. She was festering away in some nursing home or other. There she is.'

Gabrielle handed her a picture. A handsome woman, not pretty, with slightly frizzy hair, stared at the camera, a smile not quite breaking across the square features. Karen looked at it in silence, uncertain of what to say. Gabrielle seemed to be off in one of her customary orbits and Karen waited politely for her to land.

'She was very pretty,' Karen said.

'Not quite the belle, but near enough,' she replied.

By the time Gabrielle had finished showing her the photographs they ended up agreeing on several pictures that would be excellent. Karen turned and took another look at the area where The Garden was growing and then she made her way to find Caroline.

'Patisserie Valerie,' Karen said to the taxi driver as Caroline jumped in and she followed.

'How's the skirt holding up under the pressure?' Karen asked.

'I gave up with it by ten and just hiked it up under my ears.'

'How's Daniel been?'

Caroline took a deep breath. 'He's very charming, you know. That view from his office and the meeting room is amazing. You wouldn't think you could see that much from there.'

'Don't let him be too charming. Are you getting on okay with Jane?' The taxi rounded the corner of Knightsbridge and sped on past Harrods.

'She's lovely. She showed me where everything needed to go and left me to it, said I should just ask as many questions as I want. She's been there years.'

'There are a few like that at Hamiltons,' Karen said. 'There was this kind of Royal Family that existed at the start and they've stayed. Jane is one of them. Alan another.'

'You soon,' Caroline said. 'Queen Karen of Hamiltons. Duchess of The Garden.'

Karen cringed and paid the taxi driver.

'How was your morning?' Caroline asked her as they neared the front of the queue for a table. Karen drank in the bustle of customers and waiters around her. It was one of her favourite venues for lunch, just continental enough to afford a brief escape from the shop and the sandwich bar jungle that was the alternative.

'A bit fraught. Gabrielle – the one I told you about – was squabbling with the foreman of the shopfitters. I don't know if she's deliberately obstructing me or just showing early onset of Alzheimer's.'

'Don't be wicked, Karen.'

'It's true though. She just blasts off into space. I'm waiting for her to dock with the mother ship.'

'Can I come and see where they're doing the building?'

'Of course. You can come to the party as well,' Karen said as they made their way to the table.

'Is it all women?' Caroline asked, her eye-line following one of the waiters.

'No. Mixed that night. One chance for the boys to see what they're missing. Apart from the ones who are going to work there. We've recruited ten people internally, all women, for the launch and they're looking for the rest through agencies.' Karen scanned the menu, despite knowing already that she would order the vegetarian club sandwich. 'We're going to have a dry run with the staff teams in two weeks' time.'

Caroline ordered the same as Karen and when the waiter had left, she put her hands on the table in a serious pose and looked at Karen.

'Don't be annoyed with me,' she said.

'Why?' Karen asked.

'I spoke to Gareth.'

'Today?'

'Just before you came up.'

Karen sighed, knowing that Caroline would do it despite all she had said.

'Don't tell me. He's sorry?' Karen raised her eyes sarcastically.

'He hasn't made it that far yet,' Caroline said. 'He's still denying that he went away with her. I told him I'd called Marilyn's work and his. He got really angry.'

'Did you tell him you were staying with me?'

'No. He wouldn't even think of you. If he did, I don't think he'd remember where you work or live. He couldn't remember where I worked, half the time.'

'We might have to give him that one, Caroline. I couldn't keep up with that. How did you leave it with him?'

'I didn't. I told him that I just called him to let him know that I was all right and that I wouldn't be back. We were supposed to go to his sister's wedding next month and that's all he seems to be worried about – what his family will think.'

'You're not going back to him, are you, Caroline?'

'No. Promise,' Caroline replied immediately.

Karen remembered how she had felt the night she drove with Caroline and rescued all her stuff. It had not seemed like a place where a couple lived. It had taken just less than two hours to pack and remove all of Caroline's things from his house. Karen had felt it should take longer to disentangle yourself from someone you were supposed to be living with. Instead, all of Caroline's things had stood out for her the second she walked into the house. Karen would not let her go back.

'I saw Alan Saxton,' Caroline said.

'What did you think of him?'

'Very sexy. I know what you mean about a cabinet minister. He looks so solid, and he's got that sort of magnetism. Daniel's like that too. What's Richard like?'

'He's very young and trendy. Go down and look at him in the Dungeon.'

'How will I recognise him?'

'He's the cutest and straightest thing Hamiltons has down there.'

'Which of them do you prefer?'

593

'To be truthful, and selfish, I'd prefer them both, but that's starting to be difficult. Not so much with Richard. I know he plays around a bit, but with Alan it's hard. He was knocked back by the divorce and I don't want to hurt him all over again.'

'What do you think he'd say if he knew about Richard?'

'He'd be terribly understanding, stiff in the upper lip, but I'm sure, at the centre of it, he'd feel devastated. He may find out anyway. I think the grapevine is running in overdrive through the shop.'

'Better he hears it from you,' Caroline said.

'I don't agree. In some ways, I'd sooner he hears it through gossip.'

'So you're just going to sit tight and let it work itself out?' Caroline asked, sounding unconvinced.

'I intend to do just that,' said Karen as she took a bite from the sandwich, unaware that even as she spoke, things were working themselves out and in a far stranger way than she could have imagined.

Chapter Fifteen

'*IS THIS THE* room for the interview?'

Karen looked up from the papers on her desk to be confronted by the toothy smile of a young man, probably not twenty, with long black hair that drooped in a fringe and a sculpted face that was long in lines and hard on edges. It was David's day off, which was why the boy must have ambled into her office in the way he had, and Karen was quick to capitalise on it as her mind quickly rehearsed a few lines.

'There are a number going on today,' she said, trying to sound severe and businesslike. 'Who are you?'

'Glenn Carpenter. It's for the part-time job on men's fragrances.'

'Come on in. My name's Karen Taylor. I look after recruitment here,' she lied quickly and efficiently, smiling as she slowly reeled him in.

Ordinarily, Stephen Jones, Hamiltons' personnel officer, would weed through the casual staff, but Karen saw a chance to add something special to the situation and take some workload from Stephen. She was nothing, she thought frivolously, if not a company woman. She stood and shook hands with him, crossing the room to click the door silently so he would not be aware that she was locking the both of them in. She was quickly excited and when she returned to her chair, she sat with her legs positioned so that she could move them slightly and cause the gentlest of friction between them.

He was well over six feet tall, but there was nothing skinny about him, all the signs of a good body hiding under the smart but casual clothes. His eyes were large and round, a very inviting shade of green, and his mouth was wide and pouting, giving the overall impression of an endearing gawkiness and almost shyness. He was very manly despite his youth and wouldn't stand a chance with the boy-kittens on the men's fragrances, but she didn't want to tell him that just yet. Why shatter the poor boy's illusions, she thought to herself? She picked up the first piece of paper that came to hand and pretended to study it before looking up at him.

'Tell me something about yourself, Glenn,' she said to him, moving her right leg from side to side, the back of her thigh rubbing the chair.

'Well,' he stumbled, 'I'm eighteen and I just finished my A' Levels, but I'm not going to university until next year, so I want to do some part-time work while I wait. It's sort of meant to be a year off, so I'm only looking for part-time.'

His accent had the trace of a good school, probably not public, but certainly private. Karen imagined him playing sports, mud covering his muscular legs, sweat on his brow, communal bathing. She brought her legs together and squeezed them, as though trying to smother her desire.

'What are you going to study when you get to university?'

'History, most likely. Unless I end up not going at all and just going to work.' He looked at her and she could tell he felt he had been too candid with her.

'You really should go to university. It's an eye-opener, if nothing else, and you've got plenty of time to go to work. Enjoy yourself.' She regarded him with a close gaze.

'I've worked in a shop before, on a Saturday. It was a chemist's, so I've dealt in aftershaves and things before.' He was quickly volunteering the information and seemed confused that Karen had gone into a wistful recollection of her college days and had not asked him any proper interview questions.

'How long did you work at the chemist?' she asked, her right hand disappearing discreetly under her desk, the thumb hovering over the material of her skirt.

'Six months,' he said to her, appearing to get into some sort of question-answering mode that his careers officer had probably shown him.

'Did you operate a till, process credit-card transactions, that sort of thing?'

'Yes, all of that, and sometimes I would advise people on what brand of aftershave or perfume to buy – people who were buying presents usually.'

'What's your favourite aftershave?' she asked him, hoping it would seem relevant.

'Armani,' he said and then added an after-thought: 'It's lovely.'

'Favourite woman's perfume?'

'That new Donna Karan is different. It almost smells like new suede.'

She smiled, wondering if he had rehearsed these answers, actually thinking someone would ask him what his favourite fragrances were. She had run out of things she could ask him and decided it was time to ask the important questions.

'Do you have a girlfriend, Glenn?'

'Not at the moment,' he answered awkwardly, a trace of suspicion in his voice.

'A boyfriend?'

'No,' he strained, as though all the air had been slowly syphoning from the room throughout their conversation.

'But you'd quite like to fuck me, wouldn't you?'

He stared at her in silence, the question appearing to fly at him like a jab, knocking him over and leaving him reeling.

'Don't worry,' she said, 'it's not an interview

question.'

Still the silence persisted and Karen was afraid he might burst as he sat there, his features all going awry and his skin reddening.

'I'm serious,' she said to him. 'Would you like to fuck me? I bet you read about this sort of thing all the time. Well, now's your chance to make it happen. Would you like to fuck me?'

'I . . . uh . . . I . . .'

'Glenn, I'd like to fuck you, I'll be honest. There's no point in messing about.'

'Here?' he asked her, and she knew she had him, and so did her pussy as it tightened between her legs ready to spring into action.

'Unless you have somewhere else in mind. The window-ledge?'

Karen eyed him and then with a single and dramatic motion of her arm, she swept her desk clean. All her papers, the phone, her calculator and her mobile phone crashed to the floor in a cacophony, Glenn looking around all the while as though he expected someone to burst in on them. Cleared of everything, the desk looked bigger and much more inviting. The blinds were pulled and tilted just enough to allow sunlight in but nothing else – certainly not any prying eyes from across the square. She stood up to go round the desk and he stood also.

'Stay,' she said shortly, and he fell back into his chair.

She sat on the edge of her desk, less than a foot from him, and ran her eyes over him. A green plaid shirt, very Ralph Lauren, and a pair of bottle-green chinos, even more very Ralph Lauren. He wore Timberland shoes and green socks that matched his shirt, an obvious attempt at co-ordination for the purposes of interview.

Karen put one foot either side of him on the edge of his chair, her skirt falling into the hollow of her legs. She inhaled, as though she were a conductor wielding a baton before an enormous orchestra, and she concentrated hard. While he looked on, Karen gently moved the skirt over her crotch, the sound of fabric on fabric filling the small space between them. She pushed her feet into the sides of the chair, the insteps of her shoes touching the outside of his bum on each side and it felt tight. He held her legs and his palms made cups around her calves, squeezing them with a forcefulness and passion.

As she let her head fall back a degree, she hitched the skirt up, pulling her legs back from him a fraction and lifting them. The skirt fell back against her to reveal white panties. His eyes lit and she saw him skip a breath, his own need now evident from the distended state of the front of his chinos. Karen circled her finger over the white cloth where it covered her smouldering sex. The crotch of her knickers was warm and a moistness was seeping through from the inside to the out. She kicked off each of her shoes in turn. With her bare right foot, she explored the front of Glenn's trousers, not having to search too far for the expected hardness.

After she had toyed with him just enough, she re-positioned her legs and turned her attention back to herself. She shifted the mound of her pussy back and forth under her own insistent and attentive touch, carefully kindling as though she were nursing a very delicate instrument in her hands which would gradually assume a much more menacing and forceful hunger to which they would both yield. The tip of her thumb concentrated in the vicinity of her clitoris, which rose and swelled as if it were trying to break through the soft damp fabric that arrested its development. Karen pushed her thumb into the elastic on the leg and ran it up her slit, pushing it aside and sliding easily up the well-lubricated pathway, attacking her clitoris from underneath before withdrawing the digit.

'Why don't you take them off?'

It was Glenn, bug-eyed and breathing fast.

'Why don't *you* take them off?' she replied immediately.

He leaned forward in the chair and she listened to the sound his behind made against the shiny blue leather as he reached for her knickers. Karen placed a hand either side of her on the edge of the desk and raised her bottom as Glenn whisked her panties down with the sort of speed and enthusiasm that only an eighteen-year-old could manage. Richard would have been too busy reading the label on her panties rather than staring at her pussy in the way Glenn was at that moment, fascinated and as though he were looking over the edge of some precipice, instinctively drawn towards it. Karen continued to raise herself up, hands on the desk and feet on the chair, arching her back and pushing herself up towards him, tantalising him. She dropped her behind, sitting on the edge of the desk so her legs hung over it and Glenn abruptly stood and pushed himself against her.

As he kissed her, his hands rode her skirt up around her hips and toyed with them and the outsides of her thighs, gradually encircling and approaching her where she most wanted him to. She wrapped her legs around him and squeezed him into her, the cotton feel of his chinos silken against her bared pussy, the hardness of an eager and youthful cock scarcely concealed by it. With haste, she pushed him away and undid his trousers in her favourite zipper, belt and button combination, eyeing his legs as they were revealed from under the descending trousers. He wore loose boxers of a blue denim material that had been washed to a delicate fade, a dark damp patch visible on the otherwise pristine surface of them. She felt the top of his bum just protruding from the boxers as she ran her fingers over the waistband and she pushed her hand in, feeling the warmth and the taut smoothness of one of his buttocks, the sensation sending a deep-seated spasm through her as the lust took hold.

She held him tightly as they covered each other in

hot panting breaths and she whispered hotly into his ear, 'What would you like to do to me, you dirty boy?'

He ignored her and continued to nuzzle at her collar-bone and the part of her neck that was exposed from beneath her blouse.

'There must be something,' she whispered, wondering suddenly if he was a virgin, although doubting that a cute boy like this could be at his age.

'What?' she said, not hearing him when he mumbled against her ear.

'I'd like to spank you,' he whispered, avoiding her eyes.

Karen frowned to nowhere or no one in the room, slightly taken aback by his forwardness and the timorous way he couched it. An order barked in a whisper. She pushed him back and looked at him and he had trouble meeting her gaze, obviously embarrassed. Karen turned, hitched her skirt up around her waist and bent over the edge of her desk.

His request may have been timid but once she was over the desk, he seemed to find an assurance that had escaped him previously. She felt him grip the back of her skirt and jerk it, exposing her rear fully, and then he gave it a solid and firm slap that had a gentle weight behind it. As the hand landed, it caused a ripple in her behind and the warmth quickly spread under where he had left his palm. It was not a hard slap and there was no pain as such, only something more pleasurable. Karen stretched her arms and held on to the sides of the desk, raising herself on tiptoes and making the flesh of her buttocks taut. The next smack was quicker, a faint whistle as his hand travelled through the air, and then a sharp crack that was again square on the centre of her bottom.

Against the solid wooden edge of her desk, Karen's pussy was lifted by the ridge, and as he spanked her, she was pushed against it with just enough force to make her squirm. Soon her rear end began to tingle and heat up. She knew he would be able to see her pussy from behind, pouting invitingly, and she hoped it would entice him. His left hand was still holding up her skirt and the right was now fondling her and soothing the fire he was creating on her cheeks and the wetness he was causing between her legs. After his hand rained on her several times, she felt the zip and buttons on her skirt being undone and then it was removed from her.

For a second or two, he was not touching her and she heard him remove his underwear. From behind, the smooth head of an unfamiliar cock explored her pussy-lips, tracing up and down them, hot hard flesh against soft lubricated folds of skin. As the head of it parted her, fluid escaped and she gripped the edges of the desk tighter. While his cock was delving, his hand slapped down and caught her on the top of her buttock, obviously falling from above rather than directly from behind as it had done previously. He had pushed her blouse up and her back was exposed, his hands gently caressing it and rubbing the skin as though applying talcum powder. Every now and then, the softness and intimacy of the gesture would be broken by a strike to her behind. Karen enjoyed the switches between gentle and firm, his hand teasing her and then rudely awakening her. She waited for the moment when his probing cock would stir her in the same fashion and gripped on to the desk in anticipation.

A finger, his index, popped itself slyly inside her. More deft and agile than the cock, it probed her pussy, searching her lips and entering her vagina, the walls yielding wetly to it. His finger tested her, gauged her depth and flexibility as it penetrated her, the side to side movements of it causing her to cry out for the cock that would fill her. The shape and the crook of his finger felt larger than they were, the sensitivity of her vagina magnifying their size. The sensation of pleasure it created in her felt like a noise that was slowly growing louder and louder, reaching a din that would deafen her.

'I want to see you fuck me,' she said to him, the words

issuing from her suddenly, the finger in her hesitating and then withdrawing.

Karen stood upright, removed her blouse and bra, and turned naked to face him. He stood, hands hanging loosely at his sides and cock protruding from under his shirt. His legs were muscular and well shaped, like a runner's or a cyclist's. She approached him and gently undid his shirt, starting with the buttons on the cuffs and then running from the neck downwards. As she removed his shirt, he was kicking off the Timberlands and working his trousers and underwear off his ankles. When they were both naked, he reached and fondled her breasts, tweaking at the nipples. She looked at his own nipples, small and hard circles on his defined chest.

She gripped his cock and exerted pressure on it, feeling it pulse in her hand, and then she worked his foreskin back and forth, his own fluid making the action slick and hot. The size and heat of it were perfect and she masturbated him gently as she imagined the feel of his bone-like member burrowing into her, propelled by the force of his enthusiastic and youthful body. Already she envisioned his orgasm, the tight and circumscribed nature of it as he released himself so precisely and agonisingly into her, his cock palpitating inside her and his semen spurting deeply, his whole body racked by the effort required to bring him to that point. She looked at him and imagined it all, saw it foreshadowed in the studious and concentrated manner of his face as she manipulated him with her fingers.

The desk was firm against her back. Karen lay with her feet over the edge and she re-positioned herself several times before she was happy with the position of her body and the angle at which she would be able to receive Glenn as he stood and thrust into her. Her recently spanked bottom was on the edge of her desk and her pussy was up at almost the perfect height for Glenn to crouch slightly and enter her, which, with little ceremony or delay, he did.

Karen lifted her head and watched him, wanting to see what was responsible for the delightful invasion she was feeling. She revelled in his face, a mixture of attention and reverie, and she felt completely taken by him, in his image and his physical nature. The cock which she had been handling only moments earlier was now passing through the lips of her pussy. As it made its slow and aching journey, she dropped her head back, the vision of him, his strong torso tensing and his long hair falling into his face, still imprinted on her mind. He put his hands on to her pelvis and came to rest against her, his balls against her. A long and noisy sigh escaped her and she realised that she had been holding her breath all the while he had penetrated her. Now, as though to make room for him in her, she was exhaling. She rippled herself around him and allowed her legs to part wider.

With a definite and positive stroke, he fucked her. If this had been Richard or Alan, she would have thought they were making love. But here was an eighteen-year-old who had mistakenly wandered into her office and with whom she had flirted and then been spanked by as she bent over her desk. What they were doing now, quite simply, was fucking – and Karen was loving every moment of it. Each lunge he made into her and the animalistic sound that accompanied it. The breach he made into her and the way it threw her pussy into a tumult left her with nowhere to hide from him as he found new depths and different speeds and intensities with which to reach them. Karen lay back and let him do the work, her own hand occasionally wandering to her clitoris to comfort it.

The force of his movements pushed her up and down the surface of her desk, her back moving an inch or two against the grained leather of the inset. Her toes just touched the floor, pointed towards it like a ballet dancer about to pirouette. As his cock drove home, her toes left the floor for a second before dropping back to make a soft contact with the carpet. His hips and pelvic area felt hot and sweaty as they banged into her and, as his body slapped against hers, a dull thud issued from the point of contact. She was driven back by the thrust, her legs opening slightly wider each time, roused from their gently dangling position.

Karen was impressed and surprised at his stamina, having braced herself for a somewhat quicker experience. The continued and methodical nature of his technique was exciting as she felt herself gradually lose all method and control of her own, ready to explode in a confused and disorganised frenzy. Against his ordered pattern she would offer abandon and offer to take him there with her.

Although she could not put a time on it, Karen imagined he must have been there for almost ten minutes, the hard cock in the soft warm depths. She sensed he was close to relinquishing the grip he had kept on his desire for so long, as though he had been holding his breath in the same way she had earlier as he had entered her. The fucking became more intense, a deep fervour holding them both and surrounding their bodies in a kind of heat that bound them together.

His orgasm was as she had imagined it earlier. The continuity of his movements was gone and he surrendered to it as he jerked and snatched his body upwards as though trying to lift himself off the ground. His hair flicked wildly around his face which was a contorted scowl of elation and the muscles in his shoulders and upper arms tensed and un-tensed in time with his flow into her. He yelped helplessly, on display for her and unable to hide his feelings. His semen was warm as it shot into her in several short pulses. She imagined the head of his cock, the eye opening as it forced his come from deep in him, flooding her pussy. As he came, he continued to jog his cock in her pussy, the movements much shorter and erratic. When he withdrew, she looked up and saw his pubic hair matted with juices, his cock slicked with a shining film and its head displaying a pearl of his semen.

Breathing heavily, his cock still juddering, Glenn reached down and set to work on her. He masturbated her furiously and she felt his come inside of her as he centred on her clitoris, every now and then pushing a finger into her. She shifted her gaze between his hand and his face, transfixed by what he was doing to her. Her orgasm was moments away, her rear was still warm from the spanking and her pussy still reverberating from the presence of his cock. Now, with his finger, he was finishing what she had started. In a gentle swell, she felt the climax stir inside, relieved that she was so close and already wistful at the thought that it would soon be over.

Her orgasm galvanised her; vagina moving powerfully and of its own accord, Karen subordinated to its movements and the willing victim of the wave it sent through her. She rocked and squirmed against the desk. As Glenn's hand practically grasped at her, it was as if he were trying to hold on to her very self, preventing her escape. She clung to the orgasm as if she had her arms around it and was slowly letting it release. The movements of his fingers produced stimulation in a way Karen was barely aware of. She balanced off the edge of the desk in a breathless daze.

'Is this the room for the interview?' he asked her again.

Karen wondered how long the fantasy had taken and for what length of time she had sat at her desk, staring through him and projecting his image in her mind.

'Come on in,' she said to him, standing and adjusting her skirt.

Chapter Sixteen

'WHAT TIME'S HE coming?' Caroline asked her.

Karen checked her watch. It was seven-forty.

'At eight-thirty – there's no "about" with Alan. It will be eight-thirty exactly.'

Karen fitted her earring and flicked her hair with her hand, shaking her hair and letting it settle naturally.

'I don't know why you changed. You looked fine as you were,' Caroline said, appraising her thoughtfully.

'That was my interview suit,' she told her.

'For the media, you mean?'

Karen had been interviewed by one of the Sunday supplements in connection with The Garden and with the Hamiltons fragrance. It was a useful piece of free publicity and she had given little away in the interview, hoping that what detail she did give would entice women to come along. Several of the papers were going to cover the launch party and several had been pointedly refused access.

'Exactly. For the good lady of the press. How do I look?'

'You look fine. I haven't seen you this jumpy since . . . well, ever, I suppose. This is the first time he's ever been here?' Caroline asked, though she knew the answer.

'Yes. And the last. I feel awful about this, but I think it's going to be the best way.' Karen looked at herself in the mirror, hoping her YSL trouser suit had the requisite proportions of hardness and homeliness she felt the task would require. A bitch in couture was better than a bitch in nothing at all.

'You know best. He seems like a nice guy, very polite. He spends a lot of time with Daniel.'

'Caroline, do you flutter your eyelids like that when Avendon is actually there? This is a bit schoolgirl, you know? I'll tell Daniel you're on Prozac if you like.'

Much to Karen's somewhat guilty surprise, the job she had arranged for Caroline at Hamiltons had worked out well. Caroline was enjoying it, simpering on about Daniel, using it as a way of relieving the monotony of filing, and Daniel seemed to like her. She wondered what would happen when the project was over. There was not a place for Caroline in The Garden and Karen had been keeping it from her that the auditions, as they were being called, had already happened for the women. They were left looking for five token men and that would happen the next day.

'Of course I don't flutter at him. Anyway, I'll make myself scarce.'

'Are you sure you don't mind?'

'Karen, it's your flat. I'm going to see a few of the girls from one of my old jobs. I'll be fine and I'll have more fun than you by the sound of it.'

'Promise me you're not sneaking off to see Gareth.'

'Karen. I won't be back until late.'

There was a buzz on the doorbell and they both froze and looked at each other, uncertain of what to do. Karen realised how jumpy she was. It normally took more than a doorbell to put her off her stride.

'Is it him?' Caroline asked.

'Too early for Alan,' Karen said, composing herself and going to the entry-phone.

'Delivery for Miss Taylor,' a voice crackled.

'Come on up,' she said, buzzing the front door.

It was a huge arrangement of orchids. Karen thanked the delivery boy and closed the door.

'Who are they from?' Caroline asked, sounding

curious and excited at once.

Karen looked at the card and smiled, handing it to Caroline who read it out.

'I'm in town next week and wondered if there was going to be a sequel to our movie. Do I at least get invited to the party? Chris N.' Caroline looked at her. 'Who's Chris N?'

'Somebody I met in New York, a friend of a friend.'

'Hmm. And does he get an invite to the party? You'll be a free agent again by then, won't you?' Caroline said.

'All being well,' Karen said, the first smattering of doubt staining her resolve.

When she had gone, Karen started to wish Caroline had stayed a while longer. She did not relish the prospect of fidgeting for the next thirty-five minutes while she waited for Alan to arrive. She quickly arranged the flowers in one of her many oversized and normally unused vases and was about to fix herself a drink when the buzzer rang. Only eight o'clock. She buzzed the building front door and waited for the knock on her front door, going to the fridge while she did.

'Hi.' It was Richard. He walked casually in, kissing her on the cheek on his way past.

Karen shut the door and quickly said to him, 'What are you doing here? I thought you were at a party at the gym?'

'I didn't fancy it. I wanted to see you. The pant-suit is very retro, by the way. Nice. YSL?'

She ignored him, flustered and angry. She had twenty-five minutes to get rid of him, but he had already planted himself on the sofa and did not look likely to move in any short space of time. She checked her watch, the second hand seeming to have trebled its speed, and she thought of Alan on his way to see her. This would not be a pretty scene at all.

'Let's do something really horny,' she said to him, her mind finding a foothold.

'Like what?' he asked her, a willing grin on his face.

She grabbed his hand and pulled him off the sofa,

dragging him down the hall, ignoring her own bedroom, and on into Caroline's room. She took his linen jacket off and unbuttoned the shirt, still managing to notice in the rush that it was Comme des Garçons. She told him to kick off his shoes and then popped the buttons on the fly of his Katharine Hamnett jeans and took him out of them and his 2XisT underwear. She decided to leave his socks on.

'I'll be right back. Lie down,' she said to him.

Scrabbling in the wardrobe of her own bedroom, she found what she was looking for and returned.

He looked at her with surprise as she produced a pair of handcuffs. She had bought them from a tacky tourist shop in Oxford Street.

'This is interesting,' he said, as she clicked one of the bracelets shut on his wrist and brought his hands up to thread the cuffs through the brass bedstead before locking his other wrist in.

'It gets better,' she said, making several small knots into one large ball at the centre of an Hermès scarf. She pushed the knot into his mouth and tied the gag gently at first, gradually pulling it tighter. She put her finger to her lips, indicating for him to be quiet. As a final touch, she placed a blindfold on him, the one from the courtesy kit given to her on the flight to New York. She looked at him, his naked virile body locked to the spare bed, gagged and blindfolded, the blindfold bearing a single and inappropriate word. Virgin.

The gentle tumescence of his cock was an indication that he was finding the experience not unpleasant. She sat on the edge of the bed and touched him, squeezing and fondling his balls as she watched him become erect, looking at her watch as she did so. She pinched one of his balls and from behind the gag he gave a yelp. She brought her head down and breathed over his cock, letting the hot air from her mouth circulate around him. She blew, his pubic hair moving from the draught she created, but she did not touch his cock.

The doorbell rang. Richard tensed on the bed.

'Don't worry, I'll get rid of them,' she said, jumping off the bed and closing the door behind her.

The first time Alan had been early or late for anything, she thought to herself, buzzing the front door to let him in the building. She rearranged herself and waited. He knocked on the door.

'Hello,' he said to her cheerfully, flowers in hand.

'Oh darling, let's do something really dirty,' she said, grabbing him by the lapel and hauling him through the door.

Less than five minutes later, he was in her bedroom, tied to the headboard and gagged, another scarf making do as a blindfold.

It was going to be a double header.

'I'll be back,' she said to Alan.

Karen went to the kitchen and hastily gathered several items from the fridge. In the hallway, the doors of the spare room with Richard and her room with Alan across from each other, Karen removed all of her clothes and tried to decide which door to choose.

'Okay,' she said to Richard. 'Let's play.'

His cock was still quite firm, like his body, and she felt like jumping on top of it there and then and riding it. But she could not.

'I'm naked. And I have some presents for you. I'm going to give them to you one at a time and you have to be a quiet boy. Do you understand?'

He nodded obediently and she smiled, pulling the foil lid from a carton of peach yoghurt, low fat of course. She scooped some up in her fingers and slathered it over his cock, a thin layer making it glisten in the light of the room and the member hardening under her touch. He seethed from the coldness of it, moving his legs around, the muscles in them rippling as he did so, those on his arms taut from the position in which he was cuffed. She applied more to him and he became fully aroused. Greedily and quickly, she licked and sucked at him, the peach flavour of the yoghurt mingling with his own taste. Soon, his cock was bare once more, no trace of what had covered him only seconds earlier. He pushed his crotch upwards, imploring her for more.

'You need to cool off,' she said to him, picking an ice-cube from the bowl she had brought with her and quickly inserting it into his rear, the wetness providing its own lubrication. He whined and she leapt off the bed, leaving the room and crossing the hall.

'Now,' she said to Alan, 'we're going to play and you have to be a nice quiet boy, understand?'

With a similar obedience to Richard, he nodded. His cock was not as animated as Richard's had been. She would soon rectify that. She knelt between his legs and massaged him with her deft fingers, pulling his foreskin back and forth over the head of his cock, occasionally applying pressure. It enlarged with her gentle ministrations and she was not as rough or as quick as she had been on Richard. When he was full and ready, she opened the bottle of Absolut she had removed from the freezer, took a large swig and gargled with it, the heady liquid like ice in her mouth. She swallowed half of what was in her mouth, needing the alcohol, and quickly dipped her head down to suck him, not letting the remaining vodka escape.

His body twisted and writhed – the sensation must have been a mixture of cold and sharp, the temperature of the vodka so ice cold and the alcohol a stinging pleasure. She rinsed it around in her mouth, letting it wash around his cock, swishing it back and forth, the feel of it tingling in her mouth. She imagined how that must have translated to the delicate collection of nerve-endings on Alan's cock. She threw her head back and swallowed the last of the spirit and was then back on him, lathing at his shaft and taking him deep into her. She grabbed his ball sac and closed her hand around it, feeling how the testicles moved around and off each other.

'Hold tight and I'll be right back.'

There was a damp cold patch on the duvet beneath

Richard. His cock was still erect and he wriggled when he heard her enter, trying to say something. She told him to be quiet.

'Listen to me,' she said. 'Can you hear what I'm doing?'

He became very silent and very still on the bed, no further sounds coming from his mouth or from any movements of his body. The only sound left in the room was that of Karen's hand, insinuating itself into her pussy, parting the lips and directing its attention towards her clitoris. The sounds she made were delicious, a slow and wet labial rhythm, the inside of her vagina pulsing with an appetite for him. She looked at him and saw the strain his cock was under, pushed from the inside by the coursing of his blood. He began to move again, as though trying to compensate for his inability to touch himself and her lack of touch on him.

Karen climbed over him, resting her hands on his chest and straddling his groin, her pussy far from his cock. She sank an inch and then another inch. Still there was no contact between her pussy and his unyielding cock, but Karen could feel the heat transferring between their bodies. With great care and attention, as though trying to thread a needle, she lowered her body by the millimetre. Her warm lips just brushed the underside of his cock and she pulled back the instant he tried to move upwards towards her.

'That's not allowed,' she told him.

Again she dropped her body and allowed more and longer contact, but still only seconds in time and fractions of a touch. Richard snorted through his nose, sounding both inflamed and frustrated, his cock similarly angry and fit to burst. She skimmed her pussy-lips all the way along the underside of his shaft, his cock pressed solidly back against his stomach, supporting herself on her knees and arms as she did so. Her desire was now stronger than her need to tease him and she let the touch become heavier and the contact-time longer, using his cock to stimulate herself. She became wetter and her pussy felt heavier, pulled by gravity and by the lure of his cock. She was about to reach, hold him upright, and descend on to his shaft when she remembered Alan.

'I'm going to come back when you've calmed down and then fuck you stupid,' she whispered to Richard, ignoring the exasperated murmur that emitted from him.

In the hall, she paused for breath. What had started out as a game for her, a way of trying to keep the both of them happy, had now started to make its demands on her. Her pussy was alight with the urge to be penetrated and in her mind she anticipated the power of the orgasm she would be able to unleash if she could only spend long enough with either of them to get there. Of course, there being two of them presented the opportunity for her to do just that, twice.

'I'm naughty, don't you think, Alan? Getting you all hot and then running off and leaving you. I should be punished. There's a hairbrush on the dresser here, a nice round one.'

She picked it up and spanked it solidly against one of her buttocks, the stinging sensation spreading fast across the cheek. She applied it to herself several more times, getting the hang of it. She changed hands and chastised her other buttock, crying out in a small and coquettish voice, deliberately trying to excite Alan as he lay on the bed. It was working. He was clenching and unclenching his buttocks, the motion pushing his cock up in the air while his feet moved about restlessly on the bed.

When her backside was glowing from the self-inflicted paddling she had supplied with the hair-brush, she moved closer to the bed and inspected him. His body was exceptional for a man his age, the curve and line of it dense and masculine, the limbs sturdy. She rubbed herself, the need now strong. She could not wait any longer. She mounted the bed and him simultaneously and with little grace or aplomb, grabbed his cock and pushed it inside her. Her pussy was moist and ready, his member intimating itself into her with an ease that was a joy. Karen settled on to him, not stopping her descent until their bodies forced her to stop, joined at the groin.

With her hands on his sides, she moved furiously, using the spring of the mattress to give her the required leverage, the bed squeaking in a fast whine as she did so. She made no allowance for passion, that emotion having long since surrendered to simple and unbridled lust. She ground herself into him, feeling the rub of him against her, the walls of her vagina alive to the sensations it was giving her, her clitoris quivering. She forced him in and out of her with a motion that was unswerving and without compassion for him or his needs. Karen enjoyed using him like this and knew she would return to him and finish him off when she was ready.

Her orgasm came like a dream in the night; sudden and shocking, it roused her and sent signals all over her body. She wailed and threw her body about, arms flailing, but her pussy still firmly planted on Alan's cock, using it as a pivot, a stable point from which to release herself. The freedom of her movements and the liberation of the orgasm were contrasted by Alan, rooted to the bed and bound to it, unable to do much except give her pleasure. She used him for a while longer and then cruelly deprived him of her, lifting herself off and looking at the desperate and quivering member she left in her wake, already missing her pussy. He seemed almost resigned to his fate, as though he had caught on to the rules of the game.

She kissed him on the cheek, in the area of skin between the blindfold and the gag. 'I'm going to let you think about me for a little while,' she intoned breathily, 'and then I'm coming back to give you the orgasm of your life.'

'Show time,' she said to Richard. 'I need you harder

than that. Come on, imagine me here ready to sit on you. That's better, some signs of life down there.'

Richard was gritting his teeth around the gag, his arms straining against the cuffs, as he forced his cock to become erect of its own accord. Karen watched, fascinated by the way it changed size before her very eyes like a magic trick. Her pussy was still ringing from her orgasm, the force of it echoing through her. It was good to have a hard cock in front of her and one in reserve in her own bedroom.

Karen squatted over Richard, one hand on his chest and the other lifting his cock. She rested his phallus at the opening of her vagina, letting it just wait there as she anticipated the feel of it. As always, the anticipation was sweet but the reality of the penetration was sweeter. She took him into her, made him a part of her by allowing him access to her deepest and most intimate space as though she were sharing it with him. His cock was desperately hard, its length and width perfectly expanding and plumbing her. Riding him slowly at first, she tantalised him and herself. Richard started to groan virtually as soon as he was inside her, small sob-like sounds that were pleading with her to release him from the most important shackle of all and allow him to come. Massaging her clitoris with adept fingers, Karen brought herself as near to the edge as she could without toppling over it and going into free-fall, trying to time herself with him.

Speeding up her lunges on to him and on the caress of her clitoris, she felt her second orgasm fill the tracks of the first. Where the first had boiled over, the second was from deeper within, shaking her at the foundation and making her dizzy. She made less noise, keeping it to and for herself, balling the pressure up and then letting it release in carefully timed bursts, oblivious to Richard and to the room around her. Bound and gagged by her own passion, she was both its prisoner and its guard, alternating between tightly controlled sensations and untrammelled pleasure.

When she heard him shout from behind his muzzle, she slipped him out of her and masturbated him with a cruel and heartless slowness, prolonging the agony for him. His whole body froze and seemed to bury itself into the mattress as though a large invisible weight were bearing down on him. The weight of his orgasm. As the first shot of semen left him, Karen discarded his cock and left him to it. He threw his head from side to side and writhed, arching his back up off the bed and twisting his torso before finally banging his rear up and down off the bed, desperate to try and continue ejaculating unaided by her and pushed only by himself. It was agonising even to watch and Karen quietly left him as he covered his stomach with his own semen.

With Alan, she was kinder. With a tenderness and a care that was a complete contrast, she held Alan in her hands and stroked and rubbed him. It was a pleasant way to come down from her own orgasms, to gently bring Alan to one of his own. Karen reached out with a thumb and two fingers and held Alan. She pulled his foreskin as far back as it would go, making his glans look big as the blood pumped in. Moving her fingers up and down, the foreskin sliding back and forth, she masturbated Alan in a way that she was sure would be completely different to how he did it himself. She must have held his cock differently and moved it slower or faster than Alan would have. Perhaps the feeling of a different hand performing a task so familiar to him, the insistence of a rhythm so different from one that was naturally his own, would be like a drum with a new beat.

The semen flowed out of him like a small stream. Karen squeezed and let her fingers concentrate on moving his foreskin back and forth over his phallus. Rather than erupting from him, it seeped out and ran over her fingers. Clenching her whole hand around it, she felt the warm semen course over the back of her hand, a slightly white fluid with a familiar and exciting smell. The movements Alan made were tight and discreet, in keeping with the gentle ebb of his come, and Karen continued to grip and coax him until there was nothing left but the movement of her hand.

Sitting on the floor in the hallway, she was tired and spent. Two was fun, but it was hard work and she had not realised just how hard until that moment. Right there and then, in simple practical terms, Richard would be the easiest to get rid of, simply by telling him that getting dressed and leaving immediately was part of the high-class prostitute fantasy. She would return to him, wipe him down and put his underwear and trousers back on before freeing him. Easy. But she could hardly untie Alan and tell him that while she'd enjoyed herself, it was all over and could he please leave. Not least of all because she was not entirely sure she wanted him to leave.

Karen realised that she would have to make a choice and she would have to make it soon.

Chapter Seventeen

IT WAS TWENTY minutes after two in the afternoon and Karen was reluctantly admitting to herself that trying to find five men to act as staff in The Garden had not been as exciting as she had imagined. Twenty-five hopefuls, including ten from Hamiltons, had arrived at eight-fifteen that morning as instructed. Most had come from agencies and were a range of ages, all with the criterion that they were, or almost were, model handsome. Two or three others had come on recommendation, boyfriends of women or men at Hamiltons.

Group exercises and role plays were conducted, with Stephen Jones, the personnel director, organising, supervising and taking notes. He had gone on at Karen about psychometric testing and targeted selection, wanting to be even more involved than he was. Even to her untrained eye, it had been obvious to Karen who would be most likely to fit in with the spirit and atmosphere she was trying to create in The Garden. As she watched, so she had already formed some opinions about who would be the first to go and was secretly pleased when she found that her assessment agreed very closely with Stephen's. She had held firm over only one person, reminding Stephen first gently and then strongly that his role was advisory only. With him as advisor, Gabrielle as consultant and David as assistant, the whole Garden had become a juggling act. She watched David and Stephen conferring over something, their clipboards touching, and she sighed to herself. The last thing The Garden needed was men with clipboards. Just a while longer, she told herself, and then with The Garden up and running she would be able to rise above compromise.

One thing had surprised her. That Richard had shown almost no interest in working in The Garden. Looking at the twenty-five who had streamed through the door that morning, Karen was sure, even allowing for her bias, that Richard was far cuter than any of them. Karen could understand that he wanted to stay around men's clothes as they were very much his life and she also thought he did not like the idea of working directly for her. It was a shame he had not come along in any case as he may have been able to spice the auditions up slightly.

It had not been without event, though. Someone called Michael had marched in wearing full drag and a pair of stilettos which, along with his legs, Karen would have killed for. To a dumbstruck room he proudly announced, 'My name's Christie and I enjoy being a woman ... because I can.' Karen had to politely explain that they had found all the women they needed, only to be told Christie was, apparently, all the woman anyone needed. Several minutes of discussion, some of it quite political, had followed, and Michael/Christie had left happy, a point of some sort having been made. Perhaps when we've been running a few months and are successful, Karen thought to herself. She had been tempted to include him just to annoy Stephen, messing up all his little forms and quizzes.

It was when Karen and Gabrielle had whittled the twenty-five down to ten and David had asked her if there was going to be a swim-wear round that it occurred to Karen that the whole thing had gone from interview to audition to beauty pageant in fairly swift succession. David seemed to be having more fun than she and Gabrielle, herding the men around and giving them directions. The women had all been selected over a week earlier, including those who would act as team leaders. The five males would add some drapery, what David referred to as 'eye candy'. Karen was the only real judge as Gabrielle seemed indifferent to the process, sometimes asking a bizarre question that would floor someone completely, like the date of their mother's birthday. For Karen, it was the sort of situation where she would know what she was looking for once she saw it. All of the original twenty-five were perfectly fine, a good range of ages, colours and creeds, but she felt the need to make the selection based on more than just how good someone looked. Staff would be all important in The Garden.

The Garden would open in ten days' time. Most of the shop-fitting work had been done, with a few minor adjustments required, but everything else was sound and on time. Alan and Avendon had been impressed and Gabrielle, Karen noticed, had not been slow in trying to reflect as much of the glory as possible on to herself. Gabrielle was confusing, her attitudes ranging from passion for The Garden to disinterest in it, all the way to outright opposition.

The auditions were being held in The Garden itself, which looked like a skeleton with all the rails and cabinets empty of stock, the odd logo still to go on a wall. Karen and Gabrielle sat near the bar on plastic tables and chairs, the fountain installed but not yet running, using one of the areas that would hold women's designs to interview and talk to the candidates. An overhead projector and a screen had been set up for the afternoon and Stephen Jones was gone, his work accomplished. They had told everyone who was and was not being asked back after lunch and they readied themselves for the afternoon, waiting to whittle the ten down to five.

'Who do you want to see first?' David asked.

'Who would you pick first?' she asked him.

'Graham, definitely,' came an enthusiastic response.

'For the interview, I mean,' she intoned.

'Still Graham,' he smiled.

'Graham it is. Send him in.'

David went to fetch him and Karen looked over her notes and the CV and file she had been sent on Graham. He was thirty-three, tall, well-built and had modelled. With a degree in fashion and currently working a bar-job and a day-job in a shop, he was similar to everyone else, all looking to step up a rung from where they were. He had certainly made an impression on David, who had practically waltzed out of the room. Graham reminded Karen of the beefy black models Robert Mapplethorpe had photographed, with his well crafted features and hair cut close to his head.

'What did you think of this one?' Karen asked Gabrielle, making a token gesture towards her involvement in the process.

'He seemed very personable to me and attractive, but then all ten of them are attractive in their different ways. It's such a shame we couldn't employ them all.'

Each of the successful candidates from the morning had been given some blank transparencies and pens and told to come back after lunch and give a short five-to ten-minute presentation chosen from a list of subjects all related in some way to women's fashion. All twenty-five had been forewarned about it in the letters they received, so no one had any excuse, other than lack of interest, for not being prepared.

David lingered in the room for a second or two longer than he needed to, making a second unnecessary offer of coffee before leaving, Gabrielle seemingly oblivious to all around her. Karen wondered where Gabrielle went during these bouts of preoccupation.

'Graham, nice to see you again. Karen Taylor, and this is Gabrielle. I hope the fun and games this morning weren't too wearing?'

'No. I took a module at college on management and a

lot of the things this morning were familiar. I've done this sort of thing before.'

He had donned a pair of thin-framed tortoise-shell glasses that Karen did not remember seeing on him that morning and she was intrigued as to whether or not they had real lenses in them or were just ornamentation to make him look serious for the interview.

'Where did you model?' Gabrielle asked him.

'I did some catwalk at London Fashion Week two years ago and I've done some photographic for hair salons. Last time was for *Arena*, six months ago for a feature on suits. I'd tell you what month, but a feature on suits could be any month with them.'

'Obviously you've had a chance to read the covering information on The Garden and you heard the presentation this morning. Are there any immediate questions you have?' Karen asked him.

'There are a few, but why don't I do the presentation first and then we can talk afterwards,' he said, standing and producing slides. 'I've decided to focus on accessories, bags in particular . . .'

Graham's presentation came in at almost exactly ten minutes. He was knowledgeable and funny, a relaxed presenter who made Karen feel as at ease as he seemed to be. When he was done, they talked for twenty minutes, with an equal flow of questions, and Karen felt herself grudgingly acknowledge David's judgement, however different his motivations had been.

'Just finally,' Karen said. 'We've had these sniff cards of various different fragrances made up specially. They're all famous names, some men's and some women's. Just give them a smell and say which you think are for men and which are for women.'

'That simple?' he asked confidently.

He picked up a card and sniffed it. 'Polo Ralph Lauren, men.'

The next. 'Eternity, Calvin Klein, women.'

He tutted when he smelled the next card. 'Chanel

No. 5, please.'

'Oh, this is cheeky, it's Old Spice, isn't it. Men.'

After he had been through all eight cards and identified them by name, Karen had an impressed look on her face.

'You're not a perfumer in your spare time by any chance?' she asked, half-seriously.

'Fragrances are like a hobby for me.'

She handed him one final one and he raised it to his nose, concentrating hard.

'You've got me on this one. I don't know it,' he said eventually.

'Instinctively, would you say for a man or a woman, forgetting that you don't know who it's by.'

'Actually, it's hard to tell. I'm tempted to say either.'

He paused for a moment and a look of recognition seemed to dawn over his face.

'It's the new unisex one Hamiltons is launching, isn't it?' he said, eyeing her over the rim of the glasses.

Karen grinned.

'There was just one other thing,' she said. 'Can I try on your glasses? They're lovely.'

Obligingly and with a knowing smile he took them off and both he and Gabrielle stared at her as she put them on. She was able to see perfectly through the clear window glass. She took them off and handed them back, confident they were now looking for only four people from the nine that remained.

'Thanks for coming in,' she said. 'My assistant David will be in touch.'

'I liked him,' Gabrielle said, gazing at the empty shelves.

'So did I,' Karen responded encouragingly, unused to the feeling agreeing with Gabrielle gave her.

David came in with his clipboard and laid a sheet of paper on the table.

'I suggest you see them in this order,' he said.

'Does this mean they become progressively less cute?' Karen asked him wryly. 'After this morning they've all become a blur.'

'I think if you put all ten of them together you might get one good man,' he replied. 'Is the list okay?'

'Fine.' She studied it. 'Send Edwin in in about five minutes.'

When David had left the room, Gabrielle leaned towards her conspiratorially. 'I think your assistant may be gay,' she said gravely.

'Really?' Karen said, forcing her features to remain straighter than David. 'I'll keep that in mind.'

'Such a nice-looking boy . . .'

'Let's talk about Edwin,' Karen said, cutting Gabrielle off before she could say what a shame it was.

Edwin came and went with little fanfare or razzmatazz. He too had been a fashion student with some communication art thrown in, but apart from that, he was a world apart from Graham. Edwin was gawky and nervous. Obviously a better group performer, he had seemed much more impressive in the morning sessions. After he had left, Karen felt a tinge of worry. What if they were all like Edwin rather than Graham? Each one rejected stacked the odds; more to get from less. Then her rational mind took over. So what? They didn't really need the men anyway. Just see what comes along, window-shop a little.

They had seen two more people after Edwin, both of whom were suitable and they were in the middle of the presentation of the fifth person when David burst in, without his clipboard. Karen gave him an angry stare and the person presenting stammered and stopped. David made directly for Gabrielle and leaned over to whisper in her ear. Her expression went from benign to horrified, her mouth dropping and eyebrows raising, the skin seeming to tighten on her face for a long haggard second.

'Stop everything!' she shouted, standing abruptly and knocking over the chair.

'David, what is it?' Karen asked him.

'Daniel, Daniel!' Gabrielle cried out, not giving David a chance to speak. 'We will have to stop everything. At once. Oh my God.'

David put his arm around Gabrielle, who had begun to sob and shake. 'Daniel's had a heart attack,' he said to her. 'They've taken him away to hospital. It looked pretty serious according to Jane.'

'I didn't mean it. I didn't mean it, oh Daniel,' Gabrielle was mumbling through sobs.

'Can you look after her, David?' He nodded and led her away and out of the room, followed by the bemused eyes of the prospective employee who must have been wondering if this was part of the interview, some sort of initiative test.

Karen felt a throb in her left temple, a jolt of reality as she made hundreds of quick calculations about the situation, wondering what the effect would be. She guiltily ran the worst case scenario through her mind. Recovering, she thought about what she needed to do and what Avendon would do himself or want her to do. Show must go on, she heard him boom in the back of her mind. She turned to the man whose name she had completely forgotten, the short-term memory part of her brain fried by the sudden drama.

'Sorry. We've had a bit of a situation upstairs with a relative of hers. Can you pick it up from where you were?'

Chapter Eighteen

IT WAS THURSDAY night, late, and it was the eve of the opening party for The Garden. There would be a grand opening party on the Friday night and then doors would open for business on Saturday morning. Daniel Avendon had not been seen for the nine days following his heart attack, or what was being described as his 'heart episode'. It had not in fact turned out to be as bad as it had looked at the time. Karen had been told that the doctors were concerned and that he was under too much stress, things she would have expected to hear, but Daniel Avendon did not have a heart condition as such.

The mere mention of the words 'too much stress' had sent Gabrielle into a tail-spin of contrition. Her initial reaction at the day of the men's auditions had been to try and stop The Garden and possibly the whole of Hamiltons. Gabrielle seemed to feel that she may have caused Daniel's 'episode' by her own actions and she had been to spend time with him wherever he was hiding out and that had had the ultimate effect of convincing her that things must carry on unabated. Over the last nine days, Karen had seen very little of her and when she had, Gabrielle had not asked her a single question about what was happening with The Garden. Karen ended up having to chase Gabrielle for the photographs they were going to use for the lift. Alan had taken the helm in Daniel's absence and they had seen each other only once in the last ten days, both of them preoccupied by their own work. In sum, it was not how she imagined the day before The Garden would be.

'Is there anything else you want me to do?' David asked her, looking over a list on his clipboard. 'I've been through everything here, so unless anything else has cropped up . . .'

The day had been frantic. Karen had insisted that she did not want a mad rush on the final afternoon prior to the opening party. She had been through far too many similar situations with other promotions that she had worked on. She had reached a point, she realised, where that was not the sort of adrenalin she needed any more. That morning, there had been what seemed like a million people around, all seeking her attention, and as the day had progressed, the number of people interested in her had dwindled until she was left on her own, apart from David, loyal to the end.

'You know, I think we're pretty much set here. It's scary, isn't it? The number of promos we've been through where it's been insane and here we are, biggest project ever and it's going too well.' She looked around and then let her eyes fall on him. He looked tired.

'You're getting superstitious. Don't worry. I'm sure something will go at least a little bit wrong.' He paused. 'This is going to be great, you know that, don't you?'

From most other people she knew, Karen would have taken the comment cynically, but she looked at David, who was like an earnest little animal from a Disney film, and she knew he meant it.

'David, I couldn't have coped without you.'

'Karen, you're not going to sing, are you?'

They both burst out laughing, Karen enjoying the sound of it in the empty Garden, feeling the tension release from her.

'Okay,' she said. 'Enough of the mutual admiration

society. It's getting late.' She blinked and checked her watch. It was after ten. 'I have a date.'

'So do I,' David confided slyly.

'Really? I was starting to worry you might be neuter. You should have said. I didn't mean to keep you here so late.'

'That's okay,' David said. 'It makes me look less keen that way.'

'Get out of here now,' she said to him. 'Are the flowers coming at three tomorrow?'

'Yes, after that weird balloon lady has finished. I can hold my own in a balloon discussion now. I know all about air-fill versus helium-fill.'

'It is going to be tasteful, David, isn't it? I don't want it looking like a birthday party at McDonald's.'

'Well, the balloon lady will be all right as long as we watch her and make sure she doesn't get carried away. I think she'd been on the helium when she came in last week.'

David left and Karen took a few minutes to walk around The Garden, drinking it all in like a final inspection. A captain touring the ship before some final battle. The lights seemed very bright to her tired eyes and she squinted. Karen had decided that The Garden should look ready for business when they had the grand opening party. That meant space was slightly more restricted than it might have been, but not by much, and that smoking would not be allowed at the party, which would be nicely controversial in a trivial way. She wandered through the different women's designs, the accessories section and around the bar and fountain. Continuing her backwards journey she passed more designs and was then on the long wide carpet in the entrance area, now fully lined with various palms and plants, gaps allowing people to jump off and into the lingerie or hat section. Standing in the entrance hall, she gazed up at the image of Maxwell that had been blown up to three times life-size and fitted around the false dome that had been created in the entrance, making him look like something from the Sistine chapel. Karen wished there was a light switch by the lift door that she could simply flick and all the lights would go off, giving it a sense of completeness and making it feel like it was all truly hers. The lift arrived and she left.

Richard was already at her flat when she arrived there. There was a smell of cooking and she remembered the time and felt bad. She went into the living-room, set her case down next to an armchair and threw her jacket on to the sofa. There was a note on the phone in Richard's writing saying that Caroline had called. No message. The day after Avendon was taken from Hamiltons with his heart episode, Caroline had called and in a very tiny and apologetic voice told her that she had decided to go back to Gareth. They were going to work things out properly. Karen had listened, making sounds that were neither negative nor positive. Caroline was not going back to Hamiltons either, another job for her to bail out of midway through. At college she and Caroline used to say all men *were* bastards, but some women were stupid. She stood and wondered whether she should call her. It was not her place to get in the middle of Caroline and Gareth, she thought.

'Hi honey, I'm home,' she called in her best American soap opera voice, hoping Richard was not going to be upset about the time. He was not in the kitchen, so she went to the bedroom where he lay on top of her bed, reading a fashion magazine.

'You're late,' he said to her, his eyes downcast and voice quieter than normal. She chose to ignore it.

'Big day tomorrow,' she replied, sitting down at her teak dressing table and removing her earrings. She was holding up well, but could detect the tiredness in her eyes that had been creeping up on her. She watched him in the mirror.

'Could have been a big night as well.' His tone was petulant.

'It's only ten-forty. Night's not over until the sun

comes up,' she said in a dirty voice.

'Whatever,' he mumbled, discarding the magazine and sitting up on the edge of the bed.

'When did Caroline call?'

'Just after seven. When I arrived.' He placed great emphasis on every word of the last sentence, as though speaking in capital letters to make a point.

She turned to face him. 'Richard, for Christ's sake, The Garden opens tomorrow. I can't just call time and walk out. What about when you do late Thursdays?'

'I wanted to do something special.'

The conversation was getting far too domestic for Karen.

'I only loaned you a set of keys, Richard, so you could let yourself in here tonight, remember? So you could *wait* for me? I made that clear. Please don't pull this wounded shit right now.'

'It's not about the keys or you being late,' he said to her.

'Exactly,' she responded.

'Are you seeing other people?'

She laughed. 'Of course I am. You know I am. I know you do as well. You'd better give me those keys back if they're going to make your balls this big all the time.'

'Who are you seeing?'

'Uh-uh.' She made the sound of a buzzer. 'Against the rules, remember?'

'I don't like the rules any more,' Richard said, looking away.

'So leave the game,' she came back instantly. Her words were even and the volume precise, neither too loud or too low.

He looked at her. 'Do you mean that?'

'I mean you should do what is best for you. We said all along that we were not going to get complicated. This is complicated, isn't it?'

'Whatever.'

She gave an exasperated sigh. '*Whatever*. Can't we

just re-run this scene? I come in, say hi, we ask how our days went and you give me a good hard seeing-to? Wouldn't that do, at least for tonight?'

Without a word, he grabbed her and threw her on to the bed. She said nothing and did nothing, allowing him to fling her harshly. He stuck his hands up under her skirt and ripped her underwear off, frantically pulling it over her shoes and then when he had done so, pulling her shoes off and throwing them so they fell loudly. His eyes burned like angry embers as he roughly undid and removed her skirt and stockings, fumbling frenziedly with her suspender belt. He put his hands to the collar of her blouse, where it was open, and gripped it. In one strong downward movement he ripped the buttons and in a second her top was off. He pulled her bra straps down over her shoulders and forced the whole thing off her breasts before he snapped away at the clasps behind her back.

Karen lay naked on the bed, the air inexplicably cold around her, having been crudely stripped in less than a minute. Her nudity was exciting to her under his angry gaze as he stood at the end of the bed and undid the belt on his trousers, zipping down the fly and popping the button at the top. He let them gape open and pushed the front of his briefs under his balls, allowing his cock to protrude. She opened her legs discreetly, making an area on the bed for him.

Richard gripped his cock and jerked it several times, his whole body making the required movements, and then he mounted the end of the bed. He advanced on her slowly, his cock hanging from him and pointing directly at her pussy. As he neared her, he supported himself on his left hand and his right held his cock, foreskin pulled far back. She braced herself.

'Is this what you fucking want? Is it?' he shouted at her, as if trying to be heard over noise.

She seethed as his cock pushed at her pussy-lips and entered her vagina. Her pussy was just slick enough to let him in, but the speed and the suddenness of it were still a shock to her system.

'Is this what you want?' His mouth was right by her ear and his breath was hot against it, spittle falling from his mouth on to her neck. 'A good hard seeing-to? Is it?'

'Yes,' she whimpered.

He pumped harder at her, his groin banging hers with a force that was audible.

'Is this hard enough?' he asked.

'You bastard,' she said to him, half pushing him away from her with her hands but her legs pulling on his hips to keep him inside of her. She dug her nails into the back of his shirt, pushing in as deeply as she could and he growled at her as she did.

'You bitch,' he snarled.

His cock was solid as it thrust at her. It was an intruder and did not feel a part of her in the same way it did when they normally made love. It was there serving only its own purpose and his own ends and there was a sadistic selfishness in his movements, seeking only to pleasure himself and to take that pleasure as quickly as possible. His drive into her was frenetic as though he were about to spill into her at any moment. He made grunting noises that were almost sobs as he fucked her hard and then harder still and she too cried out.

'Oh. Oh,' he moaned.

When he was about to come, she felt his cock actually swell in her pussy as his balls forced the first spurt of his come along his shaft. His face was a sneer as he grimaced at her and then fell into her, his full weight on her as his body jerked and snatched on her, his semen emptying from him into her. It was as intense an orgasm as she had ever seen him have and she gripped him tightly as he continued to come.

As quickly as he had stripped her and entered her, so he was gone from her. He pulled out roughly and stood up, his cock already going limp, some of his come on its tip and the shaft veneered with a film of her juices. He looked at her as he put himself back into his briefs and did up the button on his trousers. He was still angry, even after his orgasm, and it scared her. He pulled impatiently at his belt, looking as though he was pulling it tighter than he really needed to.

Standing at the end of the bed, he paused for a few seconds and Karen realised that he was waiting for her to say something, probably feeling he was giving her a chance. She said nothing, letting a long breath escape silently from her. He seemed to nod slightly as though acknowledging that there was nothing to say and he turned and walked out of the room.

Karen remained still on the bed, angry at him, at herself and at the whole situation. She sat up ready to speak, just in time to hear the sound of the front door being firmly slammed as he left.

'Richard!' she called out, but it was too late.

Chapter Nineteen

THERE WERE OVER two hundred people swarming around The Garden at the opening party and Karen loved it. Everything had run according to plan – as far as The Garden was concerned.

The last touches were still being put by two of the shop-fitters at four that afternoon, but they were now long gone, as was the balloon lady, the people delivering the food and drink and the people setting everything up. What remained were over twenty extremely cute waiters, an amazing spread of vegetarian food, the invited guests, the staff of The Garden and the press. People mingled with each other, snubbed each other, tried to pick each other up and got progressively more drunk on Hamiltons branded champagne. That side of things was absolutely fine.

On the other, things were very much not fine. Not at all. Richard had not been in Hamiltons that day and was not answering his phone at home. She had never seen him so upset and wondered where he was. He had promised to be her date at the party ages ago. When she called Caroline to invite her, the night before, Gareth had answered and she had just put the phone down, not wanting to get involved. Avendon was rumoured to be attending, but there was no sign of him yet and likewise with Linda and Maxwell. Chris Nichol had arrived with a model and was off somewhere, Karen not having had a chance to talk to him yet. David had temporarily disappeared. In short, she was in the middle of a large party for which she was mainly responsible and she suddenly felt very alone.

David appeared from nowhere and she made a line for him, practically grabbing at him when she reached him.

'Where have you been hiding?' she asked him, trying not to sound like his boss.

'I was showing Graham where we work,' he replied, moving aside so she could see Graham, the first man she had thought was right for The Garden. He was not, she noticed, wearing his fake horn-rims.

'Hi,' Graham said nonchalantly. 'Great party, Karen. David's been showing me your offices.'

'I can see that, Graham. Maybe you could tell him to do up his flies again,' she said as though David were not even there, looking down at his trousers as she spoke.

Graham gave a wicked laugh that subsided into a smile.

'Are you looking forward to working in The Garden?' Karen asked him.

'Of course I am. What else would I say?'

'True,' she replied. 'Cheer up, David; it's a party. We've done it.'

David seemed lost without his clipboard and nibbled on a nail to compensate for it.

'I think there should have been more balloons,' he said to Karen.

Karen laughed at him and was about to say something else when out of the corner of her eye she saw a whole set of flash guns go off at the same time. Maxwell. She turned, and there he was in the doorway with Linda, smiling politely as the photographers shouted at him to get his attention. The street entrance to Hamiltons was staked out by paparazzi and the rather large number of papers they had not invited. As she watched him, so polite and gentle, she wondered if

Linda had told him to be on his best behaviour. After a few more poses, they moved on and were quickly forgotten by the snap-happy bunch at the door. Karen excused herself from Graham and David, who had fallen into conversation and barely seemed to notice her, and went to greet Linda.

'Hello darling,' she said to Linda, who was clad in a smarter version of her normal black.

'You look great,' Linda said.

'Thank you,' said Karen, knowing she was right.

In a fit of indulgence, Karen had chosen the most outrageously expensive sequinned dress by Versace that she could find and she had arranged for her hairdresser to come into the store that afternoon and fix her hair before the party. The light caught the gold scales of the dress and accentuated her skin tone perfectly. She felt like a million dollars, which was handy because that was almost what her outfit had cost.

'Hi Karen,' Maxwell said, a spindly hand extending, his eyes on hers, thoughts on his mind, or so it seemed.

'Hello,' she pulled him to her with the hand and kissed him on the cheek, holding him for a fraction longer than she should have and several hours less than she would have liked.

'The picture on the dome looks good,' Linda said. 'It was worth all the effort.'

'Very Sistine Chapel, everyone says,' Karen told her.

Linda frowned. 'Caravaggio, maybe, but Michelangelo?' She raised her eyebrows. She looked around her, taking in The Garden.

'What do you think?' Karen asked her.

'I'd come here and shop. I will come here and shop. It's gorgeous, really. Look after Max, will you? I'm off to the bathroom.'

It was the first time she had spoken to Maxwell since that afternoon when they had been to Hyde Park and ended up back in her flat. Karen had spoken to Linda several times, but not to Maxwell. He was dressed in a jacket with matching shorts that made him look like a schoolboy. His hair was better kept than normal and it seemed a shade darker than when she had seen him last. A small ache for him started somewhere in her chest.

'How have you been?' she asked him, cringing at the formality of the question.

'Centre of attention as usual,' he said resignedly. 'I was going to call you. I wish I had. I've thought about you quite a lot. You and Linda are very similar, but I don't think I'd be able to handle two at once.'

'You and Linda look very good together,' she said, feeling like Humphrey Bogart at the end of *Casablanca*, telling Ingrid Bergman to get on the plane with Victor Laszlo.

'You know what I'm saying, don't you?' he persisted.

'Max, Linda is one of my oldest friends and I hope you're going to be one of my newer ones. Let's not fuck things up with fucking. Agreed?'

'Even the toilets are sensational,' Linda said, returning, as Karen and Maxwell held each other's eyes and then broke.

'I know. Aren't they a scream?'

'Are there toilets for men?' Maxwell asked.

'Not in here. You have to go down on the lift and use the customer ones on the next floor down.'

He tutted and walked off in a minor huff, Karen and Linda watching him go.

'I'm mad about him,' Linda said to her.

'So am I,' she said, nudging her friend. 'I'll have him on the rebound.'

'He's still got a crush on you, Karen, you know don't you?'

'He was telling me that while you were in the loo.'

'What a sweetheart. Where's your beau, by the way?'

Karen looked at her and shook her head sadly.

'Trauma time, I'm afraid. He's not coming and anyway, he would have been my date, not my beau.'

'Point taken. Next subject.'

'What are you working on at the moment?' Karen asked.

'I'm finishing up on a book and then I've got about twenty commercial assignments to do. After that, I might do a whole book of Maxwell and birds. Are you going to oversee all of this gracefully?' Linda said, gesturing to The Garden.

'You know, I really don't know, Linda. This took up so much of my time, we haven't even thought about any other promotions, especially since Daniel's been away.'

'Is he going to be okay?'

'As far as we know. He's meant to be here tonight.'

'That's the boy from that stupid film with the car, isn't it?' Linda asked.

'Chris Nichol. Sexy, don't you think?'

'He certainly is,' Linda said. 'Too sexy to be with that giraffe.'

'Linda!'

'He's eyeing you, Karen. Look, he's coming over.' Linda was talking under her breath, the party ventriloquist skills long-established.

'Karen, hi,' Chris said, hugging her. 'This is Kit,' he continued, introducing the giraffe.

'This is my friend Linda Cole. She took the photographs you saw in the entrance. Ah, and here's the man himself,' Karen said as Maxwell returned.

'Maxwell, my baby!' said Kit in a fake East European voice and Linda made a face at Karen as the two of them hugged like they were being reunited after twenty years.

'Why don't we go and get some food,' Linda said, breaking into the Kit and Maxwell hug and leading them away. 'You remember food, don't you, Max? You had some once, I remember. Kit, you'll love the vine leaves. Very you . . .'

Linda's voice trailed off as she led the two of them away like they were her children, shrewdly leaving Chris and Karen alone.

'Did you come over specially for the party?' Karen asked him.

'I'd be lying if I said yes. I'm shooting a movie here.'

'Really? You never said.'

'It was last minute. I'm taking over from someone who's, shall we say, having trouble getting to the set each day.' He sniffed loudly and widened his eyes, acting as if off-balance from the effect of drugs.

'How long will you be here for?'

'Eight weeks,' he said.

'Have you seen much of Jake?'

Chris did the famous smile. 'He's on my back all the time. When will I do the movie. It's so right for me. It's the big crossover picture. All that stuff. Will we be able to spend some time together? While I'm here?'

She looked at him, a sigh about to break from her. First Maxwell and now Chris Nichol.

'Let's take it as it comes. Is that okay?' she asked tentatively.

'It's a start, I guess,' he smiled, no disappointment evident.

Linda returned alone.

'I've left them discussing the fat content of everything on the table. They'll be hours.' Linda grinned. 'I've photographed Kit for a shoe advert, before she was mega-famous. She's grown up a lot.'

'I love the pictures with the birds,' Chris said to Linda. 'It must have been hard to shoot.'

'It took a while, but we got there. I'd say I loved your last movie, but I hardly ever go,' Linda said baldly.

There was another minor commotion at the door, similar to when Linda and Maxwell had arrived. The three of them looked around and it was Daniel Avendon, smiling broadly and looking better than Karen could remember seeing him for a long while. She stared at him, almost shocked from not having seen him for so long and in her concentration she completely ignored who was hanging from his arm in a splendid ball-gown.

'Oh my god,' Linda was saying, tugging her arm, 'it's drippy Caroline with him!'

Karen's fixation on Avendon was broken and she stared at Caroline. Mousy Caroline. Holding Avendon's arm and smiling for the photographers as if she had been doing it all her life.

'When did she become Kate Moss?' Linda whispered to her.

'I have to go and talk to her,' Karen said, launching off across the room.

Caroline spotted Karen coming towards her and she broke away from Avendon, meeting her halfway.

'Hi,' Caroline said, bright and breezy.

'Hi? Caroline, what's going on?'

'I know. I'm sorry. I should have told you. It was easier to say I'd gone back to Gareth at the time. I tried to call you last night.'

'You haven't been with Gareth at all?' she asked.

'No way. Gareth came to Hamiltons the day Daniel collapsed. He'd seen that piece on you and The Garden in the paper and his little brain actually figured out I might be staying with you. He came looking for you and got more than he bargained for. It was sad, Karen. He was weeping, begging me. I sent him packing.'

'Have you been with Daniel all this time?'

'I was there when it happened. I went with him in the ambulance, stayed at the hospital and went with him to his country retreat while he was recovering. It was only a mild episode.'

'Did you see Gabrielle there?' Karen asked.

'She came several times. Daniel needs to talk to you about that.'

'Why?'

'I promised I'd let him tell you.' Caroline smiled at her.

'Caroline, are you and Daniel. . .?' she let the words trail off.

Caroline nodded. There was a beat of silence and then they giggled and embraced.

'Was that Linda Cole you were talking to?' Caroline asked. 'I haven't seen her in years. Make sure you have a word with Daniel. I'm going to chat with Linda, even though she never liked me, and we'll play catch-up later.'

Daniel had already been monopolised by several of his regular hangers-on and Karen took the time to gather her thoughts. She wished Richard was there. Or Alan. Or even Maxwell or Chris Nichol for that matter. The alone feeling returned to her.

'Excellent. Very good.'

Daniel laid a strong hand on her shoulder and she turned and smiled at him. They hugged, Karen realising it was the first time she had ever hugged him.

'Thank you. For everything,' she said to him. And she meant it. She could not have realised it without him and his backing. She would still be standing in Alan's kitchen with an apple in her hand and an idea in her head if it wasn't for Daniel Avendon.

'How are you feeling?' she asked him. 'You look well.'

'I feel well. Extremely. Have I missed any developments?'

'I feel like I have,' she said, nodding towards Caroline across the crowded floor.

'Yes. I'll fill you in on that saga presently. We should have a talk first. Soon. Now, really.'

'Caroline said you wanted a word. Shall we go to your office?'

'I've a better idea,' he said, taking her hand.

Daniel led her to the bottom of the stairs that led up to the gantry, the one that they had agreed would give a splendid view of The Garden and of the water wall at the back. It was guarded by someone from Hamiltons security as they had decided to close it for the party for fear of a drunken supermodel taking a tumble from her platform shoes and ending up on the floor below. When Avendon approached, the man jumped smartly aside and they climbed quickly to the top, Avendon in front.

'You seem in better condition than I do,' she said when they were on the gantry.

'Mistress of all you see. All.' He looked at her and then at his watch.

'Are you all right?'

'Yes. Hate drama, though. They should be here any minute, so I should spill this one now.' He seemed to be talking to himself.

'Spill what?'

He looked at her and then concentrated on the throng below. Up on the walkway, they were hidden, the spotlights off and the gantry only dimly lit. They watched silently for a few moments. Then Daniel seemed to draw a very long breath, as if about to blow up a balloon, and he spoke.

'I thought we would be better up here. You can hear it from me that way. There is no really good way to tell it or make it sound sensible.'

They were three of the longest sentences Karen had ever heard Daniel Avendon utter and she was now intrigued.

'When Gabrielle left the shop in sixty-nine,' he continued, 'it was not to have a break. Far from it. She was pregnant. She carried the child to term and at birth it was adopted. Gabrielle named him after her father, Dick Foxton and gave him her mother's maiden name as his surname. That was how he came to be called Richard Fraser.'

Karen turned and stared hard at Avendon, Richard's name stabbing at her and sounding wrong in the context it was being used. That was how he came to be called Richard Fraser? Gabrielle was Richard's mother? She was about to say something, not even sure what, when Avendon cut her off by continuing to speak.

'Also, that gave the boy no connection to his father, Alan Saxton. The whole time was really very difficult. Indeed. For all involved. Alan was still married to Margaret at the time, and I still say they were right for each other, regardless of his dalliance with my half-sister. After the adoption, Gabrielle had no interest in the boy or in Alan. Her only interest was in keeping the two of them separated. It was ironic, really, because Alan looked after the trust fund we set up for him.'

Karen eyed him and Avendon laughed.

'Oh yes,' he said. 'He doesn't have to work. Never. Alan thought a bit of time in the trenches would serve him well before we drag him upstairs. As lovely as your friend Caroline is, I'm not in the market to sire an heir at my age. Richard will suffice. Ah, there we are, on perfect dramatic cue.'

They looked down and Gabrielle and Alan had arrived, Richard with them. Karen looked down on the scene, at a wonderful vantage point but lost for words.

'When Gabrielle found out he was working here, she felt that history, the history of our fathers at least, was about to be repeated in some manner. There was little trouble she could stir up for Alan at that point as he was divorced from Margaret and Richard knows his own mind. She had no ammunition and that's why she came after the shop, in a manner of speaking.'

Karen looked over the edge, the gantry seeming higher than it did only moments earlier, her perspective on the whole scene below shifting along with Avendon's words as they calmly reordered the world for her. The taunts Richard had made to her about Alan, the way Alan had talked about children and the photograph of the supposed nephew that he had explained away so badly when they were at his house in the country. She found some words.

'Why would she come for the shop? Wouldn't she want what was best for her son?' Karen asked him.

'Yes. Of course. She believes she is doing what is in

644

his best interests by being here. She lost someone very close to her last year and that seemed to spark this off in her. I think she felt alone and wanted to grab on to the past. Richard was the only bit available and he was linked with Hamiltons by then. Richard is the thing that binds the feud in many ways. The Avendons and the Foxtons, let alone the Saxtons.'

'What is she going to do?'

'She's trying to be mysterious, but I suspect she will transfer her holding to Richard. It will work itself out. The Garden will succeed, you know that, don't you?'

'Yes,' she replied.

'We may be relying on you heavily with this venture, I feel. And I feel confident. Extremely so. And I think they will succeed too,' he said, looking down at Gabrielle and Alan, talking intimately and seemingly drawn together by an invisible force that had been nurtured for over twenty years.

At first it was no more than a trickle and then it became a gentle flow and finally it was a cascade as water poured over the top of the grey marble water wall. The lights flashed on, illuminating the water and the gantry at the same time. All eyes in the room were upturned and after a minute or two, applause broke out. Avendon took Karen's hand and squeezed it, a grin on his face, and it was then that she realised the applause was for her. For a full minute she beamed radiantly and then searched the crowd below for the face she was looking for.

Finding it, and with her eyes fixed on his, she descended slowly into the applause.

645

Chapter Twenty

NEARLY TWO YEARS after the grand opening party that launched The Garden that Friday evening, both Daniel Avendon's words and the applause still rang in Karen Taylor's ears. And the applause went on in other ways. On reflection, many of the things that had happened at the party had laid the basis for what followed.

Now, she was taking a quiet moment, lying in bed having recently made love and about to look at a book. She reached over to her side-table, careful not to disturb the gently snoozing form beside her, and picked it up. Its title was very simple, much as Linda had said it would be when she had first mentioned it to Karen all that time ago. It was called 'Maxwell and Birds'. It had been very successful as photographic books went and she had an exhibition accompanying it at the Hayward Gallery. In their strange way, Linda and Maxwell were still an item. By capturing him so consistently and continually on film, Linda seemed to be turning the pair of them into something that extended far beyond being a couple. Karen wondered where they would go next. Linda's photography of him was stunning, many different poses and ideas, including Maxwell in cages and Maxwell wearing feathers and little else. The three pictures Linda had taken for Hamiltons to promote the fragrance and The Garden were also used, with a kind thank you